I'm an Irish author who is addicted to writing romances featuring damaged, moody, book boyfriends searching for their happily ever after.

Visit K.A. Finn online:

www.kafinn.com
(trailers, excerpts, artwork, playlists etc)

Facebook: kafinnauthor

Instagram: kafinnauthor

Additional links: linktr.ee/kafinn

BLACKJACKS BOOK 3

DEFYING SHEP

K.A.FINN

Cover design by Deranged Doctor Design
www.derangeddoctordesign.com

Photography by Furious Fotog
www.furiousfotog.com

Cover model
David Cook

Published by Cooper Publishing
cooperbookservices@gmail.com

ISBN: 978-1-914177-67-5

To Dad,
Thank you for switching off when I talk shop with Mum - especially
when we try to guess how many times I wrote the word f*ck in the book or
discuss scenes I'd prefer my dad didn't read!
Love you xx

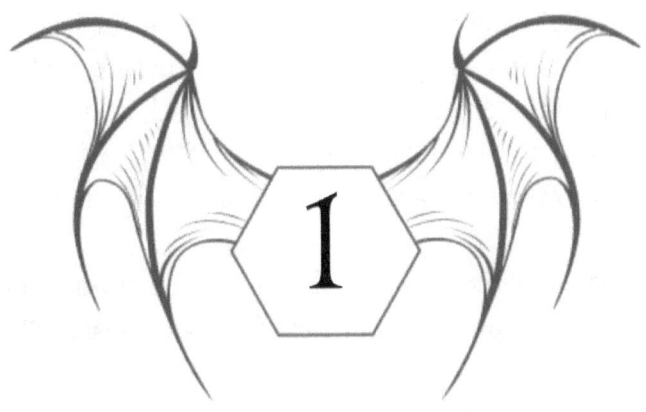

SHEP

'Fuck, fuck, fuck, and another fuck for good measure!'

Shep ducks the grenade that's thrown at him, barely missing it clobbering him on the head. He kicks the bench beside him, then curses again when he stubs his toe. 'Fuck!'

The whole training session had been a fucking disaster. He's lost his edge, or his killer instinct, or whatever made him deadly in the field. And now his toe is sore, so he's also pissed off about that.

'Do you want to go again?' Bastian asks, throwing one of the grenades into the air and catching it again. 'I've got plenty more ammunition,' he says launching one at Shep, hitting him on the shoulder.

'Ouch! Hey! Stop it.'

Bas picks another one off the ground and throws it at him, barely missing his leg when Shep twists to the side.

'Seriously? You want me to hit you back?'

'Wasn't that what you were trying to do for the last two hours?'

Shep waves his middle finger at Bas, before picking another grenade from the ground and hurling it back at him, missing him by a fair bit. 'You're too fucking fast.'

'You're too slow. So, are you going to tell me what's wrong?'

'Nothing.'

The Spaniard fixes him with one of his no-nonsense glares. 'Fuck, fuck, fuck, and another fuck for good measure? What is all that about exactly?'

'What? I'm pissed off.'

'Oh, I got that bit. Not sure kicking the bench helped.'

'Would you get off my case please! I'm having a moment here.'

Bas holds up his gloved hands and takes a step back. 'Apologies. I'll give you a minute to continue threatening the bench. Let me know when you're done.'

'Thank you. I'd appreciate that.' Shep only lasts a few seconds before he laughs along with Bas, who was valiantly trying to keep it to himself. 'Sorry. That was a bit dramatic, wasn't it?'

'A little, yes.' Bas crouches down and picks up a bulb of garlic. 'How exactly do you plan to incorporate these makeshift grenades into our arsenal? Dav won't be going on rotation armed with garlic.'

'I haven't quite thought through all the details yet.'

'I want to be there when you tell him,' Bas says, rolling a bulb of garlic in his gloved hands.

'Hey! I defeated a whole troop of evil vampire bastards in Ireland with those bad boys. Don't knock it. Plus, I don't appreciate you using my own idea against me. That was low.'

'I must admit the garlic is quite effective. But you know she's going to be pissed off with you about this?'

'Shep! Where is my garlic!'

'And here she comes,' Bas mutters, taking a step back from him.

'Hey? Where are you going? You have to protect me!'

'Oh no my friend. You're on your own.'

Shep slowly turns to face the woman, the irritation on her face reaching whole new levels. She grabs the garlic from his hand and waves it in his face.

'What exactly are you doing?'

'Training. I have to say you look particularly stunning today, Gwen. Have you had your hair done?'

Their housekeeper, cook, and unofficial mother of the group is half his height, but the look the sixty-five-year-old throws at him, has him cowering.

'This is the third lot of garlic you've swiped from my kitchen in the last week. The third! I need garlic to cook, Shep. To cook for *you*. Do you have any idea how much food you put away? Any idea at all?'

'I have a high metabolism.'

'High! It's through the roof! You like my stew?'

'Of course!'

'My bolognese? My lasagne? My pasta?'

'They're the best.'

'Do you know the vital ingredient?'

'I'm guessing you're going to say garlic?'

She shoves the garlic against his nose. 'Garlic!'

'Sorry Gwen. I was just trying out a new weapon I came up with. They're vampire grenades. You now, cause vampires are supposed to hate garlic.'

'Exactly! *Supposed* to. All fiction. You can demolish three cheesy garlic breads by yourself! You're not fighting Count Dracula. Use a rock and leave my garlic alone! You're nearly one hundred years old. Why don't you act your age!'

She storms away, stopping a few feet from him to throw the garlic back at him, whacking him on the chest.

'Ouch! That really hurt!'

'Humph,' she mutters as she walks away again. 'Maybe it does work after all.'

Shep glares over his shoulder at Bas, slumped on the bench having a good laugh at him. 'Thanks for your help there, mate!'

'I was not going to get in Gwen's way when she's in that sort of mood. I would prefer to live a little longer.'

'What about me? You not afraid of pissing me off?'

'Short answer - no.'

'Wow! Great solidarity there Bas.' He sits beside him, rubbing the spot on his chest Gwen hit. 'On the plus side, it packs quite a punch. I might be on to something there.'

'I think that was Gwen - not the garlic.'

'You think she'd be on for some training? Get her in the field?'

'Then who would cook your dinner?'

Shep nods, stretching his legs out in front of him. His damn foot still hurts from kicking the bench. Attacked and injured by a bench and some garlic. Clearly he's having an off day. He's having a lot of them lately.

'What's wrong?' Bas asks after a few minutes of silence.

'Do you ever feel like you're not on your game?'

'No.' Bas replies without hesitation.

'Nice. Thanks.'

'I'm joking. Trying to lighten the mood. Of course I have off days. We all do. That's why we train as much as we do. Hopefully we have more good days than bad ones though.'

Shep wishes it was that simple. He'd never admit it, but he's had off days every now and then. Not that he'd say it to any of the team. He's the best of the best. Admitting he struggles from time to time would kill his reputation in a second. He'd rather die than let that happen.

'How are you feeling?'

'Never better,' he lies. His body has been fucking with him ever since he got back from Ireland a few weeks ago.

He feels Bas giving him another hard glare.

'What?'

'You were injected with an enhancer and are now growing wings. That's what. I know you Shep. Be honest with me.'

Like he needs reminding of that point. His newly acquired wings are the first thing on his mind when he wakes up... if he sleeps at all.

He's a Hybrid - half-human and half-vampire. He shouldn't have wings. Ever. But thanks to the drug he was given, he's now got two fancy wing ridges down his back, and the grotesque wings had started to make an appearance a few days ago. It was only a few inches, but it was a few inches too much.

He's an abomination. Something that shouldn't exist. And he hasn't got a clue how to deal with that.

He hates that his body is changing. Hates that he's terrified the damn things will tear out of his body, but instead of just a few inches, that they will come out fully. No way he wants that to happen.

7

'I'm fine, Bas. Really. I'd appreciate if everyone wasn't watching me like I'm some fucking freak. I'm still me. Forget about the wings bit.'

Bas brushes his dark hair back from his forehead. 'You think that's how I look at you?'

'No. I was making a general comment. It wasn't directed at you.'

'I'm your friend. You expect me not to worry about you?'

Shep sighs. Bas is right. He's being a dick, but he can't help it. He's always been confident and unfazed by anything. Or at least that's how he acts. All this wing crap is freaking him out. Bas knows that, but he still can't admit it to him.

'I know. Thanks.'

Bas shakes his head, clearly getting the message. 'Do you want to try again?'

'Nah. I'm done for the day. Think the bench is done too,' he adds, grinning, desperate to lighten the mood.

It works. Bas smiles at him and gestures to the door. 'You want to grab something to eat?'

'I think I'll head out for a bit. Blow off some steam on my bike.'

'Do you want company?'

'Think I just need some time alone. Is that okay?'

Bas nods, holding the door open for him. 'Of course. Just keep your tracker on you. Nix will go nuts if you leave it in your room again.'

Shep rolls his eyes. 'Yes, Dad!'

'You're a fucking asshole, Shep!'

He blows Bas a kiss as they get to the top of the stairs. 'Love you too!'

Bas laughs as he walks down the corridor to the left, towards his room. Shep heads right and opens his bedroom door. Once it's locked behind him, he pulls off his t-shirt and examines his back in the mirror on the wardrobe door.

Two wing ridges, but nothing sticking out of them. Every time he checks he's afraid of what he'll see. That image of the large talons sticking out of his skin haunts his dreams every fucking night. Add that to the other nightmares he has regularly, and sleep is a barrel of laughs at the moment.

He showers quickly and leaves his room, before he can be cornered by Nix. Since he was injected, he's drawing far too much attention from the others. Usually he wouldn't mind that so much, but this is laced with sympathy. He could do without that part.

Reaching the top of the stairs, he pauses for a minute and closes his eyes. His senses are more attuned than other vampires. It's his special ability. His compensation for not being born with wings. Maybe he'll lose his ability when the wings come out? Then he'll be off the team for sure.

Shaking those thoughts from his mind, he concentrates on what he was doing. There's no one in this side of the house. Time to make a swift exit.

He leaps over the banisters, landing softly in the tiled hallway, then hurries through the door leading to the garage. Once it closes behind him, he allows himself to relax a little. He reaches the garage without bumping into anyone and grabs his bike keys from the safe on the wall.

All he needs is a few hours to himself. A few hours away from the looks he's been getting from the rest of the team. A few hours to wallow in a good dose of self pity, before heading home again.

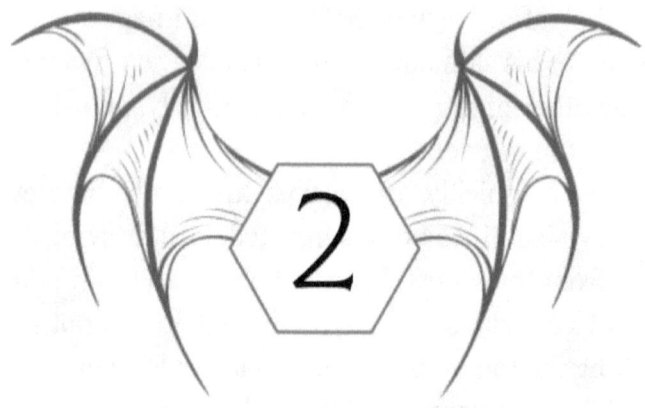

IZZY

Isabella secures her black hair into a neat bun and fastens the buttons on her blouse. Getting a job at The Lair isn't something she will ever be putting on a CV, but for now, it will help to keep a roof over her head while she completes her studies.

The reputation of the club is well known. Loud music, cheap drink, dark corners, and very few rules. She's just grateful the bar staff uniform is a pair of black pants and a black blouse. Simple, yet it covers everything, and working in The Lair that was the most important thing.

The clientele tended to be a little on the rough side. The bands that perform here are the big draw. The shows only take place once a week, thankfully, but tonight is one of those nights. The music tended to pull in the crowds, meaning she is in for a long and busy night.

She goes downstairs into the bar, psyching herself up for the night ahead. As soon as she opens the door, the heat, music, and smell of stale beer hits her. She smiles at Sabrina, one of the other servers. She had met her briefly when she interviewed for the position, and instantly liked the woman. It will help having someone she likes working with her tonight.

It's still early enough, but the bar is full, the dance floor already heaving. A fake smile plastered on her face like part of her uniform, Izzy weaves through the tables, aiming for the back of the room, away from the speakers and the crowds.

Then she sees someone who catches her attention. He's sitting at the far side of the room, a bottle of beer on the table in front of him. His dark blond hair is the perfect example of a just out of bed style, the shaggy spikes ruffled and begging to be touched. He's sporting a few days of stubble on his strong jaw, and the skin on his thick neck and arms is covered in ink.

'That was quicker than I thought,' Sabrina says, leaning over so she can be heard above the music.

'What was?'

'I wondered how long it would take you to notice that particular punter.'

'Why? Who is he?'

Sabrina shrugs, brushing her blond hair off her shoulder. 'No one knows. He's a regular. That's unofficially known as his table. It's where he always sits, and no one else even attempts to go near it.'

Izzy can well believe that last part. Even from across the room there's a threatening air around him.

'As for the why? Well, you've seen him so I don't think I need to answer that question. He's flipping gorgeous. As if that wasn't enough, the guy has a delicious Yorkshire accent. I mean it's melt-worthy. I can guarantee it sends shivers down most members of staff when he speaks on those rare occasions.'

'So why is he sitting alone?'

'Oh, he won't be for long,' Sabrina answers with a smile. 'Listen, I like you Izzy. You seem decent so I'm going to tell you how it is with him. He's gorgeous, polite, sexy as hell, tips well, never gives any trouble, but that doesn't mean he isn't trouble.'

'You've lost me.'

Sabrina nods over to him. 'He's about to prove my point.' She looks over to the man and sees a tall blonde-haired woman talking to him. He leans over and speaks to her then stands and walks up the stairs, the woman hurrying after him.

'Where's he going?'

'The owner Marty put aside a room for him to use.'

'Use?' Izzy asks, not understanding what Sabrina is saying.

'Sex Izzy. He comes here for sex. He'll show her the time of her life, then come back down the stairs and leave. So as nice and all as he is to look at, unless you want to be added to that particular list, you'll avoid him.'

Sabrina saunters off to deal with a table, leaving Izzy watching the man hold open the door at the top of the stairs, so the woman can walk through.

Before she can turn away, he looks directly at her. Even though he's at the other side of the room, she can feel the intensity of his look. But then his face softens. He smiles at her, his eyes seeming to glow.

Sabrina was downplaying his looks. Even in the dim lights the man is without a doubt, one of the sexiest men she's ever seen. His glowing eyes captivate her, refusing to let her look away. The woman tries to get his attention, but he's focused on Izzy for some reason.

Maybe because she's new? If he's here all the time surely he'd know all the staff too. He's probably just staring at her because he hasn't seen her before.

But there's something more primal in his look than just mere curiosity.

He folds his arms, leaning on the railing in front of him as he unapologetically stares at her.

But for some reason he's not making her feel uncomfortable in any way. It should do, but there's something else there she can't put her finger on.

Maybe she's seeing things that aren't there.

The woman grabs his arm, clearly unimpressed by his complete lack of attention. He speaks to her quickly, whatever he says leaving the woman pouting like a child who has just been reprimanded.

He pushes upright before looking back down at Izzy, the smile he gives her just a stunning as he is.

Don't even think about asking me to swap.

She might be attracted to him but that doesn't mean she's interested in changing places with that woman.

The man tilts his head to the side, his eyes glowing brighter before he steps back and opens the door, ushering the woman inside. With one last look at Izzy, he closes the door behind him.

Izzy blinks, feeling as if she's coming out of a daydream.

'You don't waste any time, do you?' Sabrina says, coming up behind her.

'I'm sorry?' Izzy says, still trying to get her head back in this world.

'I saw that deep moment you just had with Sexy Accent.'

'What deep moment?'

'All that intense staring. You've caught his attention. I've never seen him like that with someone before.'

While that is nice to hear and gives her a confidence boost, she's still not sure exactly what just happened. 'I'm a new face. That's all it was.'

Sabrina grins at her. 'Of course that's all it was. Now how about we both do some work. We're not going to get many tips standing here drooling over the clientele.'

13

SHEP

'Where the fuck are you?'

Bas doesn't usually curse, especially by text, so clearly he's pissed off. He's due on rotation in about an hour, so Bas is no doubt getting his nose out of joint. He's not late... well, not yet. He has just enough time to get home, changed, and head out.

Behind him, the woman is stretched out on the bed, her naked body covered in a fine sheen of sweat. He hadn't done much as usual. Just lay there and let her be with him. Let her use him. She wasn't complaining though and seemed to enjoy herself.

That makes one of them.

She traces her hand down his back, the sensation turning his stomach. Shep gets to his feet, quickly pulling on his boxers in case she gets any ideas about having another go.

'You're leaving?'

'Yeah.'

He quickly gets dressed, ignoring her pleas as she attempts to get him to stay. The only thing he wants to do is get the fuck out of here, scrub his skin until it's raw, then beat the shit out of something in the training room.

He gets dressed in record time, then heads down the back stairs, stopping at the coat check-in to grab his helmet and jacket. As he bursts through the exit, he stops by the wall, taking a few long deep breaths to steady himself.

That woman is upstairs still coming down from her high, and he's down here trying not to puke, disgust and disgrace going over him in waves.

His phone buzzes again, pulling him out of his negativity. Bas again.

He gets to his bike and swings his leg over the saddle. After firing a quick *Relax! I'm on my way* reply to Bas, he pulls on his helmet and

14

starts his bike, but doesn't ride away. Instead, he looks over his shoulder at the flashing neon light over the door.

The Lair is probably at the bottom of the list of places to visit when popping into the city, but it has everything he needs. Plenty of dark corners, women who want to see to his needs, and an owner who is happy to look the other way.

He wasn't expecting *her* though. Not for one minute. That new bartender had grabbed his attention and refused to let go. If given the choice, he would have ditched that woman he'd been with and headed back down the stairs.

As blunt as it sounds, he doesn't usually pay much attention to anyone around him. Or even notice what the women around him look like. It was more about having those few minutes of validation. About that temporary relief it offers, before that crippling emptiness returns.

It wasn't all about him though. Every woman he was ever with, always left the room satisfied. But that's as far as it went. He never wanted, or even considered anything more. Even wanting to have a brief conversation wasn't on the cards.

He hadn't noticed her before, and he has no idea why. Maybe she's new? Maybe he's just been so deep in his head he hadn't seen her. The poor woman must be desperate for cash if she's working there. The place is a fucking dump. She is seriously hot though, brightening up the gloomy bar for the first time in all the years he's been going there.

What he needs to do is put the bizarre experience behind him. It's not like he has a choice either way. No doubt she'll have heard about his reputation from her co-workers. Fuck, she saw him walking up the stairs with another woman. Unless she's the type of woman who fancies a quickie in a dark corner, there's no way she'll want anything to do with him.

He's well and truly shot himself in the foot when it comes to having anything other than a brief fuck with anyone from that place. But until he saw her, he hadn't considered anything more than that with anyone, full stop. Not to mention the small detail that he's a vampire and she's human. The two don't generally mix well.

Whatever!

It's done.

Best to get all thoughts of her out of his mind and focus on kicking some True Order ass.

But heading back to Wales, and potentially going up against some True Order vampires, isn't something he's in the mood for tonight. Usually, he's more than ready to have a good tussle with the bad guys, but he doesn't feel like it anymore. He hasn't felt ready to go up against anyone for the last few weeks. He's kind of free-falling, waiting for the bone jarring impact that will probably take him down for good.

Wow, that's a great fucking mindset to bring onto the street with him! Bas needs him to have his head in the game when he's with him tonight. They go out in pairs for a reason - back up. If one half of the team is second guessing everything, they're not much good.

As he rides out of the car park and heads back to the compound, he tries to get his head clear of all the shit that's swirling around in there.

The fucking wings that are waiting to pop out of his back and turn his life to shit, are always on his mind. Like a ticking time bomb he has no control over. He doesn't do well when he's not in control. He lost too many years under the control of someone else. Giving it up now is not an option for him. Not that he has a fucking choice right now.

Shep absently rubs his side. The injection he was given left a visible mark. A constant reminder that his body is mutating. He's growing wings he shouldn't have. That's bad enough, without thinking about all the other horrible things that could happen.

What he knows for sure is that, since he was injected in Ireland, he's been off kilter, and he hates it. Hates what it's done and is still doing to his body. Hates that he doesn't know how far it will go. He doesn't want fucking wings! No way.

Male Hybrids don't have wings. It's not the way their species is built. After being jabbed with that drug, he doesn't fit into either category.

He's a *hybrid* Hybrid. A freak. An anomaly.

As soon as he gets out of the city, he accelerates, letting the Ducati loose on the quiet roads. The speed, the freedom, helps ease some of the tension left in his body.

As messed up as it sounds, sex is like a drug of sorts. As much as he shouldn't like it, it's one of the few things that makes him feel anything.

Unlike every other moment of his life.

He's a shell. Has been for as long as he can remember. Joking and fighting his way through every single day. The only time he feels like he has even a tentative grip on his fucked-up life is when he's having sex.

It's not about him. It hasn't been for years. It's all about feeling worthwhile. But that's also the part that makes everything so much more fucked-up.

He curses and pushes the bike harder. He can't allow his head to go back there right now. His best friend is depending on him to have his back tonight. Bas deserves to get him at his best. Both of their lives depend on it.

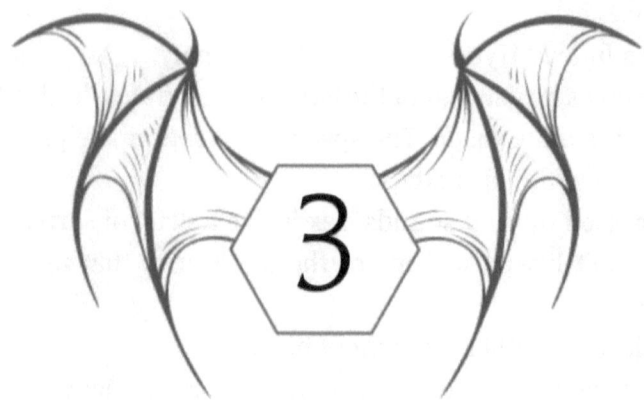

WiLLOW

'You decent?'

Willow waits outside her brother's room, but there's no response from inside. She knocks again and, after leaving her waiting for another minute, he opens the door. 'What?'

'Can I come in?'

Shep steps aside then gestures to the wardrobe. 'I'm just out of the shower. Give me a sec.' He disappears inside the walk-in wardrobe, and Willow hears hangers being slid aside as he searches for something to wear.

'Where did you go today?' she asks as she sits on the couch. 'I thought we were going to train together.'

'Damn it! I completely forgot. I kicked Bastian's ass then headed out. Sorry, Wills.'

'I heard he kicked your ass.'

'Who are you going to believe? Him or your brother?'

'Him.'

He sticks his head out the door and glares at her. 'Fucking charming! Thanks Sis.' He winks, before disappearing back into his walk-in wardrobe.

'Is everything okay? You keep heading off alone.'

He curses to himself. 'What? No. It's fine. Just needed some air. Took the bike out for a bit.'

'You were gone for six hours.'

'You keeping tabs on me now?' he asks, as he steps out of the wardrobe, towel still around his waist.

'Of course not. I'm just worried about you.'

'I'm fine, really. Living with these knuckleheads all day, every day, kind of grates on a guy's nerves. Just needed some time. So, what's up?'

'Do you have a few minutes to talk?'

'Five max. I'm on rotation with Bas and there's a small chance I'm a little late. Where the fuck are my damn trousers?' Willow glances around and finds them on the chair at the end of his bed. She whistles and throws them to him when he turns around.

'Thanks.' He brings them into the bathroom and changes quickly, as she busies herself by picking clothes off the floor and throwing them down the laundry chute by the wardrobe.

When Shep steps back out, he's swapped the towel for his fighting combats. She hands him a t-shirt which he accepts with a smile, as he sits on the end of the bed and pulls on his boots.

Not for the first time Willow can't help but stare at the series of burn marks running from his waist to just under his armpits on both sides of his body. She made the mistake of asking him about them once and was quickly and savagely shot down. Whatever happened to him, he clearly doesn't want to talk about it and that upsets her. Although they grew up apart, she always thought they were close.

Shep had gone out of his way to contact her on a daily basis while they were away from each other, ask how she was getting on and make sure she didn't need anything. When she found out he was one of the Blackjacks, she immediately wanted to join the team and fight with him.

But he had been against it. Typical big brother stuff, but she persisted and finally convinced him to set up a meeting with Nix. The rest is history. But less than a year on she's still trying to find her place on the team. She's so new and, as much as she loves Shep, he can be a little overprotective of her in the field.

When they're out fighting, he still sees her as his little sister - not a team member. Perhaps it will change in time. Perhaps one day he'll see her as an equal in the field.

He sits up straight and looks at her as he runs a hand over his blond spikes. 'So, what's up Wills?'

'It's Mum.'

As if on cue, his whole demeanour changes. The light-hearted Shep is shoved aside, as the no nonsense version comes out to play. 'Willow...'

And he used her full name. Willow ploughs on regardless. 'It's her birthday next week. She's having some people around. She wants you there.'

Shep tugs the t-shirt over his head, the protesting seams barely hanging on as he takes his mood out on the material. 'We've been here before. I told you not to mention her in front of me.'

'But I'd like you to be there. Please come with me.'

He shakes his head as he storms back into the wardrobe. She hears the hollow bang of metal, followed by a thud, as he slams the gun safe closed again. He marches back out, pulling his holster on and sliding his guns into place. Once he's roughly shoved everything where it should be, he pulls his jacket off the back of the door and slams the wardrobe shut.

'Are you finished having a tantrum?'

'No!' He thumps his fist against the wardrobe door again. 'Now I am. I need you to back off! So help me Willow, I love you to death. You know that. But as far as I'm concerned, that woman is dead. I'm sorry you're stuck in the middle, but that's how I feel. Do you hear me?'

'I hear you. I hear you every time you say that, but you still haven't told me why?'

'What the hell does it matter why? We don't get on. End of story.'

'You haven't seen her for years so maybe things will be different?'

He slams his hand against the wardrobe again, splitting the heavy wooden door. 'Enough! Drop it, Willow. I mean it.' He looks at the ground and takes a deep breath as he gets his temper under control. 'Aren't you supposed to be training with Nix tonight? If you're not taking this seriously, she can find someone else to take your place.'

And there he goes, shoving her away again. It's his MO when she brings up their mother. But calling her place on the team into question is a step too far. She gets to her feet and prods him in the chest. 'So that's how you're playing it? I ask about Mum, and you threaten to get me thrown off the team! Brilliant! Thanks. Great brotherly thing to do.'

He pushes her hand away. 'Stop over-reacting. I didn't mean it like that Wills.'

'And we're back to Wills. You're sticking to form at least.'

'What the hell does that mean?'

'What it means, *Shepherd*, is that you need to get over whatever your issue is with Mum. Dad is dead. She's all we have left. How the hell do you think I feel knowing my brother hates our mother for some unknown reason? You're sticking me in the middle of a seriously awkward situation. It's not fair, Shep.'

His arms drop to the side, and he has the decency to look ashamed. 'I'm sorry about what I said, but it's complicated, okay.'

Willow steps right up to her brother. He's got a good foot on her and who knows how many pounds, but she's far from intimidated.

Out in the field she knows Shep is a force to be reckoned with. She's seen trained True Order fighters have second thoughts when faced with him, but not her.

Before he knows what she's planning, she kicks his legs from under him and straddles his broad chest when he crashes to the ground.

'What the fuck!'

'Complicated? That's the best you can offer me? You are my brother and she's our mother. I will not stop trying to fix whatever the hell is going on with you two.' She leans closer to him. 'By the way, if you ever threaten to get me thrown off the team again, we're going to have a serious problem. I answer to Nix - not you, Shepherd. Do you get me?'

His deep navy eyes glow as he glares up at her. 'I get you,' he grinds out. Willow gets to her feet and doesn't bother offering him a hand up before she leaves, slamming the door behind her.

She hates arguing with her brother, but he can be so infuriatingly stubborn at times. Actually, most of the time. There's just no talking to him.

Willow storms into her room and sits on the edge of the bed. She didn't mean to drop him like she did. It was a rash act that she regrets. He's not well. The last thing he needs is an injury on top of that.

Willow wipes the tears from her face. Her family is falling apart, and there's nothing she can do about it. Her father is dead and her brother hates their mother for some reason. With the added strain of Shep's condition on top of that, she's struggling to keep it together.

She's trying so hard to be strong for him. Shep has always been there for her. No matter what she needed, she could absolutely depend on him to help her. No one could ask for a better big brother. But now she wants to give him a little of the support and help he's given her over the years. She wants to be there for him. But he won't let her.

It's no surprise really. Shep has to be strong in front of others. He might complain and act the idiot from time to time, but under it all he is unflappable.

Not this time though.

She knows he's hurting and he's scared. But the worst part is that he's pulling away from his friends, pulling away from her.

She's losing her brother a little more each day, and she can't figure out a way to bring him back. Fighting with him, pushing him to talk won't work. It was stupid to think otherwise.

Brushing her tears away, she lies down on her bed, hugging her knees to her chest. There's a chance the drug he was given will kill him. It's been mentioned once just after he was injected. But Fletch, Fallon, and Nix had been careful not to mention that point around her since then to spare her feelings.

She closes her eyes, trying to stop the tears from falling, but it's useless. She can't lose him. As irritating as he is, Shep is her world. He needs his family around him - especially now. That includes their mother.

She doesn't know what his problem is, but she's not going to let it rest. No matter what it takes, she'll get her brother and mother in the same room again.

SHEP

'Where the hell have you been? We were due out half an hour ago!'

Shep glares at Bastian as he pulls open the door of the grey Land Rover and climbs inside. 'Don't you fucking start! I've just about had it with today and I'm seriously fucking close to killing someone.'

Bas holds up his gloved hands in front of him. 'Don't take your bad mood out on me. What's wrong with you?'

'Will you just drive.' Bastian glares over at him. 'What? We're late aren't we. Fine!' he says when Bas gives him a look. '*I'm* late. There! I admitted it. Now will you just drive before I'm forced to shoot you.'

Bastian clenches his jaw but puts the car in gear and pulls out of the garage. Shep enjoys the peace while it lasts. But he's known Bastian long enough to know the conversation is far from over. Bastian is his best friend. Has been since the Spaniard joined the team. He's genuinely one of the most solid vampires Shep has ever met. But he's not going to let Shep stew for long. He'll want to talk.

'So, are you going to enlighten me?'

That didn't last long. 'It's nothing. Forget it. I just had a tiff with Willow.'

'Did she kick your ass again?'

Shep growls as he looks sideways at Bastian. 'I might just kick *your* ass if you don't shut up.'

Bastian curses in Spanish which usually means he's massively pissed off. It takes a lot to push Bas that far.

'I'm sorry, okay. I've just had it up to here with criticism today. I just need to beat someone up, then I'll be dandy.'

Bastian glances over at him. 'I'd like to remove myself from that list of options - just in case you have me on it.'

Shep scrubs a hand over his face and tries to calm down, but it's not working all that well. He's so wound up, and he doesn't know why. He's fought with Willow so many times about their wretched mother, but this is more than that.

He can usually blow it off within a few minutes. He doesn't get wound up. Not like this anyway. And the pounding headache isn't helping anything. It's the drug messing with him again. It has to be.

'Are you listening to me?'

He looks over at Bastian. 'What?'

'It's going to be a long night if you either want to beat me up or ignore me. What's wrong with you? You're stressing me out.'

'I'm fine. I just hate when I get into it with Wills. Landing me on my ass was a new finish I wasn't expecting. I was a dick to her, and she put me in my place.'

'She dropped you?'

Shep slowly turns to glare at his best friend. 'Yeah. It's fucking hilarious! And if you tell anyone I was dropped by someone half my size, I *will* put a bullet in your pretty head.'

'You were dropped by a trained Blackjack. You should be proud. She's coming along well.'

'I know, and I am, but that doesn't mean she has to use it in our personal life. It fucking hurt.'

Bastian laughs and glances over at him again. 'What was it about?'

'The usual.'

'Your mother.'

Shep nods as he looks out the window. Nix is sending them to Hereford tonight. There hasn't been much True Order activity there lately, but it's as good a place as any to stretch his legs.

'I'm assuming you don't want to talk about it.'

'You're assuming right.' They've known each other long enough to know it's not a topic Shep ever wants to go near, and thankfully Bas is on board with that. Fuck knows his friend has enough skeletons in his own closet without adding Shep's to the mix.

The silence stretches on until they get to Hereford and Bas pulls into a car park just outside town. They'll make the rest of the journey from above, sticking to the rooftops so he can pick up any scents in the air.

Bas uses his magic hands to open the locks of a factory, and they make their way to the roof. Shep closes his eyes and breathes slowly and deeply as he tries to tune into his senses.

'Don't shout at me.'

He groans and opens one eye to glare at Bas. 'I'm trying to do my thing here.'

'I know. I'm just thinking back to your problem.'

Shep closes his eye again. 'Which problem is that? I've been told I have a few.'

'Your mother and Willow.'

He groans again, louder this time, but doesn't open his eyes.

'You're seriously messing with my calm. I gotta concentrate to do this.'

'Have you thought about asking your mother to speak to her?'

'And there goes my calm.' He turns to face Bas and levels his now glowing eyes on him. 'No. Can't say I have thought about speaking to my mother about Willow, because, strangely enough, that would mean speaking to the bitch, and I'm sure I've mentioned the fact I'm not speaking to her, so not sure how that would work exactly?'

'Stop being awkward, Shep. She's going to keep pushing you to talk to her. You know she will.'

'Yeah well she'll just have to get over it.'

Bas laughs as he sits on the edge of the wall running around the top of the building. 'Let me know how you get on with that. She gets her stubbornness from you. She won't drop it. You know that.'

Bas has a point and that irritates the fuck out of him. He hasn't spoken to his mother for years. Talking to her isn't even at the bottom of his to-do-list. 'Whatever.'

'Did you seriously just respond with whatever? How old are you?'

'Older than you, so shut the fuck up.'

'Shep—'

'I will literally throw you over the side and drop you on the concrete. Please, please, please shut up about it. Willow will be fine.'

There's no reply, which just irritates him even more. He's here to do a job and that doesn't include talking about his mother, so he turns his back on Bas and closes his eyes again.

Thankfully, he picks up on a scent that takes his attention from Willow to some good old hunting. 'That way,' he says, pointing to the left. 'Three males.'

'Order vampires or civilian vampires?'

'Order. They're all carrying. I can smell the gun oil.' He opens his eyes and grins at his friend. 'Can we go and play?'

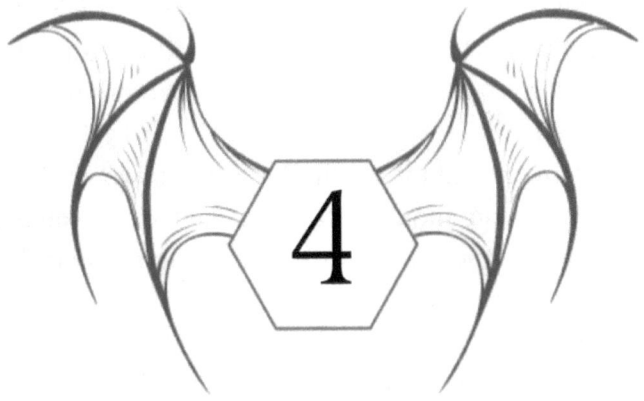

FALLON

She's a highly trained fighter, well able to take down most adversaries. Fallon doesn't do nervous. Never has. But there are some things she can't fight, no matter how hard she tries.

Standing next to Austin's bedside as Fletch examines him, she wishes she didn't feel what she does. The broken shell they found in the lab a few months ago, has been transformed from a barely alive skeleton to a healthy man.

His brown hair is growing out, the soft spikes the exact same colour as his eyes. The huge tattoo of a horned steer skull on the left side of his chest seems to enlarge every time she sees him as he gains weight.

As well as being spectacular, the tattoo is the only distinguishing mark he has on his body. They named him Austin because of it, but the more time she spends with him, the more she is convinced the name is the right one for him. Until he can remember his own, it suits him perfectly.

He still needs a lot of meat on his bones, but it won't be a fast process. They've started him on solid food and he's already putting on weight. In fact, his body is recovering from starvation a lot faster than Fletch expected.

But his recovery had hit a wall. For the last two weeks he's stalled. He should be up and about by now, but he hasn't even attempted to get off the gurney. And that's worrying both herself and Fletch. Hence the thorough examination.

At least now, Austin is calmer. They still chain him by the ankle to the gurney, but he has room to move around if he wants. She hates seeing him restrained like that, but it's for his safety as much as theirs.

He's never once fought against the chains or complained about them. He knows the Blackjacks are trying to help him, so he doesn't hide in fear when they're around him. He's far from relaxed, but whatever else is going on with him, he knows they saved his life. He knows they took him from that glass examination cage where he'd spent who knows how long.

He turns to look at her and she can't help but smile. She shouldn't let him get to her the way he does. Letting her guard down can only hurt her in the long run - especially when it comes to Austin.

They have no idea who, or what, he is. To look at him you'd think he's human, but his blood tests say otherwise. In truth, they have no idea what Rhain and his people did to him in the lab. Until Austin speaks to them, they will remain in the dark.

Unless of course Ethan can ask Rhain what he did, but they're not keen on letting the other side know they have him.

'You're doing great, Austin,' Fletch says, as he checks the notes he's already made. 'Now I reckon it's time to see if we can get you on your feet. It must be boring being stuck in the bed all the time.'

Austin drops his gaze to his legs, suddenly seeming a lot smaller than he did a moment ago. He's not happy about that idea for some reason, but it's time. If he doesn't get up, his mental health could begin to suffer. No doubt it's already taken a hit after what he's experienced. It's time they give him a little normality after all that.

Fletch lifts the head of the bed so they can sit Austin up. 'How about we start by getting those legs of yours moving again. We don't want to take this too fast. Can you wiggle your toes for me?'

Fallon looks down at his legs, waiting for him to do as Fletch asked. But nothing happens. She turns back to Austin, and immediately knows something is wrong. This is more than just being anxious. He's not looking at his feet, instead focusing on his hands, clasped in front of him.

'You okay?'

He clenches his jaw as he focuses intently on his hands. His breathing quickens as he frowns.

'Austin?'

After another minute of intense staring at his hands, Fallon nods to Fletch. Understanding what his sister means, he leaves the room, closing the door behind him. Fallon pulls up a chair and sits beside Austin's bed. She slowly reaches out and places her hand on his leg, squeezing it.

He doesn't acknowledge the contact. Nothing at all. He doesn't tense under her touch like every other time he'd been touched. 'Austin?'

He looks up at her, then down at her hand on his leg. It's barely noticeable, but when he shakes his head, then nods towards his leg, her stomach drops. Fallon stands and squeezes his leg. 'Can... can you feel that?'

He shakes his head, his eyes glassing over.

She takes a breath to compose herself, then places her hand on his foot. 'That?'

Another shake of his head.

Shit! 'You can't feel anything on either leg? Can you move them at

29

all?'

He shakes his head again.

She wasn't expecting that. Never even crossed her mind that there could be something wrong. 'When did you lose the feeling?'

He shrugs.

'Okay.' This is so frustrating. 'I'm going to get Fletch.'

Austin lies back against the bed and stares up at the ceiling, dismissing her. Fallon goes outside and walks over to her brother.

'What's up with him?'

'He has no feeling or movement in his legs at all. He doesn't know when he lost it.'

'Fuck!'

'There's nothing on his scans or x-rays to explain it, is there? Did I miss it?'

Fletch sits on the bench by the window and tucks his hair behind his ear. 'No. They were clear. There is a condition called hysterical paralysis. It's brought on by trauma. If he's remembering what happened to him in that lab, it could be related to that.

'Or it also could be down to something Rhain and his goons did to him. I wish I knew. Did they just hurt him or experiment on him? Is this a delayed reaction to something he was given? Fuck! Okay, we should get back in to him and see what we can do for him.'

He holds open the door for Fallon and joins her at Austin's bed. 'My sister told me about your legs. Are you okay for me to take a better look at your legs and back? All your scans and x-rays are clear, but there's always a chance I missed something.'

He nods and, for the next hour, does anything and everything Fletch asks him to do. But there's still no reason they can find for the lack of feeling in his legs. Fletch leaves them alone, as he goes back to his office to carefully check all the results again.

'Are you hungry?'

Austin nods again, but he's as depressed as she is. After calling Gwen in the kitchen to order some food for him, she sits back on the

30

chair beside him and crosses her legs. She should leave him alone and go back to her room or do some training. He doesn't need a babysitter, and even if he did, it shouldn't be her.

She's not built for this sort of thing. She fights. That's what she's good at. Offering consolation or compassion is far beyond her capabilities. Thankfully, Gwen arrives with a tray of food for him, breaking the awkward silence.

'Here you go Austin. Are you sure you don't want anything yourself Fallon?'

'I'm fine for now, thanks Gwen.'

She takes the tray from Gwen and places it over his lap. 'It's chicken and rice with some vegetables. We don't want to overload your stomach yet.' She sits back in the chair and watches him eat. 'How is it?'

He smiles a little and it's the best thing she's seen. 'I'll take that as pretty good. Gwen is an incredible cook. She'd want to be, with Shep in the building. He's got one hell of an appetite.'

She lets him eat in peace for a few minutes, before she asks the same question she asks every day. 'Do you remember anything at all about who you are?'

He glances up at her, then back at his dinner, before shaking his head once.

'It's okay. Hopefully in time the memories will come back.' Fletch said it's even odds, but she hasn't mentioned that fact to Austin. The poor guy is going through enough without adding that to it. They had determined his memory was taken the same way Court's was. That doesn't give them much hope. Court is still desperately trying to remember anything about his past.

As for why he's not talking, there's no medical reason for that either from what Fletch can make out. She wants to hear him talk. Wants to hear his voice, but he hasn't attempted to utter a single word since he woke up. Perhaps in time that will come too.

Or perhaps, like his legs, something had been done to take that from him.

Fallon watches him eat. The irrational pull to him had refused to lessen as time went by. Initially she presumed it was just pity. Emotions like that rarely affect her, but she'd challenge anyone not to feel something for him and what he's going through.

As the days have passed, she has to admit to herself that maybe she's attracted to him after all. Even for a half-starved man, he's caught her attention on many levels. And that irritates her. She can't afford to develop feelings - whether rational or irrational, for the man.

It's ridiculous.

Yet, she continues to spend too much of her free time with Austin.

She stands and rubs her hands on the legs of her jeans. 'Right. I have to go to work. I'll stop by later to see you.'

He nods and Fallon can feel his eyes on her back as she walks towards the door of his room. 'Fallon?'

She freezes at the sound of her name. Fallon spins and looks over at Austin. He just spoke and it was to say her name. She somehow manages to keep her calm exterior in place. 'Yes, Austin?'

She knows he spoke, but she wants to *see* him say something. She wants to see that stunning mouth move as he talks. Austin frowns and licks his lips. 'Thank you.'

His deep voice is better than she could have imagined. There's a faint trace of an accent but she can't figure it out from those few words. 'For what?'

He pauses, the frown growing as his mouth opens and closes silently a few times before he speaks. 'Saving me.'

Fallon nods, unable to speak, thanks to her throat suddenly going dry.

Austin looks back down at his dinner, then continues eating as if nothing major has just happened. 'We weren't going to leave you there.' She sits down again on the chair beside his bed. 'Do you remember anything about your time there?'

He nods as he chews. 'Some things.'

32

A part of her was hoping he wouldn't say that. The brief bits she picked up from Court and Nix don't paint the best picture. 'What did they do to you?'

He shakes his head. 'I don't know. It was silent.'

'Silent? What do you mean it was silent?'

He frowns again, shaking his head. He's struggling to either find his voice or the right words. She's unsure what it is but she'll give him time. Just hearing his voice after so long is incredible.

'Inside,' he says eventually. 'It was quiet inside. I saw people being dragged from their cells. Saw them coming back unconscious. Then they did the same to me.'

She takes a second to calm down. The anger isn't a new thing. But experiencing it when hearing about his captivity takes her by surprise. 'What did they do when they took you from the cell?'

'I don't know. They gave me something to knock me out.'

The more he speaks, the clearer his accent becomes. It's got an almost French twang to it, but also something else. 'Where are you from?'

His chocolate brown eyes lift from his plate. 'I don't know. I don't know anything.'

'It's okay,' she says, trying to keep him relaxed. 'I think you might be from New Orleans, or somewhere around that area. The more I hear you speak, the more your accent is coming through.'

He silently looks at her, not commenting on that. What can the guy say? He doesn't remember, so it's not going to make a difference to him.

'I'll let you get some rest,' she says getting to her feet. 'You'll need your strength.'

'Fallon?' She turns again as she gets to the door. 'Tell Gwen the food is nice.'

She smiles and nods, before leaving him to finish his dinner in peace. She locks the door behind her, stealing a quick look at him on the screen before she leaves.

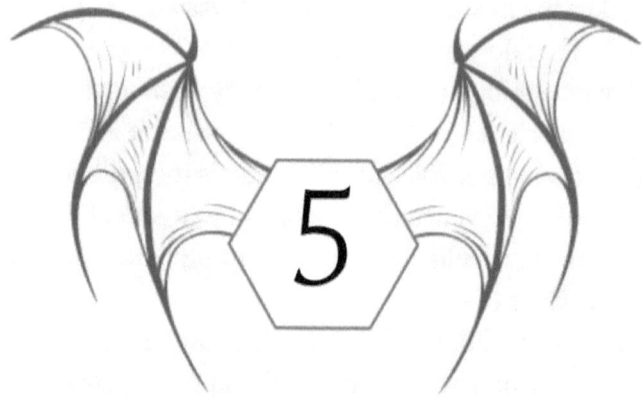

5

SHEP

When he came out tonight, he was wound up like a fucking spring, itching to take it out on some pesky True Order fighters. Unfortunately, as blowing off steam sessions go, this was far from successful. If anything, he's still hyped up, adrenaline coursing through him.

He's annoyed that he has sex with that woman at The Lair. Pissed off about the fight with Willow. Irritated that Bas probably feels like he can't depend on him because he was late.

He could do with wiping the last twenty-four hours from his memory. Start again, not that it would be any different. This is what he does now.

He pulls Bas to his feet, examining him as his friend wipes blood from his face. Bas had been clobbered at the side of the head, but still took down the fighter responsible. He's fucking lethal in the field. Not as lethal as Shep, but not too far behind. Or maybe that's wishful thinking. Bas is a stone-cold killer through and through. One of the nicest guys you can meet, but that's what makes him so deadly.

'You good buddy?'

Bas nods as he steps over the body. 'My head is ringing, but I'm fine.'

'I took care of the other two.'

Bas snorts, brushing his hand over his dark hair. 'Is that so? I thought I took down two and you helped by killing the third?'

'Helped? Are you fucking serious? I did more than help. I'd imagine the knock to your head is causing a bit of confusion. Two for me. One for you.'

Bas squeezes his shoulder as he walks by. 'Okay my friend. Whatever you say.'

'Hey! You totally didn't mean that.'

Bas just grins as he takes out his phone. 'Check them while I call this in.'

Shep searches the fighters' pockets, pulling out a vial and some syringes from the inside coat pocket of the one Bas took down.

'I'm willing to bet my dinner on this being a sedative.'

'Fuck! Boss? It's Bas,' he says when Nix picks up. 'We took down three Order fighters in Hereford. They were carrying sedatives. It looks like a hunting party.'

He pauses while she speaks, then nods and ends the call. 'She wants us to stay here another few hours. See if any more show up.'

'What are we going to do with this lot?'

Bas looks around then points up. 'The roof. Out of the way of humans, but still somewhere The Order can find them.'

'Oh great! So, we're lugging three bodies all the way up there? Okay. I have a plan. How about we each carry the dickheads we killed?'

'So, you'll take two and I'll take one?' Judging by the badly concealed grin on Bastian's face, he's on to him, but fuck it. He'll give his friend this win if it keeps him happy.

'You look tired.'

Shep straightens, glaring at Bas. 'I just took down a few fighters.'

Bas picks up one of the bodies, hefting it over his shoulder. 'That's not what I mean. You've been disappearing a lot lately.'

Shep bends down to lift another body from the ground. 'It's all good, Bas. I just need space every now and again.'

'Maybe try not to be late again. Nix keeps track of that.'

He curses to himself. He forgot about that. He drapes the Order fighter over Bas's other shoulder then hauls the last one off the ground. Shep holds open the door, letting Bas through ahead of him. 'Point taken.'

He follows after Bas, climbing the stairs, the stench from the fighter's cologne assaulting him. 'Fuck this guy is ripe. He needs to spray a little less cologne on himself when he's heading out.'

'He's dead,' Bas says as he reaches the first landing. 'I don't think it matters how much cologne he's wearing. Are you going to talk to Willow?'

'Fuck Bas! We're lugging bodies up a stairs and that's what you want to chat about?'

'What would you like to discuss then?'

'How about you for a change? Everyone is talking about me at the moment. I reckon it's time to shine the spotlight on someone else. You been up to anything exciting lately? Any developments in the love department?'

Bas kicks in the door at the top of the stairs and walks through without answering. No surprise there. Bas wasn't a fan of talking about his own life.

Well?' he asks as he follows him, dumping the Order fighters behind the door.

'Nothing exciting. I spend most of my free time waiting for you to show up.' He grins at Shep. Bastard isn't going to answer the question.

'Okay,' he says, wiping his hands on the legs of his combats. 'I've got a question for you. If you answer it, I'll drop the subject.'

Bas turns to face him, his arms crossed defensively.

'Males, females, or both?'

'What?'

'Which do you prefer? You know there's no judging with me, I'm curious. I'm asking as a mate, Bas. I'm genuinely curious because I think I know but I don't want to assume.'

'What do you think?'

'I'm thinking you're a fan of males over females. But I don't think both. I'm heading more towards the male side of the scale.'

Bas gives him a long hard look before answering. 'Take this as one of those rare occasions you're right. Can we go now. His cologne is making me ill.'

Bas holds open the door for him this time, following after him down the stairs and back to the car. He didn't think Bas would actually answer that question. He'd suspected for a while.

On the rare occasions the team went out in public together to socialise, Bas tended to keep to himself. It's the interactions between Bas and Ethan that gave him the niggling suspicion. He'd bet both arms that Bas is attracted to Ethan.

He's also willing to bet that Bas isn't happy about that attraction. Bas played by the book. He might be a career thief, but the male has scruples and a strict code. Having a thing for his boss would be pissing him off.

Poor fucker is heading to an unhappy ending there. But you can't help who you're attracted to.

'You?'

It takes Shep a minute to register the question. He sits in the driver's seat of the car, settling in to wait and see if someone arrives to collect stinky and his mates from the roof.

'I'm a fan of the females.'

Bas laughs as he sits in beside him. 'I know that. You make it obvious. I meant are there any developments in your love life?'

'Nope. Not a thing.' Being strangely attracted to a human bartender isn't a development. More of an inconvenience. 'Can I ask you something?'

'You already did,' Bas says, lying back in the seat.

'Not about that. Have you ever met or seen someone and you just got this jolt. Like a shock or something like that.'

'Do you mean an instant attraction?'

'Well yeah, but it sounds stupid when you say it like that.'

Bas turns around to face him. 'Hold on. You didn't ask me if I prefer males because you have a thing for me, did you?'

Shep is like a deer in headlights for a minute. What the fuck is he meant to say to that? It's not helping that Bas is giving him one hell of an intense look.

'Okay, right...'

Bas laughs loudly, thumping him on the shoulder. 'I'm joking with you! Besides, I have taste. You're not my type.'

'Phew, plus also I'm kind of insulted by that. Why the fuck not? I'm a catch.'

'Perhaps to some.' He stops smiling as he rests his head against the headrest. 'Who did you have the instant attraction to?'

'No one.' He's not so sure he wants to talk about this out loud. It's fucking ridiculous to have been so wrapped up in someone he's never even spoken to.

'I was honest with you. To put it in simple terms, I'm gay, Shep. Now I'm asking you to be honest with me.'

'Fuck! When you put it like that, I can hardly be a dick about it, can I. Okay so I was at a club and there was this woman. I didn't even talk to her. Her scent just hit me. It was like I'd been punched in the gut.

Then I saw her and… well, she's gorgeous Bas. But I've never had that instant attraction. Have you?'

'Have you gone back to see if it was a one-off?'

No response to his question. That's Bas telling him he's done talking about himself. 'I'm kind of afraid to. If it was a one-off, I'd be a bit bummed. But if it happens again, what the fuck am I meant to do?'

'How about you try talking to her.' Bas laughs at the confusion on his face. 'This could be harder than I thought. How about you see if you have the same reaction first. It might just have been your hormones. You're continuously going through puberty.'

'Hey! I can't help it if I'm young and full of life. Maybe you should take a leaf from my book. You are a decade younger than me.'

'I'm more mature. There's nothing wrong with that. And stop changing the subject. Go back and see what happens. I presume she's human?'

'Yep.'

'Small steps. See if it was hormones or something genuine.'

Bas turns away to look back out the windscreen. He's about to ask him again if he's attracted to anyone to see if he'll open up about Ethan, but he stops himself. Bas looks downright miserable as he stares ahead of him. He's poked into Bas's private life enough for one day. Maybe he should think about his own.

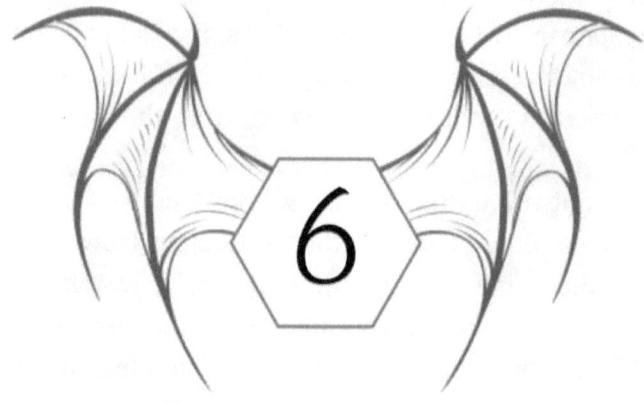

SHEP

He removes his helmet and rolls his shoulders, the muscles cracking as they move. He's wound so damn tight he'll put someone in the hospital if he doesn't release some of the tension - quick. He looks up at the flashing neon sign at the side of the building and inwardly groans at his choice. He hates The Lair, but right now, it has exactly what he needs.

Her.

That damn bartender.

Okay so that's a bit unfair. It's not her fault he can't stop thinking about her and that sucker punch to his gut when he caught her scent.

He'd heard other vampires talk about the irrational pull towards a potential mate, but he always put it down to stupidity or foolishness on their part. How can someone have that hold on someone else within seconds of meeting? It's totally far-fetched.

But now there's a slight possibility he gets it. Maybe? But maybe not. It might just have been his raging vampire hormones that got the better of him. It wouldn't be the first time that happened.

He curses to himself and swings his leg over the saddle of his black Ducati. This woman he's obsessing over is human. Massive flaw in the plan. Vampires and humans don't belong together. His parents were mixed race and it ended in a disaster. But that might just be because his mother is a bitch. It doesn't mean it would be like that with every mixed couple. Davyn and Thea seem to be managing just fine.

Considering Dav is the last male he'd expected to see in a relationship, that's a fucking miracle.

His plan tonight is to see that human bartender again, realise he's being completely ridiculous, then move on. Nice and easy. He was just tired and fed up the last time.

The bouncer nods when he sees Shep, stepping aside to let him in. Even if he wasn't a regular, the human wouldn't have been stupid enough to try and stop him. Especially when he's in one of his *don't you fucking dare mess with me* moods.

He doesn't bother checking his coat and helmet at the desk. He won't be here long enough. Just long enough to see the bartender, get his head back on track, then get the fuck out of here.

The sickening smell of drink, sweat, drugs, and sex hits him like a physical blow as soon as he opens the door. It's a nasty combination and one he plans to avoid tonight. The place is heaving, which doesn't improve his mood as he fights his way over to the bar.

Three separate women try to get his attention on his way through the room. It's less than he would usually attract when he's here. He must be losing his touch, or else they can pick up on his vibes. He's not hiding the fact he's pissed off.

When he finally reaches the bar, he sits on the stool that suddenly becomes available when he glares at the previous occupant and orders a coke. After assuring the bartender that he really just wants a

41

coke, he is served his drink.

He takes a sip and grimaces. It's warm. Shep pushes it away from him and looks around the room. Scantily clad humans writhe on the overcrowded dance floor, most of them completely missing the beat in the music.

But there's no sign of the woman. So much for his quick in and out. Maybe she's not working tonight. He closes his eyes, then tries to block out all the irritating human banter around him. He can still remember her scent from the other night. It's ingrained in his senses, refusing to leave him be.

Then he picks up on her. His tracking usually only works for vampires, but occasionally he can pick up on a human scent. And she's easy to find. She was here earlier. Her scent is diminishing, so it must have been a few hours ago. His gums throb around his canines as her scent surrounds him, instantly turning him on.

Fuck, she smells good. Really, really good. He turns his head trying to follow her scent, but it disappears when it reaches the main door. Fuck! He missed her. Of course he did. It's not like he's going to catch a break. Story of his fucking life.

Just before he opens his eyes, he smells the club owner, Marty, a good minute before he makes an appearance beside him. The man epitomises everything he dislikes about humans.

The badly fitting suit shines under the strobes, his jewellery is attempting to be something resembling gold and is obnoxiously large, while his thinning hair wishes it were as big. The gel only helps to highlight his stark white scalp through the thinning locks. The man is trying too goddamn hard to be something he's not. He's trying to fit in, to be recognised as someone to be in awe of. Shep doesn't even pity him.

'Good to see you again so soon.' Marty holds his hand out, but Shep ignores him. After a minute, he pulls it back and laughs to hide his embarrassment. 'Do you need a private room tonight?'

He shouldn't. What he should do is go back to the compound and get some sleep. Put some distance between himself and this place.

But he can't. Thanks to her scent he's got a serious hard-on he needs to deal with. Before he can stop himself, he nods and Marty grins. 'Your usual room is vacant. It's ready when you are.'

Go home Shep. Stand up and leave!

But the sensible voice in his head is going to be ignored. The brunette beside him makes sure of that. She catches his eye and smiles, spinning on her stool to face him. Why not? He's stressed out and pissed off. Might as well do something about it.

He pushes away from the bar and leans over to speak to her. 'You want to head upstairs?'

Please say no. Please!

'I'd love to.'

He doesn't bother to smile, or show that he's in any way excited, because he's not. It's a need, not something he wants. Something he's been trained to offer without argument.

The crowd parts in front of him, as he makes his way over to the stairs at the far side of the dance floor, with the woman trailing after him. He places his hand on the banisters and immediately pulls it back again. 'I hope that's drink,' he mutters as he wipes his sticky palm on his leathers.

He pauses at the top of the staircase, as an unwelcome but familiar thickness settles in his throat. There will be plenty of time afterwards for a good dose of shame. Right now, he needs to do this.

Just before he closes the heavy door behind him, blocking out the noise from the club, he catches her scent again. She's back. Fuck! He scans the room below him and his stomach tightens when he spots her. And she's looking right at him. And at the woman hanging off him.

The bartender frowns as she takes in what's happening. She won't care. Why should she?

But he doesn't need enhanced hearing to pick up on her sharp inhale. She's upset. Why?

The bartender fiddles with her dark hair, tucking it behind her ear, before turning away and speaking to one of the other employees. She takes a tray from the bar and weaves through the crowd, collecting glasses from tables.

'Are we doing this or what?' the woman asks, pulling at his jacket in an attempt to get him to move.

He wants to move all right. He wants to go after the bartender and apologise, which is stupid considering he's got this other woman ready to go and he's never even met the bartender.

His body needs the release, but instead of shutting off from what's about to happen, his mind is on that bartender and the look on her face. The disgust. The disappointment. All aimed in his direction.

All the same things he feels every time he leaves that room after fucking some random woman.

Her scent hits him again, the impact almost physical. He grabs onto the railing in front of him as he tries to ignore it. But it's like ignoring Dav when he punches you in the gut. It's not possible.

He focuses on the door at the end of the corridor and tries to get his head in the game. This is the best he can hope for. The best he deserves.

Before he can give in to all the other emotions threatening to take over, Shep takes the woman's hand and leads her into the room at the end of the corridor.

IZZY

She hadn't seen the man again for a few nights, but that didn't mean she had forgotten about him. Far from it. Each night she had hoped he'd visit the club, which is ridiculous. She'd heard about him from a few of the servers. Each one had backed up what Sabrina had said. He comes here for sex.

Perhaps she's a little old fashioned, but she has always preferred to get to know someone before she took that step with them. Considering he doesn't seem to be a fan of talking to anyone, she needs to put all thoughts of him from her mind and get on with work.

But there he was. In the same place she had seen him before. She'd caught his eye again tonight. This time however she had turned away. Leave him to his fun and games upstairs. She wasn't going to interact with him or play any part in whatever he was thinking while he was looking at her.

Thankfully, the club is busy, so she easily gets caught up with work for the next hour. She has no idea what makes her turn around, but she does just in time to see him walk down the stairs alone. Maybe the woman is still fixing her hair and make-up after their time together? He stops at the bottom of the stairs and looks directly at her again.

This time though he doesn't smile. If anything, he looks downright miserable. The utter sadness she sees in his face for the briefest of moments isn't what she was expecting. He turns away from her, making his way through the crowd towards the bar. He orders a drink, downing it as soon as he is served. He orders another, this time taking it over to the seat he was in when she first saw him.

Izzy goes back to her work, but she can't stop looking in his direction. Each time, she catches him looking at her, turning away when they realise they're looking at each other. Another woman approaches him, but whatever he says to her has her scuttling off, her cheeks flushed with embarrassment.

She continues collecting glasses, her attention moving back to him every few minutes. He doesn't appear to have ordered another drink. He's just leaning on the table, his head propped up on his hand, the other one turning the glass.

'He has got you hook, line, and sinker.'

Izzy laughs at Sabrina, moving behind her to unload her full tray. 'Would you stop it!'

'Relax! You're only human.'

Izzy takes a cloth from behind the bar and wipes her tray, again glancing down the length of the room to the man who is still looking at his glass. 'He's not that good looking.'

Sabrina snorts loudly. 'Oh, would you leave it! Of course he is. Seems to be on a bit of a downer today though. Hey, maybe that woman was a bit of a disappointment. Might have left him unfinished.'

'Oh, stop it!'

'What?' Sabrina asks, grinning widely. 'He could be sitting down there waiting for someone to give him a hand.'

'I'm leaving,' Izzy says, laughing as she walks away from Sabrina. She's never worked with someone like Sabrina before. She certainly keeps the long hours here interesting.

Izzy wanders around the room, walking past the man to deal with some tables on the other side. He moves his attention from his glass to her. Time slows for Izzy as she passes him, his cologne hitting her over all the other smells in the room. But it's his eyes that yet again capture her.

Why do they always look like they're glowing?

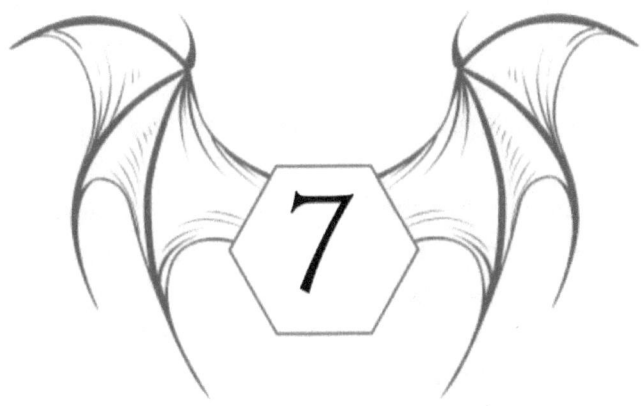

ʃHƐP

Well, that didn't go to plan. Not that he actually had a plan as such. It was more of a see how it goes kind of situation.

And judging by the fact all he can smell is her, wherever he is in the bar, he's got it bad. Fucking vampire hormones are well and truly kicking his ass.

He's managing to do a fairly decent job of that himself.

Why did he have sex with that woman? It's the same fucking story every single time. He needs sex. He has sex. He hates himself.

For some reason though, seeing that bartender before and after his trip upstairs only added to the overall grotty feeling he's experiencing.

He's caught her looking at him a few times, but then again, he's been doing the same. Whatever this thing between the two of them is, he needs to end it. Yeah, she's hot as fuck, and her scent is hitting him like nothing else has ever hit him before, but it can't be anything.

His hormones are just going to have to cop on to themselves and move on. He knows fuck all about that woman but he's adamant he won't be taking her upstairs with him. It makes no sense to him in the slightest, but there's no fucking way he's going to do that with her.

It's not like he'd be able to even if he wanted to. The look on her face when she saw him at the top of the stairs had been a serious mood killer.

What he should do is get the hell out of here and go home. So why the fuck is he occupying a seat at the back of the room nursing a warm beer he doesn't plan on drinking?

His helmet and jacket are on the seat, keeping anyone from sitting beside him. Not that they would anyway. His irritation is no doubt giving off *keep away* vibes.

He's ninety-five years old. Even for someone his age, the number of people he's had sex with is excessive. It could easily have surpassed four figures at this stage. But not once has he been so intrigued by someone before. Not one woman had interested him in the slightest.

For the first time in nearly a century, he's lurking in a bar he hates, just so he can have another few minutes watching a woman collect dirty glasses and empty bottles. He should be on his way home to scrub all traces of sex from his skin. That's what he usually does. She's even managing to distract him from that, which is quite an achievement.

He picks up the beer, taking a swig just to make it look like he's not completely weird. That horse has bolted, but it's worth a shot.

Shep leans back in the torn leather seat, scanning the room instead of leering at her. Not much chance of that. She really is beautiful. Her black hair is wrapped in a neat bun, but he'd guess it's fairly long judging by the size of the bun. Her blue eyes meet his every now and then, lingering before she looks away. She's either interested in him or thinks he's disgusting.

Probably the latter.

He could do what Bas suggested and get off his ass and talk to her. That's usually how this stuff is done. It's just a pity he's a virgin when it comes to dating. He's never even kissed someone.

That's what makes this whole thing so impossible for him. How do you explain that you're ninety-five years old and never kissed someone? It's a fucking joke!

Resigned to being miserable for the rest of the night, he takes another drink from his beer. He'll give it another ten minutes then leave and put this whole thing behind him. There's a chance he'll grow a set and talk to her, but he wouldn't bet on it.

IZZY

Why is he still here?'

It's not as if he's enjoying himself in the slightest. He's ignored multiple efforts by many women to engage him in conversation and is still on his second drink. He just seems to be deep in his head, ignoring everything around him.

Except her. She's caught him looking at her a few times in between staring at his beer. She has no doubt it would have shrivelled up under the fierce glare he's giving it had it been a person.

He suddenly shoves the drink aside, scrubs a hand over his face, and stands up. He grabs his jacket from the seat beside him, and shrugs it on, then picks up the motorbike helmet.

Izzy realises a little too late that, in his rush to leave, he hasn't noticed her heading towards a table near him. The man ploughs straight into her, sending her flying back towards a table. He catches her before she hits it, propping her back on her feet and holding her steady.

He keeps his hand on her arm as he examines her, his grip firm and strong. 'Damn it! Sorry about that, love. I was miles away. You okay?'

She nods, unable to voice any answer thanks to the mortification of nearly falling on her ass in front of him. It doesn't help that his deep, husky voice mixed with the Yorkshire accent, is stunning. She could easily listen to him talking for hours.

His eyes settle on her arm, and she could swear he growls. 'Fuck! You're bleeding.'

She glances down and notices that she's caught her elbow on the corner of the table. 'It's okay, really.'

'Blood doesn't usually mean it's okay.'

'I'm fine. I should get back to work.'

'Like hell you are! You're going to stay right there and let me take care of you. No arguments.'

Once she nods in agreement he goes over to the bar, speaks to one of the servers, and comes back a minute later with a first aid box. 'C'mon. I can't hear myself think in here.'

He leads her into the storeroom to the left of where he was sitting. He leaves his helmet on a box of crisps, then shrugs off his coat, laying it on a crate of beer. 'It's not a plush armchair but it'll have to do. Take a seat and I'll see to your arm.'

She sits on his coat as he drops down on one knee in front of her and takes her hand in his, carefully turning her arm so he can see the cut. 'You hurt anywhere else love?'

She hears the words, but all she can concentrate on is the heady spiced tones of his cologne, mixed with the scent of his leather jacket. He's so close to her it's all she can smell, and it's distracting in such a good way. Having him on one knee in front of her isn't helping either.

His navy eyes lift to meet hers when she doesn't answer. They're beautiful eyes but absolutely no glowing. That just proves she was seeing things every other time.

'You okay love? You've got a weird look on your face. Not that I'm saying your face is weird, cause it's not. Far from it actually. But you're coming across a bit confused. But I'm probably not helping with my need to fill this awkward silence I created by nearly killing you. Might be best I shut up.'

He winks and she laughs. 'You don't have to shut up, and I assure you I'm fine. Really.'

'You sure? 'Cause you seemed to zone out on me. Did you hit your head? I've done that a few times myself. Wouldn't recommend it.'

She rubs the back of her head even though she's uninjured. 'No. I definitely didn't bump my head.'

'So, any other bumps I need to deal with?'

This time she actually takes a few seconds to assess her body before shaking her head. 'Just my elbow. I'm so sorry about this. I'm so embarrassed.'

He smiles and God help her - he's got a dimple. Just one on the left side of his mouth. 'What do you have to be embarrassed about? I'm the idiot who wasn't looking where I was going. I could have really hurt you.'

Izzy smiles at him, completely out of anything remotely interesting to say. Or even uninteresting. There's nothing. Her mind has upped and left the building. For some reason she's turned into a blushing mess at the one time when she could really do with being cool and collected.

Instead of making an even bigger idiot of herself, she decides to keep her mouth shut and just watch him cleaning her wound. His touch is gentle as he dabs the gauze over her skin, wiping the small trace of blood from her.

Even on one knee, he's tall. He's got to be a good bit over six foot. And he clearly spends a lot of time in the gym. But it's his hair that she can't stop looking at. It's even more touchable up close. If he looks like this now, how would he look just out of bed?

Why is she even thinking like that? She needs to remain aloof.

51

Composed. Unaffected by his touch.

He finishes cleaning her elbow and fixes a plaster over the cut. When he slowly lifts her arm and kisses the plaster, his navy eyes locking on to hers, she turns scarlet. Her aloofness instantly vanishes.

'That feel okay?' he asks in a deep voice that sends a shiver through her.

She nods as she swallows in a desperate attempt to find enough moisture in her mouth to speak. No wonder he has a near endless supply of women willing to go upstairs with him. He has the sexiest voice she's ever heard.

'You've gone all weird on me again? Are you sure I haven't given you a concussion?'

'What? No. I'm sorry. The cut feels really good. Thank you.'

He lowers her arm and nods. 'Glad to hear it.'

'Can I get you a drink as a thank you?'

He glances up at her, and she focuses on his incredible eyes again. 'I'm grand love. If anyone should be buying the drink, it's me for you.'

'We're not really allowed to drink while we work. But I could get you another if you want?'

Izzy doesn't take it as a good sign when he stays silent for a good minute as he considers that. 'Better not. I've got to run. I'm working later. Wouldn't want to be late. My boss would kick my ass.'

The disappointment is hidden as she smiles at him. 'No. That wouldn't be good at all.'

He smiles again and she swears her insides turn to jelly. What is it with this guy? She knows nothing about him, but one thing is clear. He is without a doubt not someone she has any business looking at the way she is. In fact, what she should be doing is walking away and leaving him to it. He just did her a favour by calling an end to this before she finds herself somewhere she doesn't want to be.

'You sure you're okay, love? I can have a chat with Marty - get you the night off.'

'I appreciate that really, but I'm fine. It's just a small cut.'

He packs away the kit and stands up, holding out his hand so he can help her up. She places her hand in his, gasping when he pulls her upright as if she weighed nothing. But he doesn't let go of her hand. And she doesn't try to slide her hand from his. His palm is warm, the skin rough and calloused against hers. Whatever he does it's a manual job.

He leans forward as he moves closer to her. 'I'm here a lot and I haven't seen you before. Are you new?'

'I started about a week ago.'

'That explains that then. I was sure I'd have remembered you if I saw you before. Anyway, I better let you get back to it. Apart from hurting you, it was nice to bump into you.'

'It's just a scratch. Forget about it.'

He grins again and that blasted dimple makes a comeback. And now she's focusing on his mouth, which is absolutely the wrong thing to do.

'Not sure that's possible.'

When she catches a glimpse of a piercing in his tongue, she has to force herself to look away, but then his eyes catch her attention. She's never seen eyes like his before. They appear to be glowing again, but that's probably a figment of her overactive imagination. It has to be. Something about this man is throwing her off kilter in a way she's never experienced before. It's as if the air around him is charged, heightening her body's reaction to him.

'What's not?' she asks, not quite sure what they're talking about. The only thing she can concentrate on are his eyes.

'I'm not sure I can forget about you so easily.'

His head tilts to the side, his attention solely on her mouth. He seems as confused as she is right now.

Is he going to kiss her? Is she going to let him?

Never mind letting him, if this intense staring keeps up, she's going to kiss him first.

Izzy has no idea who moves first, all she knows is that one minute she's a few inches from him, and the next her lips are against his.

Izzy groans against his mouth, desperation suddenly taking over. His pierced tongue invades her mouth, and she can't get enough of it. She's been kissed quite a few times in her life, but nothing comes remotely close to the way he's kissing her. It's all consuming.

She places her hands on his arms which are still hanging by his side. As soon as she touches him, he breaks the kiss, shaking his head as he takes a step back. 'Sorry love. I didn't mean to lunge on you like that.'

'No apology needed. I probably should apologise too. I'm not sure who instigated that.'

His addictive smile comes back, taking away the sudden awkwardness that comes over her. 'Better go before I get into trouble. It was really nice to bump into you.' He picks up his helmet then grabs his jacket from the crate. 'Take care love.'

She watches him go, leaving her feeling like some love-struck puppy. That was weird. Not the kiss as such. That was amazing. But he didn't hold her or even touch her apart from the kiss itself. He was rigid in front of her. If she were to hazard a guess, she'd say he was extremely uncomfortable about the kiss as a whole.

She's still replaying the kiss a good few minutes after the door has closed behind him, only coming back down to Earth when Sabrina bursts through the door.

'Oh. My. God!'

She rolls her eyes at Sabrina, trying to manoeuvre past her to get back to work.

'What?' she responds, attempting to get her head out of the clouds where it's bouncing around.

Sabrina gestures towards the door. 'You and Mr. Sexy Accent heading off in here. Alone. What happened? Tell me all!'

'Nothing really. He just cleaned my arm then kissed me and left.'

Sabrina's mouth opens and closes a few times before she screeches. 'You are kidding me!'

'No. Why?'

'Hold on one teeny second there. He what? Kissed you! Sexy Accent kissed you? Are you sure?'

'What are you talking about? Of course I'm sure. I know I don't get out a lot, but I still have a fair idea what it's like to be kissed.' Not that his kiss was anything like any kiss she's ever had before. He may not have held her, but his mouth and tongue were more than capable of driving her crazy.

'What was it like?'

'Sabrina!'

'Oh come on! Tell me. I'm going through a dry spell. I need info like this to keep me going.'

Izzy sidesteps her, escaping into the crowded, noisy club. 'I'd prefer you didn't get off on images of me, thanks all the same.'

'Spoil sport! Okay, just tell me, was it good?'

She sighs dramatically. 'Yes. It was good. Fine!' she says when Sabrina gives her a bemused look. 'It was pretty amazing actually. There! Are you happy?'

'Not really. It wasn't me he was kissing, but there you go. I'm happy for you.'

Izzy laughs at her friend's reaction. Seems he's got to her too. 'It was nothing. He bumped into me. Then kissed me for no apparent reason. That's it. Why is everyone so captivated by him? I don't see the attraction.' Of course she does, but she's going to make a concerted effort to act otherwise.

Sabrina rests one hand on her hip and hits Izzy with a *yeah right* look, and she can't blame her. 'He's a great tipper, never causes any trouble, is polite, has an accent to get wet over, is the perfect advert for why people should use the gym. Oh, and he's gorgeous! That's why.'

'Okay, you might have a point.'

'Actually, that was quite a few points. Plus, I have never ever heard of him kissing anyone before. Not once.'

That surprises Izzy. 'But he's well known for taking women upstairs.'

'Yes, but it's also well known that he doesn't *kiss* them. Loads have tried, believe me, but it's not what he does. Apparently, he just hadn't found the right person to kiss. Until now?'

'Oh stop! You're blowing this completely out of proportion. No one knows anything about him. Like you said, he just comes here, stares at his drink, has sex, then leaves. Do you not think it's all a little weird?'

Sabrina shrugs as she checks her reflection in the mirrored back to the bar. 'Who cares? With the crowd this place pulls, I'll take weird over some of the other options.' She leaves Izzy to it, heading off to clear some glasses from a rowdy table in the corner.

Sabrina might have a point. Looking around the room, that man is probably at the normal end of the scale. Izzy busies herself by tidying the area behind the bar. Why did he kiss her? She just assumed it was what he did. That he was coming on to her like he did with so many others.

So, if he wasn't doing that, why did he kiss her?

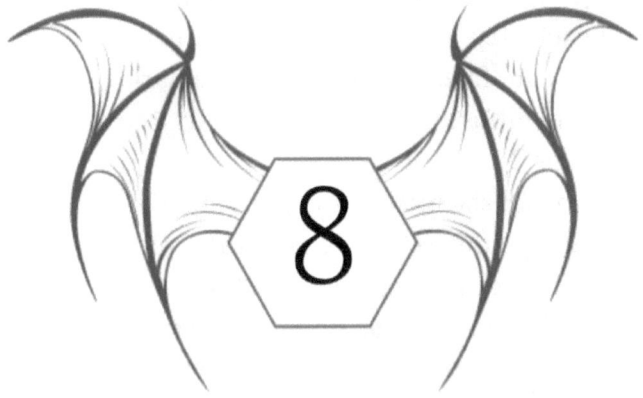

8

SHEP

As soon as he pulls in beside Bastian's bike, he knows he's in trouble. Nix is standing beside the Bus, her arms folded and a seriously pissed off look on her face. He looks around, but it seems he's going to be the lucky recipient of her wrath.

Just what he needs right now. He's already fucked off at himself for what happened in The Lair. He kissed her. Him. What the hell was he playing at? It was as if his brain just decided to shut off and his instincts took over.

Why is he thinking that's a terrible thing? Kissing is a perfectly normal part of life. Well, to everyone except him. But it wasn't all that bad. Until she touched him, he'd been enjoying it. It's just a pity he didn't have a fucking clue what to do. He knows he was supposed to hold her or at least touch her in some way. Standing like a fucking statue while he kissed her was stupid. The poor woman probably thinks he's an even bigger idiot than she already did.

Best get this over with so he can crawl into bed with a good load of self loathing. He turns off the engine, then leaves his helmet on his bike. With each step he can feel the anger coming off Nix in waves. He stops in front of her and puts his trademark grin on his face in a vain attempt to diffuse the situation...whatever that situation is. 'Hey Boss. What's up?'

Without a word she mounts the steps into the Bus and, with a sigh, he follows. She points to the nearest seat and he lowers onto it. Nix remains standing so she's clearly in lecture mode.

'Any idea why I'm less than happy with you?'

He shrugs, not trying to be flippant, but realising a little too late that's exactly how she would take it. 'Not a clue.'

'You were meant to be on rotation tonight.'

'Shit!' He completely forgot. No wonder she's pissed. That's not on. He never misses work.

'Yes, Shep. Shit indeed. Leaving aside the fact I had to call Davyn in to work instead - which by the way, he's a little annoyed with you about, you were also ignoring your phone. Fallon and Willow are out looking for you.'

'I'm sorry, okay. I was busy and lost track of time.'

Nix shakes her head. 'Yeah, well that's not good enough. You can't just disappear. Not now. Not with everything that's going on.' She lowers onto the seat opposite him going for the softer approach. He's seen all of this before. Getting on her wrong side is something he does too often.

'When Court disappeared, I looked to you for support. And you were there - for me and the team. You were invaluable.'

'It's fine Nix. I don't need you to give me a hug and tell me I'm still important now he's back.'

'You arrogant ass! I wasn't saying that. I was saying that the male who stepped up to the mark is all but gone. We can't depend on you anymore, and that's a big problem for me. Your head is somewhere else, and that won't work out in the field. You could get someone killed, Shep.'

He pushes back in the seat and crosses his arms. He's beyond caring if he's being defensive because that's what he damn well is. This team is everything to him. Every single time he's in the field he gives his all. Having that questioned isn't sitting right with him.

'My head is my business Nix. You going to get Davyn on the couch and walk the counsellor line with him? Or Bas? What about Fallon? Let me know how that goes.'

'We're not talking about the others - we're talking about you. Talk to me, please. I care about you Shep. I want to help you, but I can't if you push me away.'

'I don't need help. I'm tickety boo. I swear.'

'Tickety boo? Seriously?'

'Look, I'll apologise to Dav about tonight. If I survive that, I promise I'll do my best to be... well, better.'

'This isn't a joke Shep. What we do saves lives. It also risks them. Mainly ours. If your head isn't in the game, I need to know.' She pauses and drops her eyes briefly. He knows what's coming next. 'How are you feeling?'

'You mean have I sprouted any wings yet?'

'Fine. Yes. I was trying to be sensitive.'

He snorts and looks away from her. 'No point in trying, Boss. I've got wings growing in my back. It's not exactly something I can change.'

'I know. So, are you going to answer my question?'

He shrugs and looks back at her. 'Physically I'm fine. Some pain from time to time, but nothing I can't handle. Fletch and Fallon are keeping an eye on me. A fucking close eye.' Too close an eye. He's practically living in the damn infirmary at the moment.

'Yes, well that may be down to me. I did ask them to monitor the growth. For your sake, Shep. Rhain was specific about when we should give you the drug to stabilise your alteration.'

Like that is meant to make him feel any better. Having the vampire responsible for Court's memory loss tell them how to make sure he survives whatever is happening to him, is hardly a comforting thought. Far from it. But Fletch had checked the drug. There's nothing suspicious in it. Or at least nothing that they can tell so far. Guess they'll just have to wait and see if the wings come out, then he can be the guinea pig for the drug.

And boy is he looking forward to that!

'I'm just worried about you.' Nix squeezes his arm, and he drops his defensive attitude a little. 'So please keep that in mind and don't disappear on us again, like you did tonight. After Court and Davyn, I could really do without losing any of you again.

'I don't want to ground you, but I will if I feel you're unintentionally putting the team at risk, as well as yourself. I know you. I know you'll go down fighting every time. I'd prefer if you all came home instead. I need you all to come home every time - preferably in one piece.'

He nods, trying to keep himself from talking. The way things are going for him, he'd just put his fucking foot in it again if he says anything. He knows where she's coming from. Her job is to make sure they're all safe, and it's not a job he envies.

Nix waits for a reply or comeback of some sort but realises after a minute it's not going to make an appearance. 'Off you go. And make sure you apologise to Dav,' she shouts after him as he hurries from the Bus.

Well, this is great. Not only is he freaking out himself, but he's also got Nix questioning his place on the team. She may not have said as much, but that's what it boils down to. He's a fucking liability and that's not something he's ever been. He doesn't plan on starting now.

His phone vibrates in his pocket, so he pulls it out. Fucking Fletch again calling him in for a check-up. Barely resisting hurling the phone at the wall, he walks back down the stairs and heads to the medical centre for more poking and prodding. Maybe if the damn wings burst out everyone will leave him the hell alone. He's more than done with all this fussing and worrying.

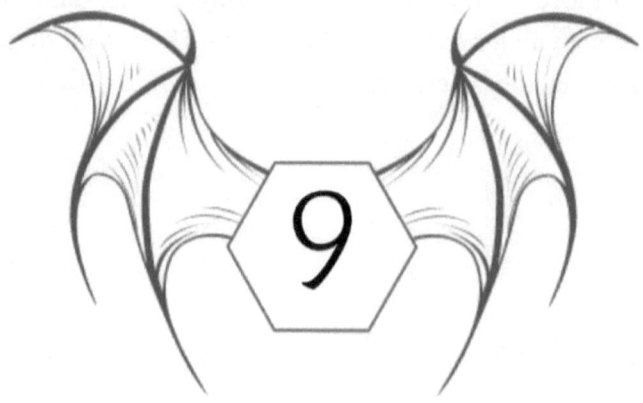

SHEP

The sickly-sweet scent of her perfume assaults him, coating his nose and throat as it always does. Her velvety smooth hand traces down his chest, her perfectly manicured nails scraping against his abs as she touches him, feels him, caresses him.

She moves lower, her nails scraping against his skin. Just before she reaches her target, Shep wakes, scrambling up the bed to get away from the memory. He gasps for breath, his heart racing in his chest, as he tries to separate the nightmare from reality. The scars along his sides and legs burn, each one coming alive as the nightmare fades.

Then his fucking back joins in the fun. He rubs his back against the headboard, but the itch won't let up. His damn skin is driving him crazy.

Shep kicks the bedclothes off his legs and slams his fists onto the mattress. He needs sleep, and to escape from the nightmares, but sleep only brings more, and he's gone beyond tired at this stage. His brain won't shut down. It's always like this when he's overtired. His head takes him back to his previous life, back to a time when he lived in fear and dread. A time he wants to forget more than anything.

Why the hell did he go to The Lair? Was he trying to prove to that bartender that he really is a lost cause? Someone not worth spending the time to get to know?

Because his performance would have done exactly that. Idiot!

It's not like he hasn't been slightly attracted to any of the women before, but his thoughts about that bartender are completely different. This is a whole new level of attraction that's refusing to let up, and that's not what he needs right now. He's got enough shit going on in his life without adding her to the mix.

And yet here he is, sitting in his sweat soaked bed, thinking about her. A few minutes after a nightmare and yet he's smiling. He wants to kiss her again. Wants to have another shot at doing it right this time.

But that all depends on her.

He climbs out of bed, and turns on the shower in his en suite, getting in while the water is still cold. He doesn't care. He just wants to wash the feeling of the nightmare from his skin. As the shower gel slides down his body, his attention is drawn to the burn scars again.

Being with the women in The Lair means he gets to be in charge. There's no talking - just fucking. He's good at it. Fucking brilliant in fact, so when he tells them to mind their own fucking business when they ask about the scars, they do as they're told. No one would risk pissing him off and having him leave the room.

He's got an impressive ego at the best of times, but he knows he's good at fucking. He was trained by the best after all.

He should want to add the bartender to that list, but he doesn't. It's not that he doesn't want to be with her. He just doesn't want her to be with him.

Massive difference.

He gets out of the shower, drying quickly before pulling on his trousers then ducking under the bed to look for his boots.

He jumps when someone bangs on his bedroom door.

'We're going to be late! Again!'

Shep opens the door, smirking at Bas as he leans on the door frame. 'It's my thing. If I'm on time too often, Nix will expect it every single time. Then I'll be late once and I'm back to disappointing her again.' He sits on the end of the bed and laces his boots.

'Under promise and over deliver?'

'Exactly,' Shep says as he searches for a clean t-shirt. He really should sort out his laundry before he has to go out naked. 'Found one!'

Bas peers into his room, shaking his head at the clothes strewn on the floor. 'How do you live like this?'

'My living arrangements have fuck all to do with you, so mind your own business!' He puts on his t-shirt before shutting his door behind him. 'C'mon. I wouldn't want your perfect attendance record to be tarnished by the likes of me!'

FALLON

She is the first to arrive with Fletch, which is a bit unusual. Nix and Court tended to lead the way. Fallon takes her seat in the meeting room, her brother beside her. She's nervous. Also unusual.

'What do you think Nix is going to say?'

Fletch shrugs. 'How am I to know what she's thinking? Just relax. You're stressing me out.'

Easier said than done. Austin's future is about to be decided, and she's nervous. Willow arrives next, with Dav closely behind. Nix and

Court take their seats a few minutes later.

The couple are going from strength to strength. Court's memory loss isn't getting between them. Fallon gives herself a mental slap. What is she doing? She really is pathetic. Next, she'll be comparing herself and Austin to Nix and Court! It's hardly the same thing. Nix and Court are in love. Austin and herself have barely exchanged a few sentences.

Shep and Bas arrive together. Another regular event. Without Bas to keep him to schedules, Shep would be late for everything.

Ethan hurries into the meeting room, removing his suit jacket before he sits down. 'Apologies for my tardiness. I was held up.'

'So, what do you have for me?' Nix asks Fletch, getting straight to business.

'Austin is progressing well. He's on solid food, is putting on weight, and even said a few words to Fallon.'

'He spoke?' Court says. 'Does he remember anything?'

Fallon shakes her head, hating the disappointment she sees on Court's face. He's desperate to figure out how to restore his memory. 'I'm sorry. He can't remember anything of any importance. His cell was soundproofed for some reason. All the procedures were carried out in a different room. He was knocked out when it was his turn.'

'There's a chance he is remembering through his dreams as you are,' Fletch offers. 'But may not be able to process what he's seeing. To be perfectly honest with you all, I'm surprised he's still with us. Any progress he makes is a bloody miracle.

'It also turns out our guest might be from New Orleans. Fallon picked up on an accent when he finally decided to speak. I've checked missing persons for that area, but there's nothing that matches his description. Apart from his accent, we're still in the dark.'

'Is he a danger to us? Why stay quiet and decide to speak now?'

He glances at Fallon before he answers. They'd spoken about this at length before the meeting and came to an agreement. It doesn't mean Nix and Court will be on board, but it's worth asking - for Austin's sake.

'I don't think he's a danger to us,' Fletch says. 'He's been here for months and been nothing but a pleasure to work with. As for why he wasn't speaking, well that might have been down to checking us out. Stay quiet until he knows he's safe. There has also been another unfortunate development.

'We can take the chains off him as he can't walk. I have no idea why. His spine appears to be undamaged, but as of now, he's paralysed from the waist down. I don't know if it's a delayed reaction to the trauma he suffered or something Rhain and his men may have given him.

'All I know is that, until very recently, he was able to move his legs and now he can't. I think we can move him to one of the secure rooms. Give him back a little of his humanity.'

'Shit,' Nix mutters to herself. 'As if he hasn't been through enough. When did he lose the feeling in his legs?'

Fletch shakes his head. 'He has no idea.'

Court looks at Nix and not for the first time, Fallon is amazed how they seem to communicate without words.

'Agreed,' Court says. 'He's been locked up for too long. He deserves more at this stage.'

'But,' Nix interrupts. 'You keep an eye on him. We still don't have a clue what he is, or what was done to him. That's the bit that could end up biting us in the ass. We need to stay vigilant.'

'Of course,' Fletch says. 'His blood work is still exactly the same as when he was first brought in. He is human for the most part, but I agree, something was done to his blood. We'll be keeping a close eye on that.'

'Good. Shep, I want you to secure a room for him. He may not be able to walk right now, but I don't think we should relax just yet. Make sure the best of the best can't get out of that room. Locks and restraints on standby, just in case.'

'Will do Boss.'

'Great. Ethan, you said you've found out some information on the guys Shep and Bas dropped the other night?'

'Indeed I have Nix,' Ethan replies as he straightens his tie. Fallon can't think of one occasion when he hasn't worn a tie. He probably wears a fucking tie with his pyjamas!

'From what I can ascertain they were all affiliated with The Order. Which means they are still acquiring vampires for testing.'

'So Rhain is still looking for a cure?' Court says.

'Perhaps, but he hasn't given any indication that he's continuing with his work. When he lost Court, he also lost his chance of finding a cure for his Blood Fever.'

'Seems he's not to be trusted.' Bas says. The look that passes between Bas and Ethan is one she's seen many times. An unspoken conversation between those who are more than mere teammates. As long as it doesn't interfere with the working of the team, Fallon couldn't care less who is fucking who.

Ethan dismisses Bas's concerns. 'He is to be trusted as much as any informant can be. We take his information with a pinch of salt until it's been verified.'

Fallon glances over at Shep. His expression is closed off, hard and emotionless. Every time Rhain is mentioned he goes into himself. Shep is strong and fearless in the field. But, when it comes to the injection and his wings, he's terrified. And she doesn't think less of him because of that.

'Talk to Rhain,' Nix says. 'Ask that bastard exactly what is going on. If he's still experimenting on vampires, I think our trust, however minuscule that is, might have run out. He might have helped us get Davyn out, and drip fed us information over the last few months, but that doesn't wipe the slate clean. Not even close.'

'I'll arrange a meeting. A few of the Elder families reached out to offer us their support. It seems word of what The Order might have been doing has got out. As much as The Order may want to strengthen Prime numbers, some of the original families don't agree.

'We've received a healthy contribution that will help to ensure we can continue doing what you all do best for a while longer. I'm happy to fund the Blackjacks as long as I need to, but I'm not about to turn away funds if offered to us. Thank you for convincing your mother, Willow and Shep. Her contribution especially was incredibly generous.'

Fallon joins with the rest of the team staring at Shep when he snarls loudly. She's been in many battles with the male, but never heard anything so vicious from him before.

'Problem Shep?' Nix asks.

'No.'

He's got such a fucking problem, but thankfully Nix lets it drop. Fallon can't blame her, and she's not interested either. Whatever issues Shep has with his mother are his. All that matters is that thanks to her, the team are financially secure for a while longer. More time to keep fighting. More Order bodies to drop.

And that sounds perfect to her.

'Okay, so Ethan, you talk to Rhain. Shep, Fletch, and Fallon, I'll leave you to sort out Austin. Everyone else, keep your guard up.'

Fallon leaves with the others, keeping far away from Shep and the less than restrained anger coming from the male in waves. She's got other things to think about right now.

Moving Austin from the cells to a room of his own is putting a smile on her face more than it should. It's about time that male had a little of his humanity given back to him.

ЅHƐP

He shouts, swinging his fists at his attacker. Willow ducks, barely avoiding his punch to the side of her head.

'Don't sneak up on me like that! What the fuck were you thinking?'

She launches at him, slamming her palms against his chest, driving him back against the punchbag he was leaving blood on.

'What the fuck Wills!' He pushes back, not using his full strength in case he hurts her. Her only response is to attack him again, so he pushes back, using a little more force. 'Back off!'

She swipes at him, using her training to give him a good wallop to his chest, followed by one directed at his jaw which he blocks.

His sister attacks him for a good two minutes, hitting his chest and face before she finally screams and, with one final shove in the chest, pushes away from him.

Shep leans against the wall, wiping the blood off his lip as Willow paces in front of him. He's seen his sister pissed off with him before, but this is a whole new level.

'You done, or do you fancy having another go at me for no fucking reason!'

She laughs as she spins around to face him. Her blonde hair is hanging over her face, her eyes full of anger and he's getting the full force of it. 'No fucking reason? Did you really just say that? You growled Shep! They mention that Mother is helping to fund us, and you growl.'

'Of course I growled Willow! What did you expect me to do? Clap my hands and sing her fucking praises?'

'Why not? Is that so much to ask? Or maybe you could just be grateful? How about just saying thank you? Instead, you sit there at the table with the rest of our team and growl. What the hell are they going to think?'

'What does it matter what they think? All that matters is the sun is shining out of Mother's ass yet again. Isn't she great!'

'Stop it! I can't talk to you while you're like this. You're impossible!' Willow scrapes her hair back from her face, the anger draining away, to be replaced by the usual hurt and disappointment left behind every time his fucking mother is mentioned.

There was nothing positive about her donation. It was done to get the upper hand yet again. Maybe get her a step closer to Willow? Honestly, he couldn't give a fuck. All he knows is that it's a calculated move - nothing more.

'I can't keep doing this with you Shep. I can't.'

'I'm not asking you to do anything, okay? Your relationship with her is your business. The last thing I want to do is get in the middle of that. I really don't. But I will not sing her praises for her donation, okay? We don't need her money. Every single penny Ethan brings in to the team is—'

He stops himself before he says anything else, but Willow jumps on him again. 'Is what? It's old inherited money just like Mum's is. What's the difference?'

Shep runs out of fight. There's no point explaining that he knows exactly where their mother got her money. All that's going to happen is that it's going to drive a bigger wedge between them, and he can't take that. 'You're right. There's no difference. I should be grateful for any funding we get. I'm sorry. I'm just in a mood.'

Willow gives him a long hard look, before cracking a small smile. 'I don't believe a word of that, but I appreciate you saying it.' Willow walks over to him, so he holds his hands up in front of him to block any potential strike. 'Relax,' she says, slapping his hands playfully. 'I'm not going to beat you up...again.'

'I let you win.'

'Of course you did.' She nudges him in the side as she leans against the wall beside him. 'Just don't see everything she does as suspicious.

Please? For me? And the extra funding will take some pressure off Ethan. That's a good thing, right?'

He nods and crosses his arms, rubbing the scars on his side as he thinks about what to say to end this conversation. He loves Willow. Loves her so much he'll do anything for her.

Even if it means grinning and bearing it when it comes to that woman. Even if it means pretending he's okay about her dirty money paying for him to do his job.

He catches Willow looking down at the burns marks peeking out from under his t-shirt so quickly covers them again. There's no choice. He either pretends or tells her the truth about their mother's part in how he got each and every one of those marks.

'You're right. We need the funding and it will help.'

'So, you'll lay off her?'

He pulls her into a hug, resting his chin on the top of her head. Everything he's done in his life so far is to protect her. To keep her safe. But more importantly, to make sure she never finds out what he the mother she still loves did.

'No problem, Wills. No problem.'

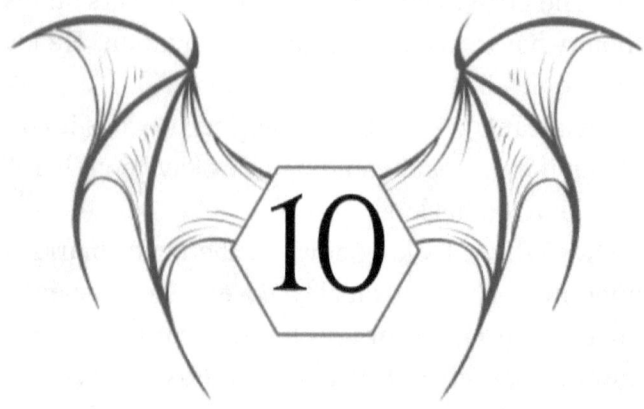

10

IZZY

'Go over to him.'

Izzy laughs as she wipes the spilt beer from her tray. 'I will not. He came here for a quiet drink. Leave him alone.'

If only she could follow her own advice. She spotted the man as soon as she stepped into the bar. Watching him with the woman the other night had affected her more than she expected. But as much as she was disgusted by the ease at which he took her upstairs, she's still drawn to him. Still thinks about their brief kiss. Still can't stop looking at him.

Like right now.

And he's looking at her, a sideways smile on his face and his navy eyes glowing eerily. She must be overtired. There's no other explanation for it.

'He's been here for an hour and dismissed every woman who has tried to approach him. And unless I'm imagining it, those eyes of his have been on you for the entire time.' Sabrina places a bottle of beer on Izzy's tray and turns her around to face the man. 'Go! Or I'll be forced to make a move on him myself, and there's no way he'll be able to resist my charm.'

'All right!'

Izzy picks her way through the crowd, feeling his eyes on her the whole way. She places the drink on the table, and he hits her with a winning smile. 'Well hello there! Fancy seeing you here.'

'Strange that, considering this is where I work.'

'Yeah, as opening lines go it wasn't my best. I don't suppose I can convince you to take two minutes and sit.'

'Okay, just for the record, I'm not interested in heading upstairs with you. I'm sure there are plenty of women here who would jump at the chance, but I'm afraid I'm not one of them.'

Something crosses his face as his eyes drop to the bottle of beer in front of him. Was that shame she saw? Or regret? Maybe neither and she's seeing things again.

'Ouch!' he says, the grin coming back like a mask. 'That's put me in my place, hasn't it? Well, for the record, I wasn't going to mention anything about upstairs. I was kind of hoping you'd fancy sitting and having a chat with me for a few minutes. Nothing else. Not that I'm not—'

He stops himself and holds up his hand. 'Okay, not going to try and explain what I meant and get myself into a hole I can't get out of.' He shrugs and his dimple makes an appearance. 'I'd just like to talk to you.'

Izzy sits on the stool at the far side of the small table and examines the man. He's bigger than she remembers, and even though he's incredibly attractive, there's a hardness to him, an edge. His eyes are on her, but they're also darting over the room, checking out every person near him. He's on guard, ready to pounce if he needs to.

It's what he'd do if he did indeed pounce that she's not so sure of.

'What happened to your lip?'

He touches the cut at the corner of his mouth then grins. 'Ah. Well, that was my sister. We were working out together and she clobbered me.'

She can't help but be impressed. If his sister can do that to him, she must be one tough cookie.

'Can I ask you something?'

He takes a sip of his beer before answering. 'What's a good-looking guy like me doing in a place like this?'

Izzy laughs as he grins at her. 'It's like you took the words out of my mouth. Spooky!'

'Isn't it? Well, to answer your question,' he says, leaning on the table, the shirt sleeves straining to contain his inked arms. 'I can't get enough of the ambience.'

'Ambience?' she says, looking around her. 'What ambience is that exactly?'

'Okay, got me there. How about the music?'

'You're a fan of 80's music?'

'I'm an eclectic kind of guy. I like a lot of things, but there's nothing wrong with the 80's. The music was a hell of a lot better than some of the computer-generated shit that's around right now.'

'Computer generated shit?'

'Yeah. You know like some of the dance music. I'm a fan of music that was actually made by people using instruments. Old school stuff.'

She has to agree with him there. They have a similar taste in music. It's not a big deal. 'So, it's the music that brings you here?'

He shrugs. 'Probably not. Would you believe me if I said I didn't know? That I just ended up here one night, and then another night, and another.' He leans closer, his dark, spiced cologne replacing the ever-present smell of stale beer and sweaty bodies. 'But I now know why I was drawn to this place.'

Her mouth dries again, as her heart races in her chest. She doesn't usually react to guys like this. Never had the instant infatuation she's read about and seen in the movies. If anything, she scoffed at it as something that would, and could never happen in real life.

But this is real life and she's swooning over this stranger. 'You do? Why?' Her voice comes out as a squeak, but he hears it over the music.

'I was waiting to bump into you. Literally,' he adds with a seductive smile.

He reaches out, his fingers brushing along her arm. Goosebumps race across her skin as he lifts her arm from the table so he can examine the cut. His thumb brushes over the small mark left on her skin.

'It's healing nicely. Glad I didn't do any permanent damage.'

'There's barely any mark left. Nothing to worry about.'

He rubs his thumb along her skin one last time before gently placing her arm back on the table. 'I'll watch where I'm going in future. Wouldn't want to knock you off your feet again now, would I?'

'Is that what you did? I thought you were just clumsy.'

The man laughs as he leans against the back of the chair. 'Busted! I was trying to make it sound a hell of a lot better than it was. You know, less clumsy lout and more suave mysterious stranger kind of a vibe.'

'Oh. Right. Going from clumsy to suave is quite a jump.'

He shrugs again. 'I'm hoping it's manageable. Anything I can do to help get things heading in the right direction? Maybe get you a drink when you finish? See if I can be on my feet around you without knocking you over again. You feeling brave enough to give it a go?'

Her first reaction is to say yes. But then she thinks back to the last time he was here when he'd taken that woman upstairs, and she has second thoughts.

As friendly and attractive as he is, does she really need to be another notch on his belt? He may be saying all the right things, but has he said all this to everyone else he's been with? Is it part of his routine? If it is, it's pretty enticing.

'As tempting as it is to see if you are as suave as you seem to think, I'm going to have to pass. Thanks anyway.'

He actually looks disappointed to hear that.

'No problem love. Can't say I blame you. Probably wouldn't risk it myself if I were you.' He picks up his coat and helmet from the seat before standing up. 'I better let you get back to work.' He leans over, his breath warm on the side of her face as he gets close to her ear. 'See you again. Hopefully, next time your friend won't have to convince you to talk to me.'

Then he's gone, swallowed up by the crowd.

SHEP

For three hours tonight he had waited out of sight down the road. He wasn't in the mood to be approached by anyone.

He wanted to see her, and only her.

He had no interest in looking for anyone to have sex with tonight, and he should. It's been a few days. Usually he's so wound up, he'd need that release to blow off some of the pent-up steam. But not tonight.

All he wants is to experience that instant chemistry he had felt with her, once again. The energy that overwhelmed him when they kissed.

The second he sensed her close by, he'd headed towards The Lair, hoping she'd come over to speak to him. After the other night he wasn't sure about approaching her himself. He needed her to make the first move to speak to him, instead of him chasing her.

He walks along the corridor leading to the car park, smiling to himself as he replays their conversation. That instant chemistry was still there. It hit him as soon as he saw her, as soon as he picked up on her scent.

She is fucking gorgeous. Her dark hair, those stunning blue eyes, the way her mouth moves when she talks. He's never noticed something like that before. He could just watch her speaking all day. It was hypnotic.

But then she turned him down. Put him firmly back in his place.

That's a first for him too. No one has ever said no to him. He knows she's attracted to him. He can sense it from her. But she's different. It won't matter how much she wants him, nothing will happen unless he can convince her he's not a total womanising dick.

How the hell does he do that? Yes, he's had sex too many times to count, but it's not how she thinks it is. It's a need, not a desire.

He slams his fist against the wall, wincing when he cuts it on the bricks. Like that is going to make a difference. He'll never be able to have anything remotely normal with the bartender. Never be able to have what he desperately wants. To finally move on.

What he needs is a break. From everything ideally. He's fed up, tired, and maybe even a little scared. The uncertainty of his future is scaring the hell out of him.

What the hell is he doing with however long is left of his life? Fighting and fucking. That's it. Not the best legacy to leave behind if these wings do end up killing him. But that's all he's been doing for the last few decades. Surviving from day to day, using whatever means he can. He laughs, he jokes, he takes the piss as much as he can.

But in truth he's hiding, trying to forget, pretending he doesn't care about anyone or anything.

It's all fake. He's fake. Now he's in a worse mood and just wants to crawl into bed and sleep for a few hours.

As he climbs the stairs leading to the car park, his world spins on its axis. He braces himself against the wall and shakes his head, trying to clear his vision. Maybe he's dehydrated. Probably overdue a feed knowing him. He tends to leave it to the last minute.

Unfortunately, his body isn't happy about waiting. There's something seriously wrong. He's not going to make it to his bike, let alone the compound.

He stumbles up the steps from the basement, nearly dropping his helmet down the stairs. After sitting on the steps for a minute, he slides his helmet onto his wrist, giving him both hands to pull his ass up with help from the banisters.

He's rough as hell and it's got nothing to do with lack of blood. It's the fucking drug. It's not helping that the wings are shifting inside him turning his stomach.

He pauses as he reaches the car park and vomits into the nearest pile of garbage he can find. Deep in his body, the alien wings stir, stretching and pulling at his skin. If he had a knife on him right now, he'd cut the fucking things out of his back.

Shep wipes his mouth on his sleeve and grips the wall, using it to straighten. His bike is only a few feet away, but when he looks up at it, the damn thing is swaying from side to side. He rubs his eyes, and the image stills a little, but his vision is still fucked.

He leans against the wall and closes his eyes, taking a few minutes to concentrate on just breathing. He needs to get back to the compound to sleep off whatever the fuck is going on with his body.

It's at times like this he wishes he could do that dematerialising shit vampires in the movies can do. He's a good hour from home. Even if he does get over to his bike, riding it back to Wales isn't an option.

But first things first - he needs to get to his bike. He straightens, turns to face his Ducati, then puts one foot in front of the other, until he finally reaches it. Leaning heavily on the handlebars, he drags his leg over the saddle and sits down, hanging his helmet on the handlebars as he catches his breath.

That took a ridiculous amount of time and energy, and now he's actually on the bike, he doubts he's going to be able to get much further. If he can't balance walking up the stairs, how exactly is he planning on riding the bike back to the compound?

He leans forward, resting his head on the bike when everything spins again. Yeah, he's fucked.

That's as far as he gets. Any plan to start the bike fades away in a blur of pain. He roars as something sharp pushes through his back, piercing his skin and his jacket.

His last conscious thought is that his bike is about to get well and truly fucked up, as both he and it fall over when his lights go out.

.

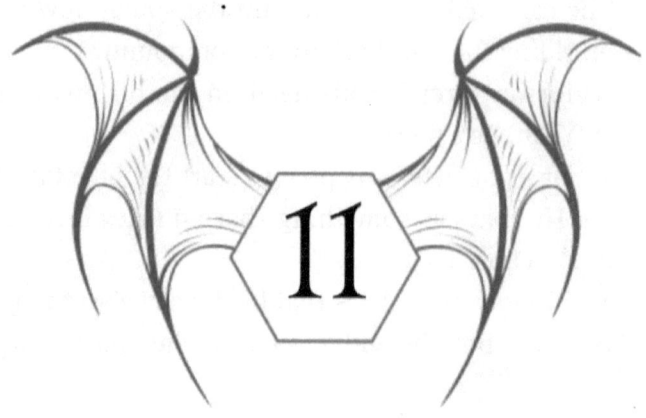

IZZY

As she steps out of The Lair, she pulls up the collar of her coat, tucking her head down as far as she can manage. The biting wind is doing a decent job of penetrating her bones. She hurries up the stairs from the basement of The Lair and across the car park.

Her Pajero is waiting faithfully in the corner under the one working streetlight, waiting to take her away from this dump and back to her apartment. She fumbles in her bag for the keys, but her fingers are so cold she drops them on the ground.

As she bends down to pick them up, she spots something on the ground at the far side of the car park. She grabs the keys, takes her phone out of her pocket and, ignoring all common sense, creeps around the back of the car to get a better look.

In the shadows she can make out the silhouette of a motorbike. It takes her a few seconds to realise it's on its side. She moves a little closer, then throws her hand over her mouth when she realises the rider is lying on the ground behind the bike.

She races across the car park and crouches down beside the prone figure. It's the Yorkshire man. 'Oh my God! Hello? Can you hear me?'

He groans but doesn't respond. He left the club two hours ago. Has he been lying out here in the cold since then?

'Okay, hang on, I'll call for an ambulance.'

'No,' he mutters, suddenly opening his eyes, then roaring in pain as he spasms, his body jolting on the ground as if he's been struck.

Izzy grabs for her phone, dropping it when he suddenly reaches out to her, his eyes squeezed shut in pain.

'I can't. No hospital.'

'You're in agony. And you've cut your face. It's really nasty. Stop being stubborn and let me get you medical attention.'

His eyes open slightly, and he searches for her face, finally settling his navy eyes on her. 'No... please. I can't go to hospital.' He tries to push himself upright, cursing as he gets to his knees before falling forward again. He manages to brace himself before he hits the ground, rolling to his side to avoid whacking his face.

'What the hell are you doing?' she says, as she retrieves her phone from the ground. 'You shouldn't move. Just lie still while I get you some help.'

He cups his head in his hands and groans. 'Fuck!' he shouts as he lets go of his head and arches his back. 'I can't...' he swallows and closes his eyes. 'No hospital. I just need rest. I need to go home.' He vomits on the asphalt, rolling the other way to avoid the mess.

'You're vomiting blood. That's it! I'm calling an ambulance.'

'No! I just need to go home.'

'Where's home?'

'Wales,' he mutters.

'Wales! Great. Of course you live in Wales. Why can't you live down the road?'

81

Izzy looks down at her phone then back at the man. He needs a hospital - there's no question of that, but there's also no question that she can do anything to force him to go. She sits back on her legs and glances over at her car.

Is she really going to do this? She doesn't know this man from Adam. He comes here for drink and sex. Does she really think inviting someone like that back into her personal space is a good idea?

He attempts to get up again, but slumps to the side, landing beside the foul-smelling bin against the wall. He closes his eyes as he breathes heavily through his mouth.

Whether it's the worst idea she's ever had or not, one thing is clear. She can't leave him on the tarmac beside a bin full of who knows what from the club. 'If you won't go to hospital, will you let me take you back to my place? You can rest there.'

He looks up at her through pained eyes. 'Why?'

She shrugs. 'I honestly don't know. All I do know is that I can't leave you here. I'll bring my car over. Will you be able to get into it?'

He doesn't reply for a minute as he stares at her. 'Yeah. I think so.'

Izzy gets up and hurries over to her car. She carefully backs it up to the man and opens the back door. After a few false starts he manages to drag his body into the vehicle and collapses across the back seat.

Izzy closes the door and moves around to the driver's side before stopping and going back to his bike. She takes the key from the ignition and slips it into her pocket, then picks up his helmet from the ground.

There's not a lot she can do about the downed bike. It's far too heavy to attempt to right without help. She sends Marty a quick text asking him to get one of the bouncers to lock up the bike. Hopefully, he'll look after it. The Yorkshire man spends a lot of money in the club. That should work in his favour.

As she climbs into the front seat, a heavy hand drops onto her shoulder, startling her. 'Shit! Don't scare me like that.'

'Sorry. Thanks for this.'

She looks at him in the rear-view mirror and nods, still no more convinced about her plan than she was a minute ago. In the back of her car, he appears so much bigger and intimidating.

But he's been a customer at the club for a good while from what she knows. No one she's spoken to has had any problems with him. Fingers crossed that still stands when she gets him home and she's alone with him.

AVSTiN

Since he woke up in this strange place months ago, each day has been terrifying for several reasons. He's been scared before, so many times. But what he went through before they rescued him - before she rescued him - is like nothing else he's ever experienced before.

He can't remember one second of his life before he woke up in that glass cell. But he remembers most things since then. He wishes he didn't. He wishes he could forget, but the memories keep him company while he's asleep as well as awake. Nightmares more like it. Constant nightmares.

He watches Fallon as she reads through test results. So many tests, but he doesn't mind. It's not like it was in *that* place. It didn't take long to realise these people are trying to help him. Here he's treated like a human instead of an experiment. Here he's not hurt.

She flicks her long auburn braid over her shoulder as she glares at the screen. He knows she's trying to figure out why his legs won't work now. Just another thing to add to his list of confusing things he doesn't remember. Was it something that was done to him in the lab, or is this delayed reaction to what he went through when he was there?

Whatever the reason, he hopes Fallon and her brother can figure it out.

She glances at him over her shoulder and smiles, before turning back to the screen. He's alone in the world. As far as he can remember he has no one and nothing. But he wants her. Not that he can ever have her. He may not have said much since he was rescued, but that doesn't mean he wasn't watching and listening.

Just because these people saved him didn't mean he was going to openly trust them straight away.

After what he's been through, trust isn't something he has a big supply of.

Over the months of watching and waiting he had learned a lot about his rescuers. He knows he's safe here. They wouldn't have spent so much time and effort rehabilitating him if they meant to do him harm.

But it's Fallon over everyone else here that catches his attention the most. Hers was the first face he remembers seeing when he woke up here. She's the one he looks forward to seeing. She's the one he misses when she leaves.

Being around her makes him believe he has a future, that he can possibly claw back a bit of his life, whatever that may be. Makes him believe he can live without fear controlling him.

Fear is all he's known for too long. Every single time they took him from his glass cell it had hurt so much. He doesn't know what they did to him, but the pain after is something he grew to know all too well.

Until they forgot about him.

The day they stopped coming to his cell, stopped experimenting on him, stopped hurting him, was the day he accepted he'd die in that cell.

Until Fallon and her friends saved him.

She's a strong, fierce, and beautiful warrior. Her tall body is that of an able fighter, someone more than capable of defending herself and others. He's disabled, barely able to pull his weak body up the bed without help. He can't do anything for himself. Not yet.

But he's going to hope. That's all he really has. Hope he can walk again. Hope his memory comes back. Hope he can take charge of his life. Hope she notices him as something other than a pity case she needs to look after.

'Do you want anything to eat?'

He shakes his head, but she crosses her arms and frowns at him. She's not going to let him stay silent now he's finally decided to speak. 'No. Thank you.'

He loves the smile she gives him in return. He hasn't seen her smile often, but she should. Her green eyes light up when she does. If he gets that reaction from her when he speaks, he'll keep it up. His throat is irritated but he doesn't care. It had been months – possibly years since he had reason to speak. Doing so now is uncomfortable, but he's sure that will ease in time.

'I was thinking about breaking you out for a while. Nix said we can get you out of your room. Maybe take you into the courtyard for some fresh air? That sound good?'

It sounds so good he can't help smiling. But then he remembers his legs. Unless she's going to carry him, he'll have to be taken outside in a wheelchair. That's not something he's so sure he's ready to accept.

Fallon leans on the edge of the bed, the impressive muscles in her arms shifting as she adjusts her position. 'Hey. I get it okay. Not too keen on being pushed out there? But I'm positive you don't want me lifting you.

'I've been in a wheelchair myself when I've been injured. You've got to look at the bigger picture. Fuck knows you must be sick of the sight and smell of this place by now. Let me do this.'

How can he say no to that? 'Thank you.'

When she smiles again, he feels a little better. She's right. He wants to go outside. He can't remember the last time he breathed air that wasn't pumped into the room.

Fallon disappears outside returning a few minutes later with the dreaded chair. Fresh air. It's worth it.

'You okay for me to help you into the chair?'

He nods, answering her aloud when she flashes him a look. 'Thank you.'

She steps up beside the bed and lifts his legs, bending them at the knees so she can slip one arm under and the other behind his back. Whatever humiliation that hits at the fact he's being carried like a baby, disappears when she holds him. The first thing he notices is her scent. It's woodsy with a hint of vanilla. Simply perfect for her.

She easily lifts him off the bed and into the chair. As she crouches down to place both his feet on the steps of the chair, he does his best not to let the humiliation get to him again. But it's not easy. He may not remember what he was like in his old life, but he knows he's not keen on accepting help. He hates it.

'You good to go?'

He nods as she pushes to her feet, rubbing her hands on the legs of her tight black jeans. He turns his eyes away from her legs. He needs to stop this nonsense. Needs to stop looking at her as someone he could have anything more with.

She grips the handles of the chair and brings him out into the corridor. He hadn't seen much of the compound since he was brought here. They don't fully trust him, which he understands. If he could tell them what was done to him, he would, but he has no idea. He wasn't conscious for any of the procedures.

But all thoughts of that place disappear as she opens the door at the end of the corridor and pushes him into the garden. The sun has set, the moon hanging high in the sky, lighting up the area. A cool breeze ruffles his hair and sends a rash of goosebumps over his bare arms.

It's heaven. So much better than he could have imagined.

Fallon crouches down in front of him, her brows drawn tightly. 'Are you okay?'

'Yes. I like being out here.'

She gestures to his face. 'You're crying. I'm guessing that's because you're happy then, not upset?'

Embarrassed, he quickly wipes away the tears. 'I'm sorry.'

'About what? Who knows how long it's been since you took a lungful of fresh air. It's bound to get to you. That's normal.'

He laughs at that. 'Normal? Is there such a thing in this new world, cher?'

The smile is quite different to what he's seen from her before.

'Cher? What does that mean?'

He didn't realise he'd said that. 'I don't know. It just came out. I'm sorry.'

'Never apologise for allowing what's in your nature. It came from you, from the *real* you. That's good. You're breaking through. Fighting back.'

'It's all I've got left to give.'

She doesn't say anything, but the look in her eyes sends a shiver through him. Was she proud of him in that moment? Fallon tends to keep her emotions well hidden. But the more time he spends with her, the more emotions creep out. Coincidence perhaps? The delusions of a broken man more likely.

'You know what Austin? You might have a point there. The longer I fight, the less surprised I am about what we encounter. Nothing seems to faze me anymore. I'm not sure that's a good thing.'

'Do you get scared?'

'When I fight?'

He nods.

'Sometimes. Fear has a time and a place. Out in the field isn't the time. It can make you second guess yourself. Make stupid mistakes based on emotion instead of fact. That leads to injury or death.'

He can't imagine what it's like to be in a situation like that. After being with them for a while, he has picked up on some of what they do. He's also seen the bandages and the scars when she comes home. 'Why do you do it? Why do you fight?'

Her stunning green eyes turn towards him again. 'I fight for those who can't fight for themselves. I fight so vampires of all breeding and bloodlines can be free. I fight so no one else has to go through what my friends went through. What you went through.' She turns away and shrugs. 'We should all be free. Anything else is unacceptable.'

He believes every word she said. This is something she's passionate about. Something she deeply believes in. He doesn't doubt she would die to protect others. Die for those who can't fight for themselves - like him.

He can't have that. He won't have that. But the idea of being able to defend himself, to fight for himself is ridiculous. He can't walk, so he's already a burden on the team.

But in that moment, looking at her in this stunning garden, he makes a silent promise to her not to be one of those she needs to protect. He will pay Fallon and the rest of the team back for their kindness, for their medical attention, for saving his life.

'Fallon? Will I ever get my memory back?' When she can't meet his eyes, he knows the truth. 'Okay.'

'No Austin. It's far from okay! You and Court had something taken from you and we aren't going to stop until we figure out a way to undo this. I promise you that. Until then we take each day at a time. You're getting stronger. I can see the improvements.'

'But what if you can't figure out what I am, cher? What then? What if I can't walk again?'

'Then we do what we always do. We adapt. We improvise. We fight. And I'll help you.'

'Why? I'm grateful, but curious.'

She pushes to her feet and stands beside him, looking up at the sky. 'You're a fighter Austin. You should have died within a few days of being rescued. You're still alive. I want to see how far you can go.'

It's a good answer, one he couldn't agree with more. He wants to see how far he can go too. He's had a few second chances at this stage. Maybe he's stronger than he thinks he is.

He glances up at the spectacular warrior beside him and smiles. Maybe with her help he can actually be useful. Maybe she can help give him a reason to keep fighting.

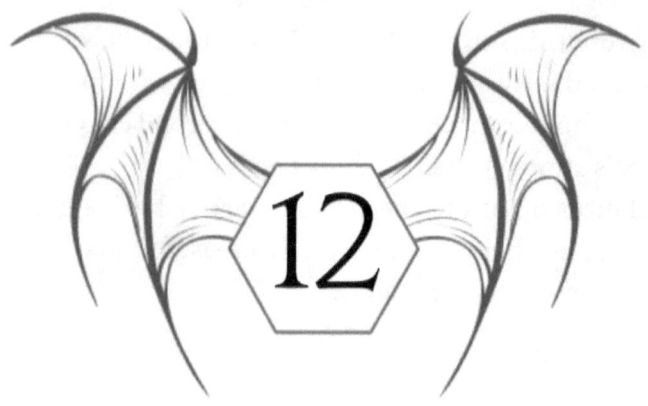

IZZY

How did she get herself into a situation like this? For every minute of her six-hour shift, all she had been looking forward to was a hot bath, glass of wine, and the next chapter in the sci-fi thriller she was reading. Finding an injured man in the car park hadn't been part of her plans.

Especially *that* man.

She peers around the archway separating her kitchen from her living room. Yep. He's real and he's sitting on her couch, struggling to take off his t-shirt.

She hadn't wanted to see him again. Couldn't bear to get all flustered and potentially make a gigantic fool of herself, by either blushing or being unable to stop looking at him. Each brief encounter with him had been electrifying.

She's being absolutely ridiculous. She knows that. Whatever she's experiencing isn't real. He wouldn't be as popular with her colleagues unless he could lay on the charm. That brief kiss, the way he tended to her, everything he said and did, it was all part of what was no doubt a well choreographed performance he did repeatedly.

But... oh God he smells so good!

His cologne is filling her apartment, the dark spiced scent doing nothing to help relax her.

For the ten-minute drive back to her apartment, the man had remained slumped across the back seat, his eyes closed as he breathed heavily through his mouth. Thankfully, he had been able to get himself out of the car and up the steps to her apartment.

Leaving him to get undressed, she fetches her first aid kit, a bowl of water and some towels, and a quick glass of wine to steady her nerves.

She's not afraid of him. All one-on-one interactions she's had with him so far, had shown him to be kind, and not in any way threatening. And the servers in the club wouldn't have been climbing over each other to attract his attention if he was a threat. It's more that the man they're climbing over each other to get near, is now sitting on her couch with no top or trousers on.

Yep. The stunning man is in a nice pair of navy fitted boxer shorts and nothing else.

This is going to be interesting.

'Do you want to lie down?' she asks as she joins him in the sitting room. 'I'll pop your clothes in the wash. I'm not even going to hazard a guess at what you were lying in when I found you in the car park.'

'Thanks. I'd prefer not to think about what's on them,' he says, groaning as he stretches out on her couch. 'The smell is enough to turn my stomach.'

She crouches down in front of the washing machine and begins to bundle his clothes in. But his t-shirt catches her attention. The back of the black material is caked in what looks like blood, but that's not what gets her attention. It's the long cuts down each side of the back that confuse her. It looks like he was stabbed in the back. She checks his leather jacket and finds similar cuts on that.

She turns on the machine then goes back to the man. 'Can you roll onto your front?'

'Why?'

'There are slices in your jacket and t-shirt. You must be injured so I want to check.'

'My back is fine. No cuts.'

'But that's impossible. Your clothes are ripped. It must have gone through.'

He pushes upright and turns, giving her a fleeting glance at his back. It's difficult to see it clearly in the dim light, but she can't see any cuts. There is blood though so surely there must be a cut somewhere.

He lies down, hiding his back from her again. 'See. It's all good. Whatever happened it just got my clothes.'

Something weird is going on, but she doesn't push it. Best deal with his visible wounds for now. 'Are you okay if I clean this cut on your face? It's full of dirt.'

He nods his head. 'Yeah. Go for it.'

She places the basin of water on the coffee table and kneels down on the floor beside the couch. Now she's up close to him, she realises he's really pale and there's a fine sheen of sweat on his skin.

'So, I guess we're even now.'

She smiles as she squeezes out the cloth. 'Oh, is that what you think? You cleaned a small cut and stuck a plaster over it. I took you back to my apartment in my car and I might have to use two plasters on this one. How exactly are we even?'

He laughs, then winces. 'Ouch. Shouldn't laugh. So, you're saying I have to sweep you off your feet again?'

She lowers the cloth and shakes her head. 'Do you ever stop?

You're injured.'

He grins and her eyes are drawn to his dimple. 'I'm one of those guys who knows what he likes.'

'Is that so?'

'Oh yeah.'

'And I presume you're going to tell me that you usually get what you want, right?'

He shrugs. 'I'll let you know later.'

Izzy scoffs, dabbing the wound again. 'How about you stop talking and let me concentrate.'

He smiles again but doesn't respond, leaving her to continue her first aid efforts.

It takes a few minutes to clean the wound then place a plaster over it. She quickly assesses the rest of his body, trying to check for any other injuries and not use the time to marvel at him, thought he is worth marvelling at.

'You okay love?'

She drops the cloth at the sound of his voice. 'Sorry. You startled me. What did you say?'

He swallows deeply. 'Are you okay?'

'Me? Yeah. I'm not the one in pain lying on my couch. What happened to you? You seem to be sore in more places than just your head?'

'Just tired. I've been working a lot lately. Just overdid it a bit.'

She sits back on her legs and crosses her arms as she glares at him.

'Not buying that one, are you?'

'Strangely enough, no.'

'It's kind of embarrassing.'

'I think we've moved past that now. I won't laugh.'

'I got jumped.' He laughs but stops and sucks in a breath. 'Ouch. Keep forgetting not to laugh.'

She doesn't know this guy at all, but that was a bare-faced lie.

Someone like him doesn't get jumped. He's got to be at least six-two and fairly solid. He's not getting jumped. It's ridiculous. Admitting defeat, she shakes her head and tidies away her first aid kit.

He closes his eyes and lifts his arm over his head, hiding his face from view. He may have lied about what happened to him, but he's not lying about being tired. He does look exhausted.

Izzy glances down at his side and frowns. From the waist of his boxers to his armpit are a series of burn scars. Each one roughly the same length and depth in his skin. It's almost like tally marks that you would see on cell walls. The marks continue down the side of his leg, stopping just at his ankle.

She makes a quick calculation. Fifty-six lines on his side. Representing what, she has no idea, but it can't be good. Izzy's eyes drift to his face, startled when she sees he's looking at her. Izzy's heart pounds in her chest as his dark eyes glance down at the scars. He drops his arm, covering them again. He swallows deeply, then focuses on the back of the couch instead of her.

'Can I ask you something?'

He opens his eyes again and smiles one of the most unenthusiastic smiles she's seen so far. 'Sure.'

'What's your name?'

He releases the breath he was holding. Clearly, he thought she was going to ask about the marks and is more than relieved she didn't.

'You don't know my name?'

'Well, no. I'm not sure anyone in work knows. We call you the Yorkshire man.'

He laughs at that. 'Fuck me! That's hilarious. I've heard the servers talk about him. I thought he was this mysterious punter I'd never seen. Didn't occur to me that they were talking about me. As if there were two Yorkshire guys who went there.'

He pushes up onto his elbow, wincing again. She's more than positive there's something else wrong with him. The man holds out his hand and hits her with that winning smile he gave her when they first met. 'Hello. Although I am indeed from Yorkshire, and that name is kind of cool, my real name is Shep.'

'Shep? Is that your first or second name?'

'Both. I'm one of those mysterious guys with only one name. Adds to my appeal.'

'Is that so?'

'Oh yeah.'

'So, it's just Shep?'

'Okay, so technically my name is Shepherd, but I'll get in a serious grump if you ever call me that,' he adds with a cheeky smile. 'What about you?'

'I'm Isabella. But I'll get in a serious grump if you call me anything other than Izzy.'

He smiles and slowly lowers back onto the couch. 'Nice to meet you, Izzy. I know I'm pushing my luck and all, but could I crash here for a bit? It's a lot to ask, I know, but I'm not feeling the best right now.'

'That's fine. I'll get you a blanket.'

'Thank you, Izzy. You're an angel.'

She can feel Shep watching her as she empties the basin of water in the kitchen. After leaving the bowl in the sink, she puts the first aid kit back in the bathroom, then takes a spare pillow and blanket from the airing cupboard.

When she brings them back into the living room, he's asleep. The lines of pain that had been etched around his eyes have softened and his breathing is steady.

Feeling like the pressure is off her a little, Izzy carefully drapes the blanket over him then sits on the armchair opposite him.

She's seen and met a lot of men over the years. Too many men, but no one like Shep. And it's not just down to his looks, even though he's gorgeous. His massive body dwarfs her couch, her entire living room in fact.

There's something about him that intrigues her. He can't be that much older than her - perhaps late thirties to early forties, but there's an air about him that makes him appear older.

While she's not thrilled about sleeping with a strange man in her house, she's exhausted. All she can do is make sure she locks her door and hopes he's out for the rest of the night.

She goes into the kitchen and fills a glass with water, before pausing to look at him again. 'Goodnight.'

She closes the living room door before walking down the corridor to her bedroom, locking the door after her.

As she tucks under her duvet her thoughts keep drifting back to Shep, asleep on her couch. She likes him. She barely knows him, but she can't deny the attraction. Maybe she can have a proper chat to him over breakfast.

With that thought in her mind, she falls asleep.

BASTIAN

He's usually known for being calm and collected. Others show their emotions in stressful situations. He doesn't. It's a skill he learned many years ago, and one he still uses when he's out of the compound. Occasionally inside too.

The team are important to Bastian. They're his family. But that does not mean he drops his guard around them. Distance protects. Another thing he learned a long time ago.

He slams his palm against the steering wheel, startling his companion. His emotions are fighting against his hold on them, and that could put Ethan in danger. That's unacceptable.

The car ride from Ethan's office to the park has taken place in silence which, given his current mood, suits him just fine.

He pulls the car to a stop at the entrance to the park and turns off the engine, still not giving Ethan his attention. It's childish, but his irritation is too strong to ignore. He's focusing all of that on the steering wheel he's squeezing in his hands.

'Are you going to be in a mood with me all night?' Ethan asks from the passenger seat.

'I am not in a mood.'

'If this isn't a mood, I'd hate to see you when you are actually irritated.'

'Do you think this is a joke?'

Ethan shakes his head as he unfastens his seat belt. 'Of course not. It's incredibly serious. That's why you are here with me and not one of the others. I trust you. I want your quiet calm. Or your usual quiet calm.'

Bas slowly turns to glare at Ethan. 'It's my job to protect you, so that part is always non-negotiable. My usual quiet calm is struggling with the fact you are deliberately putting your life in danger. That makes my job more difficult, and I take that seriously.'

Ethan rests his hand on Bastian's leg, but he doesn't drop his glare. He's too fucked off to even register the out of character contact. Ethan sighs and pulls his hand back. 'I understand what you're saying, but it's my job to keep the Blackjacks operational. I'm sorry you're angry with me, but I'm getting out of the car. It's up to you if you come or not. I'm not going to force you.'

He clenches his jaw as he glares out the window. Ethan is right - as usual, but he's still uneasy about the whole fucking situation. Even if he wasn't having sex with Ethan, he'd still be unhappy about letting him out of the car. But Ethan is his boss. And Bas has never gone against Ethan or Nix.

He shoves open the car door, nearly tearing it off the hinges when he kicks it. As Ethan joins him, Bas checks his guns are to hand and ready to be fired if necessary.

'Thank you, Bastian.'

'I'm just doing my job. But don't push me, Ethan. If I sense trouble, you will do what I say.'

'Of course. I always do, don't I?'

Bas pulls his jacket from the back seat, wincing when he shrugs it on. The wound he received when he was fighting in Ireland has healed, but the damage had been extensive, leaving him with pain when he sits still for too long. Each day he's getting stronger, but the pain is refusing to leave him.

'You should have let Davyn take your place tonight.'

'I protect you!' He didn't mean to growl that remark. All he is doing is proving to Ethan that he is letting his emotions interfere.

'I know you do, but you're still in pain.'

'Why don't you say that louder so every vampire within earshot can hear?' He gestures to the path ahead of them. 'After you. I've got your back.'

Ethan shakes his head and turns away from him. Bas hates being in a pissy mood with Ethan, but he can't help it. It's becoming more of a regular occurrence as the days go by. And he knows why.

Everything to do with Ethan throws him off his tightly controlled path. Emotions are getting mixed in with rational thinking, and that's a dangerous combination. Their personal relationship is getting in the way of their work as Blackjacks.

His feelings for Ethan are getting in the way. Feelings he needs to keep to himself more than he has of late. Their relationship is physical. Nothing more. Or that was the initial plan.

A plan he is struggling to stick to.

The wind shifts, sending Ethan's scent in his direction. He smells incredible as always. Looks incredible too. The well-bred male is from an old bloodline, well spoken, superbly dressed, and a true gentleman in every way.

On the other hand, he is the complete opposite. He's nothing but a runt from the streets of Barcelona. No family, no bloodline worth mentioning, a highly skilled thief and contract killer. Looking at them you wouldn't match them to each other in any lifetime.

Until they're alone and Ethan is his to play with.

But if things keep going the way they are tonight, there will be no playing once this meeting is done.

Ethan sits on the bench and Bas takes up position a few feet away. Ethan is watching him, but Bas isn't about to continue their conversation out in the open. It can wait until after Ethan is safely back in the car. His gums throb when he notices a familiar scent. 'He's here.'

Ethan turns in the direction Bas is looking, rising to his feet when Rhain steps out from around the corner. The males shake hands, which only serves to aggravate Bas further, before they sit. Rhain casts a quick look in Bastian's direction, then dismisses him, turning his attention back to Ethan.

'Thank you for coming.'

Ethan nods curtly. 'I hope you're going to make it worth my while.'

'Of course I am. I wouldn't wish to irritate you or your companion. He seems to be in a particularly hostile mood tonight.'

Ethan smiles and Bas growls. 'He doesn't agree with these meetings. He believes it's an unnecessary risk. I would highly recommend you don't prove him right.'

'Understood.' Rhain takes a file from the inside pocket of his expensive looking coat and, after glancing briefly at Bas, hands it to Ethan. 'That's all the information I can gather on members of The Order of which I am aware. Barton is my main contact. If your friend over there would like to remove him from the equation, I will be eternally grateful. I despise the male greatly.'

Bas doesn't respond to that. He'd like to remove Rhain too, but it's not his call.

Ethan flicks through the pages, nodding slowly as he scans the information. 'I'll have a thorough look at this. Thank you.'

'How is your team member faring? The one who was injected.'

Bas doesn't hold back the growl, snarling at Rhain, giving him an eyeful of his fangs.

'Bastian. Please.' Ethan's command keeps him in place. Just. He doesn't want Rhain speaking about his friends. It's his fault Court has no memory and Shep is growing wings.

'He's well. That's all I'm willing to say on the matter. I am working with you, but that doesn't mean I trust you.'

Rhain nods. 'Yes. Of course. I do hope in time I will earn that trust.'

'Not likely,' Bas says, resting a hand on one of his guns. He's never wanted to put a bullet in someone so badly. And he's put a lot of bullets, in a lot of people, over his lifetime. Ethan isn't impressed by Bastian's interruption, but he couldn't care less. Even speaking to Rhain is a step too far in his eyes.

'I need to ask you something,' Ethan says, bringing the attention back to him. 'Are you still taking vampires for your project?'

'Why do you ask?'

'Answer his question!' Bas is getting to the end of his patience tonight.

'No,' Rhain replies, shaking his head. 'My side of the operation has been shut down. There were many projects being carried out in my labs. I don't have details on quite a few of them. My sole concern was finding a cure for Blood Fever. The Order has loftier plans.'

'Such as the drug our fighter was given?'

Rhain nods. 'Precisely. I did attempt to find out what they were planning, but I was unsuccessful. They were holding a Rougarou for a few years. I dread to think what they were using him for.'

That gets Bastian's attention. He's heard stories of those creatures. The werewolves come from Cajun folklore and, until Rhain mentioned them, he assumed they didn't exist.

He glances at Ethan, catching the same look in his eye.

Austin.

'I wasn't aware they existed,' Ethan says, looking away from Bas.

'Some do not believe vampires exist,' Rhain replies. 'It's foolish to assume we know everything that goes on in this world.' He shrugs. 'It matters not. The creature was lost in the chaos after you destroyed my lab. If The Order are still collecting vampires, it is without my knowledge.'

He looks over at Ethan, frowning. 'Have you evidence to the contrary?'

'We intercepted a team armed with sedatives.'

'I see. That's worrying.'

Bas growls before he can stop himself. 'You took Court. Now you find that practice worrying?'

'Ignore him,' Ethan replies, seriously pissing off Bastian.

Bas rolls his eyes. He trusts Ethan and Nix without question. Always has, but this truce with Rhain is testing that trust. Working with someone associated with the enemy is foolish.

Rhain looks at him again. 'You don't believe I'm genuine?'

'No,' Bas answers. 'You don't do the things you've done, then wake up one morning and have a change of heart.'

'Is that so? You don't believe in second chances? You don't believe someone could do questionable things, then decide to turn their life around?' Rhain glances down at Bastian's gloved hands then back at his face, raising his eyebrows.

Bas tightens his grip on the gun. He can't know. There's no way Rhain has any idea about his past. No one knows. So why did he look at his hands like that? Does he know about the tattoos? Does he know what they mean?

Rhain smiles at the confusion he's caused. 'Perhaps there is the odd time someone is genuine about changing their life.' Rhain stands and fastens his coat, keeping his attention on Bas. 'I'm just asking for the chance some of us deserve. A chance to right some wrongs. That's all.'

He shakes Ethan's hand and nods to Bas. 'I'll see if I can find out what The Order are up to, but don't hold your breath. I'm not in favour with them as I used to be. Enjoy the rest of your evening.'

Bas stares after him, waiting until he's disappeared around the corner before he releases the breath he was holding.

'Are you all right?'

He nods, his attention still on the empty path. 'Back to the car.'

Bastian waits until Ethan is in the car before he slides in himself and puts on his seat belt. The bizarre exchange with Rhain has left him feeling extremely uncomfortable. If you could even call it an exchange.

'What's wrong Bas?'

'Have you spoken to him about me?'

'Rhain? In what way?'

'Have you told him about my past?'

Ethan shakes his head, his eyes going wide. 'No! Of course not. Everything about your past is confidential. The same goes for every member of the team. Only Nix and I know, and what we know has come from each of you. Why do you ask?'

'No reason.' The gang Bas used to belong to is well known. It's possible Rhain somehow found out about that part of his past, as much as he did everything in his power to hide it. Ethan doesn't know the name of the gang and neither does Nix. He intends to keep it that way.

He reaches out to start the ignition, but Ethan rests his hand on his arm, pushing it back down again. 'I think we need to talk.'

Bas would rather not. He's too wound up and wants to get on the road. Ethan isn't safe until he's far away from here. Far away from Rhain. He can protect him without question, but that doesn't mean he is willing to take unnecessary risks with Ethan's life. 'We can talk when you are back in your building. I want to get you away from here.'

'No. We're talking now, even if I have to pull rank on you.'

Bas sighs and turns to look at him. 'What would you like to

discuss?'

'First of all, I'd appreciate you drop the attitude with me.'

'And second?' he replies, clearly irritating Ethan. He's not usually so disrespectful, but irritation is winning tonight.

'Second, I never took you for a hypocrite, Bastian.'

'What are you talking about?'

'Before you left for Ireland to put a stop to Davyn's father, you made it perfectly clear the team comes first. I agreed, even though I was worried sick something would happen to you. But I gave the green light in spite of my concerns. Then I get a call to say the team was successful. That Davyn had taken control of his father's people.

'Which was amazing, until I was told you were injured. The very thing I was dreading had happened. Do you have any idea how I felt being stuck in the UK, while you were fighting for your life in Ireland?'

'I wasn't fighting for my life.'

'Your stomach was sliced open from one side of your body to the other. You nearly died.'

'Nearly. I'm fine.'

'You're still in pain so no, you're not fine. But that's not my point.'

'Well, what is?'

'This is the exact same situation from the other side. You think I'm unnecessarily putting myself at risk and you're not happy about that. But it's something I need to do for the good of the team.'

'It's hardly the same thing. Rhain has given us little to get excited about. How do you know he's not playing you?'

Ethan shrugs. 'I have no idea. Perhaps he is. All I can do is take each meeting, each piece of information at a time and go from there. But you need to keep in control. I can't do my job if I'm worrying about you losing your temper and decapitating him.'

'I don't lose my temper.'

'I know you don't, and that's the part concerning me the most. I've never seen you so on edge like you just were with him. You are becoming less composed. A few months ago, you wouldn't have let Rhain bother you. Now you can barely restrain yourself around him.'

'I don't trust him.'

'I know, but you need to distance yourself when we're in situations like that. You're protecting me, not the person you're sleeping with. That's the way it has to be, remember?'

Bas turns his attention to the window. Of course he remembers. They tell each other often enough how the team has to come first. It's repeated so many times he's sick of hearing it at this stage. But it's difficult to put the team first when he has feelings for Ethan. Feelings he needs to suppress for the good of the team.

It doesn't matter what's good for him.

He pulls off his gloves and flexes his fingers. He's wound up and pissed off with himself for blurring the lines when out in the field. He's the level-headed one. He's solid. Dependable. Doesn't react impulsively. Never. That's why he is so lethal. But he's losing his edge. Losing his control. And it's all since he blurred yet more lines with Ethan.

Ethan's perfectly manicured, soft hand wraps around his rough one, covering the vile pattern inked on the back of it. He doesn't usually take off his gloves in public. Ethan knows the marks tattooed on the back of both hands weren't his idea, and he knows how much Bas hates them, but that's as far as he's gone on that subject. No one outside of his old gang knows what they mean. That was his old life. This is his new one.

Or was, until Rhain looked at his hands and gave him that knowing look.

'Are you okay, Bastian? This isn't like you.'

Bas turns back to him and attempts a smile. Being pissed off at Ethan for doing his job is unfair. He wouldn't appreciate if Ethan pulled that one on him. 'I shouldn't take this out on you. I apologise. Rhain... he just really irritates me more than most people I've met.

That male has a way of hitting a nerve.'

Ethan laughs at that. 'Really? I'd never have guessed. You hid that remarkably well. I don't think he has any idea!'

'Is that so? How about I tell him next time?'

'How about you don't? As much as you dislike him, the Blackjacks need the information he has in his head. Perhaps you could wait until we extract that information before you put a bullet in it?'

'I'll do my best.'

'I'd appreciate that.' His thumb runs over the side of Bastian's hand. 'Are we alone?'

Bas closes his eyes, concentrating on the sounds and smells around them. Nothing but Ethan's addictive cologne. 'We are. Why do you ask?'

Ethan rests his hand on Bas's thigh, moving slowly up to his groin. 'You're tense. Will you let me try to help you relax?'

'What exactly did you have in mind?'

Ethan's hand grips his dick through his combats. 'I want you in my mouth.'

He wasn't expecting that. Ethan usually prefers to keep things firmly behind closed doors as much as possible. If he were to use his bodyguard common sense, he'd say no. It's not safe here. He can't protect Ethan if he's being sucked off at the same time.

But when Ethan's hand tightens on his dick, his other side takes over. The side that needs to take control of Ethan. The side that puts him in charge of his boss.

He looks around but can't see or hear anyone else for miles. His senses in that regard aren't remotely comparable to Shep's, but he can usually pick up on sounds or scents from miles away.

'Are you sure you want to do this here?'

'I want you in my mouth now, so it's going to have to be here.'

'You're not usually so demanding.'

'You're not usually so hesitant.'

'I'm trying to do my job, Ethan.'

'Would you prefer if I ordered you to unzip your trousers?'

Bas smiles in response. He's not used to Ethan being so forward. It's something he doesn't dislike. Having Ethan challenge him when they're alone could make for some interesting sex. He's not a fan of relinquishing control.

'When we're alone, I give the orders Ethan - not you.'

He unbuckles his belt then unzips his combats, moving his gun and knife out of the way so Ethan doesn't hurt himself. Ethan was correct when he said he needed to relax. A mix of adrenaline and being close to Ethan has turned his dick to stone. He pushes his hips forward then grabs Ethan's tie, pulling him down to his dick.

'Take it all.'

Without hesitation, Ethan takes him deep into his mouth, the contact making Bas hiss in pleasure. He holds the back of Ethan's head, forcing his dick further down his throat. Fuck, he loves seeing Ethan like this. Loves that Ethan willingly gives himself to him.

He holds Ethan in place, praising him in Spanish as he takes every inch of what Bas is giving him. He gags so Bas releases him, pulling his head up so he can kiss him, before pushing him back down to his dick.

Holding Ethan's head steady he thrusts his hips, fucking Ethan's mouth hard. He can take it. After months together, he's yet to find something Ethan isn't willing to do for him. They're well matched, each one pushing the other to their limits.

Bas turns Ethan's head to the side, watching his dick slide in and out of Ethan's mouth. The image alone is nearly enough to give him the release he needs. But he holds back. As difficult as it is, he'll push himself and Ethan a little longer. Draw it out for both of them.

Bas uses Ethan's tie to pull him up again, gripping him by the jaw as he marvels at the stunning man in front of him. Ethan's blue eyes are glassed over, his lips red, swollen, and damp from sucking his dick.

He can't resist kissing him, hungrily invading Ethan's mouth, fucking it with his tongue. His dick twitches when Ethan groans against his mouth.

Ethan is his.

He's never experienced the level of intense possessiveness that he feels for Ethan. It scares him at times how strong a hold Ethan has over him. He would raze the world to the ground for him without hesitation.

But he can't tell him that. Never can tell him. This is all he has, all he can ever have. Might as well make the most of it while it lasts.

Bas pushes Ethan back, his hand still gripping his jaw. 'Get back down there and finish me, Ethan.'

Less than a minute after giving the command, Bas comes down Ethan's throat, the release coursing through him in waves.

Ethan groans as he takes everything Bas gives him, continuing to work him until there's nothing left. Ethan slowly slides Bas's dick out of his mouth and hits him with one hell of a sexy smile. 'Thank you.'

Bas laughs as he lies back against the seat. 'You're welcome. Come here. I want to taste you again.'

This kiss is slower, but that's only because he restrains himself, and keeps his hands off. He loves the taste of himself on Ethan. If he didn't hold back, he could easily take Ethan right here. Drag him out of the car, bend him over the bonnet and sink his teeth into his skin as he fucks him. But they've already taken too much of a risk by doing what they did. He needs to get Ethan back to the safety of his building.

'That was a pleasant surprise,' he says, as they both try to make themselves presentable again.

Ethan sits back in the seat, then straightens his tie. 'I can be unpredictable occasionally, especially when it comes to getting something I want.'

'I'll remember that.' Bas finishes buckling his belt, making sure his weapons are back where they should be. 'I must admit I am more relaxed now.'

'Job done then,' Ethan says, that sexy smile back on his face. 'Now, how about you do your job and drive me home.'

Bas smirks as he starts the engine and pulls away from the park. 'Anything you say.'

'Good. And when I get home, I'd very much like if you could use me as you see fit. This was the appetiser. I would very much like to see what you have in store for the main course.'

Bas puts his foot down. He still has a hell of a lot of pent-up adrenaline to work off.

SHEP

He freezes as the door opens, the creak of the old hinges ominous in the darkness. She's coming for him again. He closes his eyes, hoping she'll leave him alone if she thinks he's asleep. Sometimes it worked. Most of the time it didn't. It really depended on her mood.

Then the scent hits him. Her perfume. The sickly flowery smell coating his nostrils and the inside of his mouth.

Shep fucking hates the smell. Hates the way it clings to him long after she's left.

The light turns on, but he keeps his eyes shut, pretending to be asleep. It's a waste of time, but he'll drag it out as long as he can.

He hears her walking over to him, the click of her expensive shoes echoing on the wooden floor. He can hear her breathing from somewhere behind him. She's not going to be fooled. Not this time.

Her fingers skim along the back of his bare shoulder, the

sensation turning his stomach. But he doesn't react. Just keeps his eyes closed and his breathing steady. Her hand brushes over his hair, her fingers tracing along his forehead again and again.

'Are you awake my pet?'

Shep jumps up and shuffles away from the touch.

But it's not her.

The woman holds up her hands as she stands a few feet from the couch. 'Hey, relax. It's me. Izzy. Do you remember me? I helped you last night.'

The only thing he's concentrating on right now is not vomiting. Her voice is still ringing in his head. The way she used to call him *pet* in that sickly sweet tone not helping his control on his stomach.

'I found you outside The Lair last night. You were injured.'

He scrubs a hand over his face and nods. He remembers, and now he feels like a right plonker. 'Yeah. Sorry. Izzy, right?'

She nods but doesn't relax. No doubt he's freaked her out when he freaked out.

'Just didn't know where I was for a sec. Did I hit you?'

'No. Sorry I startled you. I was just going to check the wound on your head.'

He touches his forehead, feeling the plaster under his fingers. 'Yeah. Forgot about that too. I didn't mean to scare you. You can lower your hands now. I'm not about to attack you.' He smiles to try and put her at ease. It works and she returns his smile as she lowers her hands.

'How are you feeling? You look a lot better than you did last night.'

That wakes up his brain. 'Yeah. I'm grand thanks. All good! Can I use your bathroom?'

'Of course. Down the corridor to the left.' He gets up and hurries down the corridor to the bathroom and locks the door. When he faces his reflection, he peels the plaster from his skin. No cut. No scar.

He tentatively looks over his shoulder, checking his back in the mirror. Nothing there either. He'd half expected to see the tips of two wings peeking out. It's happened twice now and that's two times too many in his opinion. He's not keen on seeing those freaky talons poking out of his skin again. Gave him nightmares.

While not having two grotesque mutant wings tearing out of him is a good thing, it doesn't solve the other problem.

How the fuck is he going to explain the lack of a cut on his face to Izzy? There's only one way. He sticks the plaster back in place, hoping she doesn't notice the bruise around it is gone too. He had better get some clothes on and make a run for it before she notices.

When he steps back out of the bathroom, she's making herself a cup of coffee.

'Would you like a drink?'

'No, thanks. Did I have clothes on last night?'

Izzy gestures to the chair by the window and the pile of freshly laundered clothes. 'They're just out of the dryer.'

'You're a star. Thanks love.'

He grabs his jeans and gets dressed, while she peers at him as she sips her coffee.

Her dark hair is out, falling in soft waves around her shoulder. The oversized pyjamas she's wearing have clouds all over the pale blue material, and her feet are bare. It shouldn't do anything to him. It's fucking pyjamas. But on her, with her hair all tousled from sleep, it's downright sexy. She's downright sexy.

'Would you like something to eat?'

'No, thanks. Better head before I'm missed. Thanks for everything Izzy.'

'Are you sure you're up to leaving? You were in a bad way last night.'

He pulls on his t-shirt, trying not to rip the back any more than it already is, then grabs his boots. 'I'm feeling fine. Really.'

'But your bike is at The Lair. It's about ten minutes from here by car.'

'I could do with some fresh air. Clear my head a bit. Thanks again for helping me. I appreciate it. So, I guess I'll see you around.' He grabs his helmet and jacket from the chair by the couch and aims for the front door.

'Wait!' she says as he opens the door. 'Don't forget your keys.' She grabs the bike keys from her coat pocket and hands them to him.

'Thanks. Not going far without them. Bye.'

She watches from the doorway as he makes his escape. Shep waves over his shoulder at her, before heading back in the direction of The Lair. Hopefully, his bike is still there and in one piece. All the bouncers know it's his, so fingers crossed it's been looked after, or at least not trashed. He could do without that headache on top of everything else going on in his life.

Shep pulls on his sunglasses even though it's not particularly sunny today. As a Hybrid, he's not as sensitive to sunlight as full-blooded vampires, but the light can still fuck with his eyes if he's out for too long.

His phone rings in his pocket and he groans when he sees Willow's name on the screen. He was hoping to have a shower, some breakfast, and a few more hours of sleep before he had to deal with her again. 'Hey Sis. What's up?'

'Where are you?'

'Out.'

Her sigh is loud. 'I got that part Shep. Out where?'

'Just out. What's up? Or did you just call to have another go at me, cause I'm not really in the mood right now, thanks all the same.'

'I don't want to have a go at you, Shep. I never do. I'm sorry okay. I just hate all the tension.'

'There's no tension, Wills. It's all good,' he says, darting between cars to cross the road, ignoring the blaring of horns when he interrupts the flow of traffic.

'But you're not going to change your mind, are you?'

'Nope. Final answer.' He knows his nonchalant tone will piss her off, but when it comes to his mother, he's all out of fucks.

'Shep...'

'Don't say my name in that tone Wills. We're good. Can we just leave it at that?'

'I just—'

'Wills! Seriously, I need you to drop this. I love you to bits, but I swear the only thing you're going to do is piss me off if you don't let this go.'

'So, what do I tell Mum?'

He bites his lip before he says something that'll irreparably damage his relationship with Willow. It's not her fault. None of this is. She's caught in the middle of a situation she knows nothing about.

She knows the lie, the easy story meant to explain why he doesn't talk to their mother. But it's a lie she doesn't seem to want to buy any more. Another thing to add to his plate of things to deal with.

'Putting this as politely as I can, you can tell her whatever you want. I'll be home in a few hours.'

He ends the call, turning off his phone so she can't have a go at him again. It would be so much easier if she knew what his problem is, but there is no fucking chance he'll ever tell her. She's his baby sister. It's his job to protect her, not scar her for life. He may hate their mother, but Willow doesn't. He'd be a right dick of a brother if he destroyed Wills relationship with her mother just to keep himself happy.

When he finally gets to The Lair he's relieved to see his Ducati on its stand in the staff car park. The paintwork is scraped along the side where it landed on the ground last night, which doesn't do anything to help his ever-growing foul mood.

Now he's well and truly fucked off. His back is killing him. He's pissed about his fight with Willow. His precious bike is damaged. Izzy probably thinks he's a rude, ungrateful ass, which is fair enough considering the way he left her apartment.

He's not sure why, but that's the one that's hitting hardest. Which makes no sense. He doesn't get hung up over women. But he's getting himself in knots over her.

Shep swings his leg over the bike, wincing when he settles back into the saddle. He's so fed up being sore. Whatever is happening to his body is bad enough, but now it's beginning to affect his day-to-day life.

He pulls on his helmet and starts his bike. He should go back to the compound. He knows he should, but that's not where he heads as he rides out of the car park. He can't do anything about a lot of what's going wrong right now. But he can make sure one issue fucks off.

Time to have a heart to heart with his mother.

BASTiAN

'Does Ethan know you requested a meeting with me?'

Bas settles into the passenger seat of Rhain's car and closes the door. 'No. This is between you and I.'

Rhain nods, but thankfully doesn't comment. Bastian uncovers one hand, placing it on the door handle.

'I'm not going to lock you in, or try to trap you,' Rhain says. 'You requested this meeting, not me.'

Bas silently looks over at Rhain. The male appears ill, his eyes bloodshot and surrounded by dark circles. Blood Fever is catching up with him. 'How long do you have to live?'

Rhain smiles thinly. 'That depends on you at this moment.'

'I don't plan to kill you yet.'

'I appreciate the inclusion of *yet* at the end of that statement.'

'I didn't call you here to kill you Rhain. How long do you have to live?' he repeats.

Rhain sighs as he looks out the window. 'Months at most. I am in the final stages of Fever. The process is irreversible. Perhaps you can do me a favour and kill me before I turn into a babbling blood-crazed monster?'

'I'm not inclined to do you any favours.'

Rhain laughs. 'That, I believe! I will have to take care of that matter myself when the time is right. Now, as much I enjoy speaking about my own impending death, what do you want?'

Bas pulls off his other glove, shoves up his sleeve, then holds his arm out to Rhain. 'You know what these tattoos mean? The ones on my hands.'

Rhain nods slowly. 'Yes. I am surprised to see them on your skin. I wouldn't have thought that about you.'

'Everything on my skin is earned. Everything except those on my hands. I don't care if you believe it or not, but I didn't deserve those marks.'

'From what I know of you, I actually do believe you.'

It doesn't give Bastian any comfort. Having the marks in the first place is as bad as it gets. Whether they were given falsely or not, barely matters.

'How do you know what they mean?' he asks Rhain.

'I have been alive many centuries and have dabbled in many grey areas of our society. I came across your old gang on a number of occasions. I have to say I'm impressed that you were able to extract yourself from their employ. I was under the impression it was a lifelong membership?'

'It is.'

'So as far as they are concerned, you're dead? That makes sense.'

'Do you know what all the marks on my arm mean?'

Rhain takes a moment to examine the various images covering every inch of the skin on his arm. His eyes widen when he spots a few

116

of the more hidden images, buried in the black lines on his skin.

'I take that expression as a yes. You know these marks aren't given unless they have been earned?'

'Yes.'

'So you know what I have done, that I have proved myself time and time again?'

'I understand. Is this where you tell me to keep your exploits to myself?'

Bas covers his arm, then slides his gloves back on. Then he launches at Rhain, holding him back against the seat, pressing a thick blade against his neck. Rhain blinks in shock, his throat moving against the knife as he swallows. 'You're fast.'

'No Rhain. I'm lethal. I'm trained to kill in silence, in the shadows, in locked, sealed, and secured premises. I can bypass any security system, open any lock, take down any bodyguard. I can kill you before you know I'm there, watch the life drain out of you, then put your body on display for the world to see.'

Rhain clears his throat. 'I... understand.'

'I hope you do. I may be a Blackjack, but old habits die hard. It will not take much of a push to tip me over that edge Rhain. I strongly suggest you are not the one to push me.

'My past is *my* business. Ethan is under *my* protection. The Blackjacks are *my* family. Any threat to them will be dealt with the way I used to deal with problems.' He leans closer, digging the blade into Rhain's skin. 'And I will sleep better that night.'

He removes the blade from Rhain's neck, sliding it back into the holster on his side.

Rhain coughs as he massages his neck, frowning at the blood that smears over his hand. 'Your reputation is well founded. Perhaps underestimated. I assure you I won't make that mistake.'

Without saying anything else, Bas gets out of the car, slamming the door behind him. He turns and watches as Rhain fastens his seat belt, starts the engine, and pulls out of the car park. Only then does he walk to the far side of the park to his bike. As he walks, he concentrates on his breathing, flexing his fingers, trying to calm down.

Control has always been his strength. He doesn't lose his temper. Never acts without careful thought and planning. In the car with Rhain, that control had been dangerously close to slipping. It wouldn't have taken much to move that blade up, ending his life. And he would have slept better tonight. He always does after he kills.

SHEP

He pulls his bike to a stop at the bottom of the wide expanse of concrete facing him. The grand set of steps leads from the cobbled courtyard up to the door of his mother's country mansion.

The residence is nestled deep in the rolling hills surrounded by acres of forest and not much else. It's a nice enough place if you liked flowing fountains, grand pillars, deep balconies, and multiple terraces, but it wasn't for him.

This grandeur had been Willow's home, and to this day he doesn't know how she felt comfortable here - or how she can now survive in the compound after living somewhere like this.

They had been born and bred in Yorkshire, living there for decades before their mother decided she just *had* to move to this ridiculous heap. Shep had stayed in Yorkshire. It was his home. Or was until she changed that by making a decision that changed his life forever.

He takes off his helmet, hanging it on the handlebars of his bike, as he glares at the ridiculous mansion.

'Better get this over with,' he mutters to himself as he slowly dismounts and climbs the steps to the front door.

He rings the bell, grimacing when he hears the pompous tune sounding in the vast hallway beyond. He tries to calm his unruly spikes, then curses himself, gives up on his hair, and stuffs his hands in the pocket of his jeans.

A small, serious looking man opens the solid oak door and examines him with bucket-loads of barely contained disdain. 'Yes?'

'I'm here to see Lilith.'

The man raises one wiry eyebrow. 'Is that so?'

'Tell her it's Shepherd.'

The man frowns, his overgrown eyebrows hiding his eyes. 'As in her son?'

'Yeah, lucky me.'

The man closes the door in Shep's face but returns less a minute later. He opens the door and gestures for Shep to come in. The door is shut behind him, the ominous bang loud in the marble foyer, echoing thanks to the high vaulted ceilings. 'Lilith is this way.'

He follows the man up the stairs, taking the left side when the staircase splits in two. Everything about this place makes Shep feel out of place. He glances behind and smirks to himself when he sees his boots are leaving dust marks on the plush carpet.

Large portraits of his mother and Willow sit at either side of the corridor. Shep's sure you'd be hard pressed to find anything in the house with his name or face on it. The only hint he exists is the dust prints he's leaving on the stairs.

The butler stops at the end of the corridor and opens the door. Shep steps inside and faces the woman he hasn't seen in decades. His mother has aged since he last saw her. She looks like someone in their fifties, which isn't all too common for a vampire heading into their fourth century. Maybe the guilt is beginning to eat away at her. He dismisses that thought as fast as it comes to him. Not bloody likely.

She gets to her feet and smiles at him. 'Shepherd, how nice to see you. Would you like a drink?'

The butler closes the door behind him with an ominous click. 'I'm not here for a damn drink! I need to talk to you about Willow.'

Lilith gestures to the overstuffed sofa opposite him, but Shep shakes his head. She sighs and sits down in her armchair by the fire. 'Of course. I apologise. Is there something wrong with Willow?'

Shep shakes his head. 'She's amazing. The problem is you.'

'Me? I don't understand?'`

'Where do you get off dragging her into our mess?'

'How did I do that?'

'Inviting me to your birthday! Throwing your dirty money at the Blackjacks! She thinks that you're generous and I'm being an asshole by getting pissed off about it. Stop interfering in my life!'

'I'm not going to get in between you and Willow. But don't you dare interfere in my job. You have no right! And you have no right to send her to do your dirty work. Did you really think inviting me to your party would put you back in my good books again?'

Lilith sighs and clasps her hands together. 'I didn't send her to do my *dirty work,* as you so eloquently put it. I merely mentioned that I am planning a gathering for my birthday, and she suggested I invite you. I did not have the heart to tell her why that would be an unwelcome olive branch.'

'Olive branch? Give me a fucking break!'

'Must you curse?'

'Yeah, I actually must fucking curse. What can I say? I guess it's down to the environment I was raised in.'

She drops her gaze and wrings her hands together. 'Shepherd—'

'Don't! You need to shut down any mention of me and you patching things up. It's never happening. Make sure she knows that.

And back away from the Blackjacks. You've made your charitable donation, got the praise, now leave it alone. Leave me alone!'

'I just wanted to support my family. There was no ill will intended.'

'My family is Willow. Not you! Not ever!'

'I am painfully aware of that, Shepherd. While I would be delighted to repair our relationship, I know that will never happen.' She settles back into her chair and reaches out for the glass of wine on the ornate table beside her. 'Believe me, I know how lucky I am to have my daughter still willing to talk to me. I'm not going to push my luck with a futile attempt at a reconciliation.'

'At least we finally agree on something.'

Shep turns to leave, but Lilith clearly isn't done. 'What would you have me tell her?'

'I'm sure you can figure it out yourself. You're good at coming up with solutions to problems.'

'I don't want to cause you any more pain, Shepherd. If I make the wrong decision, I could give her hope that doesn't exist.'

Shep fights to keep his fangs in his gums, but his eyes have other ideas. His mother recoils in the chair as the glowing orbs burn into her. 'Pain? Are you fucking kidding me?'

'Forgive me. I didn't mean to upset you.'

'What the hell do you care if I'm upset? You've already done your worst. Tell Willow what you want, 'cause I honestly couldn't give a fuck. I've lived with your bad decisions for years. It's not like you can do anything worse than you already have.'

'Please Shepherd...'

'What's wrong Mother? Don't like hearing the truth? You made me this way. You and your decisions. You kept me in that place, helpless and scared, waiting for them to...' He closes his eyes and curses himself. 'I've got seven-hundred-and-fifty-three burns on my body thanks to you and your wrong decisions. Don't do me any favours now.'

Lilith swiftly wipes her eyes before she speaks. 'Shepherd, I had no idea that would happen. I didn't—'

'Don't!' Shep roars. He rolls his head on his shoulders as he tries to convince himself to calm down. He needs to get out of here - now. 'Don't you dare try to fix this or justify what you did. The best thing you can do for me is leave... again.' Without looking at the woman sitting in the chair, he turns and leaves the room, slamming the door after him.

He races down the plush staircase, adding more grubby footprints to his ones from earlier. He fumbles with the lock on the door, but finally gets it open and hurries down to his bike.

Resisting the urge to get down and kiss the machine, he grabs his helmet, shoving it on as he climbs onto the saddle. He starts the engine, speeding away from a conversation that's brought up too many horrors from his past.

SHEP

'A rouga what?'

Ethan turns on the screen at the head of the room and points to an illustration of the type of werewolf you'd see on the TV. Fully upright, huge wolf with whopping great teeth. 'A rougarou.'

Shep shrugs. 'Looks cool as fuck, but you're talking gibberish.'

Ethan straightens his blue tie as he throws a withering look in his direction. 'It's a creature from Cajun myth. Or it was. According to Rhain, there was one in the lab when you infiltrated it.'

'A lot happened during that assault,' Bas says. 'But I didn't see anything like that.'

Fallon nods. 'We would have noticed that in a cage. It wasn't there.'

Ethan pauses before he continues. That usually means he's got a revelation of some sort. 'I've done some research on this creature. They are remarkably similar to our Irish wolf friends.'

'Great,' Shep mutters. 'More dogs. Just what we need.'

'Shep!' Nix says in that disapproving tone she likes to use just for him. 'We've talked about this. Enough with the dog comments.'

Shep grins apologetically. He should have kept that comment to himself, but he's still wound up after the chat with his mother earlier. 'Sorry Boss.'

Ethan clears his throat. 'If I can continue? So, the rougarou have similar traits, however, instead of shifting from human to full wolf, they turn into a rather intimidating werewolf - half man and half wolf.'

'Hold on,' Fallon says, sitting upright in her chair. 'Are you saying that you think Austin is a rougarou?'

'Perhaps? Rhain said this creature escaped or vanished during your attack. No one has seen it since. Now, it was either killed or escaped during the confusion. Or we took him. I have no intention of asking Rhain for the description of the rougarou. No one knows we have Austin. I'd like to keep it that way.'

'Agreed.' Nix scrubs a hand over her face as she looks up at the image on the screen. 'Is there anything to say these rougarou are dangerous?'

Ethan shrugs. 'Are vampires dangerous? Are shifters dangerous? It very much depends on the individual. Fallon and Fletch? You two have been closest to him. Do you both still stand by your evaluation of him?'

'Of course.'

Shep can't help but notice that Fallon responded immediately. She's got a thing for Austin. Cute. Won't go anywhere, but it's cute. Just like him and Izzy.

Doomed from the start.

'Fletch?' Ethan asks, clearly not satisfied by Fallon's answer alone.

'I'm with my sister. He's a dream to work with. Polite, well mannered, gentle, and hasn't exhibited any threatening behaviour at all. I've spent a lot of time with him. He's never shown any sign of changing into this strange creature. And I'm fairly confident he doesn't know what he is. He doesn't remember anything that happened before he woke up in the lab. He doesn't remember where he's from. His memory loss is total, as with Court.'

'I didn't remember I was a vampire,' Court says, backing him up. 'That's a big detail to forget. It's completely feasible that he genuinely doesn't know what he is - *if* he is one of these rougarou?'

Nix nods. 'Fair point. Okay, so we keep going the way we are with him. But I don't want any human staff alone with him at any time from now on. A vampire can defend themselves if this other side does come out. Fletch? I mean you too.'

'Got it, Nix.'

'Good. Ethan? I don't suppose there's a handy rougarou kit that you can use to confirm if he is one or not?'

'If only. I've got a team on it, but it's a completely new species for us. We've never come across anything like this. It will take some time.'

'Just when I think we have a handle on the way things work,' Nix says, laughing briefly. 'I don't think there's any need to mention this to Austin just yet. Let's get the facts first, before we scare him with talk of werewolves.'

'Agreed,' Fletch says. 'He's already struggling with his new found paralysis. We can't throw this at him yet.'

'Dismissed,' Nix says, calling an end to the meeting. Shep nudges Bas in the arm as he leaves the room. 'You got an hour? I could do with kicking something.'

Bas laughs. 'And you think that will be me? When was the last time you beat me?'

'I'm sure there were many times. I just can't think of any off the top of my head.'

'That's because there are none. I have time. I could do with working off some Rhain aggression.'

'You're not warming to the guy, are you?'

Bas holds the door open for him, following him along the corridor leading to the training room. 'I would like that bastard's warm blood coating my hands.'

Shep grimaces over his shoulder at him. 'Nice! Wow, you really do hate him.'

'And you don't? If not for him you wouldn't have wings.'

'Hey! I don't have wings. Well, not yet anyway. And yes, I do hate him. Won't help my situation though. Plus, he'll get it eventually. He'll either be taken out by Fever or—'

'Me.'

Shep walks into the changing room and over to his locker. 'Exactly.'

Bas pulls off his shirt, replacing it with a tank top from his own locker. 'I dream about killing that male.'

Shep glances over at his friend. Bas has a dark side to him, but the look on his face in that moment is one Shep's never seen before. It's downright cold, and scary as hell. He fully believes Bas would tear Rhain to pieces given half the chance.

'Okay. So back to training. You fancy a bit of one-on-one combat or a full training program?'

Bas slides his weapons into the numerous holsters draped on his body. 'Full program.'

Shep follows him into the vast training room, rearranging his own weapons so he's ready to start. If Bas is in one of his aggressive moods, he's going to have to be on his game today.

AVSTiN

His nightly visits to the garden have quickly become the highlight of his day. Fletch takes him out when Fallon is doing her job, fighting whoever she fights. It's not something he wants to think about. She's more than capable of looking after herself. A part of him can't help but worry, which is ridiculous. That stunning warrior doesn't need *him* worrying about her.

Today, instead of bringing him out just after the sun sets, she had arranged to meet with him when she got off rotation. She'd been busy the last three nights, and he had missed their time together.

Over the last few days, he's noticed they are being more cautious with him. He's still in his own room, but Fletch hasn't been alone with him. He doesn't remember doing anything to make them wary. Perhaps they learned something about him? Perhaps something showed up on one of the many tests they perform on him?

Maybe he's just being paranoid after so long not trusting people around him.

He's trying to talk more, but it's not coming naturally yet. He's still getting used to the sound of his own voice. Apparently, his accent is from New Orleans, but how he ended up in the lab in the UK he has no idea. He'll just add that to the growing list of things he doesn't know.

He watches as the wind blows through Fallon's hair, brushing it back from her shoulders. She appears to have a new wound up the length of her arm, as it's covered in a thick bandage. She also looks tired. It must have been a bad night.

'Are you all right?'

She glances at the bandage before nodding. 'Better than the vampire who gave me that wound.'

'You killed him?'

'Lately it's them or us. I intend to be the one who walks away. Same goes for the rest of the team. We fight to survive, Austin. Our survival, and that of others being hunted by The Order.'

'Do you think I was hunted by them?'

She sits on the bench opposite him, clutching her hands together as she leans forward. 'Maybe. It's what they usually do. Find someone they want and take them by force.'

'How many have they taken?'

Fallon shrugs. 'No way of knowing.' She frowns as she looks at him. He could swear she's sad, but she's not easy to read. Fallon shakes her head and stands suddenly, pacing the grass in front of him as she rolls her shoulders. 'I love this time of the day, just before the sun comes up. I come out here sometimes and release my wings, let the sun hit them when it rises. Another night with The Order survived. Another morning back here with everyone safe.'

She falls quiet again, rubbing her arm as she watches the sky.

'Would you release them?' He grimaces as the words come out. He honestly didn't mean to ask her that.

Fallon turns to face him. 'Release my wings?'

'I'm sorry. I shouldn't have asked.'

She frowns at him for a long time then removes her vest top, leaving on her sports bra. He watches in quiet amazement as the two enormous turquoise wings slide out of her back, stretching and reshaping to either side of her.

Stunning. No other words can describe her. 'I can't imagine what it would be like to walk again, let alone fly.'

Fallon walks over to him, her wings stretched out to either side. 'Would you like... I can show you what it's like. If you want me to? I swear I won't drop you.'

'I'd like that, if you're sure?'

She crouches in front of him. 'Put your arms around my neck. I'm not going to carry you like you're a damsel in distress or anything like that. I'll just hold you around your waist and lift you off the ground a bit.'

He does as he's told, hanging on while she stands, lifting him from the chair. His useless legs drag on the ground thanks to being a few inches taller than Fallon, but he couldn't care less about appearing weak in her presence. Just holding her like this makes him feel better than he's felt for a long time.

'You ready?'

He nods, too nervous and excited to speak. Fallon stretches her wings, the huge limbs flapping. She pushes off the ground, launching them into the air, her wings beating to either side of her. He hangs on tight as she carries them higher, then stops, holding them a few metres above the trees surrounding the garden.

'I've got you,' she says as his grip tightens. 'I'm not going to let you go.'

He releases his death grip from around her neck, the pressure of her arms around his waist firm, as she supports his weight. Austin looks around, taking in the spectacular view. The landscape is breathtaking, trees and valleys as far as the eye can see.

'You okay?'

'Yeah. Is your arm okay? I don't want carrying me to hurt you.'

'I told you I'm not going to let you go. Stop worrying.'

'It's the first time I've been suspended in the air, cher. Or the first time I can remember. Give me a chance to get used to it.' She falls silent, so he looks around at her. She's smiling at him again. 'Why do you smile at me like that after I talk?'

'I like hearing you speak. It was something I was hoping you'd do for a long time. I'm still getting used to it. Your accent is becoming clearer each time you talk. I like it.'

'That's good, because I believe I'm stuck with it.'

He grips her tightly as a gust of wind drives them to the side. 'It'll take more than some wind to knock me out of the sky.'

Because of the way she's holding him, her mouth is right by his ear, her breath warm on his skin. Her strong body is pressed firmly to his, supporting his frail broken one as she holds him.

As humiliated as he is at being held by her, he can't help but be thankful for this moment. Being held in her arms, being able to hold her in return, is something he could never have hoped for. He can hear every steady beat of her heart, even over the rush of the wind through the trees.

He doesn't know how or why, but he can always hear her heart. No matter where she is in the compound, that comforting sound keeps him company.

He knows it's not normal in any way, that he shouldn't be able to hear her no matter where she is in the house, but he doesn't want it to stop. He's alone so many hours of the day, and hearing that sound, beating steadily, helps him feel a little less alone.

A gust of wind blows her hair aside, exposing the side of her face and her long neck. Her beautiful scent envelops him, sending his own heartbeat into a frenzy. She swallows heavily as she slowly leans back to look at him. 'Are you okay? Your heart is racing.'

So is yours. 'I'm good. Thanks cher.'

Her smile is stunning. She likes hearing him speak. Her breathing, her heartbeat, her scent - it all changes when he talks. He wishes he could offer more than just talking. Wishes he could offer her the *real* him... whoever that is. It's so frustrating.

He shouldn't be looking at her the way he is. Shouldn't be wondering what it would be like to kiss her. Shouldn't be imagining that she's looking at him the same way he's looking at her.

'You confuse me, Austin.'

'How?'

'There's a strength in you. A fight I admire. Most in your position would be huddled in the corner of a room, muttering to themselves. You face every problem thrown at you. You face your fear. Your body is weak for now, but your mind is stronger than anyone I know.'

'I don't have much choice, Fallon. I either give up and drag myself into that corner, or I fight. I'm not ready to give up, cher. Not even close.'

The smile she gives him in return is the fullest he's seen so far. 'Yeah - you're a fighter. Maybe even a Blackjack.'

He laughs, loving the way her arms tighten around him, so he doesn't fall. 'I can't see me being much use out in the field.'

'Never say never.'

He nods, not able to find a suitable reply. He'd love that, but it's so far in the future he can't see it happening.

'Would you like to go for a fly?'

'Is that not what we're doing?' he asks trying to relax his grip.

'I meant a proper fly,' Fallon says.

She lowers them both to the ground but keeps hold of him which he really likes. She can hold him forever. 'Let me show you what it's really like to fly like you had wings yourself.'

'You're not just going to throw me in the air now, are you?'

She laughs. 'No. All you need to do is trust me. I'll do the rest.'

He nods before his mouth can talk him out of it. Fallon turns him around so his back is pressed to her chest, her arms tight around his torso, holding him against her. Then she lifts them off the ground again.

Facing away from her is so different. There's nothing in front of him except the forest, stretching out for miles in all directions. He grips her arms in his hands, holding them tight around his waist.

'I'll never drop you, Austin. Are you ready?'

'For what, cher?'

'To fly.'

She beats her wings, taking him over the compound, across the trees, and out towards the horizon.

IZZY

'Damn stupid piece of shit!' She kicks at the offending wheel, and it finally relents, allowing her to shove it into the bar far enough to close the doors behind her. Izzy curses her cleaning cart, as she straightens her blouse and takes a deep breath. She shouldn't have offered to take the extra shift at The Lair. But she needed the money, so it seemed like a good idea at the time.

She can't explain why she's angry.

Well, she can.

She's angry at Shep, which is downright ridiculous. He didn't do anything wrong. Not really. Running from her flat like someone was after him had hurt a little. But it's not like he owed her anything. She'd looked after him and he'd thanked her. End of story.

So why is she so irritated by his abrupt departure?

Two days had passed since she last saw him. She's embarrassed to admit she had casually asked around the club to see if he had been in, or if anyone knew when he would be in next, but no one had any idea, which just served to irritate her even more.

She resists driving the blasted cart into the wall as she steps out into the main bar. The club doesn't open for another few hours. With the lights on full and the room empty, it's all the more evident just how much of a shithole this place is. It's badly in need of a revamp. Or even a full demolition.

The same wheel jams against the edge of the bar, refusing to free itself. 'Oh for the love of God. Give me a break!'

A large hand reaches out and pulls the cart free. She slowly lifts her head, following the hand to the tattooed arm and up to the body it's attached to. Shep smiles down at her and winks. 'I may be reading this wrong, but I'm guessing you're having a bad day?'

A tirade of abuse threatens to pour out of her mouth, but she holds it back, settling on a mature silence as she pulls the cart around the bar and away from him. She is acting completely irrationally, but she's tired and upset, so he's going to get it.

'Did I do something to annoy you? I've been told I'm surprisingly good at irritating people.'

'I'm fine. I've got work to do.'

He leans on the bar and plays with the leather bands wrapped around his wrist. He doesn't say anything else and neither does she. He just silently watches her as she tries to get on with her cleaning. Unfortunately, the mirror that takes up the wall behind the bar isn't helping. Every time she looks up, which is probably more often than necessary, she can see him.

She can't stop looking at him no matter how hard she tries. His tall body is clad in dark jeans, a navy fitted t-shirt, and a pair of Converse - quite different to what he usually wears when he's at the club. He's more casual today and she likes it.

Stop looking!

She turns away from the mirror, focusing on the tables instead of the bar. At least that way her back is to the mirror and him.

'Yeah, I've definitely pissed you off. My Spidey senses are tingling. Sure sign I'm in the bad books.'

She throws the cloth on the table and faces him, her hands on her hips. 'I was minding my own business. All I wanted to do was go home, have a bath, and read a book. Nothing exciting.'

'Right... Okay, so you've lost me.'

'I didn't ask to find you, bleeding and barely conscious in the car park. I didn't ask for any of this. But I helped you. I brought you back to my house and patched you up. Then you wake up and run like I was an axe murderer or something.'

'And that's annoying you because...'

'Because...' she pauses and drops her hands from her hips. He's got her there. She doesn't have a clue why she's so annoyed. Okay so maybe she does, but she's not going to tell him she was hoping he might stay and at least have breakfast with her. She feels even more ridiculous when the realisation hits.

She likes him and was hoping to spend more time with him. Plain and simple. 'Never mind. I have to get back to work.'

Shep watches her for another few minutes before he speaks again. 'I'm sorry I left like I did. I had to get back. I was late for work. But I really do appreciate what you did for me. I mean that Izzy. A lot of people would have just left me there. Like you said, you didn't have to help me, but you did, and I'm not going to forget that.'

She stops and looks over at him again, frowning when she realises something. All evidence of the cut is gone. It's only been two days. There should be some sign of the injury she patched up. But there's nothing at all.

'What?' he asks, glancing in the mirror behind the bar. 'Have I got food on my face or something?'

'I was just thinking that you heal remarkably fast. There's no scar

135

on your head.'

He drops his gaze, his attention on the bands around his wrist again. 'Yep. I always heal fast. It's a special gift I have.' He straightens and claps his hands together, ending that topic. 'Well, I guess I'd better leave you to it. I just wanted to make sure you were okay. I honestly didn't mean to piss you off by leaving like I did.'

'Well, I appreciate you coming to check on me. Thank you.'

Shep nods, then walks away, but stops at the end of the bar. 'What time do you finish?'

'I'm sorry?' she asks, surprised by his question.

He stuffs his hands into the back pockets of his jeans and turns to face her. 'What time do you finish work today?'

'Why are you asking?'

He looks away, the usual confidence seemingly gone. 'I'd like to thank you properly. Would you let me take you to dinner?'

'With you?' He grins and she's annoyed with herself for liking it. Why does he have to be so gorgeous?

'Ideally with me, yeah. I was kind of hoping you might let me eat food with you. As in at the same table. At the same time. Unless you want me to get you a take-away then fuck off? Because I can do that if you want.'

'Don't you mean fuck off again?'

He nods but keeps smiling. 'Ouch! Walked into that one, didn't I? The other night was complicated.' He steps up to her and holds out his hand. 'But I pinkie swear, this time I won't make a run for it.'

She quietly looks at him as her mind goes into a whirlwind. A part of her instantly wants to say no. Knows she should say no. He's a player. Someone who sleeps around. But the other part of her desperately wants to say yes. He's gorgeous, kind, charming, irritating, secretive, and more than a little intimidating. What the hell is she thinking?

'Hold on. Do you mean it was complicated as in a married kind of

136

complicated?'

He shakes his head briskly. 'Hell no! Married? Me? Hand on heart promise that I am completely unattached.'

'Okay. Yes. Dinner with you would be lovely.' She frowns as the words pop out without any consideration for her brain.

'Really?'

'What the hell!' She hooks her little finger with his and shakes. 'I finish at nine, but I'd like to get changed after, if that's okay.'

Shep smiles and any doubts disappear. Oh she is in so much trouble. 'Do you want me to pick you up, or meet you somewhere?'

'How about I meet you at The Crossroads pub at ten.' She doesn't want him anywhere near her apartment again. Best to keep temptation far away if possible.

'I'll sort it out. See you then.' He takes a step towards her, then changes his mind and retreats from the room. Izzy lowers on to the nearest chair. In her head, she's already back in her room rifling through her wardrobe, trying to think of something suitable to wear.

This is ridiculous. Why is she getting so carried away with this? It's dinner with Shep. Just an innocent dinner with someone she's attracted to.

Someone who ran out on her instead of spending even a few more minutes with her. Until now it seems. To say he's giving off mixed signals is an understatement. But she's running when he clicks his fingers, so that makes her just as bad.

At least she chose the venue. She picked The Crossroads for its relaxed dress-code and informal setting. The bar is a popular haunt, mainly thanks to its outstanding bar food and incredible live bands that flock to perform there. Being a Wednesday, there would be no music so it should make conversation easy, but there will still be enough people around so she won't be alone with him.

It's not that she feels wary being with him, but she barely knows him, and what she does know excites her a little too much for her own good. She's not exactly using the sensible part of her brain when it comes to Shep. Unless she's careful, she could easily be hurt by him.

SHEP

'How are you feeling?'

Shep sighs dramatically. 'I. Am. Fine. How many fucking times, Fletch?' The human doctor perches on the edge of his desk, arms crossed as he stares over at Shep. 'What?'

'You're lying your fucking arse off, that's what!'

'Am not! I'm fine.'

'So you're telling me you haven't had any pain? No twinges? Nothing at all?'

'Nope. Not a thing.'

Fletch points over to the screen showing the x-ray he just took of Shep's back. 'I find that hard - no, impossible to believe. The wings have grown, Shep.'

'What?'

'Not by much, but any change in size will have hit you. Sort of like I want to do right now.'

'Wow! Wonderful thing for a doctor to say.'

Fletch pushes off the desk and sits on the bed beside him. 'If I was treating humans, you might be right. But I'm not. I'm treating a bunch of macho alpha male vampires who like to lie to me. To my face! I can't help you if you're not honest with me. You know what Rhain said. Hybrids usually don't survive when they are injected with the drug you were given.'

'Yeah. I'm on borrowed time. I get that.'

Fletch pauses then speaks again, his voice softer. 'I don't mean to have a go, but I need you to be honest so I can help you. As much as a pain in the fucking arse you are, I'd prefer you didn't die on my watch. You need to talk about what's going on with you. I'm here for you, Shep. Day or night.'

'I don't need your sympathy, Doc.'

'Stubborn ass. I'm your friend so you'll take it and shut up. I am trying to help you, but I can't unless you're honest with me. Lie to everyone else if you want. I don't care, but not me.

'I need to know what's going on with your body so I can react, or step in if I have to. If I'm late giving you that stabilising drug Rhain gave us, you could die. Now I don't know about you, but I'm not keen on that happening.'

For the second time that night, Shep feels like a right dick. 'I'm sorry. My head is fucked up with all of this.'

'I'm not surprised.'

'I *might* have collapsed a few days ago. Threw up a few times too.'

'Might have, as in you did?'

He nods. 'Just felt dizzy and hit the deck. Came to a while later. Not sure how long I was down for. I had the same thing happen tonight, but I didn't actually go down this time. Just had a minor wobble.'

'How are you feeling now. Honestly.'

'Bit rough. Kind of *off*. I don't know how to describe it. And my back aches.'

'I'm not surprised it does. You're not going to want to hear this, but I don't think you should be going out alone while you're like this.'

'No way, Fletch! You're not grounding me. If you lock me in here, I'll go off my rocker. Please, buddy.'

Fletch strokes his beard as he looks over at Shep. He needs the human to get on board. Desperately needs him to. If Fletch decides Shep is too much of a risk, he'll tell Nix, and she'll take him off rotation and absolutely would ground him.

'I don't know, Shep.'

'I feel fine.' He stands up and spins around. 'See. Fine and dandy.'

'Shep, you were given a high dose of a drug I know nothing about. Let me worry about you. It's my job.'

Shep smiles at the doctor. For a human he's not half bad, and he does genuinely care about all of them. But that doesn't mean he'll take Fletch's babying. 'I get that, and I appreciate it, but I feel okay. I'm not going to lie about this.'

Fletch doesn't look entirely convinced, but he nods once. 'The slightest twinge, you come back to me. No questions. And no more hiding the truth from me, or next time I *will* ground you. You hear me?'

'Loud and clear, Doc.' Shep hurries from the room before Fletch can change his mind. He pauses just around the corner and leans against the wall. Okay, so maybe saying he feels fine was a little extension of the truth. He mostly feels fine, but not entirely. He's exhausted, but if he told Fletch that, he would never have been allowed to leave.

Shep pushes off the wall and forces one foot in front of the other until he finally reaches the main house. He'll grab some food, then try to sleep for a few hours. Heading over to see Izzy this morning has tired him out for some reason. He can usually go out on his bike for hours, but the measly sixty minutes had nearly wiped him out. Maybe he should take one of the cars tonight to their date?

He can't help but smile to himself. He's going on his first date. About fucking time.

'What happened to your bike?'

He jumps as Bas steps out from the shadows under the staircase. 'Do you wait to jump out and scare me?'

'Believe it or not, I have a life, so no.'

'Right,' Shep says as he continues heading towards the kitchen. 'Well, I'm hungry, so can we walk and talk.'

Bas sits on one of the stools at the vast counter, as Shep searches in the kitchen for some food. He finds a container on his shelf in the fridge filled with Gwen's bolognese. He pops it in the microwave with half a dozen slices of cheese topped garlic bread.

'You look tired.'

'Thanks Bas! Love having these chats with you.' Bas glares, so he smiles apologetically. 'Sorry. Yeah, I am, hence the cranky mood. How did things go with Rhain?'

Bas raises one eyebrow. His friend knows he's changing the subject, but he lets Shep get away with it. 'Infuriating as usual. I have to trust Ethan and Nix know what they're doing.'

'It's all any of us can do,' Shep says as he sits opposite Bas with his plate of food. 'Ethan usually knows what he's doing.'

Bas drops his gaze as he nods.

'What's up?'

'I worry he is putting too much faith in Rhain. We know what he did to Court, to Dav, to Austin. That deserves retaliation, not friendship.'

'Oh, don't worry Bas,' he says around a mouthful of pasta. 'We'll retaliate all right, and then some. But we need to make sure we get what we can from him first. You know that.'

Bas nods again. If Shep had a better grip on his own life he'd ask about Ethan. But he's in no position to ask anything, so he keeps his mouth shut.

'Your bike?' Bas asks, helping himself to a slice of garlic bread.

'The paintwork is scratched to shit, but the body isn't damaged. I'll have to strip it back and respray sections of it. I'll be able to get her back to the pristine condition she was in before.'

'Before what? You didn't say how it happened.'

'I fell off.'

Bas scoffs. 'You're a highly trained vampire with excellent reflexes. You don't fall.'

'I might have passed out, then I fell.'

Bas curses in Spanish as he shakes his head. 'Are you okay?'

'Yep. Signed off by Fletch.'

'Who assisted you?'

He shovels another forkful of pasta and meat into his mouth. 'Assisted me with what?'

'You passed out. I presume someone helped you?'

'Okay, so that woman I was telling you about found me. Let me stay in her place overnight, then I rode my bike back here. It's all good.'

'I presume you felt the same attraction?'

Shep nods as he chews.

'Does she know you're a vampire?'

'Of course not! I'm just this attractive guy who she came across and helped. It's not a big deal.'

Bas nods as he silently stares at him, so he concentrates on his dinner. Bas can be really fucking unnerving when he just stares. He's really fucking unnerving most of the time.

'What do you plan to do?'

Shep shrugs. 'Finish eating my dinner.'

Thankfully, his phone buzzes in his pocket at the same time as Bastian's. He's grateful for the distraction, but both phones going off means only one thing.

Nix needs them, which means he can kiss goodbye to his nap before his big date with Izzy.

SHEP

As they wait for Nix to finish her call, Shep looks around her office. Court is lounging on the couch beside the desk, reading through more reports. Still unable to remember anything beyond a few years ago, he spends most of his free time reading old reports, seeing if anything jogs his memory, but so far nothing has worked.

Shep's not sure what's worse - not having a fucking clue who you are or having wings popping out of your back. They're both probably as bad as each other for very different reasons.

Willow, Bas, Fallon, and Dav occupy the other chairs scattered around the room. They don't usually take meetings in Nix's office. Something is up. The rushed meeting mixed with the tense expression on their leader's face says as much.

Nix puts down the phone and faces them. 'Sorry about that.' She turns the laptop around and shows Ethan on the screen. 'So, we're all here. What do you need to tell us Davyn?'

Shep does a double take. Dav rarely talks, let alone calls a meeting. This is so much more than one of their usual problems.

'I had my latest report from Fergus. It's not good.' The vampire Davyn had left in charge of his late father's vast estate in Ireland has been a lifesaver. Dav may be a lord by name, but any interest he had in taking his seat at the head of the house was killed a long, long time ago.

His father had been a sadistic brute of a male, and his death should have meant the death of the family name and all it stood for. Deciding not to raze the castle and everything in it to the ground, is a decision he knows Davyn still regrets on a daily basis.

'What's happened?' Court asks, straightening on the couch.

'The Whelans have disappeared.'

'They've what?' Ethan asks.

'Disappeared. Bas brought them back home after they helped us take down my father, then nothing. Vampires and wolves fucking hate each other, but the four brothers swore allegiance to me. They're under my protection. None of my men have seen or heard from them since I left Ireland.'

'I don't like the sound of that,' Nix says, and she's not the only one. He's not a fan of the fleabags. The vampire and wolf shifter bad blood goes back generations. He's not even sure exactly how the feud began. But by the time the Whelans had helped them storm Dav's father's castle, he had warmed to them slightly. Murt, Fionn, Con, and Garret were decent enough - for wolves at least.

'Could they have landed themselves in trouble with the other wolves for helping us?' he asks.

Dav shrugs. 'It's possible. Murt wasn't one for following the rules. I doubt he would have cared either way. But from what Fergus says, Murt could have placed his clan in trouble when he sided with us.

'Himself and his brothers are under my protection, so they should have been in touch at least once. It's not right that no one has heard anything from them. It's like they've vanished.'

'I did a lot of research on our new allies after they went home,' Ethan says. 'I wanted to know as much about them as possible considering how helpful they were. It seems there are actually five siblings. Four males and a female.'

'Murt never mentioned a sister?' Nix says.

'She's been missing for decades. Presumed dead by most, but of course, the brothers don't believe that.'

'So are you saying their disappearance is somehow linked to their sister?'

'I'm just saying that one Whelan has already vanished. Now the remaining four have followed too. I agree with Davyn. Something isn't right. Murt could very well be the one to challenge the old ways when it comes to the wolves in Ireland. That may have ruffled a few feathers among those not so keen on a new and more united future.'

Nix turns in her chair to face Davyn. Shep knows what's coming and so does Dav. He's frowning, which isn't anything new when it comes to Dav, but it's a bit more intense than usual.

'What?'

She smiles apologetically. 'How would you feel about taking a trip back to Ireland?'

'I'd rather kiss Shep.'

'Hey! I take offence at that!'

'I couldn't give a fuck if you do,' Davyn replies. 'It's the truth.'

'I know you really don't want to go, but like you said, the Whelans are under your protection. It's your house. None of us can do it for you and believe me, I would offer if I could.'

Dav growls to himself as he glares at the floor between his boots. Shep doesn't blame him. Dav's legacy is an old castle staffed by people who were tortured and abused by his father for centuries. Himself included. It's not somewhere Shep would be racing back to either. It's also where he was jabbed with the enhancer so overall, the castle is full of bad memories for a lot of people.

'I'll go with you,' Court says. 'I'm sure Thea will want to tag along too.'

'I've got nothing planned,' Shep says. 'I'll go with you.'

'No you won't,' Nix says, instantly killing his buzz.

'Why not?'

'You know why. There's no way you're leaving the country. The best place for you is here.'

'Ah Nix come on! I'm fine!'

'Do you want me to bench you indefinitely, because I will?'

He closes his mouth before the next argument comes out. She will too. One more word and he'll be watching everyone else head off on rotation and he'll be stuck here on his ass. 'Got it.'

'Glad to hear it.' She gives him what he could swear is a sympathetic look, but he doesn't want that. He wants to be treated like a fucking member of the team.

'Fallon? You okay to go with Dav?'

Fallon nods as she leans forward in her chair. 'We have your back Dav.'

'Fine. I'll go. What do you want me to do?'

'Just see if you can find out if they're okay. They put their lives on the line to help us. We owe it to them to make sure they haven't been punished because of that.'

'Fine.' Davyn's curt response is the final word he says on the matter. At least with Court and Fallon heading over with him, he'll have support. And Thea will have his back in a different way none of the rest of them can.

Nix smiles at Dav, but he's back focusing on the floor again. 'Head out in a few hours. The sooner you find them the better. That's it everyone. Make sure Dav, Court, and Fallon have what they need.'

Shep gets to his feet, ready to make his escape with the rest of the team, but Nix isn't ready to let him go that easily. 'Not you Shep. Sit.'

Groaning to himself, he turns and puts an award-winning smile on his face. 'What's up Boss?'

'How are things with you?'

'Me? Perfect. Why?'

'Are you going to keep this up, or will you actually try to answer the question?'

'That depends.'

'On what?'

'On whether you'll bench me for opening my fucking mouth.'

Nix points to the seat on her right. 'Sit down.'

He sits, trying not to be an ass about the situation, but he's not doing a fantastic job.

'I'm worried about you Shep. You're clearly tense. You haven't laughed or joked for ages. I miss you. And I know you have a lot to deal with, but you're not alone. Each and every member of this team are here to you. I'm here for you.'

Now he feels like a total ass. 'I know Nix. Thanks. But it's like you said. I have a lot on my mind. I'm waiting for these monsters to tear out of my back. Kind of puts me on edge.'

'Of course it does. I just don't want you taking chances in the field.'

'I'm not going to put the rest of the team at risk. I'm a damn good fighter Nix. These fucking wings won't change that.'

'Oh would you calm down! I'm not having a go at you! At ease!'

He reins himself in. She's right. He's on edge and taking everything as an attack. 'Sorry Boss.'

'This is what I'm talking about. You're so wound up. My main concern is your well-being. The rest of the team can take care of themselves. Do you want some time—'

'No! No,' he repeats, a little quieter this time. 'Please Nix. I'm okay.'

She hits him with a long hard look which he returns. He's not going to back down from this.

'Fine. I want you to have daily check-up's with Fletch. That's not a request!'

'Yep. No problem, Boss.'

She shakes her head, but gestures towards the door. 'Go on.'

He jumps up, hurrying from the room before she can change her mind. He races back to his room, grabs a clean shirt, sprays on some cologne, then leaves again.

He's excited about meeting Izzy tonight. More excited than he remembers being for ages. The part he's most excited about is spending time with her out in public, talking and eating together. He's never done that.

Shep grabs his jacket from the back of his bike where he dumped it earlier and takes his keys from the safe.

'Where are you going?'

Shep jumps as Bas steps out of the shadows. The fucker is seriously stealthy. 'You trying to give me a heart attack or something? Would you please stop doing that!'

'My apologies.'

'Yeah, well you're not a thief anymore, so you don't have to skulk around in the shadows.'

Bas leans against the wall, his arms crossed as he gives him a wry smile. 'Stop changing the subject. Where are you going dressed up like that?'

'Out. I'm a big boy. I don't have to tell you. And I'm not dressed up. It's a shirt.'

'Exactly! I didn't know you could operate shirt buttons.'

'Oh haha. You're a fucking comedian do you know that?'

'Oh dear. You are in a bitchy mood, aren't you?'

Shep shrugs on his jacket, then grabs his helmet from the handlebars. 'Yes Bastian. I'm a total bitch. What can I say? Now stop bugging me and mind your own business.'

He's not in the least bit surprised when Bas steps in front of his bike and just looks at him. His friend's face is unreadable which it usually is unless he's smiling. Bas is pretty much a closed book. 'What?'

'I'm concerned about you. I'm just asking where you're going in case something happens. I know you're going to meet that woman and I'm happy for you. But you're not on your game at the moment. I'm going to be concerned about you.'

'Oh, lucky me!'

Shep yelps as Bas hauls him off the bike, throwing him against the wall and holding him there. 'Being scared doesn't give you the right to be an ungrateful ass. I know what it's like to feel like you have no control over your life. What it's like to wonder if each time you wake up it will be the last. Thinking about how your life will finally end. I know okay! I've been there.'

Shep is stunned into silence for a moment at Bastian's outburst. Bas rarely raises his voice. He's more of the cool calm kind of guy. But it's what he said that fully floors Shep. What the fuck happened to him? He opens his mouth to ask, but Bas releases him and takes a step back.

'No Shep. This is about you, not me. I just wanted you to know I have an idea of what you're going through. It's not the same I know, but I'm not a stranger to fear. I know how it eats away at you, makes you question everything you do, everything you are. Push the others away, but don't push me away. We're friends.'

He nods, then surprises himself by pulling Bas into a hug. He's not usually a fan of being touchy feely with the rest of the team but fuck it. He needs to do this - for Bas as much as himself.

When he releases Bas, his friend looks just as confused as he feels. 'I wasn't expecting that.'

'Yeah, well join the club. I appreciate you looking out for me, and I know I'm being a right pain in the ass. I'm not coping well with being coddled like this. It's ruining my vibe.'

'What vibe would that be?' Bas asks with a small smile.

'You know. My vibe. My kick ass warrior vibe I have going on. You know the one you're so jealous of?'

Bas laughs as he shakes his head. 'And there he is again. Back to joking.'

'I'm not doing that to brush you off. Not this time. I'm just trying to lighten the mood a bit. It's getting too gloomy for me.'

'We can't have that now, can we? Are you going to tell me where you're going or not?'

'Not,' he replies as he swings his leg over the saddle and starts his bike.

IZZY

She glances around the room at the other occupants. Compared to some of the women here tonight, Izzy feels overdressed. Her black pencil skirt, jade sleeveless silk shirt, and matching heels shows enough skin, without screaming desperation.

She wipes her damp palms on the seat of the chair to either side of her. The bar is busy but not too crowded. Shep had reserved one of the booths at the back of the room. It was private, but still not out of sight of the bar or other patrons, and she's grateful for that. Clearly, he's trying to make her feel comfortable and she appreciates it.

She rummages in her clutch for her lipstick, reapplying it as she waits for Shep to arrive. He's not late. She arrived early. It was either that or hang around at home and get increasingly stressed about the meeting with Shep. It's been a long time since she last went on a date, and nerves have well and truly taken over. It's not like it's even a date as such. It's a thank you meal - nothing more.

A thank you meal with a man she appears to be ever so slightly attracted to. Why does she have to like him? Why can't this be an innocent meal, instead of something her mind is turning into a big romantic gesture?

Especially with Shep.

He's a massive question mark. A big unknown in every way. Who has one name? Musicians and actors yes, but in everyday life people tend to have a first and a last name. Does that mean he's hiding something? Is he hiding from someone? Maybe the police? What if he's a major criminal and she's about to have dinner with him?

Oh stop it!

Too many nights alone buried in a book has given her an overactive imagination. She's sure he's not a criminal. Hopefully.

Then she spots him coming through the door, and her worries transform to excitement. Wearing a navy shirt with the sleeves rolled up which shows off the ink on his arms, with a pair of navy jeans, carrying his jacket and helmet, he is quite a sight.

He easily stands a good head above everyone else in the room which helps him find her in the crowded space. When he smiles and makes his way over to her, her heart seems to beat in time with each of his long strides.

Shep sits beside her, his broad body filling the booth. 'Hey. Wow, you look absolutely incredible.'

She blushes before she can stop herself. 'Thank you. You too.'

'Glad you noticed. I even ironed my shirt after we made our arrangements. Rare occurrence believe me.' He winks and nods down to her glass. 'Fancy another drink love?'

'Thank you. Gin and tonic would be great.'

'Not a problem. I'll be back in a sec. Mind my seat.'

He stands and makes his way over to the bar. A scantily dressed woman gyrates beside him, attempting to get his attention in the most obvious way.

An irrational twinge of jealousy hits her as the woman brushes against him. Shep takes a small step to the side, separating himself from the woman, much to her obvious annoyance. He eventually gets their drinks and makes his way back to their table, sliding back in beside her.

'There you go love. So, do you come here often?' He cringes at his question, slapping himself on the forehead. 'Wow! Sorry, that was just about as clichéd as you can get. Not the best start, huh?'

Izzy meets his eyes, and her stomach tightens. His blue eyes seem to be glowing in the dim light. Putting it down to tiredness mixed with the effect he has on her, she licks her lips as she gets herself together.

'I've been here a few times, and it was a perfectly acceptable question.'

'Clichéd though.'

She smiles, resisting the urge to reach out and brush her fingers through his messy hair. She can't see Shep as the kind of man who spends hours grooming himself, so she's guessing his hairstyle is natural. She knows men who could easily spend a fortune on their hair and still come nowhere close to looking like he does. And while she's never been a fan of facial hair, Shep instantly changed her mind.

Everything about his carefree, messy look is seriously appealing to her. If he looks this good groomed, how amazing would he look after rolling around under the covers... naked?

Stop it!

'It was a bit clichéd, yes, but I'll let you away with it. You've already knocked me off my feet, so why not add another clichéd moment to the list?' She takes a sip of her drink when his smile does things to her a mere smile shouldn't.

'Now hold on there one second. I swept you off your feet - not knocked! My comment was corny as hell but sweeping you off your feet was genuine. I was genuinely clumsy and not looking where I was going. Two completely separate incidences. But when you say it like that, my track record isn't stellar at the moment. I'm usually a lot smoother. I am quite a catch I assure you.'

'I'll have to take your word for that Shep. All evidence to the contrary so far.'

He leans closer, trapping her in his gaze again. 'You don't believe that. In spite of my performance, you're drawn to me. Just like I'm drawn to you.'

He blinks, releasing her from his hold, then sits back in the leather seat. 'How was work?' he asks, suddenly changing the subject.

'Work? Right, I guess it was as tolerable as usual. I saw that you got your bike back from the club and you obviously came here tonight on it. Will you be able to repair it?'

Shep puts his own glass on the table then grimaces. 'Mechanically it's fine but scratched to shit. It'll need a bit of work to get it back to where it was.' He glances down at his drink before looking up at her again. 'I know I've said this before, but I really do appreciate what you did for me, you know that, right?'

'There's no need to thank me, really. But I do owe you an apology for the way I was with you earlier. I was in a mood, and I took it out on you.'

He smirks. 'Ah don't worry about that. I've been told I have the uncanny ability to rub people up the wrong way. It's kind of my thing.'

Having Shep laugh it all off helps ease some of her guilt. It wasn't his fault she completely overreacted about whatever went on between them. 'Thank you. Are you okay... after what happened outside the club?'

Something she can't describe crosses his face before he quickly hides it again. 'Yeah. Sure. It's all good.'

Clearly, he's not too keen on talking about what happened, so she moves on. 'So, what do you do for a living? You mentioned that you had to get back for work.'

154

'Eh... protection.'

That she can believe, but the pause before he answered doesn't go unnoticed. 'Private protection or something else?'

'Something else, in a roundabout way.' That puts an end to any further possible questions. He's a fan of remaining mysterious.

With nothing else to be said on the subject, Izzy reaches for her glass and sips her drink. She should have been expecting an answer like that from him. Everything about Shep is shrouded in mystery; his job, what was wrong with him the other night, his attraction to The Lair, his single name. Nothing is straightforward.

Does she really need someone this complicated in her life at this moment? She's a year away from completing her course. That should be her only concern, not getting in deeper with someone like Shep.

Not that anyone is getting in deep with anyone else. He asked her out tonight to thank her. Nothing more. The worst thing she can do is make this into more than it is. Which is a big fat nothing.

She risks a quick glance up at him. He's frowning at his drink, his fingers playing with the three thin leather and silver bracelets wrapped around his wrist.

He's good looking, but is that really enough? Does she not deserve more than someone who quite clearly refuses to tell her the truth about himself?

She should end this before she gets hurt. Decision made, she picks up her bag. 'I should probably go,' she says, getting to her feet. 'Thank you for the drink Shep.'

He lifts his head, frowning. 'What? You're leaving? Why?'

'This was a bad idea, Shep. I have college in the morning. I really should get an early night.'

'But what about dinner?'

'I'll pass, thank you. I honestly don't know what I was thinking accepting your invitation. This isn't me. None of this is. I like reading and studying. My favourite thing in the world is a hot bath, a good book, and an early night. That's as exciting as my life gets, and I'm more than happy about that.

'I'm only working at The Lair to pay my bills until I finish my course. I hate that place, but you're always there, so you clearly love it. Or maybe it's just the staff and locals that draw you there? I don't know.

'I do know that I've heard you like to work your way around the staff. I know that, yet here I am on a date... is this even a date, with you. Whatever. It's entirely your business. But I like simple and uncomplicated. That's not you, Shep.'

He pushes his drink aside and sits sideways, facing her. 'Sit down Izzy.'

'No. I really—'

'Sit!'

She stares at him, startled into silence at his abrupt command. But she sits anyway, more to stop him from attracting attention by raising his voice again. 'I'm sitting.'

'You're at The Lair because you have no choice. It's paying your bills, right?'

She nods, not sure where this is going.

'I go there because I have no choice either. It's complicated, and a long story, but it's something I need to do. I can't explain it and it'll make no sense to you. Fuck knows it makes no sense to me, but I need to keep going back there. It's... maybe a little familiar in a strange way.' He pauses and shakes his head. 'My life is stressful. So is my job. I guess it's kind of like a release for me. A way to unwind.

'And I know things seem... weird with me and I'm sorry about that. My life is complicated. Always has been, but I'll be as honest as I can with you. Stay please. Let me buy you dinner as planned, and I'll tell you everything.'

'You mean you'll tell me as much as you can.'

He grimaces, then smirks. 'Got me there! Okay, I'm going to lay all my cards on the table. I like you, Izzy. I really do and I mean that. It's been a hell of a long time since I liked someone enough to spend more than ten minutes with them, let alone ask them to dinner. That's the truth. I hope you believe that much.'

She does believe him. It's been a long time since a man has said those words to her, especially one that gets to her the way Shep does, but is that enough? Can she stay, knowing that he can only be honest and open with her up to a point?

He sits back, watching her as she decides what to do. What the hell! 'I'll have the house burger, sweet potato fries, and a portion of mayo.'

That smile of his makes an impressive reappearance before he stands up and gestures towards the bar. 'I'm going to order the food now, before you change your mind. Back in a sec.'

Izzy sips her drink, watching him speaking to the bartender to order their dinner. 'What the hell are you doing, Izzy?' she mutters to herself.

She's having dinner with an attractive man. That's it. Nothing strange about that. Millions of people do it every day. What happens after that is entirely down to Shep and how open he decides to be with her.

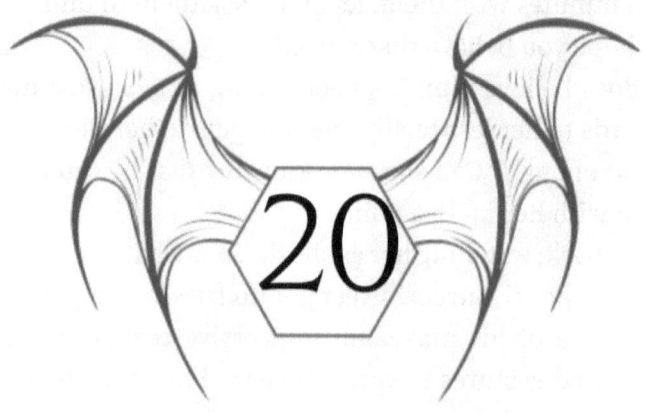

ςΗ≢P

He thought he'd blown it. For a few minutes there he was convinced she'd leave and that would be it. Not that he could have blamed her. But it's not what he wanted.

It's been a long time, if ever, since he cared whether the person he was with was interested in sticking around or not. It's not that he doesn't want more, it's just not something he ever gave much thought to.

Maybe he does want a relationship? Maybe deep down he does want what Court and Nix have? Maybe he is slightly envious of Thea and Dav? Until recently, he'd never let his mind get carried away for too long with thoughts like that.

He's a fuck up. A seriously messed up vampire, with so many shameful secrets he wouldn't know how to begin explaining them to anyone. He can't even bear thinking about it himself, let alone the thought of opening up to anyone else about what he's done. Being in a relationship would mean sharing all that shit, and that's not something he can consider.

And even if, in some bizarre turn of events, he actually did open up about what had happened in the past, and who and what he is, he'd then have to watch the woman run for her life and never see her again. He has no fucking doubts there would be an epic dust trail in her wake. Nobody in their right mind would want anything to do with him if they found out the truth.

Which is why he has meaningless sex with random strangers at The Lair. She's right about that part. He's worked his way through most of the staff there - sometimes multiple times. Talk about messed up. He's so far beyond messed up he doesn't know how to describe himself.

Izzy licks some mayo from her finger. Fuck, he wants to be with her so badly. All the other women he's been with have thrown themselves at him. Chased him. Come on to him. She's not doing anything like that, which just makes him want her even more.

And it's not like she's playing hard to get. She's just being herself. Taking things slowly. Making sure he's not some weirdo.

She might just have lucked out there.

Her dark hair slides over her shoulder and he has to make a conscious effort not to sweep it back in place. She's so different it's throwing him off completely. Most of the other girls are working at The Lair for tips and fucks. It's what it's known for. There's more to her than that. So much more, and he knows he's barely scratched the surface.

He likes her. He really does, even though he shouldn't. Maybe the fact she's different is what's attracting him for the first time? She's certainly beautiful. He thought that from the minute he nearly knocked her flat.

She doesn't deserve a flawed male like him to go anywhere near her, but he can't keep away. Since he first saw her in The Lair, he can't stop thinking about her.

If she has reservations about him sleeping his way through the staff at The Lair, he can only imagine how she would react if she knew he's a vampire fighter. If she knew he can never be with her like that. That he can never let her close to him in *that* way.

The best he can do for her is buy her dinner, then try to release the sensible part of his brain again and get out of her life for good.

'Are you really going to eat all of that?' she asks, pointing to the two portions of chips, huge burger, and side salad he'd ordered.

'Just watch me. I'm a big guy. I've got a healthy appetite. So,' he says, trying to act semi-normal in front of her as he tucks into dinner. 'You said you're working at The Lair to pay for your course. What are you doing?'

'I'm studying architecture,' Izzy says, as she wipes her hands on her napkin. 'I couldn't settle on a course when I left school, so I took a few years off. I enrolled as a mature student and am loving every minute of it.'

'Wow,' he says, genuinely impressed. 'How long have you got to go?'

'A year,' she replies, pulling a face. 'I suppose it's not too bad.'

'You got any family here?'

She shakes her head. 'I'm an only child. My parents own a restaurant, so architecture was my way of getting out of running the family business. I wanted something of my own. To stand on my own two feet and have my own life.'

Shep stares into his drink, slowly turning the glass in his hand. He totally understands wanting to break away from family. 'How's it all going for you?'

'So far so good. Working at The Lair wasn't exactly on my list of dream jobs, but the money's good and the hours are pretty perfect. As long as I wash my brain out as soon as I get home, it's all good.' She lowers her glass and places her hand over her mouth. 'I didn't mean that to sound the way it did.'

'Don't worry about it.'

'It's just some of the people who go there... Damn it! I mean... oh shut up, Izzy!'

He laughs as she smacks herself on the forehead like he did earlier. 'Hey, you didn't say anything wrong. I'm a big boy. I know what the place is like. Believe me. So, you've been dodging the subject since the food arrived. What do you want to know about me?'

'Maybe it would be easier to ask what you can tell me?'

He leans on the table as he gets his story straight. No lies. No matter what he tells her it will be the truth. 'My name is Shepherd, but I absolutely prefer Shep. Like I said, that's my full name. Always been that way. I have a baby sister, Willow, who I still think of as a child instead of an adult - apparently. I'm denying all charges. I work in protection in Wales where I live with my sister and the rest of the team. And yes, I am the typical overprotective, pain in the ass, big brother.'

'Why do you come all the way to The Lair to blow off steam?'

'I go there because it's... the people who go there...' he doesn't want to finish the sentence. Why does mentioning The Lair in earshot of Izzy make his skin crawl? 'Well, you know.'

She looks at her drink as she nods. 'And the car park? When you collapsed, what happened? Why were there cuts or slash marks on your t-shirt and jacket?'

I collapsed because I was injected with a fucking rotten poison that's altering my body. 'I'm sick.'

It's the truth. A massively watered down, highly edited version, but it's all she's getting. He wasn't expecting her face to drop the way it does at his statement. Fuck. Maybe he should have stuck to a lie? Should have said he was tired or some other shit like that.

'Oh God Shep! What's wrong? And please tell me to mind my own business if you want. Actually, forget it. I shouldn't have asked. It's got nothing to do with me.'

'No. It's fine. I'll spare you the fun details if that's okay, but I get pain and dizziness from time to time. A few seizures and seriously unpleasant vomiting have added themselves to the mix lately. The other night I was just walking up the steps when I felt dizzy and then my lights went out completely when I was on my bike about to set off for home.'

She accepts his answer, not mentioning the slash marks on his clothes which he's grateful for. Hearing that he's sick has overshadowed everything else. He feels shitty about that, but he wants to be as honest as he can with her. For some reason it's important to him.

'Are you going to be all right?'

He shrugs. 'I don't know. I hope so, but my doctor hasn't fully figured out what's wrong with me, or how to get it under control yet. Guess I'll just have to wait and see. Anyway, I don't really want to get all down in the dumps about it. I'd prefer to enjoy the meal. And the company of course.' He smiles and winks at her, loving the smile she gives him in return.

IZZY

He's sick. Seriously sick. She has no doubts he was playing down his illness, and all she did was push him to talk about it.

Izzy tries to keep the conversation flowing between them as they finish their meal but is finding it difficult. Her question about what had happened in the car park had come from a good place. She was genuinely concerned about him after finding him like that, but she had never considered he was ill.

It's his business though, and she's not going to push him for more details. His entire demeanour altered while he was speaking about it. The usual light-heartedness she's used to had dimmed quite a bit. She should have just left it. Now she feels guilty for bringing the mood of the evening down quite a bit.

He's been distracted since he spoke of it. The topic had changed a few times since then. It's clear he's trying to keep things upbeat but, like her, he's struggling.

'How many colleagues do you live with?' she asks, desperate to find some subject that won't drag him down further.

'Too fucking many at times,' he says, his grin coming back for the first time in a few minutes. 'There are nine of us altogether. Seven on the team, a girlfriend of one of the guys, and a doctor who makes sure we're in tip top condition. A few support staff too but they tend to keep to themselves.'

'Wow. That's a lot of people under one roof. It must be a big house.'

'Not big enough. We've all got our own space, but I like to get away as much as I can. My boss is one of the people I live with.'

'Oh. That must be interesting!'

'You think! It's a fucking nightmare at times. She's decent and all, but you kind of feel like you're always on the clock.'

'And only one girlfriend?'

He nods as he pops a chip into his mouth. 'Well, my boss is with one of the team and another is going out with someone off the team. It's not easy to find time to see people when you're always working.'

'But you have time to go to The Lair,' she says, smiling to take the sting out of her words.

'Like I said, it's a stress relief.'

'Do you find time to... see people? Outside of The Lair I mean?' She's not usually so forward, far from it. Something about the way he is with her gives her a confidence she's never really felt before when out on a date. Maybe it's the way he's looking at her? She doesn't know how he's doing it, but every time he looks at her, it feels like everyone else in the room vanishes. It's just the two of them.

Shep hasn't looked at one other person all evening. Not once. It's her and only her.

He leans closer to her and targets her with his dark blue eyes. 'I haven't been interested until I nearly gave a certain person a concussion by knocking her off her feet.'

She wasn't expecting to hear him say that. Izzy licks her lips and stares at his mouth. She wants him to kiss her. It makes no sense and he's still as wrong for her as someone can be, but something about him has captured her.

Shep leans across and cups her face in his hand. His palm is surprisingly cool as he runs his thumb across her lips. The smell of his cologne fills her nostrils, sending sparks of excitement through her body.

His lips meet hers taking all the air from her lungs. His kiss is strong and unapologetic, more so than the first time. His hand weaves through her hair, pulling her close to him. His tongue pushes into her mouth and she can't stop her moan when she feels his tongue piercing again. Shep wraps a strong arm around her, pressing her to his solid chest, his tongue turning her entire body to putty.

Shep moves away from her mouth to kiss along the side of her neck, the barbell in his tongue pressing against her skin. Her eyes close as his warm lips caress the sensitive skin under her ear. His teeth graze her flesh and this time the moan does escape. His grip on her tightens, his kisses turning more frenzied along her neck, his teeth scraping her, making her moan again.

Then Shep freezes and moves away from her.

It takes her a few seconds to come out of her daze and open her eyes to look at him. 'What's wrong?'

He shakes his head. 'Nothing. I just need a second.' He leaves the booth and disappears into the crowd, heading in the direction of the toilets. Izzy watches after him, the euphoric high she was just on, drifting away as the seconds tick by.

Something is seriously wrong with him. She saw the look on his face. He was scared.

DAVYN

He's never been one for making conversation or small talk. It wasn't something he was taught, or even picked up on over his long life. Being locked in a cage for most of that time had put survival at the top of his list - not useless things like chit chat.

But his silence as the helicopter nears his father's castle has nothing to do with his inability to make small talk. He's trying not to panic. Trying not to demand they turn around and go home.

Davyn loves Ireland, always has. But what his father did to him ruined that. Now being here makes him sick. Turns him into someone he doesn't want to be. As head of his deceased father's house, a lot of people look to him for leadership. He's no leader. Never wanted that. Just because he's a lord doesn't mean he has the first clue how to act that way.

A small hand slides under his, holding it firmly. He flashes Thea a quick smile. He's glad she's here with him. She centres him, keeps his head straight.

As much as he doesn't want her to be a part of his old life, he wants her in his future. The two are intertwined, so he doesn't have a choice. And he needs her right now. If he's going to set foot in that castle again, he needs her by his side.

'Are you okay?'

He shakes his head. No point trying to hide it from her.

She slides her finger under his chin, gently turning his head around to face her. Thea reaches up and removes the eye-patch from over his damaged eye. 'This is for Murt and his brothers. And I promise I won't leave your side.'

'Thank you. I love you.'

She kisses the scarred skin over his damaged eye before replacing the eye-patch. 'And I love you. You can do this.'

He nods before looking back out the window. His stomach tightens as his father's castle - his castle - comes into view. The monstrous stone structure is imposing in its appearance and its location.

Perched on the edge of a cliff, the fortress clings to the headland and can be seen from miles around. If he had his way it would be rubble, but dozens of servants live there. They have nowhere else to go. His father had abused them for decades. Giving them a roof over their heads is the least he can do for them.

Fallon brings the helicopter down in the field just in front of the castle, then joins himself, Thea, and Court in the cargo hold. None of them say anything. They're waiting for him to make the first move.

The sooner he gets this done the sooner he can go home. He stands and hits the control to open the back hatch. With Thea's hand still firmly in his, he crosses the field, each step bringing him closer to the huge double doors. They open before he reaches them and Fergus smiles at him.

'Welcome back sire. My apologies, Davyn.' He quickly corrects himself when he uses Davyn's title instead of his name. He's no one's *sire*. 'Thea! Such a pleasure to see you again.'

She hugs him tightly. 'Good to see you again, Fergus. How are things going?'

He nods and smiles. 'Well. Come in and we can talk out of this chilly night air.' He greets Court and Fallon before leading them into the castle.

Each step Davyn takes only adds to the chill that's crept into his bones. Each vampire they pass bows to him. Old habits die hard. When they reach the main hall he has to force himself to enter the room. Even though all evidence of the pedestal and rack have been removed, the memories hit him like a blow as he looks around the room.

He'd been put on display in front of his father's throne. Beaten and humiliated for days. Lost his eyesight to a broken glass and finally had his fangs sawn off, his mouth sewn shut, and his wings sewn in place. All carried out by his father. The Binding had nearly killed him, starved him in the worst way.

But he'd survived... barely. Some days he's not so sure how far he's come. Some days he still has to check his lips aren't sewn shut before he opens his mouth after he wakes. Some days he can't listen to running water without thinking about his submerged cell.

Thea has no idea of his fears. No one does. She worries about him too much as it is. He's far from the male she deserves. He's a broken lord with an horrific past and uncertain future.

He crosses his arms, hiding the tremors that come to life. Her blood is keeping Blood Fever at bay, holding it back. But it's still there, like a faint whisper he can't escape.

'Why don't we talk over here sire? Apologies, Davyn.'

Fergus drags him out of his head, gesturing over to the table that now sits where his father's throne once sat. He'd burned that monstrosity along with the Binding rack.

They all take a seat at the table, Davyn being left at the head of it, which he is less than comfortable about.

'How long are you staying?'

'Not long,' he answers, ignoring the disappointment on Fergus' face. He still wants Dav to rule from Ireland, from this castle, but it won't be happening any time soon. He left Fergus in charge and plans to continue keeping an eye on things from Wales.

'I see. Is there a particular reason for your visit? I know you are less than keen about being here, so it must be important.'

'What do you know about the Whelans and their last reported sighting?'

Fergus frowns as he considers that. 'I'm afraid I do not know anything other than the information I already gave you. Just after you left, Murtagh contacted me to say they had reached their home and wanted to thank you for your help. Nothing since then. Do you believe they are in trouble?'

'We think they might be,' Court answers for him. He's not in the least bit bothered by that. Court is second in command. He does this stuff all the time.

'We've checked our records, but they're sketchy at best when it comes to the wolf/vampire relationship,' Court says. 'You've been here for a long time Fergus. Is there anything else you can tell us? Any information you know that could help?'

Fergus nods slowly. 'Perhaps. When I realised the brothers had not been in touch, I checked some of Davyn's father's records. I am not up to date with computers or modern technology, however there are centuries of records in his room. There is mention of a punishment for wolves who betray their own.'

'Betray?' Court asks.

'Yes. The feud between our kind and shifters dates back to our ancient past, but in some circles, it is still forbidden to mix with the opposite race. According to what I found, it is still strictly forbidden for a wolf to associate with a vampire.'

'Fuck,' Dav mutters. 'Helping us could have been seen as betraying the other wolves.'

'Yes Davyn. I fear it would have been.'

'When they swore allegiance to me, that would have been the final kick.'

'Did the records mention anything about the type of punishment?' Thea asks. He can feel her worry, hear it in her voice. She's not alone. This doesn't sound good for the Whelans.

'There are various punishments mentioned. Murtagh and his brothers are from an old clan. Even though from a well-respected family, Murtagh's conduct has always been outside of acceptable norms in the wolf community. He likes to do things differently, as I'm sure you have figured out.'

'Yeah.' Dav says. 'I got that when he bowed before me. What does that mean for him and his brothers though?'

'Some of the punishments talk about physical harm, but that would not work for the Whelans. No one would want to hurt them in that way for fear of retaliation. I believe they may have been stripped of their possessions, their title, and their land, before being banished.'

'Fuck! Where to?'

'That I don't know.'

Dav sits back in his seat and looks over at Court. 'What now?'

'You said you have records from Davyn's father. Would it be possible to bring them with us to Wales? It might not be a bad idea to catalogue everything. Could be something in there that will help.'

'Of course,' Fergus says. 'I'll make sure we box everything so you can take it with you. It's of little use to me here. While you wait, would you like dinner?'

'No,' Dav responds before anyone else can have a say. 'Just the records.'

Fergus nods and stands, hurrying from the room. 'We'll help him,' Court says nodding at Fallon.

Thea slides onto his knee once they're alone. 'You can stay for dinner if you want.'

'I don't want. I don't want anything to do with this place.'

She strokes her fingers through his hair, but it's not relaxing him as usual. 'All the people living under this roof are looking to you for protection. They lived in fear, now they're safe and happy.'

'I should have killed his name, his legacy, destroyed this place,' he says looking around the vast stone room. 'By leaving it standing it's a fucking monument to him. It was my prison for decades, Thea. It shouldn't still be standing.'

'Now it's home to all these people. Maybe over time those bad memories will start to fade? Maybe the people under your protection can bring laughter and happiness back into the castle? Maybe you shouldn't see it as being a monument to him? Perhaps it can be a monument to your mother? To Ronan?'

He never thought about that. His mother and his mentor Ronan, both died by his father's hand. They were the only good thing he remembers about his life in this place. The only light in the smothering darkness.

They loved him. For so long, they were the only ones who did. 'You might be right.'

Thea smiles, looking pleased with herself. 'You're only just figuring that out? As someone who doesn't have a connection to this place, as a structure, the castle is spectacular. Slightly ominous though, but that's nothing a splash of colour won't help.'

'Are you saying we paint the walls?'

'Of course not! You told me your mother used to draw all the flowers that grew in the gardens around the castle.'

'Yeah. My father flattened everything. He didn't want his many enemies to be able to sneak up on him.'

'So fix that. Ask the people who live here to help restore the castle and grounds to its former glory. To a time when your mother lived, when your grandfather ruled. Rewrite the legacy. You've already started with everything you've done so far. Take it to the next step.'

He kisses her deeply, trying to show her exactly how much he appreciates having her in his life. 'I'll speak to Fergus. Get him to oversee it. I still want to leave within the hour, but maybe next time, I might not be so dead against coming back.'

SHEP

He bursts into the toilet and goes up to the mirror. Even without checking, he knows that his canines have extended. Not fully, but enough for Izzy to notice if she was looking. Or if she kissed him again. No hiding the bastards if she was that up close and personal with him.

He splashes cold water on his face, willing himself to calm down. It was a damn kiss. Just a kiss. He looks back at his reflection. He thought his reaction to the first kiss didn't mean anything. That he got carried away and his hormones took over.

But he was wrong. It had felt the same – better even. He had actually moved his damn body this time and touched her. It felt so right.

Maybe everything he's experiencing is a normal reaction? He immediately dismisses that thought. It's Izzy. Kissing her, holding her, being that close to her, had hit him straight in the dick. He'd been turned on by just being near a woman. That was a first.

He bends over, resting his forehead on his hands. He should have just stayed away from her. He has no right to get anyone else involved in whatever is going on with him and his fucked-up life. Even though it's the last thing he wants, he has to end whatever is going on between himself and Izzy. He has no choice. If he reacts to a kiss like this, he can't allow things to go further as much as he wants it. He'd out himself as a vampire and then she'll run.

He examines his reflection again and grimaces when his fangs are still clearly visible. There's only one way to get rid of them. It has been a few days since he fed, so he's fighting a losing battle. Unless he feeds, they're not going away. Shep steps out of the bathroom and looks around. He has to find someone quick. Izzy doesn't deserve to be abandoned while he's getting his shit together.

A man stumbles towards him on his way to the bathroom. With no other option available, Shep drags the man out the emergency exit into the alley at the back of the bar. He throws the man against the wall, takes a deep breath, and sinks his teeth in.

The warm, alcohol laced blood may taste disgusting, but it's just what his body needs. His fangs lengthen, his eyes changing as the full effect of the blood hits home. He braces his palms against the wall trying to keep from touching the other man's body.

The man grows limp between his arms, so Shep pulls his teeth out and lowers the guy to the ground. He wipes his arm across his mouth and leans against the wall as he gets the other side of himself under control. Taking a few calming breaths, Shep finally feels his teeth retracting. It's then he senses he's not alone with the man. He turns his head to the side and his blood-filled stomach lurches when he sees Izzy standing in the doorway, her hand over her mouth and her eyes open wide.

Shep turns to face her, but she steps back, shaking her head. 'Oh

173

fuck! Izzy, please. I can explain.' Can he? Even given a few years he doubts he'd be able to explain what she just saw.

Her feet continue moving back as she shakes her head.

He reaches out to her, but she holds up her hand. 'Don't! Keep away from me!'

Without another word, she turns and disappears into the bar. Shep wants to follow her but stops himself. Chasing after her will just freak her out even more. He'll follow her home. Make sure she gets there safely, then try to explain himself while she's away from a crowd of people.

DAVYN

He's tired, but thoughts are swirling around his head since he left Ireland again, refusing to let him get the rest he needs. He's survived days without sleep. He's well used to it, but that life is behind him. Or so he had thought.

As Davyn looks at the boxes of files from his father's office, he realises that chapter of his life will never truly be behind him. He's lost the sight in one eye, has too many scars to count, and a pair of wings that, although repaired by Fletch's doctor friend Annie, still bear the scars left by his father.

He slumps into the chair at the head of the table in the compound library. The fire burning in the hearth is doing nothing to take the chill from his bones.

He dreads to think what's in those boxes of papers. Did his father document every kill, every death, every life he took? Has he got an account of the money he made from locking his own son in a fighting pit to kill, or be killed?

Perhaps he noted down the day he killed Davyn's mother because she was trying to sneak her son out of the castle to give him a better life?

It's his job to go through those papers. But he can't. It's got nothing to do with the fact that he really doesn't want to know how much of a cretin his father actually was. He can't read.

Thea has been teaching him, but he's nowhere close to being able to read any of these papers. Which means he's going to have to delegate it to someone else.

He's going to have to open up those horrors and allow someone else see his father's true colours.

Davyn jumps when Thea wraps her arms around him from behind. 'Sorry. I didn't mean to scare you.'

He pulls her around so she can sit on his knee. 'I was in my head. Why aren't you asleep?'

'I was, until I realised you were gone. Why aren't you asleep?'

'I can't stop thinking about what's in there.'

Thea gets off his knee so she can pull one of the boxes closer. She picks up a leather-bound diary and flips through the pages. 'It's all handwritten. According to these dates, it goes back centuries.'

'Probably further than that. I wouldn't be surprised if some of my grandfather's notes are in there. I owe it to everyone in that castle to sort through all that. So many lost their families to him. He took people and sold them or put them in the fighting pits. Vampires would just vanish from the castle, never to be heard from again. A lot of ghosts could be laid to rest for so many families thanks to those books.'

'I had better get started then.'

It takes him a few seconds to register what she just said. 'You?'

'Your reading is coming on well, but this is too much for you right now. I'm at a loose end at the moment. I can get all this onto computer. Make it easier to search for information.'

'I can't ask you to do that. I have no idea what's in those books.'

She laces her fingers with his. 'I'm in love with you Davyn. We're in this together.'

'And I appreciate that, but this is too much.'

'Let me do this for you. The information in there could tell us where the Whelans are. Or where their sister is. It's important someone goes through it. And I've been thinking about what we said in Ireland. About leaving a new legacy.'

'Right. Should I be worried?'

'You know me.'

'That's what I'm afraid of.'

'Shut up! Anyway, I was thinking that I could liaise with Fergus about the gardens. If you want me to, of course? I don't want to interfere. I just know that it's not really your thing. I thought I could look after that with Fergus. It would leave you to do other important *lord of the manor* and Blackjacks stuff.'

'Where did I find you?'

'I think I broke into your bedroom?'

'That sounds so wrong when you say it like that.' He gathers her in his arms, holding her close as he looks down at the boxes of files. 'Are you really sure about this?'

'I'm sure. I'll get started in the morning.' She takes his hand and leads him towards the door.

'Where are we going?'

'To bed,' she replies with a wink. 'Those boxes will still be there in the morning. You need to get some sleep. When was the last time you slept for more than a few hours?'

'I know that face. It's not your sleeping face.'

She grins as she leads him up to their room. 'You might be right.'

IZZY

A vampire?

Is Shep actually a real-life vampire?

Izzy slams her apartment door closed behind her and locks it securely, checking the bolts twice just to be sure.

He can't be. Vampires don't exist.

She walks into her living room, goes back to check the door again, then lowers onto the cream couch, still shaking her head. She squeezes the front of the cushions in her fists as she slowly rocks back and forth. Images are racing through her mind. Images that don't make any sense. Images that can't make sense.

Unable to sit still, she pushes to her feet and finds her way into the kitchen. It takes two attempts to close her trembling hand around a glass and take it from the cupboard. The bottle of bourbon she keeps for special occasions finds its way to the counter and she pours a large measure. Izzy drinks it in one go, refills the glass, and leans against the counter.

She spots her laptop on the table next to the coursework she had planned to work on this weekend. She laughs to herself. There's not much chance of that happening now. Not with her mind filled with... what exactly?

What did she see? The vampire thing is a stretch. Maybe Shep was making out with that guy in the alleyway? Did he kiss her in the bar, decide he wanted someone else, then race off to find a guy?

Izzy pulls the chair out, sits down, and powers up the laptop.

But that doesn't explain what he was doing to the guy's neck. Or the blood she saw when Shep pulled away.

Or the fangs.

Izzy scrubs her hands over her face. She saw fangs. She's sure she did.

Her fingers hover over the keys and she laughs to herself again. Is she really thinking about doing this? Another mouthful of drink convinces her to go ahead.

An hour later, the drink has barely registered with her body. Usually, a mouthful will send her over the edge, but two glasses hasn't had any effect. Perhaps what she's reading is helping to keep her sober.

After reading through all the usual vampire lore, she manages to find a few articles which only serve to back up what she thought she saw outside the pub. The reports are unverified, but there is mention of people seeing or witnessing vampires in the UK. People who feed from the blood of others. Who have heightened strength and speed.

There's even mention of some having powers, but she dismisses those reports which makes no sense. Why is she so willing to believe everything else, but the superpowers is the part she's struggling with?

She slumps back in the chair, staring at the image of a man with fangs on one of the websites. It's an artist's rendition, but for some reason she can't stop staring at the teeth.

Shep's were larger. She's sure of that part.

Is Shep a vampire?

Vampire. Even the word sounds ridiculous said aloud. 'Vampire,' she repeats to herself, laughing harshly at the notion.

'Sounds stupid out loud, right?'

The glass crashes to the ground as she scrambles from the table. The block of knives by the cooker falls over onto the counter as she grabs for the largest one. She points it at Shep standing in her living room, irritated when her hand refuses to stop shaking. 'What... how did you get in here?'

'Bedroom window was open.' At least he has the decency to look embarrassed by his breaking and entering. 'I needed to talk to you. To explain.'

She laughs harshly, forcing her hand to remain steady. 'Explain?

What's to explain? I know what I saw. Well, I think I know.' She shakes her head, again feeling like an idiot for believing what she saw. 'You were... you bit him... didn't you?'

'Can you please put the knife down. Don't really feel comfortable talking to you while you're waving that around.'

Her hand trembles as something clicks in her head. 'Hang on. You bit his neck. You were kissing my neck in the bar.' Her hand moves up to her neck. 'I felt something...' She meets his eyes. 'Were you going to...'

He takes a step forward, shaking his head vigorously. 'No, Izzy. You have to believe that. I would never bite you.'

She waves the knife at him. 'Believe you? Why would I believe anything you have to say? You drank someone's blood! Just get out of here.'

Shep moves faster than she expected, grabs the hand holding the knife, forcing it down by her side. 'I'm not going anywhere until you listen to me.'

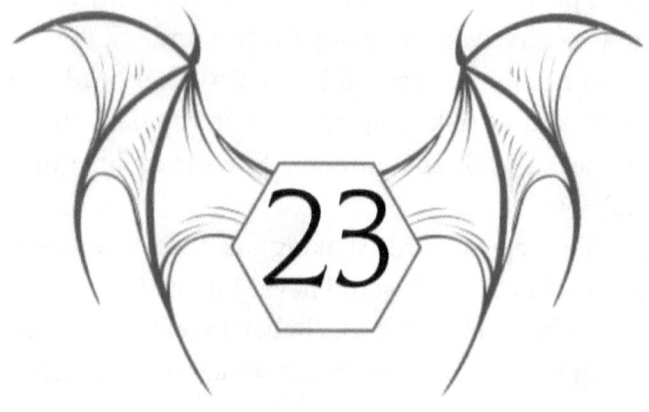

SHEP

'Are you going to kill me now? Bite me and drain my blood? Throw my body in the ditch somewhere?'

Shep leans against the counter, as far from Izzy as he can get in the small kitchen. He would have preferred to sit in the living room, but he was pushing his luck even being here. Getting comfortable isn't on her to do list - not with him around anyway.

He'd watched her pace her living room, then her kitchen. Down a fair amount of drink, then head to Google. He knew at that stage she'd have her head filled with all sorts of fantasy crap, but he couldn't convince himself to step in. He wanted to. Wanted to set the record straight, however fucked up and unbelievable that record is. But he stayed outside like a fucking stalker, watching her through the window.

It was generally frowned upon when a human is brought into their world. There was no choice in this case though. He couldn't leave her going mad wondering what the fuck she saw. He'll just have to deal with any repercussions later.

'You honestly believe I could hurt you?' Out of everything that happened tonight, that's the killer statement.

She laughs harshly. 'I don't know who, or what you are. Why aren't you arguing the vampire thing with me? Why aren't you saying that I'm crazy? That there's no such thing as vampires.'

'It's more complicated than that.'

She pauses and smiles wryly as she looks at the ground. 'Complicated! Of course. What was I thinking? Everything about you is complicated. It's not like you've really told me anything about yourself. Why should you explain this to me now?

'Or maybe it's simpler than that. Maybe you met someone you wanted to be with while on a date with me. A man, but hey, why not? I did say my life was boring. Having my date dump me for a man, while on a date with me, would serve me right.'

'Izzy—'

'That's probably my fault though.' She laughs to herself as she continues to shake her head. 'No one ever mentioned it was a date. That was all in my head. I'm not someone you'd want like that. But after seeing what I saw, I'm glad I'm not.'

Shep runs his hands through his hair and curses to himself. She's given him an out. An uncomplicated way to excuse what she saw. A way that will allow them both to go back to their own worlds and continue as if nothing happened.

So why isn't he grabbing it with two hands and running?

He looks at Izzy and knows why. He likes her. Really likes her. For the first time in nearly a century, he is actually interested in someone for something other than sex.

If he goes along with what she's saying, he will lose her forever. No one in their right mind would be with someone who cheated on their first date - especially with someone of the same sex. It was a bit of a downer for any continuing relations.

On the other hand, if he tells her the truth, she'll be showing him the door pretty damn fast. It's a *lose lose* situation for him. Might as well go out honourably.

He rests his hands to either side of him, squeezing the counter in his hands. 'Fuck!'

'What?'

He looks at her and smiles to try and ease some of the tension. 'Okay, so I am a vampire, Izzy.'

She freezes and stares over at him.

Shep stops holding back the other side of himself. Izzy's mouth opens in fear as his canines drop and his eyes glow. 'You don't have to be afraid of me, Izzy.' Even as the words come out, he knows it's one of the dumbest things he could have said. She's alone in her kitchen with a real-life vampire. Of course she's going to be fucking scared!

She reaches behind her and grabs the string of garlic from the vegetable rack against the wall. She holds it out to him, shaking the bulbs in his direction. 'Come any closer and I'll use it.'

Shep sighs, doing his best not to laugh at her. 'Damn stories. How exactly are you going to use it? You going to whack me on the head with it or something?'

She looks down at the garlic, then back at him. 'It doesn't repel you, does it?'

He shakes his head. 'To be honest, I'm quite partial to anything with garlic in it. I'll easily demolish a plate of cheesy garlic bread without stopping for a breath. And just for the record, holy water won't do a thing either, and neither will crucifixes.

'We can also go out in sunlight. After a while it'll sting our eyes, but that's just because they're super sensitive. I won't burst into flames or anything dramatic like that. On the other hand, a stake to the heart would probably work, but it would kill most people.'

Izzy slowly lowers her hand, dropping the garlic on to the table. 'So, none of the stories are true? There's no way of protecting myself from you?'

Ouch! That one fucking hurt more than he thought it would. He shrugs it off, hiding the fact that comment was like a kick to the gut. 'We've been around a long time, Izzy. The stories have a grain of truth, but it's a bit like Chinese Whispers - details get muddled over time.

'I do need blood to survive, but not every day. Once every week or so is enough, and no, we don't kill to feed, and the donor won't change into anything when we bite them.

'We are stronger and faster, heal quicker than you do, which comes in handy. We're not immortal but take a hell of a lot longer to age. There are some vampires who are five hundred years old. Maybe more. But we live *with* humans. We don't hunt you or want to do anything to you. I swear.'

He waits until she's looking him in the eye before he goes for the next part. 'And you don't need anything to protect yourself from me. Please believe that. I would never hurt you.'

She holds his gaze for a few seconds before she finally looks away. But she doesn't argue, so hopefully his sincerity hit home.

'You heal faster?' The smallest semblance of a smile breaks out. 'That explains your miraculous recovery after you collapsed. Before you made a run for it, I noticed the cut had healed.'

'Yeah. Like I said, it comes in handy from time to time. And that's why I made a run for it. I didn't want you to notice.'

The silence hangs for a few minutes, so he leaves her to it. There's a lot to process, and he'd rather give her time, than push her and risk losing her.

Not that he has her, but any small chance is better than a hard no.

'So, where does that leave me?' she asks, finally breaking the awkward silence. 'Are you going to feed off me?'

He curses and shakes his head. So much for her believing a fucking word he'd said. 'Damn it, Izzy! No. When I leave, you're going to be in exactly the same condition you were in when I came here.'

'Did you say the same to that man you fed from?'

Shep's fangs retract into his gums as he takes a step towards her, but she moves further away from him. 'I didn't kill him. I swear. I was just...' He trails off not willing to finish the sentence.

'You were just what? Feeding? Drinking his blood? What do you call it?'

'Doing what I have to do to survive.' He moves to the side of the room and massages his neck. He can't shift the tension that's been building since he was outside watching her. He's not even going to think about the tight sensation spreading across his back. No way he's going to acknowledge that. He feels unbelievably crap, but he's not leaving here until he knows she's going to be okay.

'What about our survival?'

'I told you, we don't kill when we feed. I swear. Listen, I can't help what I am, Izzy. And I get that you probably want fuck all to do with me now. I can't blame you.'

'Are your friends like you? Is your sister?'

He nods. Nix is going to tear him a new one when she finds out about this. 'The team are all vampires, but one of the guys is in a relationship with a human woman.'

That seems to surprise her. 'Really?'

'Yeah. They're crazy about each other. It's... I don't know... nice, I guess. Gives the rest of us hope.' He didn't mean to say all that. Staying on his feet is taking all his concentration right now, leaving his mouth to run away on him.

He looks back at her, but he can't seem to focus. He blinks, but either she's doing a bizarre side-to-side dance on the walls, or he's about to embarrass himself in front of her. He steadies himself on the worktop and takes a few deep breaths, but the sensation of falling intensifies.

'Shep? Are you all right?'

He nods, or at least he thinks he does. It's difficult to tell with the room spinning the way it is. When he opens his eyes again, his ass is on a chair he doesn't remember sitting on, and Izzy is crouched in front of him, staring at him. 'What happened?'

'You looked like you were about to faint, so I brought you over to a chair.'

'I don't faint. Pass out maybe, but not faint.'

He's so relieved when she smiles at him. 'Consider me corrected. When you said you were sick, you were telling the truth, weren't you?'

'Yeah. Not really something I'd joke about. Everything I told you tonight was the truth.'

'So, your ability to heal faster...'

'Does fuck all with actual illness. Just applies to injuries.' He takes the glass of water she offers him, downing it in one go. 'Sorry about what just happened.' It takes a few attempts to get himself back on his feet again. 'I'll leave you to it.'

Shep hands the glass back to her and smiles. 'I know I've hit you with a lot tonight, and most of it is going to take time to sink in, if at all. But I really did enjoy your company tonight. That was genuine. I hope one day you can believe that much at least.'

She doesn't reply. No surprise there. She's just looking at him, a strange expression on her face.

'How are you getting home?'

It wasn't the response he was looking for, or expected, but at least she's talking to him. 'My bike is down the road.'

'Are you okay to ride your bike? I don't want a replay of the other night.' He could swear there's a faint trace of a smile, but it disappears again.

'I'm good. No collapsing again. Been there, done that.'

Izzy stays in the kitchen as he heads over to the door. He wants her to say something, anything to make this shitty feeling go away, but he's all out of luck tonight. What does he expect? He's being selfish even looking for comfort after what he just threw at her.

He closes her front door behind him and looks down the street to where his bike is parked. Might as well head back to the compound. Nothing else to do around here except feel sorry for himself.

SHEP

'Jesus man, would you just sit still for one measly minute!'

Shep groans and forces himself to stop squirming. 'Sorry Fletch.'

The doctor goes back to poking and prodding him. He's been at it for a good ten minutes, and any patience Shep had, has well and truly fucked off. His head is still with Izzy. Has been since he got back to the compound.

What the hell was he thinking coming clean like he did? He should have just walked away and left her to it. Should have just accepted it wasn't ever going to go anywhere, and just let her get on with her normal, uncomplicated life.

But he didn't want to. He likes her. Likes being with her, likes talking to her, likes it when she touches him.

That got to him more than anything else. Too many people have touched him over his life. After a while he had learned to block it all out. The sensations, the revulsion, the pain. It was the only way he could stay sane.

But when Izzy touched him he actually *felt* it. The shiver that went through him was pleasant. More than pleasant. And as for what he had felt when they kissed...

He thought he'd been permanently damaged. Was convinced that he couldn't have anything other than one-night stands - or one hour stands. Sex. Meaningless sex. That's all he has ever had. Calling it anything different is being delusional.

He's never had anything else. Never felt anything before. Never thought he could, or that he even wanted that.

Now he's not so sure.

'Any sensitivity there? Shep? Hey! I kind of need you to answer, or this might take a few hours.'

Shep shakes himself out of his thoughts. 'What?'

'I asked if there was any sensitivity there?'

He shakes his head.

'Anything there?'

'How about I say ouch if you hit something that hurts?'

Fletch takes off his gloves and faces him, arms crossed. 'You're fed up.'

'You think? No offence Doc, but you've been giving me this personal not-such-fun back massage treatment for weeks. I like you, but this is getting ridiculous.'

'I know. And I'm sorry. I wouldn't be doing my job if I didn't keep an eye on you.'

'I reckon we'll both notice when the wings actually do come out. I'm getting the impression they'll be difficult to miss.'

'I think you might be right there. Any other weird sensations you've been experiencing?'

He knows he should mention the whole passing out incident when he was in Izzy's house. But he doesn't. The idea of being benched forces him to keep his mouth shut. He's already on shaky ground as it is, without giving Fletch more ammunition. 'Nope. All good.'

Fletch gives him a long hard look, before grunting. 'Yeah. Like I believe that for a minute.'

He smiles, doing what he can to convince the doctor, but he knows Fletch can see right through him. 'So, how's our newly vocal friend over there doing? He saying anything else?'

Fletch glances at Austin lying at the far side of the room, staring at the wall, waiting to have his daily check up. They're both part of Fletch's daily routine at this stage.

'He's still a bit on the quiet side with me, but not so much with Fallon. It seems my sister has been able to turn him into a veritable chatterbox compared to what he was.'

Shep looks over at the thin man. He thought the guy would give up within a few hours of being brought back to the compound. Seems he's more stubborn than they thought. That's something he appreciates.

'I have those results you were looking for?'

Shep smiles at Thea as she joins them in the examination room. 'Hey.' Their relationship is still somewhat strained. He knows it's his fault - like most things are. He can either bend over backwards to help you or cut you off if you get on his wrong side. Unfortunately, she found her way into the latter camp. He's trying to get her back on the other side, but it won't be a quick fix.

When Court's daughter first came to live with them they'd got on pretty well. But then he was a dick and blamed her for Dav getting caught and tortured. It wasn't her fault... well, not really.

Okay, so she did disobey Nix and get herself into trouble. Not something he can really have a problem with. It's not like he hasn't disobeyed a few orders himself over the decades.

But her disobedience resulted in Dav being captured.

And he took that badly, shouting at her in front of everyone, telling her she was to blame for everything.

Since then, he's tried to put things right, but deep down he kind of still does blame her, and she's no idiot. Dav's mate is one smart woman. She knows full well he still blames her and, as a result, she's been avoiding him.

Awkward.

'Hey. How are you doing?' she asks, her smile still on the nervous side.

'Yeah. I'm good thanks,' he says, smiling widely to try and convince her he doesn't have an issue. 'Those my results?'

Fletch nods as he reads the information. 'Your DNA is still altering but it's slowing down.'

'Meaning...'

'Meaning I haven't got a fucking clue what it's doing.'

'Oh wow! Thanks Doc. Way to put your patient at ease.'

Whatever comeback Fletch is about to offer up is forgotten when Austin shouts out from the other side of the room. Shep watches in confusion as the guy scrambles backwards, making a desperate bid to climb through the wall to escape something.

Shep follows Austin's line of sight, frowning when he realises Thea is the source of his freaking out.

'It's you,' Shep says, getting off the bed to put himself between Austin and Thea.

'Me what?' she asks, her attention on what's happening on the other side of the room.

Fletch takes her by the shoulder, slowly moving her back towards the door. 'Shep is right, love. He's freaking out because of you.'

'What did I do?'

'Nothing,' Fletch says as he opens the door and ushers her out. 'He's all over the place at the moment. Best you leave for now and I'll try to figure out what's going on. Could you be a pet and send my sister down here. He seems to be calm when Fallon is around.'

With one last confused glance at Austin, she hurries from the room, leaving Shep and Fletch facing the thin, yet surprisingly energetic man, still trying to drag himself up the bed. 'Any ideas?'

'Not one. Best we wait for Fallon. She'll be able to get through to him. Knowing our luck, we'll just scare him even more.'

Less than a minute later, Fallon bursts through the door, looking more flustered than Shep has ever seen her look before. Could the hardened female have a soft spot for the broken man? Usually, he'd be right in there with the jeering and sarcastic remarks, but not in this case.

First, you don't take that line with Fallon. She'd castrate you without blinking. Second, whatever happened to Austin isn't something you laugh about.

'What happened?' she asks as she slowly approaches Austin, hands out in front of her.

Fletch shrugs as he steps out of the way to let her get past. 'He saw Thea and freaked out. I have no idea why.'

Fallon takes over, dismissing the two of them as she slowly makes her way over to Austin. 'Hey Austin. It's okay. You're safe. Calm down.'

'It was her!'

Shep does a double take at the sound of the voice coming from Austin. It's deep and a lot stronger than he would have expected from someone so frail.

'Her who?' Fallon asks.

'It was her!' Austin says, his voice stronger than before. 'I remember her from that place. She was there. She was one of them!'

Fallon shakes her head as she takes another step closer to Austin. 'That was Thea. She's a friend. She lives with us. You don't have to fear her.'

He frowns, taking a minute to process what Fallon just said.

Shep hasn't spent a lot of time with this guy, but so far he can't help but be impressed. He's not what he expected. Faced with an unfamiliar situation he's still relatively calm and coherent. Apart from the initial freaking out, he's accepting Fallon's explanation.

Austin nods slowly, his eyes still on the door. 'She's familiar Fallon.'

Fletch pulls up Thea's photo from her medical file and points to it. 'This is Thea. Are you sure you've seen her before?'

Austin examines the photo, the frown growing as he stares at it. 'I thought it was her. This woman is familiar. Not the woman herself, but similar to her. She was at the lab. I know she was.'

'Thea was captured by The Order. She would have been there the same time as you. Maybe you saw her when she was a prisoner?'

Austin shakes his head at Fallon. 'No. The woman she looks like was part it. She was one of them. Not a prisoner.'

'Shep, I think we need to have a chat to Nix,' Fletch says, as he watches his sister help Austin back down the bed. 'I'm not liking that reaction. Any idea who this Thea lookalike could be?'

'Unless he's confused, and it was actually Thea? Who knows what the fuck he went through.'

'He's settled,' Fallon says as she joins them. 'What the fuck happened?'

'Thea was delivering some paperwork and he just freaked out,' Fletch says. 'He say anything to you about what happened in the lab?'

Fallon glances over at him before she shakes her head. 'No. But I know he hasn't seen Thea since we rescued him. She didn't visit his cell while we were holding him there. You going to tell Nix?'

'I think we should,' Fletch says. 'Something weird is going on.'

'You can say that again,' Shep says, just relieved the attention is off him for a while. 'I'll call Nix. See if she wants a meeting.'

He leaves the siblings to look after Austin while he grabs his shirt and makes a speedy get away.

SHEP

If it wouldn't have almost certainly landed him in the infirmary, Shep would have laughed at the look on Court's face. He's seen their second in command pissed off before, but not very often. He wasn't hot-headed. Like Bas, he had the whole *calm under pressure* air about him. Except when it came to his daughter.

That is one area you'd do best to avoid if you wanted to walk away after.

Shep has to give it to Dav. The guy must have a death wish to go anywhere near Thea. Shep has a lot of time for Court, but that doesn't mean he'd ever want him as a future father-in-law.

'For once I'm with Dav on this point,' Court says, his voice cold and proving the pissed off vibe Shep was getting from him. 'There is no way in hell I'm going to let you give Rhain a photo of my daughter.'

Nix takes a deep breath before she continues. Good luck to her.

Being in a relationship with Court doesn't mean she's going to be able to change his mind about this. 'I understand your reservations, but he's already seen Thea. He captured her, so giving him a photograph—'

'Exactly!' Davyn growls from the other side of the table, backing him up. 'He took her!'

Shep is fairly impressed Dav managed to keep his reply to those few words. If he was in that position, he'd be a bit more physical in his response. He gets why Court and Dav are less than thrilled about involving Thea in anything to do with the dickhead Rhain. But Nix has a valid point. That particular horse bolted a few months ago.

'Do you want me to wipe that grin off your face?' Davyn barks at him.

Shit! Busted. Shep holds up his hands. 'Nope. It's all good. I'm fully with you on this, Dav. All the way. No arguments!'

Nix taps the surface of the table, drawing their attention back to her. Not that it's going to make the slightest bit of difference. With Court and Dav against this plan, she's not going to come out of this one without a fight.

'Austin recognised Thea. Leave aside who she is to all of us. Court, you spoke to Thea. She didn't see Austin in the facility Rhain brought her to, right? There's no way she's mistaken about that.'

'True,' he replies, grinding the word out between clenched teeth. 'She was brought straight to the room. Rhain was the only one she saw.'

'So how does he know her? How is Thea familiar to him? I'm all ears. If anyone around the table knows how Austin could possibly have seen Thea, or her likeness before, please let me know. Any ideas at all? I'll take it no matter how bizarre.'

Shep meets the eyes of his teammates. No one has any ideas. And by the growl Dav releases, he knows it too.

'Rhain has been playing ball with us so far,' Nix continues. 'All I'm asking is for Ethan to show him a picture of Thea and go from there. I have no intention of bringing Thea to him, or vice versa. I'm just talking about a photo.'

'Do you trust him?' Court turns his attention to Bas, sitting beside Shep. 'You've met with him a few times. What's your feeling on him?'

'He's dying,' Bas says. 'Blood Fever has a firm hold on him. I don't like him, and I don't trust him, but he appears genuine when he says he wants an end to The Order. I doubt he has enough time left to be considering placing himself at the head of the table. I may be wrong, but I don't believe that is his intention. Ethan believes he is an asset. I trust his judgement.'

The room falls silent as Court and Dav look at each other. Each male wants to protect Thea for different reasons. Lucky Thea having those two watching out for her.

Court nods once, but he's as far from happy as you can get. Dav on the other hand bares his teeth, the growl deep in his chest as menacing as Shep has heard. He's seriously pissed. After a tense pause, he finally nods.

'Do it,' Court says, answering for the two of them.

'Thank you. I'll contact Ethan and ask him to arrange the meeting. Now, Shep, how are things with you?'

He wasn't expecting the attention to be turned to him. 'You what?'

'How are you?' she asks again, all eyes turning to him which isn't in the slightest bit awkward.

'Me? Good. Why? You all know something I don't?'

'I think she means your back,' Willow hisses at him across the table.

'Right. Thanks Sis. Still all good. What!' he says when Nix sighs and hits him with a seriously unimpressed look. 'I'm fine, Boss. Really. No gruesome talons sticking out of my back at the moment. No offence to any of you here that have talons.'

Not the best way to put an end to that topic. Insulting more than half his teammates wasn't planned. 'I'm sure they're great and all. Probably useful too. Kind of yuck when they stick out of your skin and wave at you though.'

His attempt to lighten the mood falls flat on its face. He's either losing his touch, or they can see right through him. He's not sure which one is worse.

'I'm dealing with it, okay? One day at a time.'

That seems to work. The team focus on Nix again, taking the spotlight off him.

'That's all you can do. Don't take any chances though.'

'Got it Boss.' *Please change the fucking subject!*

'Okay. That's it for now. We'll see what Rhain has to say and go from there.'

He hangs back as the others file out of the room, but Bas isn't in a rush to leave. 'Do you want to train?'

'Nah,' Shep says as he pushes to his feet. 'I'm beat. Might just get some sleep.'

Bas narrows his eyes. 'You? Sleep? What's wrong?'

'Not you too. There's nothing wrong. I'm just tired. Besides, you have to go watch Ethan's back. Protect our founder and all that noble stuff you do.'

'What does that mean? Nix put me on his detail.'

'I know! I didn't mean anything by that. Like I said, I'm tired.' Bas doesn't drop the frown. He's always on edge whenever Ethan is mentioned. Shep has never broached the subject with him. Fuck knows he wouldn't want Bas to ask him about his personal life. It's an off-limits area. Always has been.

He's best mates with Bas. Has been for a hell of a long time, but he knows he's still in the dark about most of Bastian's life. That doesn't mean he's not aware of certain aspects. He knows Bas was part of a gang for most of his life. He knows Bas's tattoos are badges of honour, or maybe symbols of a life he ran from. He knows most of those

196

badges resulted in the loss of someone's life. He knows Bas hates the marks on his hands.

And he knows Bas is sleeping with Ethan.

They're hiding it well enough, but he's seen the looks that pass between them. Bas is protective, but with Ethan it's a whole other level. Whatever. It's his business. If his mate can find happiness in all this crazy, fair play to him.

'Honestly, Bas. I didn't mean anything by that. I'm all over the place.'

Bas's frown eases. 'I'm here for you, Shep. I won't go to Nix with anything you say. You can trust me. I'm worried about you.'

'I know. And honestly, I really am tired. I just want to crash for a few hours. You find out what the fuck is going on with Thea and Austin.'

Bas's dark eyes bore into him for a long time before he finally nods. 'Get some rest. We can train tomorrow.'

'You mean I can kick your ass tomorrow?'

Bas grins at him. 'You wish, my friend. I can kick your ass every day of the week.'

'Oh, we'll see about that.'

Bas laughs as he turns to the door. 'We will.'

'Hey, Bas!'

He stops and looks at Shep.

'Be careful out there. I don't trust Rhain. This whole situation is weird, and I don't like it.'

'I agree. Ethan believes Rhain can be of value to us. I'll do my job until we've used Rhain for everything he can provide. Then I'll kill him.'

Before Shep can respond to that, Bas leaves, his heavy footsteps fading as he walks away.

IZZY

'Can I buy you a drink?'

Izzy puts on her best smile, hoping it doesn't come across as a grimace, as she sidesteps the drunk customer. 'Thank you, but I'm fine.'

'Oh that you are!'

She doesn't hide the grimace this time. The stale beer he breathes all over her turns her stomach. Izzy takes cover behind the bar as she checks her watch. One hour left and still no sign of him.

'He's not here,' Sabrina says as she joins her behind the bar. 'It's been a few days too. That's not like him.'

Is it her fault? Is he avoiding The Lair because of what happened... or didn't happen between them? Maybe he has important vampire things to take care of.

That whole scenario is still mind boggling.

'Hey?' Sabrina says, nudging her in the side. 'Are you away with the fairies?'

More like away with the vampires. 'Sorry. I was miles away.'

'Looking for Mr. Sexy accent?'

She laughs, trying to make light of the situation. Her friend thinks she's pining over a gorgeous guy she's attracted to. What would she think if she knew she was actually lusting over a vampire. She'd probably think Izzy had lost her mind.

Maybe she has?

'He's not that sexy.'

Sabrina snorts loudly. 'Right! Of course not! Who would find that body, that face, that accent in any way sexy? Not you, right?'

'Okay! So maybe there is something about him. But he's so far off my usual type it's not even funny. I don't date guys like him.'

'Hot guys?'

'Oh would you stop with the hot and sexy stuff. I'm being serious.'

'So am I,' Sabrina says with a wink. 'So, what if he's not your usual type? Which by the way I don't believe in. You're attracted to someone, you're attracted to them. End of story. As long as he treats you right what does it matter?'

'But you know what he does here.'

'He has sex with women every now and again. So what? He's not dating any of them. Plus, from what I've heard, he's nothing but the perfect gentleman with every single one of them. And in case you missed out on this one teeny fact - he's never ever taken any of them out to dinner.'

'Yeah well that didn't end well unfortunately. I don't think I'll be seeing him again.'

'Don't be so hard on yourself. We all have bad dates from time to time. He'll be back. You'll see.'

Sabrina hugs her, then hurries off to collect glasses. Shep won't be back. The more she thinks about it, the more convinced she is that he's gone.

RHAİN

As he watches the males walking down the path towards his car, the more certain he is that they are in a relationship. The level of protectiveness Bastian has for Ethan is hard to ignore, and much greater than that between an employer and his bodyguard.

It is a relationship he can't help but be jealous of. He has people in his life, too many at times. But they are there because of duty or payment. His bodyguards will put his life before theirs, but only because he's paying them to.

There isn't a doubt in his mind, the formidable Blackjack would give his life for Ethan because he chooses to. Not for duty or payment.

That is something Rhain has never had. Even his own parents were focused on duty and appearances. Love, affection, and such things were irrelevant. And Rhain believed that to be true too, until recently.

Perhaps facing his own mortality had given him a new sense of what's important. And right now, watching Bastian and Ethan, he yearns for what they have. Or at least what he believes they have. He will never ask the question, knowing it would be his last.

He had entertained many females over his long life, but nothing that lasted longer than a night. Sex was a physical release and nothing more. He never wanted anything more. Being predisposed to blood addiction had stopped him from letting anyone close. Not that he had found anyone worth letting close.

As if to add insult to injury, a tremor decides to work through his hand. 'Not now,' he mutters, keeping his attention on the approaching males. His Blood Fever isn't something Ethan or his mate need to know about. If he is to survive this truce, he needs to at least appear strong.

Bastian opens the passenger door and peers into the car. Rhain tries to hide the tremors, but he fails. Bastian gestures to Ethan, who hurries over and sits in the passenger seat. Bastian takes up position outside the car, his glowing eyes keeping watch over the two men.

'Take your time,' Ethan says as he settles into the seat. 'We're in no rush.'

Rhain would respond, but the cramps escalate, taking the air from his lungs. He reaches for his jacket pocket, but the syringe slips from his hand, falling between the seat and the door. Bastian opens the door and picks up the syringe.

'Where do I inject you?'

Rhain manages to hold out his arm, gasping as the cramps twist at his gut.

Bastian shoves up his sleeve and injects the contents into Rhain's arm, before passing the syringe over to Ethan and shutting the door again.

As he waits for the drug to take effect, he has no choice but to lie in his seat, riding out the cramps, while his enemy keeps watch over him. It's humiliating and instantly kills his reputation with the males.

Ethan takes out his phone, responding to emails as he waits. Instead of drawing attention to what he's going through, the Blackjack founder is doing the opposite. And while he's under no illusions Ethan's bodyguard is watching out for Ethan as opposed to him, having his looming presence outside the car offers a little comfort.

He has no idea how long passes, but eventually the cramps ease enough for him to find his voice again. 'I... apologise.'

'No need.' Ethan taps on the window, waiting until Bastian walks over to him and opens the door. 'Can you fetch some blood from the car.'

'I'm not leaving you unguarded.'

'I can barely... speak,' Rhain says, hating the weakness in his voice. 'I assure you... I am no threat.'

Bastian growls at him. 'I decide what's a threat to him, not you.'

'Bas, please.'

The bodyguard mutters something under his breath in Spanish, before slamming the door and storming off. 'I trust... that was not... a polite comment.'

Ethan smiles as he watches after Bastian. 'Oh, it was far from polite, believe me. How are you now?'

'Enjoying my life.' He smiles as he says it, but Ethan is no fool. He knows exactly what's in store as the Blood Fever progresses.

'Your condition is worsening?'

'Unfortunately.' Thankfully, Bastian arrives back with the blood, and he could not be more grateful. The Spaniard may have laced it with poison while he was gone, but at that moment, Rhain couldn't have cared less.

He accepts the bag of blood, piercing the top with his fangs and drinking greedily. It's exactly what his body needs, the liquid instantly re-energising his sore muscles. 'Thank you.'

Bastian just slams the door again and goes back to keeping watch. That male would kill him without a second thought, and no doubt, sleep like a baby afterwards. 'Before I forget. I received... some troubling news as I was leaving for this meeting. The inside pocket of my jacket.'

Ethan reaches into the back seat and finds the piece of paper. 'Is this it?'

'Yes. Open it.'

He does and his face drops. 'Where did you get this?'

'That picture is circulating among some not so friendly types. Nothing to do with The Order, however. It seems that your man Shep is being looked for.'

'And quite a hefty bounty on him to sweeten the pot. You have no idea who is behind these flyers?'

Rhain shakes his head. 'No. But I believe that photograph... is from quite a few years ago. Perhaps just after he transitioned?'

'Perhaps,' Ethan says, not giving anything away as usual. 'So why now?'

'I don't know. The only thing I can think of is that someone from The Order is linked to this other group. That wouldn't be difficult. They have tentacles everywhere. The Order have been keeping an eye out for your man because of what happened to him in Ireland. I would imagine it's just bad timing.'

'Perhaps,' Ethan says again. 'Thank you for telling us.' He slips the page into his own jacket, glancing at his bodyguard as he does so. Something unspoken passes between them, before the Spaniard turns away again.

Rhain can feel his strength returning little by little, but even though Ethan and the Blackjack will protect him, he'd much rather be back in his own house where he can recover in relative safety. 'So how can I be of assistance, Ethan?'

'Are you sure you're well enough?'

'This is part of my life. Delaying until I feel better could leave you waiting for quite some time.'

Ethan takes a photo from the inside pocket of his coat and hands it to him. 'Do you recognise this woman?'

Rhain takes less than a second to examine the photograph. 'Of course I do. Quite a feisty human.'

Ethan glances at Bas through the window. He's glaring at Rhain. He clearly didn't appreciate that comment.

'Was she in any other areas of your facility while you had her? Would she have met with anyone else you kept there?'

'No. My man brought her straight to the facility, and she was secured in the room until Davyn rescued her.'

Ethan meets Bastian's eyes, before sighing. 'Thank you anyway.'

He slides the photograph back into his coat, clearly disappointed with the answer.

Rhain has faced so many do or die situations in his life. Decisions he's had to make in the moment, without any prior planning or foresight. It's not how he likes to do things at all. Meticulous planning had kept both him and his businesses alive for many centuries.

Or his businesses at least. There was no escaping his mortality.

Or the fact that he's about to say something that could very well end his life a lot sooner than Blood Fever had planned.

'I trust Court has not regained his memory?'

'The memory you took from him. No. He hasn't.'

Of course they're still upset about that point. If he had a way of giving Court back his memory he would, but that's not possible. Not that having those memories would serve the male in the slightest. There are things in Court's past that should remain forgotten.

Instead of leaving them alone, he's about to pull one out and hand it to Ethan, with no regard for Court yet again. But he has no choice. This is much bigger than Court. It's bigger than any of them. And Ethan needs to know. It's not as if Court will forgive him either way.

'Court's daughter is the image of her mother.'

That not only gets Ethan's attention, but also that of the bodyguard outside the car. He turns to face them, his thick arms folded across his chest.

'Her mother? You know Thea's mother?'

'No. I don't know her. Very few do and I'd imagine that's the way she likes it.'

Ethan turns in his seat to face him. 'What are you talking about?'

'Her mother, Court's old girlfriend. She now sits at the head of the True Order, Ethan. She's my boss.'

ETHAN

The car ride from the park to the compound takes place in silence. Usually when he is alone with Bas, they talk. Their time alone is limited, so they make the most of it. Leaving aside the incredible physical relationship they have, Ethan is growing fonder of talking to Bas, sharing snippets of his day with him.

It's a foolish thing to do. They don't have a relationship. They have sex. Continuously blurring the lines is going to end up in hurt - his.

He glances over at Bas, his throat closing as the reality of his situation hits again. His situation. His problem. His pain.

Bastian is sticking to their agreement. Ethan can't. Not any longer. He's completely in love with Bastian. His scent is filling the car, his cologne consuming him, keeping him aroused, and his heart beating rapidly. That's what Bas does to him. And it's beginning to affect his job.

It began when Davyn wanted to go back to Ireland to kill his father. The thought of sending Bastian into battle had terrified him. He'd delayed making his decision, only by a few hours, but that was unacceptable.

He can't run the team properly, can't send them out to fight, if he's going to be overprotective of Bastian. It's not fair on the vampires they help, it's not fair on the rest of the team, and it's not fair on Bastian.

'You're quiet.'

Ethan smiles at Bas when he looks over at him. Bastian's opal eyes glow, the deep green and brown swirling in a way that makes him weak. 'I'm just considering what I need to do next.' It's not a lie. There are many things he needs to consider on different points.

'You are going to tell Court.'

Bas isn't asking a question, but Ethan needs to talk. Needs to take his mind off his heartbreaking situation. 'Of course I am. He deserves to know. I'm not sure how to broach the subject with him. I can't say I've come to terms with it myself yet.'

'Do you suspect Court of having links to The Order?'

That's something he's been asking himself since Rhain told them. It has completely thrown him. 'I can't see that. Court has been with the Blackjacks nearly from the team's inception. He has never given us a reason to doubt him. If there was an affiliation with The Order, then why was he taken and used in Rhain's project? Why does he have no memory? It doesn't make sense.'

Bas doesn't reply as he guides the car into the underground garage of the compound. There's no answer Bas can give.

He pulls into the designated spot and turns off the engine. Only then does he turn to face Ethan. 'Are you ready?'

Ethan is far from ready, but he can't put this off. He gets out of the car and walks with Bastian to the meeting room. He'd called ahead, so Nix should be there with Court. This isn't a matter for the team.

Only Nix and Court, then, when Court feels the time is right, Court can speak to his daughter.

'I have training with Fallon,' Bas says as they reach the end of the corridor.

'Of course. Are you free tonight?' he asks before he can stop himself. He needs to back away, not keep going back for more.

'No. I'll drive you home when you're ready, but I can't see you tonight. I'm on rotation.'

He nods as the instant worry hits him. He can't keep doing this. Bastian is a fighter. This is what he trains for. It's what he excels at. The last thing he needs is Ethan worrying about him. Holding him back.

'Good luck with Court.'

'Thanks.' Without another word, Bas turns away, disappearing around the corner.

That was peculiar. Unusually abrupt. Perhaps Bas is tired, or maybe worried about the connection between The Order and Court?

'Ethan?'

He looks over at Nix as she steps out of the meeting room. 'I'm coming.'

He closes the door behind him and takes his seat towards the top of the table. Nix is at the head with Court to her side. The second in command appears pensive, his pale blue eyes hard and cold as he stares over at Ethan. 'What did Rhain say?'

Straight to the point as usual. The least he can do is return the favour. 'I'll do my best to relay this as he did to Bastian and me. He said that Thea is the image of her mother.' He holds up his hand, pleading with Court to let him finish. 'According to Rhain, Thea's mother - your ex - is the head of The Order.'

The silence that follows carries on for what feels like an age. Nix and Ethan keep their attention on Court, as he comes to terms with what he just heard. And he's not the only one. Ethan knows Nix well enough to see the confusion, the questions, going through her mind.

'What else did he say?' Nix asks as Court frowns at the desk.

'Nothing. That's all he knows. He's met her a few times while on Order business, but he has no idea of her name, or anything else about her. All he knows is that she controls The Order.'

'Are you sure he's telling the truth? He could just be fucking with me again. He knows I have no memory. He could be saying all this to throw me off track.'

'That's true,' he says. 'I can't see why he would want to do that. I doubt he's expecting you to go back to him and allow him to continue using your blood. He knows he's lost you. Plus, he's helping us to a certain degree by feeding us information. I can't see what his angle would be.'

He pushes down the twinge of jealousy that hits when Nix takes Court's hand. Being envious of his friend's public relationship is not going to help his situation.

'I agree with Ethan,' Nix says, drawing his attention. 'Rhain didn't know Ethan was going to ask about Thea. He had no reason to have this story fabricated just in case someone asked. If that was the case, he would have offered that information weeks ago.'

Court lets go of her hand. 'If she's the head of The Order, there's a chance I'm linked to them. It might not be a good idea to continue giving me free access everywhere.'

Nix takes his chin in her hand, turning his head to face her. 'You are not linked to The Order! We all know that.'

'How can you know that? I don't know! I was in a relationship of some kind with their leader. She's Thea's mother. That sounds like a pretty important fucking link. How the hell am I going to tell Thea about this?'

He gets to his feet, pacing the meeting room as he draws his hands through his hair. 'If I was in a relationship with this woman and she's head of The Order, she must have known I was in the lab with Rhain.'

Ethan nods. 'I would presume so.'

'Did she arrange for my capture? Arrange for my memory to be taken? Why? Why didn't she want me to remember her?'

'I presume it was to protect herself. Maybe protect you too.'

Court spins to face Ethan. 'Protect me? My life only began when I escaped from the lab. I've lost over a hundred years of memories. How the fuck is that protecting me?'

Court is usually calm and cool under pressure, but he can't blame him for being upset. 'I wish I had more answers for you Court. I really do, but as of now, this is all we know. The fact she may have instigated having your memory taken tells us a lot. It tells us there's something in your head she doesn't want us to know.'

'What use is that, Ethan? None of my memories have come back. Apart from a few vague flashes in my dreams, there's nothing. I can't even remember most of what I dream about. If there is something there, it's not coming out in a hurry.'

'We haven't given up working on a cure. All my medical staff are on it. Every single sample and scan we've taken from both you and Austin is being repeatedly picked apart. We will find a solution. I promise.'

Court sighs, leaning against the wall and crossing his arms. 'I do have faith in you and your people. I just can't help feeling that whatever was done to Austin and I is permanent. Fuck!' he shouts, slamming his fist back against the wall.

'I don't want anyone to say a thing to Thea. Not yet. Until we know more, this stays between us, okay? Make sure Bas knows to keep his mouth shut too. She's still coming to terms with me being her father. I don't want to throw this at her just yet.'

Ethan nods. 'Of course. I'll have a word with him when he drives me home. I'll leave you to process this.'

'Yeah. Thanks. And I do appreciate you telling me. I'm just not thrilled with this situation.'

'I understand. I'll talk to you later Nix.'

She flashes him a tight smile, before turning back to Court. Ethan leaves the room, shutting the door behind him. He really feels for Court. The last few months have thrown so much at him. Having this now added to the pile won't be a quick or easy thing to come to terms with. Far from it.

They need to unlock Court's memory somehow. It has now become imperative to find out what he knows.

IZZY

'Didn't feel like breaking in today?'

Shep smiles sheepishly. 'Yeah, sorry. I didn't think you'd appreciate being scared twice in one week.'

Izzy leans against the door, blocking his entrance to her apartment. Not that she would be able to stop him from coming in if he really wanted to. 'What do you want?'

'To talk. Ideally inside, but I totally get if you're not interested.'

She examines him for a few seconds, then looks up and down the road. 'Are you sure... is it safe?'

'You mean am I safe?'

Izzy nods once.

'I promise I'm not going to hurt you, Izzy. I just want to talk. Please?'

She nods again and steps aside, letting him in. He goes into the sitting room and waits until she joins him and points to a chair. Shep sits in the armchair and clasps his hands on his knees. He's not used to the nerves he's experiencing. It's ridiculous that he can fight without a second thought, but being close to Izzy makes him a nervous wreck.

Izzy sits on the couch opposite him and looks over at him, but it's a very different look to the one she gave him when they were out together. He doubts she'll ever look at him that way again. She's scared of him. 'How are you?'

Izzy laughs without humour. 'How am I? A few days ago, I found out vampires are real. How exactly would you imagine I would be?'

'Yeah. Sorry. Stupid question. This is all kind of new to me too. I've never had to explain all this stuff to someone before.'

'Why are you here Shep?'

'You've had a fuck load of information thrown at you, and I guess I just wanted to make sure you were okay with it all. Maybe answer any questions you have?'

She snorts loudly. 'No. You're here to make sure I'm not going to tell anyone that vampires are real. If you are real? Maybe I was imagining the whole thing?'

Any minuscule chance there was, that she could somehow put all this behind them and pick up where they left off, has vanished. She's not going to get over this. 'I didn't come here to intimidate you, Izzy. I'd never do that. And while we'd prefer our existence is kept on the down low, that's not what I care about right now. It's you.'

Shep mentally kicks himself. He's never said that to anyone before. He's off his game in more ways than just that. He rolls his shoulders trying to release some of the pressure that's building across his back. He swears his skin is being stretched to its limits, and the sensation is sickening. He's so fucking uncomfortable in his own body.

Izzy narrows her eyes as he squirms in the seat. 'Are you okay?'

He forces himself to pretend his body isn't about to be torn to pieces. 'Me? Yeah. All good.'

'You look pale. Paler than the other day I mean.'

'Vampires don't get great tans. It's not really our thing.'

The briefest of smiles makes an appearance. 'You like making light of things, don't you?'

'Sorry. I don't mean to. I'm just trying to diffuse an awkward situation with humour. That's my thing.'

Izzy leans back on the couch and tucks her legs under her. 'Were you serious when you said I can ask you questions? And you'll answer them - not just brush me off?'

There goes his chance to make a run for it. If she's willing to talk to him he's not going to go anywhere. He'll stay with her as long as he can. To hell with the pain. It should pass... hopefully. 'I promise I'll answer whatever questions you have. I don't want you to be scared of me Izzy.'

She nods and a faint smile appears, which is awesome. Maybe he can turn this around.

'Do you just randomly pick people to... feed from? Like do you attack them without giving them a choice?'

He shakes his head, disturbing the ball of pain he thought had dissipated. 'No. We have a list of donors we use. Every single one of them walks away after we feed. They also donate blood, so we have a stock for emergencies. It's all voluntary. No one is forced to do anything.

'I was an idiot that night you caught me. I hadn't fed for a few days, and it caught up on me. I grabbed the first person I saw... well, the second. I stopped myself from biting you. Okay so that makes me sound like an ass, but I'm not. I genuinely only usually go for one of the donors. I'm not a fan of picking up a takeaway.'

He grimaces as the words come out. 'Right, so that sounded so much worse than I meant it to. Like I said, I'm not used to having to explain all this. And I'm not doing a fantastic job.'

213

Izzy holds up her hand to stop him before he continues rambling. 'I appreciate you not adding me to your takeaway list. Do these donors change into vampires when they're bitten?'

'No. You're either born vampire or human. No changing.'

'Oh, okay. And the sunlight thing is really a myth? And the garlic?'

'Yep. I have no idea why the garlic thing took off. It's ridiculous. Love the stuff myself. As for sunlight, pure blood vampires, those who have two vampire parents, are more sensitive to natural light. Hybrids like me, with one human and one vampire parent can handle sunlight. But our eyes are super sensitive, so it can hurt if we're out for too long. No bursting into flames though.'

'Hybrids? There are mixed blood vampires?'

He nods, instantly regretting the sudden movement. Fucking head is killing him. 'Of course. I'm half-human. My mother is a vampire, and my dad was human.'

Her eyes narrow a little and she discretely shakes her head.

'What? You can ask me anything.'

'I was just wondering, it's probably a rude question, but how old are you? I mean you look like you're in your mid to late thirties, but I'm guessing you're not.'

'I'm ninety-five.'

Izzy stares at him for a long few minutes. 'Excuse me? You're ninety-five?'

'Yep. Heading towards a century. In vampire terms I'm a baby. Loads more fuel in my tank.'

'Wow!' She rests her head on her hand, silently watching him as her brain tries to come to terms with all of this. 'I kissed a ninety-five-year-old! That's a first for me.'

He laughs when she smiles at him again.

'When you said you worked in protection, what did you mean?'

'Like humans, there are good and bad vampires. We're the good guys. We fight the bad guys. That's it in a nutshell.'

214

'You can say that again. A ridiculously small nutshell. Fight how? Are you talking about physically fighting or...'

'Yeah. It gets physical. We're a team of kick ass highly trained vampires, who protect anyone who needs protecting. There's a whole world out there Izzy that humans know nothing about. Vampires are only the tip of the iceberg.

'There are other creatures for want of a better word. Some good, and some really horrible dicks. But we're really fucking good at our job. That's why humans don't know what goes on. I mean they do see things from time to time, but it's so rare that no one believes it. We survive in the shadows Izzy. It's the only way.'

'How many more creatures are there?'

Shep doesn't want to freak her out any more than he already has, so shrugs. 'Not many. Vampires have the strongest number. And for the most part, we're all good guys. There are just a few who want to ruin it for everyone else.'

Izzy wraps her arms around herself. 'I'm not sure any of this is helping. I thought it was weird enough with just vampires. How many people in my life could be other beings? Do they have powers like on TV?'

'Not like that, no. We have some extra abilities, but—' He stops himself there. 'Actually, maybe to humans they could be seen as powers.'

That gets her attention. She sits forward again. 'Do you have powers?'

'Kind of. I can sort of see what happened in a location by concentrating. I'm like a vampire bloodhound, but instead of tracking a scent, I can see the image of what happened. It's hard to explain.'

'You can see the past?'

'Yeah, it's a little more complicated than that, but that description works. But I can't see the distant past. Just a few hours. But I can track an actual scent for much longer and further.'

'So, if you wanted to find me in the city, you could?'

He nods. 'If I drank your blood I could then track you wherever you are.'

'Well that's not exactly comforting.'

'Izzy, I told you. I'm not going to hurt you.'

She tucks her cardigan around her, hugging it tight. 'Well I'm sorry if it's going to take me longer than a few hours to believe you. This is a lot to take in Shep.'

'I know.' He pauses as one of the wings shifts inside his back. Something isn't right about this. The pain hasn't let up even a little while he's been here. In the back of his mind, he knows what's happening. But knowing it and accepting it are two different things.

'Are you all right?'

Faced with all this world changing information, and yet she's asking about him. 'I'm good. Just a twinge.'

'Can I get you anything? You look like you're in pain.'

'It'll pass in a sec. I'm more worried about you and all this stuff I'm telling you.'

She gets up and fills a glass with water in the kitchen. Izzy passes it to him before sitting down again. 'Sip that. I don't want you passing out on me again.'

'Thanks.' He takes a sip, but it threatens to come back up when the wings shift again. They're coming. Whether he likes it or not, the fuckers are working their way out.

RHAIN

The female smiles as he enters the room, her naked body laid out on the sheets ready for him. She's pleasing enough, but that's not what he's interested in. It's her blood, her body that he needs.

Rhain clenches his fists, attempting to hide the residual tremors. The attack had been one of the worst so far. He thought after what happened when he met Ethan, that he'd have a few days of relief, but he was wrong. They're coming faster and harder.

And, if that wasn't enough, the increased need for blood after each attack is concerning him. The addiction is stronger than he ever expected. If he continues to deteriorate at this rate, he has mere weeks left until he's gone.

The female spreads her legs as she beckons him over with a seductive smile. He's not attracted to her. It's been a long time since he's been attracted to anyone. Sex has become something he requires, not enjoys.

Foreplay and kissing have been disregarded as unnecessary and a waste of time. All females he's with are required to be ready for him when he enters the room. It cuts out any time wasting. He doesn't have enough time left to waste it on ensuring his sexual partner is warmed up.

He undresses, ignoring the way her eyes widen when she sees his body. It's not the first time. No one expects a pampered aristocrat like himself to have the body of a trained fighter. A body that's slowly fading away. It's only a matter of time before his sickness attacks that too.

His fangs drop as he releases his wings. The vast silver wings slide into place as he lowers onto the bed. She turns her head to the side, giving him access to her neck so he can feed. Rhain slowly slides a finger inside her, grateful that she's more than ready for him.

The growl isn't planned, the sound coming from deep within him, surprising him as much as her. It doesn't seem to concern her. Quite the opposite. She moans loudly, writhing under him as he gets into position. His dick and fangs sink in at the same time, pinning her to the bed.

The second her blood hits his tongue, a primal urge takes over, fuelled by the taste of blood. He growls, thrusting into her with more force, his fingers digging into her wrists, as his fangs tear at her neck.

But he can't stop.

He doesn't want to stop.

His wings tear at the floor to either side of the bed, ripping the expensive carpet as he feeds, the frenzy building the more blood he takes.

When the haze fades, Rhain pushes back from her and slowly slides out. He takes a long breath, fighting to get his fangs to retract. Then he looks down at the woman. It doesn't take a medical degree to realise she's dead. Her neck is torn apart, her lifeless eyes staring at the ceiling over the bed.

'Sire! What happened?'

The shock of what he just did masks the irritation he would have had at Geraint's intrusion. His butler tries to get his attention, repeatedly calling his name, until he finally looks up from the body. 'I killed her.'

'Yes, sire. You did. We need to get you cleaned up and dispose of the body. Come with me.'

'I didn't mean to kill her,' he says, slowly climbing off the bed. He slides on the underwear Geraint passes to him, then allows himself to be guided from the room into the adjoining bathroom. Geraint points to the rim of the bath. 'Sit and I'll clean the blood from you.'

Rhain glances down, only then noticing the blood smeared on his chest. Did he bathe in her blood? Wipe it on himself? 'I can't remember what happened.'

Geraint wipes a warm, wet cloth over his skin. 'Your Fever must have taken over. I've heard it can happen.'

'I didn't mean to kill her.'

'Stop speaking about her. It's not a concern. She was a whore and she's dead. It's not the first time you've taken a life, and it won't be the last.'

'She did nothing to deserve her death. I kill for a reason. There was no reason for this.' He's never felt remorse after he's taken a life. Not until this moment. She was brought in to feed and service him. Not to die.

He has always respected the women he was with. He might not have felt anything for them, but they still deserved to be treated correctly. He's never lashed out, never been harsh or rough with any of them. It was important to him that they enjoyed their experience and wanted to come back time and time again.

He looks into the bedroom at the body until Geraint shouts at him. 'Stop! It's done sire.'

Geraint has never raised his voice to him. He has served Rhain's family for too many years to count, but it was a master and servant relationship. 'Excuse me?'

'I apologise for overstepping my position, but this regret will not serve you in any way. Mark this down as another kill. Nothing more. This show of weakness will destroy you if seen by the wrong people. You are feared and respected. Showing remorse over killing a whore is doing nothing to solidify that reputation.'

He really wishes Geraint would stop calling her a whore. It's no more deserved than her death was. 'I want her body returned to her family. It won't help ease the loss, but I also want them to be generously compensated.'

Geraint isn't on board with that, but he keeps his mouth shut. Rhain appreciates his help with his affairs, but if he keeps answering back, Rhain might have to change their arrangement.

Frustrated with the entire situation, he pushes to his feet, swiping at Geraint's hand when he tries to push him back down. 'Leave me! I've told you what I want. Make sure she's taken care of.'

Before Geraint can answer back, Rhain leaves the room, not looking back at the woman as he walks to his quarters on the top floor of the house. A few months ago, he would have taken to the air and entered through his balcony from the outside. But he can no longer fly. His sickness had taken the strength from his wings, grounding him.

First agonising seizures, then useless wings, and now losing control when he feeds. What fun will come next? He slams his bedroom door behind him, hoping that Geraint takes the hint and keeps away.

He strips out of his clothes, dumping them in the chute in the bathroom, then steps into the shower, turning on the water. It cascades down his body, turning pink as it washes the female's blood down the drain.

The scent of it is everywhere, filling his nostrils with every breath. He holds his wings wide so the water washes the blood off them too.

It feels like it's everywhere, coating his skin, soaking into his pores, smothering him in shame and guilt.

Rhain grabs a bottle of shower gel from the shelf, pouring half the contents onto his hand. He scrubs his skin and hair, using his nails to scrape at his flesh, desperate to ensure all traces of blood are removed.

It takes nearly twenty minutes of scrubbing before he's satisfied his skin, hair, and wings are clean. He pulls a towel from the rack, wrapping it around his waist before going into his bedroom.

He's too tired to pull his wings back in, so he leaves them out. It's only a matter of time before he's too weak to release them at all.

He needs a distraction, something to take his mind off what he just did to that poor woman so he sits at his desk, his wings spread to either side, and logs on to the computer.

An alert notification pops up on his screen. It seems someone has been trying to access his financial and business information. He sits back, staring at the screen.

It's not Ethan or any of his team. They have no reason to delve into his business. No, there's only one person who would have the gall and stupidity to do that.

He smiles to himself. He's going to enjoy confronting the weasel about his meddling.

IZZY

She can see there's something wrong with him. He's been acting strange since he arrived, but it's getting worse. Shep squeezes his eyes shut and holds his breath for a few seconds. He's in serious pain and doing a lousy job of hiding it.

She may be angry and confused, but that doesn't mean her feelings for Shep have disappeared. He sucks in a breath again and curses. Izzy wishes she knew what was wrong with him, but she doesn't want to pry into his private life, especially about an illness - vampire or human, whatever it may be.

'Shep? What can I do?'

He shakes his head and leans forward, burying his head in his hands. 'Nothing. Sorry, I need to go. I don't feel so good.'

He tries to stand, but falls to one knee and roars in pain, startling her. Izzy scrambles off the couch as he rears up, clawing at his back. He pulls his phone from the back pocket of his jeans but drops it as the pain hits him again. Izzy tries to grab for the phone, but Shep growls when she approaches. 'Sorry! Keep away, please.'

'You need help. Can you slide your phone over. I'll call your friends.'

He fumbles for his phone and unlocks it, then slides it across the floor to her.

'What name should I search for?'

Instead of responding, Shep's glowing eyes target her, and he snarls, showing her a little too much of his impressive fangs for her liking. Izzy grabs the phone from the floor and slowly backs away from him.

He lunges at her again, so she quickly moves into the kitchen, standing behind the table, as if it will offer any protection. If a six-foot tall vampire wants to come after you, a table won't do much to deter them.

Izzy scrolls through his recent calls, stopping at Wills, presuming it's an abbreviation for Willow.

Shep drops to his hands and knees, breathing so hard she's surprised he hasn't passed out. Then he screams, stopping her in her tracks.

Izzy can't stop herself from taking a step closer to him. There's something sticking out of the back of his t-shirt. Something that looks like a claw or a talon.

Shep releases another agonising howl, and Izzy staggers back in horror as two enormous wings tear out of his back. Blood darkens what's left of his t-shirt and coats the wings as they move and appear to reshape themselves. Whatever is happening, Izzy can't take her eyes off the horrific sight.

She only spurs herself to move again when Shep crashes to the ground. The wings follow suit, one taking down her small bookcase as it falls to the ground.

Then silence returns. She licks her lips and takes a step closer to him. 'Shep?'

Nothing. He's still breathing, so he must just be out cold after whatever the hell just happened to him. Before anything else bizarre happens, she taps Willow's number and licks her dry lips again, as she waits for the call to be answered. 'Shep?'

'No. Sorry. My name is Izzy. I'm...' What exactly is she to him? 'I guess I'm Shep's friend. I need to show you something. Can I turn on the video?'

There's a brief pause before Willow replies. 'Okay.'

Izzy smiles as Willow appears on the screen. She could be Shep's twin with the exact same hair and eye colour as her brother. 'He needs ... I don't know what he needs. Best I just show you.' She turns the camera around trying to fit Shep and his wings in the image.

'Oh God! When did they come out of him?'

The fact Shep's sister isn't surprised by the wings registers with her. 'They just tore out of him a minute ago. He's unconscious and I haven't got a clue what to do for him. You need to come here. Please!'

'Okay. Hang on.' Izzy watches as Willow appears to run down a corridor and she hears more voices.

'Hi there, Izzy.' A man with a beard and dark blond hair tied back in a bun smiles at her. 'My name is Fletch,' he says in a thick Scottish accent. 'I'm Shep's doctor. Can you show me what's going on with him?'

She turns the phone around and Fletch curses quietly. 'Right. So there's a tracker in his phone. We're on the way to you. Is he unconscious?'

'Yes. He collapsed after the wings came out.'

'But you're sure he's breathing?'

She slowly moves closer and nods. 'He's definitely breathing.'

'Good. Any other injuries you can see?'

'There's a lot of blood from his back, but I don't think he's hurt anywhere else.'

'That's something. Now Izzy, is there anything on the wings? Like a fluid or liquid? Don't touch the wings. Just tell me if you see anything on them.'

She leans closer and nods. 'Yes. There's a clear gel-like substance on them.'

'Okay, that's good. That will protect them. Just try not to touch his wings until that's been absorbed. They're incredibly delicate at this stage. Any damage could affect him long term. We'll be with you as soon as we can.'

'Will he be okay? I mean is there anything I can do for him?'

'He should be okay, but I really need to check him. And you've done all you can for him at the moment. Just keep your distance in case he wakes up. Those wings will take a little getting used to. We're on the way to you. Sit tight.'

Fletch ends the call and Izzy stares at the phone screen. There's a picture of Shep and Willow as his background. He has his arm wrapped around her shoulder and they're both smiling. The image in front of her on her living room floor is vastly different. It wouldn't be out of place in a horror movie.

She crouches down beside his head and reaches out to brush his hair off his sweat soaked forehead. Fletch may have told her to keep away, but she can't leave him like this.

Even unconscious his brow is furrowed, his breathing laboured. She hates seeing him in pain. Hates seeing anyone in pain, but it hits harder with him. He's light-hearted, always joking or smiling. This is such a contrast.

Izzy runs her hand over his hair, trying to soothe him.

He must like her. There's no other reason for him to take her to dinner, or to visit her at home twice. It's more than just making sure she was going to keep what he *is* a secret.

As confused and cautious as she is about what he is, she knows she likes him too. Since that moment in the bar when she saw him properly, he'd caught and held her attention.

Leaving aside the vampire thing and the new addition of the enormous wings, she still feels the same. He still makes her smile, in spite of the bizarre situation.

One of his wings twitches, so she gets up and moves out of the way. She has no doubt they'd tear her flesh apart if one of his talons got close enough.

With nothing to do but wait for his vampire friends to come to the rescue, she makes herself a strong coffee, then leans on the door frame to watch over him.

IZZY

Since she began working in The Lair, Izzy has seen her fair share of odd things. It was part of the deal in that place. But when she opens her apartment door to find seven huge vampires on her doorstep, odd takes on a whole new level.

A tall man with a thick beard and long hair moves to the front and holds out his hand. 'Izzy? I'm Fletch.'

She nods, her attention still on the gang he brought with him. 'Are you all... you know?'

Fletch shakes his head. 'Six vampires and one human.' He lifts his hand. 'And that would be me. I know this is a bit of an ask, but do you think we could come in? This lot don't exactly blend in.'

'Yeah. Sure. Come in.' She steps aside, pushing back against the wall as the group of vampires invades her apartment. Once everyone is in, she shuts the door, hanging back, unsure of what to do.

'Izzy? Can you come in here?' Fletch says from her living room.

She skirts around the vampires, trying not to look at them too closely, squeezing into the living room where Fletch is examining Shep. 'Is he all right?' she asks when she pushes past them to join Fletch, who is crouched on the ground with a red-haired woman beside him, and Willow. In real life the likeness to her brother is uncanny.

Fletch nods as he searches in his bag for something. 'From what I can tell, he's going to be fine.'

'So why is he unconscious?' Willow asks.

'Poor guy is exhausted. He's just released two flipping big wings. Wings, I might add, that weren't fully formed when I last took an x-ray of his back. His body has just gone through a massive change. He's going to be worn out for a bit.'

'Hold on,' Izzy says, not quite believing she's involving herself in this discussion. 'What do you mean he didn't have wings?'

'I mean Shep is a Hybrid - human and vampire blood. That means he shouldn't have wings.'

Izzy looks past him to the unconscious vampire with wings on her living room floor.

'So, what happens now?' Izzy looks over her shoulder at a beautiful woman with long deep brown hair. She doesn't know anything about this woman, but she can tell she's in charge. The way she carries herself, the confidence and calmness she brings with her is impossible to miss.

'We need to give him Rhain's drug. Those wings need to be stabilised.'

'Are you sure it's safe?' Willow is holding Shep's hand, tears streaking her cheeks. The poor girl is worried sick.

'It's safer than not giving it to him and taking a chance. It's your call Boss.'

The dark-haired woman nods once. 'Do it. Can we move him?'

227

'Not yet. We need to wait for the protective coating to absorb. If we move him now we risk permanently damaging the wings. He may not want them, but I doubt he'd appreciate if we fucked them up for him.'

'How long is that going to take?'

'A few hours.'

The dark-haired woman turns to face Izzy. 'Are you okay for us to hang around here until it's safe to move Shep?'

Izzy nods. 'Sure. Make yourself at home.'

The leader holds out her hand, shaking Izzy's firmly. 'I'm Phoenix, Nix. This is Court, Fallon, Davyn, and Bastian. You've already met Fletch and Willow. I'm sorry for bursting in like we did. Thanks for looking after Shep until we got here. It must have been terrifying watching him like that.'

'Yeah. It wasn't good. Excuse me. Can you give me a minute?'

She walks as fast as she can without running, into the bathroom and locks the door behind her.

What the hell is going on? Seven vampires are in her apartment. Seven trained vampire warriors in her small apartment. With her. One of them may be unconscious, but that doesn't even out her odds in any way.

She sits on the lid of the toilet and focuses on not completely freaking out. But how do you not freak out in this situation? What if they decide she knows too much and can't let her live? They could take Shep away with them and leave her body behind.

She screams when someone knocks on the door. 'Izzy? It's Willow. Can I come in?'

This is it. Her time is up.

'Please Izzy. You're safe with us.'

She slowly pushes to her feet, then unlocks the door.

'Thank you. Are you all right?'

Izzy nods. 'Never better.'

Willow holds out her hand. 'Nice to officially meet you. I'm Willow.'

She gingerly takes Willow's hand, shaking it. 'You too. Izzy.'

Willow smiles and it somewhat puts her at ease. 'Why don't you come back into the living room. It's your home and we have no intention of taking over or driving you out.'

Willow holds out her hand, smiling when Izzy takes it. 'Come on. Let's see how Fletch is getting on with my stubborn brother.'

RHAiN

He woke up in one of the worst moods he remembers being in for a long time. He's not usually one for good or bad moods. He gets up, goes about his business, then retires to his quarters to sleep. He's been angry of course. Many times, and when that happened, he usually took care of the rage by dispatching the irritant.

At his age he can't be bothered dealing with irritations. It's not worth it.

Perhaps his mood swings are down to the growing weakness he's experiencing. He's not a weak male. Never has been. Rhain's bloodline is as long as they come. Each Prime ancestor as pure in blood as is possible. He's royalty in all but name.

Which is why he's dying slowly and painfully. He's not used to feeling so weak, so helpless. When he walks into a room others cower. He is respected and feared - both reactions entirely justified.

If he loses that respect or fear, his enemies will attack. Everything he's worked for will be destroyed. He's already had to step away from the laboratory he invested a fortune in creating. As soon as the Blackjacks attacked he had no choice but to shut down operations, putting an end to his chance of finding a cure.

A cure he had within his grasp. Court was the secret to his survival. Not a cure as he had hoped, but Court's blood was the only thing that dulled the pain, killed the tremors and cramps.

For a while at least, he felt in control of his life again. Until the male escaped and that relative *normality* slipped away.

Perhaps in time Court may be open to donating some of his blood, but Rhain doubts it. Thanks to him, the second in command of the Blackjacks has no memory.

And once Ethan tells him Thea's mother is the head of The Order, Court would be even less inclined to help. Court's blood is the one thing that would give him more time, but any glimmer of hope he may have had seems unlikely now.

Hence the foul mood.

And he couldn't think of a better way to put that bad mood to use.

His True Order contact runs a small investment business in the city. Its main purpose is to funnel funds to The Order, but Barton still considers himself a business mogul with a healthy portfolio. It's just another reason to despise the male.

He arrives at the outer office and is met by a youngster who is clearly disinterested and not hiding it very well.

'Yes?' he asks without lifting his eyes from his computer screen.

This receptionist isn't helping Rhain's mood. 'I would like to see Barton.' His tone should tell the male in front of him that he is serious, but the idiot either isn't listening, or doesn't realise how close he is to having a deadly issue.

'About what?

Enough of this! Rhain reaches down and grabs the male by the back of the head. He slams the receptionist's head against the wooden desk over and over, until the front of his skull caves in, smearing blood all over the screen.

Once he wipes his hands on his handkerchief, Rhain turns to Barton's door and walks in without knocking. The weasel has done the same to him enough times.

Barton freezes when he sees who's just disturbed his peaceful and no doubt boring afternoon. 'Rhain! How did you get in?'

Rhain steps aside and gestures to the remains of the receptionist. 'He had an attitude problem. I took care of it.'

Barton's mouth opens and closes a few times, as he stares at the blood now dripping onto the floor from the desk. 'You can't just come in here and kill my people! This is my company!'

Rhain settles into one of the leather chairs in front of Barton's desk and smiles. 'Oh. I apologise. I thought that's what we do now.'

'Excuse me?'

'I heard you've been delving into my business. Why are you asking my business acquaintances questions about me?'

Rhain nearly laughs aloud when Barton's face takes on a strange red hue. The irritating vampire had paid handsomely for information on Rhain and his businesses. Payments he no doubt thought would ensure silence on behalf of the recipient.

Unfortunately for him, Rhain still holds more respect than Barton does. If given the option to get on Rhain's wrong side or Barton's, there would be no need to consider.

'Loyalty is something you should familiarise yourself with. I reward those loyal to me. However, I am known to punish those who fuck with me. Do I make myself clear?'

Barton nods quickly. 'I was just doing as instructed.'

'By whom? Who wants to know more about me?'

'Those higher up the food chain. That's all I know. I like you Rhain. I really do. But we all answer to others.'

Rhain stands and leans on the desk, bringing himself so close to Barton he can smell nothing but the male's cheap cologne. It reminds him of cat urine. Suits him perfectly. 'You like me?'

Barton swallows, then nods. 'Of course.'

'Interesting. You see, I think of you in the same way I think of a fly. Irritating. Unwanted. Always buzzing in my ear when all I want is peace. That's you Barton. I honestly don't care who orders you to do what. If you ever interfere in my personal business again, you will wish I had crushed your skull like I just did to your receptionist.' He reaches out and straightens Barton's tie, pulling it a little too tight. 'I don't want to have this talk with you again.'

Barton nods quickly, so Rhain taps him on the cheek. 'Good. I'll leave you to your business then.'

Without a backward glance he walks past the corpse sprawled on the desk and down to his car. Geraint opens the back door as he approaches, then climbs in the other side once he's closed the door again. 'Where to?'

'Home.'

Geraint shuts the partition between the chauffeur and the back of the car before he speaks again. 'Did the meeting go as planned, sire?'

'I think Barton got the message. Perhaps the blood on your shirt helped to make your point.'

'I think it helped.'

'But you're still concerned?'

'Of course I am,' he says as the car pulls out of the underground car park. 'Someone told him to delve into my life. Why now?'

'Have you done something to displease The Order?'

Rhain shakes his head, gratefully accepting the drink Geraint passes to him. 'You know me. I always play by the rules.' He smiles, but Geraint just shakes his head.

'Oh, I know you sire.'

Rhain sips his drink as he looks out the window. The Order have never asked questions about him before. Not until now. The only difference is his contact with the Blackjacks. Have The Order somehow found out he's meeting with Ethan?

It's highly unlikely, but not altogether impossible.

Which could mean he's in a great deal of trouble.

SHEP

Everything hurts. His skin feels too small for his body and there's a weight sitting on his back that's fucking sore. Shep groans but doesn't even bother to open his eyes. He just wants to go back to sleep and hide from the pain.

'Shep? Look at me.' It sounds like Izzy, but he's not sure. The ringing in his ears is distorting the sound. 'Please Shep. Can you open your eyes?'

It takes a ridiculous effort, but he manages to do it. For some reason Izzy is crouched on the floor, peering down at him. And why is he on the floor? 'Hey Izzy.' He winces and groans again. 'Sorry. Feel like shit. What happened? Did I pass out?'

'Yes, but it's a little more serious than that.'

Izzy reaches behind her and takes something large from someone. She holds the mirror in front of him, and Shep stares in horror at his reflection. He looks as shite as he feels, his skin pale and slick with sweat, thick black rings under his eyes. But that's not the part that turns his stomach. It's the fucking huge wings sticking out of his back that he's not on board with.

He has wings. This can't be happening. He doesn't want wings!

Shep tries to scramble up or back, he doesn't know which way. All he knows is that he needs to get away from the wings. Which makes no sense. Deep down he knows they're attached, but that doesn't mean he's ready to accept that. 'Get them off me! Get them off me!'

Fletch and Bas appear from somewhere, holding him down on the ground, not letting him up.

'Shep, you need to calm down,' Bas says, holding his arms down firmly on the floor. 'You will only damage your wings if you move. Please stay calm.'

'Stay calm? Are you fucking serious?' Calming down is the last thing on his mind. He hears furniture falling and things breaking, but still tries to get up. 'Please get rid of them! Bas, please, please! I don't want them! Please!'

He's begging. Even through the panic and confusion, he sounds fucking pathetic. But he can't handle this right now. He can't handle the sensation of the wings on his back. 'Take them off!'

'Look at me!' Court's command breaks through his panic. Shep looks up, realising a little too late that Court is about to get into his head. Court's pale eyes glow and, even though Shep tries to resist, Court works his freaky eye thing on him.

'It's okay, Shep,' Court says, his voice low and soothing in a strange way. 'We're going to help, but you have to try to remain calm. Can you do that for me?'

He has no idea whether it's Court or exhaustion, but the panic diminishes. Shep closes his eyes and takes a minute to get himself together. Which is ridiculous. It'll take a hell of a lot longer than one measly minute to process any of this.

He can still feel Court in his head, but he doesn't mind. Whatever he's doing is stopping him from attempting to tear the wings off his back.

'You need to lie still. Can you do that?'

He nods against the floor and Court releases him. He doesn't have the energy to move anyway. When he opens his eyes again, Izzy is lying on the ground, facing him, her head propped up on her hands. 'You've destroyed my living room,' she says with a grin.

'Sorry about that.'

'I think I can forgive you. Fletch wants to strap your wings so you don't accidentally decapitate someone. After that they'll help you off the floor. It can't be too comfortable.'

'Yeah. Right. Not sure comfort and me will be getting up close and personal any time soon.'

She reaches out and squeezes his hand, somehow easing the fear Court had already suppressed, a little more. Even after everything that's gone on between them the last few days, she's looking out for him.

'I know you're freaking out and I know you're scared,' she says, her voice lowered so the others don't hear. 'You have every reason. I'm freaking out too. But Fletch seems to know what he's doing. All your friends are here for you. Your sister is here for you. And I'm here for you too, okay?' She smiles and he feels a little comforted.

'Thanks. And yeah, I'm kind of freaking out. I'm sorry about your living room. If I'd known they were... if I'd known the wings... I would have stayed away. I swear. I didn't want that to happen here. I didn't want it to happen at all, full stop. But wrecking your house wasn't in my grand plan.'

'It's just a bookcase. Don't worry about it.'

He groans when something is wrapped around one of his wings, pulling at it.

'Sorry,' Fletch says from behind him. 'It'll take a few minutes to wrap your wings.'

Izzy squeezes his hand a little tighter, bringing his attention back to her. 'So, your friends seem nice. And they used the door instead of a window which I appreciate,' she says with a wink.

The bandage pulls against his wing again, turning his stomach. The sensation is alien and seriously sickening. He doubts he'll ever get used to it.

'And Bastian is your best friend?'

Shep nods. 'He's the only one who can put up with my natural charm.'

Izzy laughs. 'Natural charm? Is that what you call it?'

'I'd also call it being a stubborn ass,' Bas says from somewhere behind him.

Bas is also trying to distract him, but nothing is working. Nothing will be able to mask the weird sensation of his new wings being touched. He hates it. Hates them.

Fletch appears in front of him again, crouching down to bring him closer to eye level. 'They're safely wrapped up. Ready to get off Izzy's carpet?'

'I don't know if I can get up.'

Bas and Fletch take an arm each, helping to lift him up. As soon as he's upright, his head swims. He tries to stay conscious, but it's a lost cause. Whether he faints, or goes for a manly passing out, Shep couldn't really say. All he knows is that when the darkness comes, he welcomes it.

RHAIN

The pain consumes him. Every muscle. Every bone. Breathing is difficult. Moving is impossible. All Rhain can do is wait and ride it out, counting down the seconds in his head until it passes.

It's getting worse. Each attack lasts longer. The recovery time after each one dragging on longer.

He's also down to just twelve doses of serum. With the attacks hitting with greater frequency, that doesn't give him long. Once the serum is used up, recovery will take days rather than hours. Blood Fever will dig its fingers deeper into him.

He stops counting when he gets to three thousand and fifty-six. What's the point. Counting only depresses him. Once the cramps ease a little, he reaches out and calls for Geraint. 'I need help.'

He cuts the intercom before his butler can respond. Not being strong enough to climb off his bed and get the serum, is adding to the depression that's threatening to take him deeper.

Thankfully, Geraint arrives, disturbing his dark thoughts.

But his butler doesn't arrive alone. Rhain tries to push himself upright, but he's as weak as a baby. Barton smiles as he saunters across Rhain's expensive carpet. 'How the tables have turned.'

'What's all this? Geraint? Why did you let this cretin in?'

'Oh, he called me,' Barton says with an irritating smile plastered on his face. 'Called us actually.'

Six more males invade his personal space, blocking his exit which is ridiculous. He can't get off the bed, let alone try to escape from the room.

Ignoring the Order males, Rhain turns to Geraint. 'Why did you do this? I've known you my whole life. You served my father before me.'

'And I would have continued to serve you, but you have made it impossible lately. You are growing weak, sire. Weak and foolish.'

'You told me getting into bed with The Order would be the end of me. But I never thought it would be by your hand.'

'The reason I served your father for so long was because he never aligned to any one group. You were too weak to stand on your own, so chose The Order. Then you reconsidered and sided with the Blackjacks. Your complete lack of resolve is disgracing your father's memory. I had no choice but to seek help getting you on the right path again.'

'You're an idiot, Geraint!'

The next move is timed to perfection. If he had the energy, Rhain would probably applaud the timing. But when Geraint's head is removed from his shoulders by one of the Order males, Rhain can merely sit and watch as it falls to the ground with a wet thud.

Geraint served him well, but his betrayal has ended his life. If not ended by The Order, then Rhain would have taken care of the task himself.

Barton steps over the fallen body and smiles down at Rhain. If he had the strength to strangle the irritant, he would.

'I think you know what happens next?'

'I'm going to hazard a guess and say *she* would like to see me?'

Barton nods. 'She would. I'd ask you to get dressed, but I don't have time to wait. I'm sure she won't mind if we bring you in, in your underwear.'

'Whatever she wants.' He would rather die right here and now than go anywhere with Barton, but he's not going to let the male know he's fazed in the slightest by what's going on.

Which of course he is.

He's being taken to his death. In any other circumstances, he'd happily oblige. But this is The Order. He knows death by their hands will not be fast, or in any way, painless. Quite the opposite.

He's not keen on having his mouth sewn shut so he can slowly starve. However, after handing Davyn over to the same fate, perhaps it's only fitting and what he deserves.

Barton steps aside and two of the males come forward, one carrying a hefty set of restraints.

'I guess it's time to go,' he says, throwing the duvet off his legs.

His wrists are secured behind his back, the whole while Barton keeping a satisfied smile on his face. Once Rhain is firmly restrained, he is dragged to his still unsteady feet. Barton gestures to the door as he steps to the side. 'After you.'

The walk down the stairs and out to the waiting car is slow and painful, the males half dragging, half carrying him, helped in no way by Barton giving him a nudge from behind, every few steps.

Once Rhain is shoved into the back of the car, Barton slides in beside him. 'Burn it,' he says to the Order male, standing by the car.

Rhain watches as his home is set alight, the glow from the rising flames burnt into his vision as they drive away.

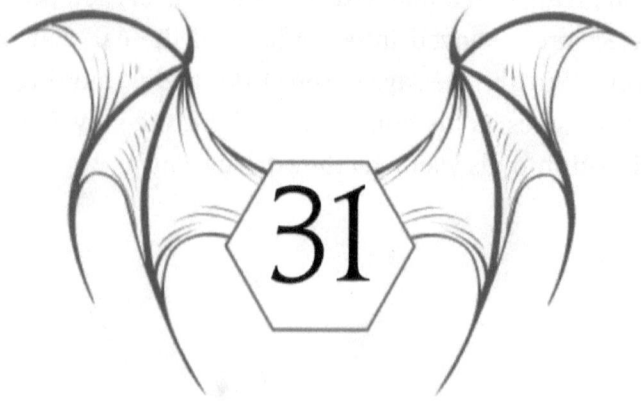

IZZY

No doubt all of this will hit her a lot harder once things calm down. For now, her worry is taking charge. Worry about Shep. Worry about this new world she's living in. Worry about monsters lurking in the dark.

As Izzy stops in the doorway to her bedroom she tries to process the sight in front of her, sprawled across her bed. Fletch, Bastian, and Davyn had carried Shep into her room after he collapsed again. They wanted to take him home, but Fletch wasn't happy to move him too much, so right now, her house is home to a lot of large, intimidating vampires.

She glances over her shoulder, but everyone is in the kitchen and living room, tucking into some pizza they had ordered. She couldn't write this stuff if she tried. A few days ago, vampires lived in books and films. Now they're eating pizza in her kitchen!

Maybe she'll wake up from this strange dream... or nightmare, in a while?

Izzy creeps around the side of her bed and looks down at Shep. Learning he's a vampire was enough of a shock, but the two enormous wings on the bed behind him are something entirely different. The wings are wrapped in a bandage of some sort to protect them, until Shep is ready to pull them back into his body, whatever that means? The bandages are also keeping the razor-sharp talons away from flesh... and any more of her belongings.

Izzy quietly kneels on the floor next to him and leans on the edge of the bed. He looks so peaceful now and she's grateful for that. The shock of waking up to find he had wings had really rattled him and she can't blame him. Watching them tear through his flesh is something that will stay with her for a long time.

She peers over at his back and the wounds where the wings came out of his body. Although there had been a lot of blood initially, Fletch assured her that was only because it was his first time. The ridged skin to either side of the wings had stopped bleeding and had already begun healing.

Izzy sits back on her legs and watches him sleep. She likes him. What does that say about her? He's a vampire. He's got wings. He's a fighter who goes out at night with the rest of the scary vampires in her living room and fights the bad guys - whoever they are?

Why is she still looking at him like she can be with him? It's just not possible. Not only are their lives as different as they can be, they're also completely different species. What she needs to do is get any thoughts of a relationship with Shep out of her mind. She was unsure about him from the start. All this new information should just prove to solidify that.

So why isn't it?

She looks up when she feels someone watching her. Willow is hovering in the doorway, her cheeks streaked with tears, and her arms wrapped tightly around her. Her brother is hurting, and she's worried about him. It doesn't matter whether they're vampires or humans. They're siblings. Nothing changes that.

Izzy pushes to her feet. 'I'll leave you alone with him.'

Willow shakes her head. 'No. Please stay. If I'm alone I'll just let my mind run away with me. I need someone to distract me.'

They sit on the carpet, backs against the wall, legs stretched out in front of them, looking over at Shep. 'I didn't get a chance to say this to you earlier with all the chaos but thank you for calling me when he collapsed. You might have saved his life by doing that.'

'Of course.'

'How did you know to call me?'

'We went out to dinner a few nights ago. He spoke very highly of you. You were the only other person he mentioned by name.'

Willow wipes her face as she looks over at her brother. 'The last time we saw each other we fought. We do that a lot,' she says, smiling thinly. 'Shep knows how to push my buttons.'

'Yeah. He mentioned he's rather good at irritating people.'

Willow laughs at that. 'Oh yeah. He's an expert at that.'

'Is he going to be okay?'

Willow shrugs. 'Fletch doesn't know. The drug he was given is messing with his body. Fletch thinks the wings will be the most dramatic alteration, but he can't say that for sure. Every other mixed breed vampire who's been given the drug hasn't survived much past this stage.'

'Oh God...'

'We were given another drug that should stabilise the changes to Shep's body. That's what Fletch gave him in the living room. We were told it should stabilise the transformation. Without it, he would die within days.'

'Will it work?'

Willow sniffs and shrugs. 'Fletch doesn't know for sure. All we can do is wait and see if it works.'

Izzy falls silent. Shep being sick is one thing. Shep potentially losing his life because of that illness is something she hadn't contemplated. He groans in his sleep, one of the enormous wings shuddering behind him, before stilling again.

'How was he infected?' she asks after a few minutes of silence.

'Davyn was taken while on a mission. He's the big guy with the eye patch,' Willow explains when she sees the confused look on her face. 'We went in to get him back. There was a lot of resistance and, during the fight, Shep was injected with something. The stubborn fool kept it to himself for a while so he wouldn't worry anyone. That's what he does.

'He never puts himself first. As long as the team is okay, he's happy. I know he plays the joker from time to time. That he seems to laugh everything off, but he would give his life for every single one of us without thinking about it. This is just so unfair. He doesn't deserve this.'

They look up as someone knocks on the open door. 'We're going to move him in about two hours,' Fletch says from the doorway. 'Nix wants him back in the compound, and I'd prefer to have some of my equipment on hand. We'll just let him rest a wee bit longer before we risk waking him up. The poor guy needs all the rest he can get.'

'Are you sure it's safe to move him?' Willow asks, pushing to her feet.

'His wings have been out for a few hours now, so I'm happy we won't do them any damage. I'd also prefer to move him while he's still drifting in and out of consciousness. He's been through enough the last few hours. We should spare him any more discomfort.'

Izzy stands, unsure what she's supposed to do now. Are they going to whisk Shep away and leave her wondering if he's going to be okay? If he was awake it would be a different situation. She'd just ask if she could tag along, or worst case, at least make him promise to let her know how his recovery progresses.

'I'd like Izzy to come too.'

She turns to face Willow, a little surprised at the request. 'I'm sorry?'

'Shep would be less than impressed with me if I left you here. You should come.'

'That's not my call,' Fletch says, crossing his arms. 'You'll need to speak to Nix.'

Willow nods and hurries from the room to talk to Nix. 'Is that really an option?' Izzy asks.

Fletch shrugs. 'It's Nix's call. If she says yes, you can tag along. But if she says no, I'm afraid that's it. Nix will put the team first. She has to. It's her job.'

Izzy wants to go with him - no doubt about that, but she's not exactly in a position to make any demands. All she can do is hope Nix agrees to bring her into their world.

32

IZZY

The drive back to Shep's home could probably be added to the list of surreal things that have happened since she met him. But after watching huge wings tear out of his back, being stuck in an armoured truck with a group of vampires is strangely normal.

Whoever these vampires are, whatever they do, there's money behind them. A lot of money. The Bus as they call it, is a hi-tech mobile unit, equipped with a small medical centre, seating for everyone, a few bunks, and a kitchenette.

But at that moment, Shep is the only thing holding her attention. He's lying on a gurney in the back of the Bus with Fletch and Fallon fussing over him.

He's still unconscious. Still far too still and pale. Izzy is worried sick, but his friends don't seem to be overly concerned, so she takes a little comfort from that.

The Bus comes to a stop, and everyone gets to their feet. 'We're home,' Willow says, getting up and following everyone off the Bus.

Izzy steps off the vehicle, finding herself in a huge garage. As well as an impressive collection of cars and motorbikes, there is a helicopter in the centre of the space. Willow takes her arm, gently guiding her to the door at the far side of the garage where Shep is being taken by Fletch.

'What is this place?'

'It's where we live and train.'

'Shep said he lives with his sister and teammates, but I never imagined it would be somewhere like this.'

'We need to be the best of the best,' Willow explains as she opens the door for her. 'Our backers make sure we have everything we need to survive.'

Izzy has nothing intelligent to say on the matter so keeps her mouth shut, following after Willow through the door, along the corridor and into what appears to be a normal house. Willow brings her through another door and into an elevator, where Fletch and Fallon are waiting for them with Shep still unconscious on the gurney.

Less than a few minutes later, Izzy is standing in a state-of-the-art medical centre, watching as Fallon and Dav carefully lift Shep onto a strange looking bed that can hold him and his wings.

Before she can ask anything else, an African American woman bursts through the door, stopping when she sees the scene in front of her.

'What happened now?'

'Hey Annie,' Fletch says, giving the woman a hug. 'Thanks for coming so fast.'

'No problem. I was due to pop in to check on Dav's wings anyway.' Annie ties back her long hair then rolls up her sleeves as she walks over to Shep. 'They seem to be full sized wings. That's good I suppose.'

'Why is it good?' Izzy asks before she can stop herself.

'It's good because, it's better for him to have full-sized wings instead of tiny little useless ones.' She holds out her hand. 'I'm Annie by the way. My friend Fletch seems to have forgotten his manners. I'm a surgeon who has the pleasure of helping out with more tricky issues from time to time.'

'I'm Izzy. I guess I'm a friend of Shep's.'

'Well,' Annie says, turning her attention back to Shep. 'Let's make sure your friend is going to be okay.'

She puts on a pair of gloves while Fletch and Fallon unwrap Shep's wings then cover their own gloved hands with a strange gel, before carefully stretching each one out along the extra panels to either side of the bed.

Annie slowly and methodically examines both of the rust-coloured wings, probing the bones and the flesh before checking Shep's back when Fallon and Fletch hold him upright.

Until that moment, Izzy hadn't seen his wings spread out to their full span. Even in this vast room, his wings are enormous. Both wings are equipped with five huge razor-sharp talons, each one the length of her forearm.

Seeing them tear out of his back had been terrifying, but seeing them spread out to either side of Shep, she realises how breathtaking they actually are.

'You can wrap them up again to keep them safe,' Annie says as she removes her gloves and throws them in the bin.

'Is he okay?' Willows asks before Izzy can get the words out.

'His wings are perfect. Considering some of the wings I've seen while helping you lot, his are the best I've seen.'

'So will they work like my wings?'

Annie leans against the edge of the counter as she considers that one. 'I can't say for sure yet. I believe you don't fly for a few months after your wings come out, is that right?'

Fallon nods. 'They're not strong enough until a few months later. We need to build up the muscles first.'

'Glad I got my homework right. Okay, so we should follow the same rules with Shep's wings. Take it slowly and see how he gets on. But as far as I can tell, they're healthy. He's incredibly lucky.'

'I'm not so sure he'll see it that way,' Willow says.

'Perhaps not, but it could have been a lot worse,' Annie says. 'Did you give him the injection Rhain provided?'

Fletch nods. 'I gave it to him shortly after the wings came out. So far so good, but time will tell if it worked.'

'Hmmm,' Annie says. 'From what I've seen of Rhain's work, he's not someone I'd like to meet. Let's see if he can redeem himself somewhat with this injection.'

She gives both Izzy and Willow a good look over. 'No offence to either of you, but you look worn out. Why don't you both get cleaned up? We'll look after Shep.'

'Annie's right,' Fletch says. 'Get some rest. He'll be out of it for a while. I'll call you if he stirs.'

Izzy doesn't want to go, but with Annie, Fallon, and Fletch creating a barrier between them, Willow and Izzy aren't going to win this one.

'How is he?' a dark haired woman asks as soon as they step out of the room.

'Izzy, this is Thea. She's Davyn's mate.'

'Nice to meet you,' Izzy says, giving her a weak wave. Her mind is still back in the room with Shep.

'He's okay,' Willow says, answering Thea's question. 'Annie is just with him right now. We'll know more once Annie has examined him.'

'Annie seems nice,' Izzy says, as the three woman go back into the main house.

'Annie is lovely,' Thea says. 'She trained with Fletch years ago. She was brought in when Davyn's wings were broken last year. She's super talented.'

'So, if she says Shep's wings are okay, she means it?'

'Absolutely,' Willow says 'I don't think it's going to make things better for Shep, but having fully working wings is better than two useless ones. It'll take time for him to get used to them, but he will. He's stubborn. He won't let them beat him.'

Willow opens a door to the left side of the landing and gestures for Izzy to go inside. The bedroom is huge, more like a suite than the room she was expecting. 'There should be a robe in the bathroom with some fresh towels. Your overnight bag is on the couch by the window. If you find you've forgotten anything in the rush to pack let me know.'

'Thanks Willow. I know I probably don't have any right to ask but can you let me know when he wakes up?'

'You have every right to ask. I promise I'll get you if I have any news on Shep. This could have happened to him while he was in the road, or alone somewhere. I couldn't be more grateful that he was with you. I mean that. Try to get some sleep. Goodnight.'

'Goodnight Willow and nice to meet you Thea.'

'We're on the other end of the phone if you need anything. All our extensions are on the notebook by the phone. Shep is tough. He'll get through this.'

'Thanks. I really hope you're right.'

The women leave and Willow closes the door. She doubts she'll get much sleep tonight. This is all so surreal she won't be able to switch off from any of it. Even if she could, Shep is still occupying her thoughts.

But at least she's here. She's in his world with his friends and family. Izzy looks down at her hands. His blood is still on them. Maybe she will have a shower and try to get some rest. She wants to be ready to go Shep when he wake up.

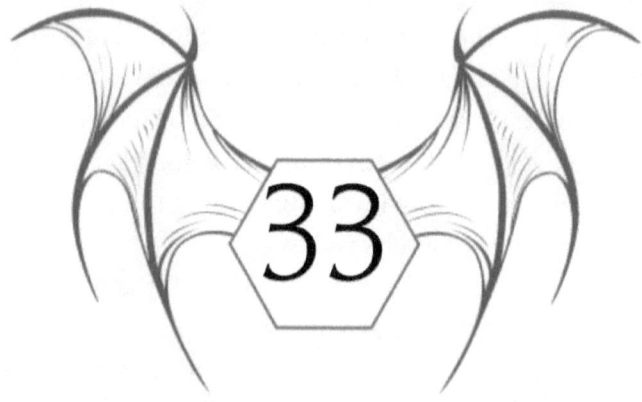

SHEP

Over the decades he's had his fair share of beatings and injuries out in the field. He's lost count of the number of times he's woken up in the medical centre feeling like he's been run over by a train.

This is so much worse.

Instead of a few muscles aching, every single muscle and bone in his body aches. He doesn't feel this bad after going ten rounds in the training centre with Davyn. The bastard always managed to do the most damage when they trained together.

He tries to flop onto his back but something really fucking painful stops him.

'You need to lie still.'

It's then he notices someone sitting beside his bed. Not someone from the team either. 'Izzy?'

'Hey.'

He frowns as his eyesight clears. How the fuck did he get back to the compound? More importantly, how is Izzy here too? 'What are you doing here? Does Nix know? Oh, please don't say you sneaked in!'

She laughs at his ridiculous question. 'Of course she knows, and how exactly would you suggest anyone sneaks in here? Willow asked if I could come back, and Nix agreed.'

That surprises him. Nix isn't a fan of bringing outsiders into the group for obvious reasons. You can't just invite humans into a vampire house without being sure about them. Which means Nix is okay about Izzy. It shouldn't matter either way, but it kind of does for some reason. Unless... 'Did she invite you back here because I fucked up so badly she didn't have a choice, or...'

'She smiled as she gave me her okay. Does that count?'

'Yeah. I guess that's a good sign. How long have I been out for?'

She checks her watch before answering. 'About fifteen hours, give or take.'

'What? Really?'

'You had us a little worried actually. Fletch has been checking on you every few minutes. He even brought in another doctor to double check.'

'He did? He brought Annie in?'

She nods. 'She was due to check on Davyn's wings, so he asked her to have a look at yours too.'

That's not a list he wants to be added to. Annie is nice and all but Fletch only calls in his human colleague when he's not happy about something. She managed to repair Dav's wings after they were broken, and she did an incredible job. That doesn't mean he wants to be one of her patients.

'I don't suppose she had any words of wisdom?' Like maybe that she can remove the wings and he can go back to living his life without having them attached.

'She said your wings are healthy and strong.'

'Great. Perfect.'

He frowns when Izzy reaches out to take his hand. 'I'm sorry.'

'About what?'

'The way I reacted when you told me what you are.'

'I told you I'm a vampire! Of course you reacted the way you did! Fuck it, you actually reacted better than I thought you would. I was convinced you'd scream and run from the room. You're handling all of this really well, Izzy.

'You found out vampires are real, had one of them collapse in your house, then these things appear,' he says, gesturing over his back. 'Then you saved my ass by calling in a whole troop of vampires, who took over your house, before bringing you back to their lair.'

'You call it a lair?'

'No. We call it the compound.'

'That doesn't sound any more homely.'

'No,' he agrees. 'Not really.' His shoulder is itching like crazy, but he doesn't want to scratch it. If he does he might accidentally hit off one of the wings, and he's not ready to feel them yet. If he keeps talking to Izzy he can forget about them. Or at least try to. Nothing like a bit of good old denial.

She rubs her thumb over the back of his hand. His first instinct is to pull it out of her grip, but he leaves it where it is. It doesn't feel too bad. Far from it.

'You scared me when you collapsed like that.'

'I'm sorry I keep scaring you. It's the last thing I want. I don't want you to be afraid of me.'

'No, that's not what I meant. I was scared because you collapsed. Scared for you.'

'You were?'

She nods as she holds his hand a little tighter. 'It didn't matter what you were. It just mattered that you were in trouble. Maybe you being a vampire isn't as big a deal as I thought it was?'

'Oh it's a big fucking deal, believe me! But if it's something you can handle - or even get used to over time, that's good. I'm not expecting you to just smile and get on with life as normal. It'll take time to get used to all this craziness.'

'That's probably true. But first things first. How are you?'

'Me? I'm fine. No problems at all.'

'You're allowed to be scared, Shep.'

Good, because he's fucking terrified. He has wings. Him. A Hybrid.

No amount of denial, joking, or making light of it is going to help him. The wings will still be there no matter what.

'What... okay what colour are they?' He could have asked a dozen questions about them, but that's the only thing he can think of right now. Knowing his luck at the moment they're probably bright pink and covered in glitter.

'They're rust brown.'

'Oh. Is that good?'

'Good in comparison to what?'

'I don't know. Pink I suppose.'

She laughs at that, and he joins in. Or does, until his wings move and put a stop to his fun again. 'Don't make me laugh. They feel weird when I do that. So is the colour okay?'

Izzy glances around the room, spotting the mirror over the sink against the far wall. She takes it off the wall and holds it up, the back facing him. 'Would you like to see?'

He does, but he also really fucking doesn't.

'You don't have to. There's no rush, but maybe seeing them will help you come to terms with them?'

'Yeah! Not so sure about that. Fuck it! What the hell?'

She turns the mirror around and there they are. His first thought is that they're big. Really fucking big. And the colour isn't too bad either. They're a dark, almost golden brown with lighter finger bones. Not too bad at all. And definitely not pink.

'See. No pink anywhere,' Izzy says, echoing his thoughts. 'What do you think?'

'They're okay I guess. It's hard to tell when they're strapped up like that.'

'Fletch said the straps need to stay on until you figure out how to use them safely. Apparently - and I quote - he doesn't want any heads to go flying.'

'Nothing like the mention of decapitation to put a downer on things. Sorry. I'm not the best of company at the moment. You may have sussed it already, but I'm not over the moon about this new revelation. Either of them.'

'Of course it's going to throw you! It would be weird if it didn't. I may not know anything about wings or anything vampire related, but I've seen how worried your friends are about you. You have an amazing group of people on hand to help you through this. And I'm guessing a few of them do have wings? You're not going to have to figure this out alone.'

But he is alone. Having Willow and his friends willing to coddle him as he gets his shit together isn't appealing in the slightest. He's the strong one. The dependable one. He doesn't take or need sympathy from other members of the team.

'Are you hungry?'

The question catches him off guard. 'Sorry? What?'

'Are you hungry? You've been out of it for quite some time. I'd imagine someone your size needs a lot of food. I thought you might be hungry.'

'Yeah. I could do with something.'

She gets to her feet and gestures to the door. 'Willow said Gwen always has the fridge stocked up for you and your appetite. I'll call her on the intercom outside. What do you fancy?'

'You're in the know about a lot of things. What else did my lovely sister say?'

'Nothing you need to worry about. She just thought the food topic could come up, so wanted me prepared.'

'How right she was. Can you just ask her for one of her chicken club sandwiches please.'

'Will do.'

He keeps smiling until she leaves the room, and the door closes behind her. Then he curses under his breath and buries his face in his hands.

He's trying his best to hold it together. To keep from freaking out with her here, but it's so difficult. He picks up the mirror and looks at his wings in the reflection. They're enormous.

How the fuck are they supposed to get back into his body? They're going to rip his insides to pieces. He doesn't even want to think about that part. They'll just have to stay out. There's no other option.

ETHAN

'He's late. I don't like this.'

Ethan agrees but isn't about to fuel Bastian's barely controlled anger by vocalising it. These meetings with Rhain are becoming an issue between them, and that's something he's less than happy about.

The relationship, if you could even call it that, is difficult enough, without adding extra stress between them.

He remains sitting on the bench as Bas paces in front of him. His arms are by his side, one hand close to the gun he has strapped to his belt, the other ready to grab the blade strapped to his thigh. Ethan knows Bastian will use those weapons if anything threatens him. It's a thought that gives him little comfort.

Bas is his bodyguard, tasked with giving his own life to save Ethan's if needed.Something Ethan is also less than happy about. Being in love with your bodyguard isn't ideal. Far from it.

Bas's dark eyes are constantly moving, scanning their surroundings, ready to pounce. It's at times like this the differences between them are more evident.

Bastian is a highly trained fighter, while he is more suited to sitting behind a desk in his penthouse office. But that's what the team is all about. Balance. He provides the information. Nix and the team act on it.

Bas flexes his gloved hands as he walks. He's more tense than usual. 'Can you sense anything?'

Being mostly human doesn't help much in these situations either. Ethan is very much dependent on Bas and his vampire gifts.

'Nothing.' He stops pacing and turns to face him. 'He's never missed a meeting.'

'I know.' Something is wrong. Rhain has been dependable so far. He looks over at Bas. There's no love lost between Bas and Rhain. 'Have you met with Rhain without me being present?'

'Yes, but I didn't kill him, if that is what you're going to ask.'

He was hoping his gut feeling about this was misplaced. 'Why did you meet him?'

'That's my business.'

The flippant, unemotional response irritates him. 'This is serious Bas. You can't arrange meetings behind my back. You answer to me, Bastian. You all do. I can't have you going off on your own and potentially jeopardising a relationship I'm working hard to build. What did you discuss with him? I need you to tell me.'

'He knew about my tattoos. No one outside that time in my life should know what they mean.'

He guessed that would be the reason behind the meeting, but it doesn't help to quell his irritation. If Rhain knows what the images on Bastian's skin mean, he's figured out something Ethan himself has tried and failed to decipher.

He had been able to deduce some of the marks meaning, but the majority of them are still a puzzle. Bastian was a thief. He knows that much, but that doesn't explain the obvious revulsion and shame Bas exhibits when he looks at some of the marks.

'And? Did he have any information for you?'

Bas falls silent which doesn't surprise Ethan. He's incredibly guarded about his past. 'So, no response? Nothing at all?'

'I've said it before. My past is my business. Rhain was alive when I left him. If you don't believe that, there's not a lot I can do about it.'

'Damn it Bastian! Of course I believe you.' Bastian has never lied to him. Not once. If anything, he's usually brutally honest.

Bas curses in Spanish as he goes back to pacing.

'Was that directed at me?' Ethan asks, knowing full well that it was.

'You, Rhain, and this relationship you are desperate to build with him. You are both delusional.'

'Is that so? Would you care to elaborate?'

Bas stops again and takes two steps closer. 'I've already told you how I feel about this. I'm not going to go over it again.'

Ethan doesn't want to have that argument again either. 'I find it troubling that Rhain misses a meeting after he told us the identity of Thea's mother. I don't believe in coincidences.'

'What do you want to do?'

He looks over at Bastian. 'You're not going to like it.'

'When it comes to Rhain, that's a given. You want to go to his house, don't you?'

'If something has happened to him because he's been helping us, I need to know. He owns half a dozen properties in the area, but my team hasn't been able to narrow down his regular home.

'It's time we dig a little harder. We need to find out where he lives and pay him a visit. I'd like to go back to my office to collect some files from my last delve into his life. Would you be able to drive me home after that? I don't want to force you if you have to get back.'

Bastian crouches down in front of him. For the first time ever in public, he drops his stern bodyguard mantle and takes Ethan's hand.

'I go where you go. You could never force me because that's where I want to be.'

The unexpected confession takes him by surprise. He never thought Bas would come out with something like that. 'Thank you.'

His ridiculous impulsive *thank you* deflates the situation instantly. Bas lets go of his hands and pushes to his feet. 'We'd better go.'

'I didn't mean to say thank you like that,' Ethan says as he gets to his feet, then walks with Bas to the car.

'I shouldn't have said what I did. I can't protect you if I blur the lines when we're in public.'

True to form, they have both managed to dismiss whatever they have, pushing it back behind closed doors, as if they're doing something sordid that the world can't know about.

Like his grandparents.

Like Nix and the rest of the team.

Though he doubts Nix, or the Blackjacks would have an issue with himself and Bastian being together. Not that they are together. Not really. Not the way he wants. He'll never be able to wake up next to Bas. Never be able to be seen in public together as a couple. Never be able to kiss him, to hold him.

All he can hope for are a few brief meetings. A few short hours before they each have to go back to their own worlds.

No matter how much he wishes otherwise, it's something he's just going to have to accept.

BASTiAN

He should just drop Ethan in his private garage and take his bike back to the compound. It's what he's tasked with doing. When Ethan meets Rhain or has to do anything outside of his usual business, Bas is his bodyguard. Just his bodyguard. Door to door service.

Not door to bed.

But as he unlocks Ethan's door, following his boss inside the vast and expensive two-story penthouse, he knows he won't be going home immediately.

Ethan walks across the polished tiles to the kitchen area and places his briefcase on the counter. Bastian silently watches him as he lays some files on the counter, then pours himself a glass of wine and a glass of chilled water for Bas. He doesn't drink. Vampires don't usually get drunk, but it can happen. It's not worth the risk.

'I'll get my people to begin searching for Rhain's residence,' Ethan says as he takes more files from his briefcase. 'I know he stays under the radar but we're good at what we do. We'll find him.'

Bas walks over to him, turns him around then pushes him back against the countertop.

'Enough talking. I'm not here to discuss him.'

He pulls off Ethan's tie then rips the buttons on his shirt, tearing the material off him. He runs his gloved hand down Ethan's firm chest. He may sit behind a desk most of his life, but he looks after himself. Under his expensive shirts and fine suits is a body he can't get enough of.

Ethan's belt, trousers, shoes, socks, and boxers are removed next, leaving Ethan naked in front of him. His dick is already hard, standing proud of his body. Bas pulls off his gloves, dumping them on the counter on top of Ethan's files. He wraps his hand around Ethan's dick, and Ethan groans loudly.

Bas takes Ethan's tie from the counter, then pushes Ethan over to the bedroom. He shoves him face down on to the vast bed, climbing on after him to pin him down. After securing Ethan's wrists behind his back with his own tie. Bas stands and undresses quickly. Ethan's eyes stay on him as he takes off his clothes, exposing his tattoos in all their horrific glory.

But instead of shying away from his marks, Ethan seems to like them. If he knew what they meant he might not be so keen to be alone with him.

He fists his dick, sliding his hand over it, trying to get his mind back on Ethan and off his past. He barely gets enough time with him. He's not going to waste a second of it. Bas takes the bottle of lube from the drawer beside Ethan's bed and pours it along his dick and Ethan's ass.

He will never tire of seeing Ethan laid out like this for him to use. He spreads his legs, offering himself to Bas. Someone is eager to get things going. He smiles to himself as he slowly rubs his thumb over Ethan's hole, applying just enough pressure to have Ethan groaning into the sheets.

He pushes his hips back, but Bas holds him in place, digging his hand into Ethan's hip. 'Not until I say.'

Ethan closes his eyes but nods.

'Good boy.' Bas slides his thumb in further, his own dick hardening at the sounds coming from Ethan. His restrained hands reach back, trying to touch Bas.

He grabs Ethan's wrists, shoving them further up his back and holding him in place. Bas rubs his dick along Ethan's ass. He moans into the covers, his ass pushing back as he tries to get what he wants from Bas.

And he will get it, but not yet. As soon as they both come, it will be over. He'll have to leave Ethan's house, go back to the compound to sleep alone.

'Please...'

The sound of Ethan begging him changes his mind about taking it slow. He slides inside, the way Ethan's body responds to him nearly driving him over the edge before he's even begun.

He pulls Ethan upright, nuzzling against the side of his neck as he gives him a minute to get used to him.

Then he sinks his teeth in, pinning him in place. Ethan's blood may be considered weak as it is more human than vampire. But to Bas it's like the richest wine. Ethan doesn't need to feed. If he did, Bas would make sure it was his blood and his alone that sustained him.

But as Ethan's blood can't offer him everything he needs to survive, perhaps that is best. Maybe it's just the world giving him another message, telling him that they aren't meant to be together.

He lowers them both to the bed, one hand to the side to support himself, the other hand moving under Ethan's raised hip, until he finds and grips Ethan's dick.

Ethan whimpers as Bas drives into him, his dick, teeth, and hand working him until Ethan comes with a loud shout.

Once he knows Ethan has been satisfied, he allows himself to get lost in the sensations. Lost in everything Ethan offers him.

Bas groans as he comes inside Ethan, his fingers digging into Ethan's ass as he drives in hard and deep. 'Fuck!' He shudders, thrusting into Ethan one last time before stilling. Ethan's eyes are closed, his head sideways on the bed, his fangs visible as he pants heavily. Fuck, he is gorgeous.

Pushing aside the sadness that suddenly overcomes him, Bas unties Ethan's wrists, rubbing the raw skin before gently rolling him onto his side.

Ethan groans as he opens his eyes. 'I can't move.'

'That's what I like to hear. You don't need to go anywhere.'

Ethan looks down at his stomach before flopping back on the bed. 'I have my cum on my stomach. I need to wash it off.'

'No, you don't. I want you to sleep with it on you. With my cum inside you. Reminding you of what we did.'

Marking you as mine.

He's blurring the lines again. Taking sex to obsession, but he can't help it. All he wants to do is mark Ethan. Let the world know he belongs to him. That if anyone lays a finger on him, Bas *will* kill them.

But that's not his place. It never will be.

Ethan stretches out, a sexy, satisfied smile on his face. 'Do you really think I'll be able to sleep like this?'

'You will because I'm telling you to. Do I need to tie you to the bed all night?

Ethan smiles at that suggestion. 'If I didn't have an early meeting I might not be opposed to that.'

Bas grips Ethan's jaw firmly in his hand, pushing his head back. 'Don't give me any ideas.' He kisses him, getting so lost in the moment he lies down beside him, holding him in his arms. Ethan sighs as he lies against his chest.

'I think I'm fucked,' Ethan mutters sleepily. 'Can you... will you stay for a while. I know we don't do that, but I'd—'

'Just for a few minutes.'

It's a mistake to stay, but he can't leave. Ethan feels too right in his arms. The scent of sex hangs in the air, their sweat, their release mixing to create an intoxicating perfume. He closes his eyes, listening to the sound of Ethan's soft breathing as he does something he swore he'd never do. He falls asleep holding Ethan.

ETHAN

As sleep fades away and he comes awake, the first thing Ethan remembers is falling asleep in Bastian's arms. It's something he's wanted to do for so long, but with their arrangement being primarily about sex, that was never an option.

Bas had spent many hours at his penthouse, but always left as soon as they'd had sex. Something was different about last night, and he wishes he knew what. If he knew, he could replicate it. Give Bas a reason to stay. To actually sleep with him. Wake up with him.

Ethan opens his eyes, fully expecting to see Bas sprawled out on the bed beside him. But he's alone. From the feel of the cold sheets, he's been alone for a few hours.

The high he was on when he woke, fades.

Why did he leave in the middle of the night without telling him? The only thing he can think of is that Bas regretted staying in the first place.

That's his fault. He shouldn't have asked him to stay. What was he thinking? That's not what they do. They never have. He took a step too far and potentially scared Bastian away.

As painful as it is being with him the way they are, the thought of not having him at all is too much to bear. He can't think about that.

Ethan stares at the creased sheets where Bas had been lying beside him. He should get up. His diary is full for the morning, but he can't convince himself to move.

His alarm rings beside him, drawing him out of the darkness that's taken over. He drags himself out of bed and into the bathroom.

Cursing himself and his stupidity, he turns on the shower, washing all remnants of their night together from his skin. Anger and humiliation keep him company as he dresses, his attention falling on the bed as he fixes his tie.

As he ensures the knot is correctly positioned, he can't stop looking at the bed. Memories of what Bas did to him play in his mind, pushing him further into the stomach-churning humiliation.

He asked Bas to stay. He overstepped their agreed boundaries. He was the weak one who pushed things too far and scared Bas away in the middle of the night.

Unable to bear it any longer, he grabs the sheets, pulling them off the bed and dumping them on the floor. He can smell Bastian, his deep spiced scent wafting from the sheets as he gathers them and the pillowcases, rolling them into a ball and shoving them into the laundry chute.

With that task completed he prepares his breakfast, eating it as he checks his emails.

The distraction fails less than five minutes later.

He did this to himself. Bas did nothing wrong. He stuck to their arrangement. Ethan was the one who took it too far.

SHEP

'You don't have to be here for this. I mean if you want to, I don't know, maybe grab something to eat, that's cool. I won't mind.'

Izzy takes a step closer and holds his lips closed. 'Shut up. I'm staying. And you're babbling.'

She releases him then tries to take his hand, but he grabs hers first. It doesn't make a difference if he's holding her hand, or she's holding his. Nowhere, except in his head.

'I know you're scared, but it will be fine. You'll see.'

He wishes he could vocalise how much he appreciates her being here. But all he can offer her is a weak smile. She's incredible, taking to all this craziness like a duck to water. Vampires, random wings, secret organisations. It's so messed up, but she's got it.

And for some reason that makes him believe he can do this. He can walk into the room and let his teammates help him get the damn wings back into his body. Ideally without him freaking out and running from the room so he can vomit. Which is even odds at the moment. He's not sure if it's the thought of what he's about to attempt, or the fact those huge wings will have to somehow fit in his body.

Yeah, it's probably that one. He glances over his shoulder at the wrapped wings. How the fuck are they going to fit?

'Breathe. I don't want you fainting on me again.'

'Hey! I do not faint. Pass out. Macho vampire warriors like me, pass out.'

She smirks and winks at him. Job done. He's suitably distracted.

'Come on macho vampire warrior. Show me how it's done.'

He lets her lead him into the gym where Nix, Willow, Fletch, Court, Fallon, Dav, and Bas are waiting for him. Full house. He's not sure if he should be flattered or pissed off. Probably should veer more towards the flattered end of the scale. It's not like they'd come out so they could watch this shitshow for a laugh. Because that's what it's going to be. One painful, freaky, unpleasant shitshow.

Bas walks over to him, pulling him into a quick hug. 'You good my friend?'

'Never better. Living the Hybrid dream. Who wouldn't want to figure out how to pull in wings?'

'Just like everything else in your life, you will excel at it. Then continuously tell us how much you excelled, repeatedly.'

'Thanks Bas.'

'Are you ready?' Fletch asks as he joins him at the Salmon Ladder. He remembers Dav hanging off the device when he had to pull his wings back after they were broken. He never thought he'd find himself here.

Izzy squeezes his hand, bringing him out of his thoughts.

'Whenever you're ready we can get started,' Fletch says, standing beside the ladder.

'Yeah. I'm good. Let's do it.' He releases Izzy's hand, but instead of joining the others against the wall, she stands to the other side of the ladder facing him. It's what he wants, what he needs, and she knows it.

Willow joins them. Seems she's going to be the one to talk him through this. Given the alternatives, he'll take her. Better than making a fool of himself while Fallon, Dav, or Nix try to help. He'll take Willow any day over that.

'Okay, so first you're going to have to breathe. Holding your breath won't work.'

'Yeah. Breathe. Right. Thanks Sis.'

She thumps him on the shoulder. 'Ouch! Hey watch it!'

'Stop being an ass and breathe.'

He glares at her but does as he's told. 'I'm breathing. Now what?'

'Now Fallon and Fletch will unwrap your wings. After that I'll talk you through pulling them in.'

It takes a few minutes to release the huge rust wings from the straps holding them closed, but a part of him hoped it would take longer. 'I don't know if I can do this Wills.'

'My big brother can do anything.'

Fuck! Now that's two people who have said that to him.

'Close your eyes and just do what I say. I'll help you.'

He closes his eyes, not convinced about any of this.

'Now just imagine pulling the wings into your back and let them do the rest.'

He opens one eye and looks at her. 'Just imagine? Are you fucking serious?'

Willow slaps him on the arm. 'Shut up and just do it.'

He sighs as he closes his eyes again. 'Right. Fine. Here's me imagining.' It takes a good minute until he feels something weird happening with his back. The pressure builds in his body, like an invisible hand shoving him against the rack. He clings on to the rung, using the ladder to hold himself up.

'That's it,' Willow says. 'Keep doing that.'

He hasn't got a clue what he's doing, but he doesn't argue. He leans on the rack as the pressure builds in his back, driving him forward again until he's nearly lying on the equipment, then it stops. 'What happened?'

'Have a look for yourself.'

He opens his eyes and looks in the floor to ceiling mirror opposite him. No wings. 'They went in?'

'Like a dream,' Fletch says, slapping him on the shoulder. 'Good job Shep.'

He smiles as Izzy steps in front of him. 'How do you feel?'

'Full.' It wasn't half as bad as he thought it would be. Then he tries to push himself off the rack, falling forward again. 'Why the fuck are they so heavy?'

'It'll take you time to get used to them,' Willow says. 'Stop being a wuss.'

'Right.' He pushes off the rack again, this time managing to stay upright. 'So, what now Doc?'

'Well, they can stay where they are for a few days. Then it's best to let them out again at that stage. As for flying, we'll work up to that. I'd prefer to give them a few months before we throw you into the sky.'

'Seriously Doc, you need to work on your bedside manner.' The idea of flying hadn't even crossed his mind. 'I'm taking it you mean you want to see if the drug works and they don't disintegrate, or I die in the meantime?'

'Now who needs to work on their manner? You are not going to die, Shep.'

He nods, still not convinced. But when he sees Izzy's face drop he forces himself to smile. 'I know. Just being dramatic. It's all good.'

Willow rolls her eyes at him, before walking away, followed by the rest of the team, leaving him alone with Izzy and Fletch. 'I want you to stay in the compound for the moment. You and I are going to be spending a lot of time together.'

Shep grins at Fletch. 'Ah, you just can't get enough of me, can you?'

'Oh I can. Believe me,' Fletch says with a laugh. 'You're a pain in the ass. I'll leave you to it for now. No leaving the compound!'

'Yes! Fine! I hear you.'

'Just making sure.' Fletch smiles, then nods at Izzy, before he leaves them alone with a whole load of awkward silence.

Now what?

She's been here for two days at this stage. She's got a life outside this place. A life away from him. He can't just keep her here indefinitely. 'You hungry?'

'I am a bit.'

'Come on.' Food first, then think about what he's going to do. It'll take more than a sandwich to sort that out.

Twenty minutes later, with their plates cleared while they chatted about meaningless stuff, Shep is still at a complete loss.

'So, how are you handling all of this?' As opening lines go it's pathetic, but it's all his brain can come up with.

She wipes her hands on her napkin as she nods. 'Yeah. I think it's all only beginning to sink in. Nothing makes sense, but I'm accepting that. I'm guessing that's the way things work in your world. Accepting, rather than trying to make sense of it?'

'Couldn't have put it better myself. I genuinely am sorry that you got dragged into all this. None of this was planned. Fuck, I don't think anything I've done since I bumped into you was planned.'

'Swept me off my feet you mean!' Her smile is fucking incredible, her blue eyes twinkling as she tucks her hair behind her ear.

'Yeah. Although, with the shitshow of recent events, maybe I did just clumsily walk into you and knock you over. I'm not pulling out all my usual impeccable moves. I've fumbled every second with you.'

'You've been genuine. Nothing to apologise for. I've seen a vulnerability in you that I didn't expect.'

'Ouch!' That's fucked that up then. Vulnerable isn't the vibe he was going for.

She takes his hand in hers, letting go when he instinctively pulls it away from her grasp. He didn't mean to do that. She only wanted to hold his hand. No big deal but tell that to his fucked-up head.

'That was a compliment Shep,' she says, hiding the hurt. 'It's not a bad thing in any way. The man I'd heard about in The Lair, was this *don't give a damn* womaniser. I think that's an act. Actually, I'm sure it is. You've been the complete opposite of that person with me. I believe I'm seeing the *real* you.'

She might have him there. 'What are you doing about work?' he asks, trying to change the subject. He's had more than enough attention on him today. 'I don't want you to get into trouble for missing it.'

'I took a few days off. I probably should get back soon though. I can't stay here forever.'

'No, guess not. I'm on lock-down, but I could get Bas to bring you

270

home.'

'Why haven't you tried to kiss me again?'

His mouth drops open before he can control it. He closes it again, then smiles at her. 'Wasn't expecting that.'

'Are you going to answer me? You've kissed me twice. I get the impression you don't do anything you don't want to do, so I'm assuming you wanted to kiss me. So does that mean you don't want to kiss me again?'

'No! I mean yes. Fuck, I'm making a right meal of this.'

She leans forward, bringing her closer to him. 'So, what's the problem?'

'I'm a vampire. The whole wings thing. You've had a lot to—'

'This isn't about me,' she says, interrupting him. 'Every time I touch you, I can feel you tense. You're absolutely the most confusing man I've ever met. You give off signals that say one thing, then do the exact opposite. I don't know if I'm coming or going with you.'

He wants to tell her the truth, to lay it all on the table and let her see who he really is. But he can't. If there's a chance she'd pity him or look at him with sympathy, it would kill him. He'd prefer she left thinking he's a bit of a womanising ass, than the alternative.

'Do you like me Shep? Be honest with me, please.'

He's already been honest enough with her. Freaky winged vampire is enough of an image to leave her with. 'It's not a case of whether I like you or not. It's compli—'

She cuts off his *complicated* comment by kissing him, completely taking him by surprise.

Then Izzy rests her hand on his shoulder. His head fucks him over, taking him back to that room, the stench of rosewater filling his nostrils again. He pushes back from Izzy, scrambling to get off the seat and away from the memory.

'I'm sorry. I can't do this.'

She takes a deep breath as she looks at him. He's hurt her. Made her feel like he doesn't want her, that she means nothing to him. But it's the opposite. She means too much to him to allow her to stay with him. He's broken on such a deep level he doubts he could ever be repaired. And he won't allow her to waste another minute with him.

'Right. Okay. I get it.' She nods to herself as she wipes the tears from her face. 'I probably should head back to my place.'

'I'll sort out a ride for you back to civilisation.'

She pushes to her feet, the hurt on her face like a knife to his heart. 'Thank you. I'll get my things together.'

Izzy hurries from the room and he lets her go. Every part of his being desperately wants to go after her, but this is best for her. Shep pulls out his phone and sends a message to Bas asking him to drive Izzy home.

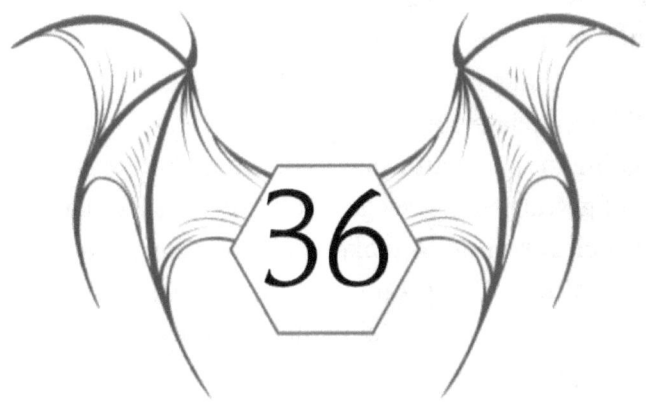

SHEP

'Why is she leaving?'

Shep shouts in surprise as Bas walks into the kitchen, his phone in his hand. 'Would you please stop doing that. I could really do without adding a heart attack to my list of problems right now.'

Bas holds up the phone. 'Like this problem?'

'She's not a problem. Don't say that. She just has to go home. She's got a life.' He picks up the plates, putting them in the dishwasher. He'd usually leave them on the counter, but he needs something to do while Bas is giving him a disapproving look.

'Have you asked her to stay?'

'Don't be ridiculous! She's not staying. Like I said, she has a life outside of here.'

Bas slides his phone back into his pocket and leans against the counter. 'You are attracted to her.'

'Of course I am. Have you seen her!'

'You seem to get on well together.'

'Again, yes. What's your point?'

'You know what my point is. Why are you sending her away, when you want her, and she clearly wants you?'

'Yeah well that's my business. I don't stick my nose into your love life, so I'd appreciate you butting out.'

'I'm going to speak out when I see you making a mistake,' Bas says, clearly not getting the message. 'And this is a mistake.'

'Yeah well it's mine to make, so back off. Can you just drive her home? I would, but I'm grounded.' He makes a hasty escape, but Bas catches up with him just outside the kitchen.

'Why are you pushing her away?'

'Oh for fuck's sake Bas! Can you let it go! It's done okay. She'll head home and I'll be fine. No problem.'

'Except you're not fine. You like her, Shep.'

He tries to push by Bas, but he won't budge. 'Fine! You want me to ask about you and Ethan? Do you want me to poke into your private life and question you about it?'

Bas looks as if he's been struck. 'What?'

'Oh don't give me that innocent look. I've seen you when he's around. You go all alpha male. I know you're on his protection detail, but you weren't meant to go that far. How do you think Nix would react to you going all gooey eyes over Ethan?'

He knew he was pushing Bas's buttons, but he never thought he'd react the way he does. Bas doesn't ever react, tending to act in a calm and controlled way.

But there's nothing calm and controlled about the way he tackles Shep to the floor. The wind is knocked out of him, as his sensitive back strikes the tiled floor. He goes straight into fight mode, but in those few seconds it takes him to get there, Bas already has the advantage.

Shep wins on weight and height, but Bas is a lethal fucker when he's fighting. There's no way he's going to come out of this one unscathed. Thankfully, Court and Fallon come to his rescue, hauling the near feral Bas off him. Court holds Bas back, while Fallon helps Shep to his feet.

'What the hell is going on?' Court asks, his no-nonsense tone instantly calling an end to the fight.

Bas says something in Spanish that is no doubt less than complimentary. He really should learn some Spanish for times like this. 'A disagreement between friends. I have to go and bring Izzy home.'

Court looks at each of them before finally nodding. 'Go on.' He turns to Fallon. 'You see if this knucklehead has done any damage to himself. I'll check on Bastian.'

'Knucklehead?' he says once Court is out of earshot. 'Bas attacked me. If anyone's the knucklehead, it's him.'

She spins him around and pushes him back into the kitchen. 'Sit down and take off your shirt. Let's see how you're doing.'

He drops onto the nearest stool then pulls off his top. He hit a nerve with Bas. One he didn't mean to hit. Now his friend probably isn't talking to him, Izzy is leaving, and his back fucking hurts.

'Aren't you going to ask me what happened?'

Fallon gently prods his back. 'No. Don't care. You in pain at all?'

'A bit. Nothing too bad. He gave me a fair wallop against the ground.'

'A wallop you deserved,' she says, handing him his shirt.

'Hey! You weren't even there.'

'I was on my way to the kitchen. He asked why you're sending Izzy away and you retaliated by throwing Ethan's name in the mix. How did you expect him to react?'

'You picked up on something between them too?'

She shrugs, leaning against the counter in front of him. 'None of my business. It was a low blow taking it in that direction. He's just looking out for you.'

'I don't need looking out for. I'm a big boy.'

'You're a stubborn ass who can't see what's in front of him. But that's what we do. It's what we all do. We're so used to doing it alone, we can't drop our emotional walls and let someone in. Twenty years down the line we're going to be a bunch of miserable, lonely fighters.'

She walks away without adding anything else to her cryptic comment. What the fuck is wrong with everyone at the moment? There are too many hormones and emotions flying around the place.

IZZY

The drive from the compound to her apartment takes place in a strangely comfortable silence. She doesn't know anything about Shep's friend, but he seems to be in his head as much as she is in hers.

Bastian is breathtaking in every way. She wouldn't usually describe a man as beautiful, but it applies to Bastian. Something about him isn't quite right though. There's something dark under the surface that she can't quite put her finger on. Something that will stop her from being fully at ease around him.

But she doesn't want to feel at ease right now. She's angry, upset, and confused about Shep. Why did he kiss her both times? Why did he ask her out for dinner? Why did he come back to the club repeatedly to see her?

She thought there was something between them. Not love in any way, but an attraction at the least. But, when she kissed him and he pulled back, it was the worst thing she's experienced. The first time she decides to make a move and she gets rejected.

Not only rejected but shown the door.

It seems he'd prefer to have sex with the women at the club, than even consider being with her. What's wrong with her? Why chase her, only to reject her? Why be so cruel?

'It's not you.'

Izzy looks over at Bastian. 'Excuse me?'

'You look confused. I presume you're trying to figure out why he told you to leave?'

'I didn't realise I was that transparent. So, do you have any words of wisdom?'

'Probably not. Shep is complicated. He jokes, pretends he is not taking things seriously, but it's a mask. He's afraid of letting anyone close to him, so he pushes people away.'

'Even you?'

'Yes. I've known him for years, but I don't truly *know* him. I believe he sees talking about feelings as a weakness. Shep needs to be strong and dependable. Anything that takes away from that is pushed aside.'

'Yeah well, I've got the message loud and clear. I just wish I knew why. It's driving me crazy. One minute he's after me, then the next he's backing away. I know he likes me, or at least I'm mostly sure he does. But the one time I try to make the first move, he pushes me away.'

Bas smiles at her. 'I can tell you care about him.'

'He's an irritating, extremely stubborn vampire, but yes. I care about him a lot. If he doesn't feel the same I'll just have to accept that. But what's with the mixed signals?' she asks, more to herself than to Bas.

Bas stays silent for a moment, before speaking again. 'May I ask you a personal question?'

'Of course.'

'You say he pushed you away when you tried to kiss him. You haven't taken things further with him?'

'You mean sleep with him?'

'I apologise. It's none of my business.'

'No Bastian, it's fine. We've kissed twice. Three times, if you include my failed attempt.'

Bas stares at her for a long minute, confusion all over his face. 'You've kissed? Nothing more?'

'No. Why do you look surprised?'

'I thought he would have been more intimate with you considering...'

He stops talking, and she knows he's trying to spare her feelings.

'It's okay. I met him at a club where he goes for sex. He's slept with countless women there. And it's not like I want to necessarily be added to that particular list. He's nice, friendly, talks to me, brings me back here for what? Does he want a new pal? Well I'm sorry. I want more. Is that so wrong?'

She blows out a breath, trying to compose herself. 'You're quiet.'

Bas smiles over at her. 'I was waiting to make sure you had let it all out.'

She laughs, feeling a little better for the outburst. 'I'm sorry. That all came out at once.'

'Venting is healthy. Did you ask him why he is treating you differently?'

'Of course I did. And now you're driving me home.'

'Ah. Not a helpful answer.'

'No' she agrees. She waves her hands in the air admitting defeat. 'What does it matter either way? He's made it clear how he feels. Maybe it's for the best. After seeing what you do, I'd probably just be worried sick about him going out to fight. I'd drive him crazy, no doubt.'

Bas glances over at her. 'You would worry?'

'Of course I would! Wouldn't you if someone you care about is putting their life in danger like that? I know you all train hard, but there are no certainties in life. One wrong step, one lucky shot, and you're not coming home.'

He nods silently, his attention on the road ahead of him.

'It still would have been nice if he had given me the option. Let me make my own mind up. But I guess he's done that for the both of us.'

'Perhaps he is just trying to keep you safe?'

'Maybe. It doesn't matter if he had the best intentions at heart. It still sucks.'

Bastian doesn't reply, so she turns to look out the window. She'd prefer he didn't see her crying anyway. The more she speaks of Shep, the harder it is to keep the tears at bay.

She knows he likes her. Unless he's a damn good actor, she can see it in his eyes. But something is holding him back. Something is keeping him from admitting his feelings.

Something he's not going to tell her no matter how badly she wants him to.

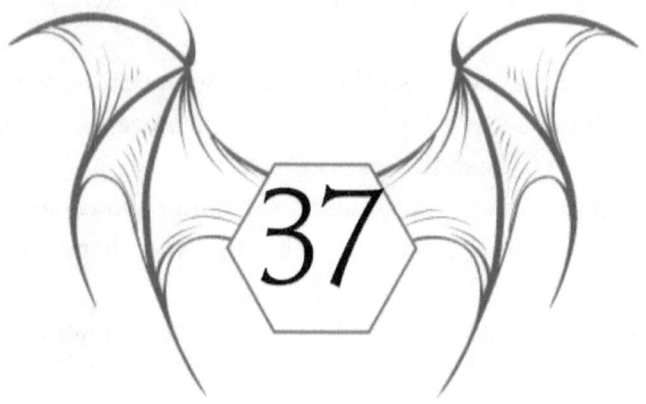

BASTiAN

As he steps off the elevator, the receptionist manning the desk in the main lobby jumps to her feet, a huge smile on her face. 'Bastian! So nice to see you.'

Amber has worked for Ethan's company for years. She's nice enough but seems to have a bit of a Blackjack groupie thing going on. Any time one of the team steps off the elevator she's all smiles and fluttering eyelashes.

Well, as long as it's a male team member. Nix and Fallon don't get on with her. He has no idea about Willow, but then, she gets on with everyone.

'Hello Amber. I'm here to see Ethan.'

'He's in his office. I'll walk you down.'

'It's fine, thank you. I don't want to take you from your work.'

'It's no trouble, really.'

'I insist.' He pushes through the double doors into the main office area before she can race after him. The attention carries on as he walks along the central corridor, passing rows of offices. The Blackjack support staff work from this level, so everyone here knows who he is.

The attention is mainly from the female workers. He knows he doesn't fit the vampire warrior stereotype, but that works to his advantage in the field. He looks younger than his years, softer and less of a threat than he is.

He's been told, with his looks, he's more suited to a career on a catwalk or magazine cover. But his arms and hands tell a vastly different story. His tattoos tell of a life spent stealing and killing. Looks mean nothing.

There's a reason he was put on protection detail for Ethan. He will kill without hesitation or remorse. It's what he excels at.

And for Ethan he would do so much more.

One of the women he passes calls his name, but he doesn't stop. He only answers to one person in this building. No one else is on his radar in the slightest. Maybe they'd all leave him alone if they knew he was fucking their boss.

That he was in love with their boss.

With his boss.

Bas has always taken his job seriously. From the day he was brought into the team, he's never disobeyed an order, or given less than his all every time he fought.

It's not against the rules to be in a relationship, no matter what type, with a member of the team. Nix and Court are in love, and they still manage to run the team as efficiently as they did when they were apart.

But this is Ethan.

And he wouldn't even call what they have a relationship. He wants it to be, but they agreed it would remain between them. Secret.

Hidden.

As much as Bas wishes it could be otherwise.

He's just delaying the inevitable. That's all he's been doing for the last few weeks. Denying that this has to happen. Trying to find some way, however minute, of being in Ethan's life as anything other than a meaningless fuck.

He hopes he's more than that, but he's not sure. All he is sure of is that he needs to do this. After speaking with Izzy, he realised how selfish he's been the last few months. Ethan hates ordering him into dangerous situations. Does he possibly worry about him too? Maybe. He's not sure, but if there's even the smallest chance he does, Bas needs to remedy it immediately.

He gets to Ethan's door and knocks once before entering. As soon as he sets eyes on Ethan, the possessiveness he feels kicks in. Ethan is his. His to protect. His to fuck. His to love.

He's never labelled himself as one of the alpha male types. Didn't give much thought to it in the slightest. Not until he met Ethan.

He clenches his fists firmly, the pain grounding him again. He can't let those thoughts enter his mind right now. Once he's alone again, he can think about Ethan. Wish things could have been different. Wish he'd been born into a bloodline that would allow him a future with Ethan. Wish he wasn't so in love with him. Wish he didn't have to walk away to save him.

Ethan's brilliant blue eyes lift from his laptop and lock onto him. 'You're early,' he says, smiling at him. When Bas doesn't return his smile, Ethan's face turns serious. 'Is something wrong?'

Bas pushes off the door and walks towards Ethan. He stops at the couch, propping himself up on the back of it. If he goes any closer to Ethan, he's going to kiss him.

'I have to speak to you.'

Ethan walks around his desk and sits on the edge of it, facing him. 'Is everything all right?'

'I believe we have run our course.' The words are forced out,

282

leaving a sour taste in his mouth. But it's Ethan's face that hits him like a punch to his gut.

'I see.'

He needs to push on. Give him no reason to doubt this is the end. 'You are a distraction. One that is beginning to interfere with my job. We agreed the team comes first.'

'I see,' he repeats. 'That is what we agreed. I apologise for distracting you. It was never my intention. I have to admit I will be sorry to end this.'

'As will I, but it is time to move on with our lives. This was never more than sex. It could never be more than that.'

Ethan nods, his face pale as he straightens his tie. 'Yes. Of course.'

Bastian is dying inside, a piece of his heart crumbling as he watches Ethan struggle to accept what he's saying. 'I suggest you ask Nix to assign Fallon to your detail. It wouldn't be right if I continued in that role. She's a formidable fighter. You'll be safe with her.'

'Yes. Thank you. I'll speak to Nix. So, that's that then.'

Bas nods. 'I'll leave you to your work.'

He opens the door, fighting to remain composed as he steps into the corridor. 'Bastian!'

Bas turns to look at Ethan over his shoulder. Neither of them says anything, but Bas can see the pain in Ethan's eyes. He returns it with nothing. He is an expert at hiding his emotions. Putting a mask in place to protect himself. It's that cold, emotionless version Ethan is met with. He hides his pain. Hides the fact he desperately wants to hold Ethan. Hides his love.

Ethan licks his lips, the lack of response from Bas pushing the point home. It's done. It meant nothing. Just sex.

'Can you please close the door.'

Bas does as he's told, blocking Ethan from view. He strides through the office, his expression, or the cloud of pain hanging over him, dissuading anyone from interacting with him. He rides the elevator to the garage, climbs on his Harley, and accelerates away from Ethan.

Ten minutes later he pulls into an empty car park outside the city and kills the engine. Only then does he allow his emotions out again. Only then does he shout, scream, roar, cry.

He doubles over the front of his bike, as the pain threatens to tear him in two. It was the right thing to do. The only thing to do. Ethan is vital to the success of the Blackjacks. Without him, there is no team.

Long term, Ethan will find happiness with a well-bred male. Probably a well-bred female. He doubts Ethan's family will allow him to be his true self. It's not what the old families would approve of.

Whoever he ends up with, Bas isn't even at the bottom of the list. With his past, he doubts Ethan would even be willing to give him a chance.

He pulls off his gloves, making a fist, stretching the tattoo on the back of his hand. It's only a matter of time before someone figures out what the marks mean. Rhain knows. Eventually Ethan will find out. Once that happened he would have lost him either way. It's better to have this pain now on his terms.

SHEP

He's tired, fucked off, and couldn't be less interested in standing around looking at a building. Being dragged from his misery to go to Rhain's house isn't improving his mood. It took a lot of digging, but the team Ethan has working for them had worked their magic and found the house Rhain lives in out of the ten or so he owns. Being a villain sure pays well.

Shep rolls his shoulders. He's twitchy as fuck, but so glad Nix let him out to play with the others. His wings have been part of his life for a week and, so far, haven't given him any problems, so hopefully

284

this is the end of his grounding. If she had told him to sit this one out, he's sure he would have put on a highly unmacho display of begging.

He needed to get out. Needed a distraction from his shitshow of a life. The last week had crawled by. He'd trained, worked on strengthening his weak wings, was poked and prodded by Fletch countless times, and slept the rest of the time.

Shep never really gave much thought to Rhain. He knew the guy was a dick. Torturing and experimenting on vampires put him permanently in the dick zone. But he never thought about what the ancient vampire was like behind all the evil villain stuff.

Did he have a girlfriend? A wife? A boyfriend? Kids?

As he looks at the charred remains of what was once a stunning mansion, he hopes to fuck the guy lived alone.

He glances over at Bas, but his friend is staring at the building, completely ignoring him. They hadn't kissed and made up yet. He'd watched Bas drive away from the compound with Izzy and had not spoken since.

'Shep? Shep! Hey! Are you with us?'

He blinks then looks around, seeing each of the team staring strangely at him. 'What?'

'I've been talking to you for a minute. Are you all right?'

'Yep. All good Boss. What's up?'

'You mean apart from Rhain's house in a pile of ash in front of us?'

'Yeah. That. I did notice.'

'Well that's something,' Nix replies with a slight smile. 'Can you see if you can sense anything that happened here?'

It was only a matter of time before she was going to ask him to use his gift. He hasn't tried since he got his wings. Probably should have, considering it's what he does, but he was doing the whole denial thing again. Might just have bit him in the ass.

He closes his eyes, trying to block out all the anxious looks he's getting from the team, and concentrates on just breathing. Easier said than done at the moment. He feels like he's always on the brink of a panic attack.

It takes a little longer than usual, but he nearly shouts out when it works.

'Shep? Why are you smiling?'

'Nothing Boss. Give me a minute.' He sorts through the jumble of images, trying to piece them together into something resembling a timeline of sorts. 'He's alive. Rhain was taken by force. He was restrained and put into a car.'

He can't usually pick up on emotions when he sees what happened, but it's hard to miss Rhain's. 'He was fucking livid. Not scared though. Fucker is tough. They made him watch as they razed his house to the ground.'

He opens his eyes, swaying slightly when he's thrown back into the present.

'I think my wings amplified that. His emotions came through clearly.'

'That could come in useful,' Nix says. 'Do you know who took Rhain?'

'I didn't recognise them, but I think it was The Order.'

'Damn it!' The outburst from Ethan gets everyone's attention. 'This is our fault! He was taken because he was helping us.'

'Don't jump to conclusions Ethan,' Nix says. 'He worked with some questionable people. We don't know why he was taken.'

Ethan storms over to her, gesturing wildly at the ruined house. 'Oh come on Nix! This is on us.'

'It's on him!' Court says. 'Rhain isn't an idiot. He knew what he was doing when he contacted you. He knew the risk and he still went ahead. It could also be down to the fact he works for The Order. I get the impression they're not keen on just letting people walk away.'

Nix holds up her hand, silencing both Ethan and Court. 'We're out in the open here. There's nothing more we can do. Back to the compound.'

Shep follows after the rest of the team, his thoughts on Izzy instead of what he just saw. He misses her so much.

She's not the only one he misses. He looks over at Bas. He misses his friend. He shouldn't have said what he did to him, but he's not in the right frame of mind to even go there with him. Knowing his luck, he'll just make things so much worse.

Seems he's all out of luck though. As they pile into the cars, Shep finds himself alone with Bastian. Fuckers must have doubled up to make sure it played out like that.

With the other cars already on the road, he has no choice but to climb into the passenger seat next to Bas. Bas glances at him before starting the engine. After five minutes the silence is killing him. 'I'm sorry okay.'

Bas snorts as he shakes his head.

'What the fuck did that mean?'

'*I'm sorry okay?* Is that the best you can do?'

'We're kind of in the car, so kissing your fucking feet, as I beg for forgiveness isn't an option.' Bas slams his foot on the brake, throwing Shep forward in his seat. 'What the fuck Bas!'

His friend turns around, hitting him with a steely glare. 'Is everything a joke to you?'

'What? No. Of course not.'

'Bullshit!'

He's never seen Bas so pissed off before. 'I am sorry, okay! I mean that. I shouldn't have said what I did. I was angry and pissed off and you got the brunt of it.'

Bas looks over at him, his eyes still glowing. 'I ended things with Ethan.'

He wasn't expecting Bas to admit there was something between himself and Ethan. He suspected it. He's sure most of the team suspected it. But as for ending things, that's the bit that confuses him. 'Why?'

'Why do you think? I'm a thief, Shep. No bloodline. No legacy. Nothing but an extensive list of crimes to my name. He's...' Bas rubs his gloved hand over his face. 'He's better. So much better.'

'But I don't get it. Did he not feel the same?'

Bas looks out the window. Shep could be wrong, but he swears that Bas is crying. 'We had a deal. Blackjacks first. He was struggling to send me out on missions. I was interfering with the running of the team. I stopped interfering.'

'I'm sorry Bas. I should never have mentioned it when I was fighting with you. It was a low blow.'

Bas wipes his face again, before looking over at him. 'Yeah Shep. It was. You're my friend, but if you ever use him to push my buttons again, I *will* kill you.'

Shep doesn't doubt his words for one second. 'Got you.'

'Good. I'm used to having you in my life. It would be a shame to have you kill you at this stage. Now, what about Izzy?'

'What about her?'

'There was no future for myself and Ethan. There can be for you and Izzy.'

'No. I've done things Bas. Things she can't be involved in.'

'We've all done things Shep. Each one of us have. Ethan and I aren't the same as you and Izzy. She's new to our world. No connections. No repercussions. You *can* be with her.'

'You and I are more alike than you think Bas. She's so much better than me,' he says, repeating Bastian's words. 'I can't bring her into my life. I barely have a grasp on it myself. The best place for her is far away from me.'

'I understand that all too well.'

Shep hates that his friend is as miserable as he is. But there's nothing he can do about it as much as he wants to. 'Are we good?'

'Yeah,' Bas says. 'We're good.'

'Thanks. I kind of missed having you around.'

'And I missed kicking your ass in training.'

'Whatever.' Shep pulls out his phone when it buzzes. He looks at the name on the screen and curses.

'What is it?'

'Nothing. Just some personal stuff I need to take care of. How about we head home?'

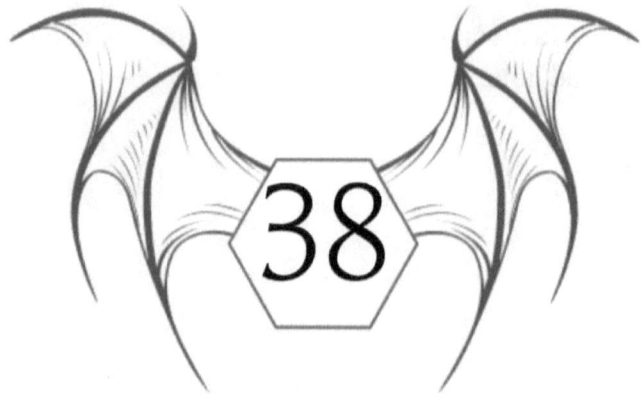

SHEP

The impressive Bentley comes to a stop beside him and the window lowers. Shep looks over at his mother, slightly surprised she managed to drive herself here. He was fully expecting a chauffeur. 'Please get in.'

His initial reaction is to tell her where to go, but if he's to get her off his back once and for all, he probably should hear her out. He swings his leg over the saddle of his bike, walks over to the car, then slides into the plush leather seat next to his mother.

'Thank you for meeting with—'

'Just say what you have to say so I can go.'

Lilith nods and takes an envelope from beside her. She holds it in her hands, but doesn't make a move to hand it over, or open it.

'Willow tells me you are unwell.'

'Fuck! I told her to keep you out of my life.'

'She was worried about you, Shepherd. You cannot fault her for that.'

'What the hell is this? Concerned mother hour? Stay out of my life!'

'I fear I cannot do that.'

'What the hell are you talking about?'

'When you were... taken to clear my debt...'

A hard knot forms in Shep's stomach. 'You mean when you handed me over to clear your debt?'

'I was not honest with you.'

'About what?'

Lilith hands Shep the envelope. He opens it and unfolds the document. He needs to read it twice before the words begin to sink in. When they do, his fangs lengthen, and he launches at his mother. He wraps his hands around her neck and growls. 'You sold me to them! Forever!'

'I had no... choice...'

'No choice? I was your son and you sold me off to pay your debt!'

'Please... Shepherd...' Shep squeezes his hand tighter, a cold calm taking over as he watches his mother struggle for breath. 'Shepherd...'

He shoves his mother back against the expensive seat. 'Fuck!'

He lets go and pushes the door open, nearly taking it off its hinges. Shep leans against the railing overlooking the valley below, and squeezes his eyes shut. Not for one second had he thought his mother could stoop any lower.

Abandoning him to her debtors was bad enough, but a minute part of him understood. If it was a toss up between himself and Willow, there's no question he would not have given himself to save her. But selling him like he was nothing more than a possession...

He growls as his mother joins him at the railing. 'Why didn't you tell me? Why keep it from me for all this time?'

'I should have told you, but I was weak.'

'So why now?'

'I thought it was over. I presumed they considered the matter closed and the contract satisfied. But I fear that is not the case. I have been contacted by someone I trust. He informs me they are looking for you.'

'Why? I was there for twelve years. I've got over seven hundred burns. The debt is settled.'

'They are not looking for the debt to be settled. That business is concluded.'

Shep snorts and turns towards her. 'That business is concluded? Did you really just say that? Selling your son to be used for sex is just business to you? Wow! Thanks Mom!'

She nods once. 'Forgive me. That was a bad choice of words.'

'You think?'

'Shepherd, they consider you their property. They want you back. Specifically, the wife of the man I sold you to, wants you back according to my contact.'

That scent of rosewater comes back to him at the mention of that woman. 'No! She's not getting me back!'

'I understand how you feel, but the contract is a legal document. My people are working on a way to undo it, but it is not looking promising.'

'You don't understand a fucking thing about my feelings, so spare me the false pity, or whatever the hell you're doing. I was chained to a bed and raped multiple times a day! Has that happened to you?'

She clears her throat, looking away from him. 'No.'

'Thought not. So don't you dare say you know fuck all about how I feel!'

'I apologise.'

'So what happens now? Do they expect me to pack my bags and happily head back to them?' When she doesn't immediately respond his stomach churns. 'Fuck! They do!'

'My informant has given me a message to pass on to you. You are to return to them.'

'Is that so?'

'Shepherd, they know about Willow. They know about your human friend, Isabella. They know everything. If you do not go with them... I do not want to think what they will do.'

He has to grip the railings to hold himself up when he hears that. The assholes who own him aren't just in the sex business. They also happen to run a group of thugs who are trained to put the pressure on, whenever they don't get their way. He can't have them looking at, or hurting, Willow or Izzy. He won't have them put at risk because of him.

'So I have to save the fucking day again? Lucky me!'

'There is one thing they do not know, however. They do not know that you are a Blackjack. This situation could be best suited to your friends and their particular expertise. Perhaps there is some way of circumventing the contract or, worst case, at least protecting you from these people?'

'So I hide for the rest of my life? Lock up Willow and Izzy to keep them safe?'

'I have no answers Shepherd. I wish I did.'

With nothing else to say, he stuffs the contract in his pocket, then climbs onto his bike.

'What are you going to do?'

'What the fuck do you think I'm going to do? I'm going to clean up after you, yet again.'

Starting with Willow and Izzy.

He knows Willow is on the training roster for the next few hours. She's safe in the compound with an army of trained fighters looking out for her. It's Izzy he's freaking out about. She's alone with no way to defend herself.

He tells his phone to call her, listening to the buzz through his helmet speakers as the call tries to connect. Nothing. He tries again, leaving a message this time. 'Hey Izzy. I know you don't want to talk to me right now, but you're in danger. You need to lock all your doors and windows. Stay put until I come and get you. Don't open the door to anyone. I'm on my way.'

He ends the call, kicking the bike up a gear. It should take twenty minutes to get to her from here. He just hopes it's fast enough.

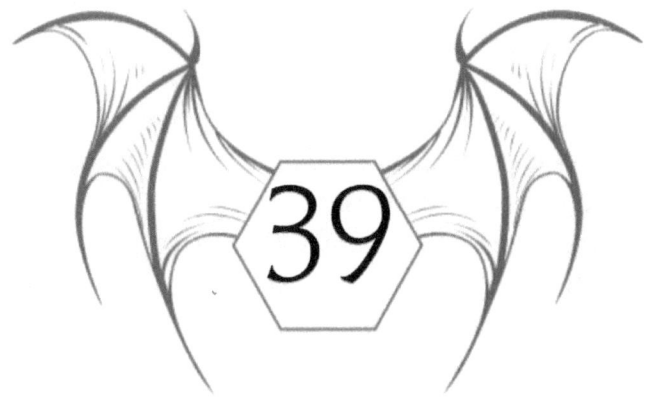

39

SHEP

Even before he gets to her street, he knows he's too late. His special ability kicks in without having to concentrate as he usually does. In his head he can hear her shouting, screaming, fighting to free herself. He can see her being loaded into a black van. He can hear the screeching of the tyres as it speeds away from her apartment.

Shep pulls up outside her house and climbs off his bike. Her door is open and, even though he knows it's empty, he pulls out his gun, holding it in front of him as he kicks it wide open.

Her cosy living room is a mess, the couch and coffee table overturned. She put up one hell of a fight. Not that it did her much good.

He walks into the kitchen, finding it empty, then checks the bedroom and bathroom. Nothing.

'Fuck!' Kicking the kitchen door only adds a new door to the other destruction in the flat. He's not usually someone who panics, but he's fucking close right now.

This is his fault. She was taken because of him. His fucking mother may have set all this in motion years ago, but he's the one that put Izzy in the firing line. He should have just stayed away. Should have thought about her, instead of keeping her in his life for selfish reasons.

His owners are sadistic bastards. He can't bear the thought of Izzy being anywhere near them for even a minute.

Then something catches his eye. There's a piece of paper tacked to the back of the kitchen door. He pulls it off and reads the note, his fangs dropping as the anger builds.

Shepherd,

I am willing to forgive you and welcome you back, but you only get one chance. Be at the following coordinates at midnight. To ensure you behave, I have taken your human friend. Your life for hers.

See you soon, my pet.

He scrunches the note in a ball then slams his fist against the wall. It's eight o'clock now. Four hours. As much as he doesn't want to involve the team, he'll need them to get Izzy back. His mistress has a horde of goons ready to kill on her command. He can't have Izzy getting caught in the crossfire.

Shep locks her front door, then climbs on his bike and speeds towards the compound.

He'll get her out. It doesn't matter what he has to do, he will make sure Izzy is as far from that bitch as possible.

Even if it means giving himself to keep her safe.

IZZY

Just breathe. Don't panic.

It doesn't matter how many times Izzy repeats this mantra to herself, panic is nipping at her heels. Not just panic, but fear too.

She wipes her face. Crying didn't help. Banging on the door didn't help. Screaming to be released didn't help.

She's checked the bedroom she's in numerous times since she woke up. The window isn't your average window. It's there to let light in, but with no openings, and glass that appears to be thicker than usual, she doubts she'd be able to break it. The small bathroom is windowless and the door into the bedroom is locked.

Until someone decides to let her out, she's trapped.

Until Shep gets her out, she's trapped.

He *will* come for her. Even through the mounting fear and panic, she knows that.

His message came in just as her flat was broken into, and she was taken, but she had heard it. He was on his way. As soon as he gets to her home, he'll know she was taken. Then he'll find her.

She looks at the door as a key rattles in the lock. A petite smartly dressed woman enters, with a beast of a man behind her. The deep plum suit she's wearing looks like silk, her hair is perfectly styled, as is her makeup. Everything about this woman speaks of wealth.

The woman stands at the end of the bed Izzy is sitting on and clasps her hands together. 'I must say I don't see the attraction.'

'Excuse me?'

'I suppose there is some sort of simple beauty there.'

'Did you take me just to insult me?'

The woman smiles at that. 'Ah. Now I see it. You're feisty. He always liked a bit of a fight.'

'He?'

'You know who I mean. Shepherd. I hear you and my *pet* have grown close of late. I have to say I'm not impressed by that. But I suppose I can't lay all the blame on you. Unless of course you knew he was mine. Did you?'

'Did I what? I have no idea what you're talking about.'

'I bought Shepherd many years ago. He belongs to me.' She takes a thick chain and padlock from the chair by the bed. 'He wore my crest around his neck for twelve years before the ungrateful bastard escaped. But that will be rectified soon enough. This will be locked around his neck yet again. Perhaps tighter this time. Perhaps this time I'll tattoo it to his skin so there's no doubt who owns him. Would you still have fucked him if he was wearing this chain?'

Bought him.

He belongs to me.

This is making less sense by the minute.

'Ah. He didn't tell you, did he?' The woman laughs loudly as she takes a seat at the end of the bed. 'Well, my dear human, the minor point he forgot to mention is that I legally purchased him a long time ago. I have the documentation to prove it.'

'You bought him?'

'Yes. In our world, a Prime can own a Hybrid. He's nothing but a mere mongrel, my *pet* to play with, to use, to rent out. And I want him back.'

'Want him back? I don't understand. What do I have to do with any of this?'

She shrugs as she picks some lint from her suit. 'Shepherd seems to be attracted to you for some reason. I took you so he will be more open to coming back to me. You for him.'

'No!'

'No? No what? You don't have a say in this my dear. You are simply a pawn. Nothing more. I will get my property back and you can go on your merry way.'

'I won't let you take him.'

The laugh is expected, and Izzy can't really blame her. What can she do to stop any of this from happening? 'He picked well. So tell me, I'm curious. Did you enjoy him?'

'What do you mean?'

'When you lay with him of course. I trained him well. He was worth nothing to us unless he could excel in the bedroom. This was his room. I had it prepared for his arrival. It was his home for the time he was with me.'

Izzy looks around the room in horror. When she first woke up she hadn't given the decoration or look of the room much thought. These four walls were where Shep was kept against his will.

'Do you like his piercings? They were my idea. One of my best. His price went up after that.'

'His price?'

'I charged for his time. You have no idea how much that vampire put in our pockets. Do his eyes still glow when he comes? I particularly enjoyed that trait of his. Of course, he only came when I allowed him to. As I said, I trained him well. And that dimple...' she groans to herself which turns Izzy's stomach.

'I have an idea,' the woman says, lifting a heavy chain from under the head of the bed. She wings it in her hand, the thick shackle moving back and forth like a pendulum of a clock. 'How about I let you use him one more time when I get him back? I'll have my man chain him down and gag him for you. Then you can play with him to your heart's content while Shepherd can do nothing to stop you. I won't even charge you for the pleasure.'

'You're disgusting.'

The smile falters. 'No. I'm a businesswoman who used one of her assets to give herself a comfortable life. You know, I'm not sure which I preferred more - when he fought against me and I had to chain him down, or when he just lay there broken and willing to please me. Which do you prefer?'

Izzy screams as she launches herself at the woman, slapping her hard on the cheek. Before she can make contact again, the huge bodyguard hauls her off, pinning her back against the wall.

The woman wipes her mouth, smiling nastily at the blood on her hand. 'My, my, my, aren't you a feisty one! Well suited to my Shepherd. It's just a pity he's mine!' She slaps Izzy so hard her teeth rattle in her jaw.

The woman grabs a handful of her hair, before throwing her onto the bed. 'If I didn't need you to get him back, I'd gut you right here and now. You stay on the bed you little bitch! Push my buttons again and I'll chain you down.'

She turns and leaves Izzy alone in the room, locking the door after her. Izzy doesn't move for a long time. She stays lying on the bed, her cheek throbbing, and angry tears on her cheeks.

She's terrified. Never been more scared in her entire life. But it's not just herself she's scared for. It's Shep. The thought of that woman getting her hands on him again turns her stomach. She has no idea what he went through or how long he was there, but that bitch is pure evil.

Izzy lies down, hugging her knees to her chest as she keeps her attention on the door.

She wants Shep to come. She needs him to, but at the same time she wants to keep him as far from here as possible.

It's not going to make a difference what she wants. Shep might still be a mystery on most fronts, but she does know one thing for sure. Whether she wants it or not, he'll hand himself over to save her.

SHEP

'Please sit down.'

He ignores Willow. He can't sit down. How the fuck can he sit down when they have Izzy! His sister should be glad he's not going fucking berserk.

The rest of the team take their seats, waiting for him to get things going. Attention never usually bothers him. He's fairly big, so gets a few looks whenever he's out. But the attention he's getting from the team surrounding the table isn't the kind he either wants or feels comfortable with. If anything, it's making him itchy.

'What's going on, Shep?' Nix asks, gently giving him a shove to get on with it.

'I'm just going to launch right in, so please let me get it out. Someone really fucking bad took Izzy. I need your help to get her back.' He slams the piece of paper onto the table. 'They want me to meet them here to do the exchange.'

'Hold on a second. Who took her? Who are they? Exchange what?' Nix asks, sitting upright in her seat.

'Just after I transitioned, my mother gave me to a group of vampires she owed money to. I was used to entertain visitors to their establishment. They kept me chained to a bed, and entitled vampires would pay for an hour with me. The female in charge, my mistress, locked a chain and her seal around my neck, then used me as her personal *pet* when I wasn't entertaining all the paying guests.'

He stands up and lifts his t-shirt. 'One burn for each hour of my time *entertaining*. Seven hundred and fifty-three hours before they gave up taking note. I have no idea how many unmarked hours I was used for, but it was a hell of a lot.'

He sits down again, keeping his eyes on the centre of the table. He can't do this if he makes eye contact with any of them, but he can hear their shocked gasps, and feel the tension, disbelief, and anger in the room.

'I made them a lot of money, so they decided to keep me for years after the debt was paid. And my dear mother couldn't be bothered coming back for me. I spent twelve years there. I kind of gave up fighting for a bit. Just accepted I'd be there until I died, not that they'd allow that to happen. She told me repeatedly that I was worth too much to them.

'But after a while they stopped watching me so closely, got complacent, and left the chains off from time to time, so I was finally able to escape. I hadn't heard anything from them since then, until my mother gave this to me a few hours ago.'

He pulls the contract out of his pocket and places it in the centre of the table. 'According to that I'm their property. My *mother* actually sold me to them! She just sold my life to those people. Anyway, they contacted her recently, and told her that I have to go back to them willingly, or they'll convince me by hurting people close to me. They said I had to get my affairs in order, but it seems they couldn't wait.

They took Izzy.'

He stops talking and the room falls silent. No one speaks for a good few minutes. While they're letting that truckload of information sink in, he targets the contract. He doesn't want to look at their faces. He's embarrassed. Downright humiliated.

Ethan finally breaks the silence from hell. 'I'll send a copy of the contract to my people.'

Shep nods but doesn't look at him. 'Sure. My loving mother already had her people look at it but can't do any harm I guess.'

Ethan opens the contract, reading through it himself, before taking a photograph of all the pages and sending it to his team back in his office building.

Fuck, he needs this meeting to end. He can't stand this attention.

'Why didn't you tell me? I thought we were close. Why wouldn't you tell me any of this?'

He forces himself to look over at Willow. The tears are pouring down her face. 'How could I tell you? I wanted to forget the whole fucking thing. It's all I've ever wanted. I've fought hard to move on from that, Wills. The last thing I wanted to do was talk to anyone about it. Please stop crying. It's okay.'

'Give me a break, Shep! How is this okay?'

'Fair enough. It's not okay, but it will be. This is a blip—'

'A blip! It's not a fucking blip Shep!' She grabs the contract and waves it in his face. 'This says you belong to someone. My brother is someone's property. Our mother sold you! Don't you dare brush this off like you usually do. It's serious!'

His announcement might have brought the room to silence, but Willow's outburst, coupled with the cursing, shocks everyone all over again. She's not usually so vocal, let alone angry.

'I was trying to protect you. That's all I've ever wanted to do.'

'And who protects you Shep?'

He has no answer for that. He protects her and his teammates. It's what he does. He's never thought about it the other way around.

'You should have said something. I've been pushing you for years to put things right with our mother. I thought it was just a stupid male pride thing with you.

'I would never have put you in that situation if I knew the truth! Not for one minute, because you're my big brother and I love you. All I want to do is protect you. It's all I've ever wanted to do.'

In that moment, he realises his little sister is stronger than he's given her credit for. He's never known her to be so sure of herself, so confident and strong. And he couldn't be prouder.

He reaches across and takes her hand. 'Thank you. I love you too. I'm sorry I kept this from you. I did it for the right reasons. Please believe me.'

Willow nods and wipes her face. 'What can we do, Nix? There has to be something.'

'There is something. Us! We'll get Izzy back and also stop anyone from taking you, Shep. I swear. Ethan? Find out everything you can about this female in charge. How many men she has. What sort of resistance we'll be facing. I don't want us to go in there blind.'

'You're not going in at all.'

The silence that follows his statement keeps going for nearly a minute, until Nix breaks it. 'I'm sorry?'

'I didn't tell you all that so you can come up with a plan to get her out. I'm going to do that. I only need you to make sure she's safe once I make the exchange.'

'What exchange?' Willow asks.

'I was with these people for over a decade. I know them. I know what they're capable of. There is no fucking way I'm letting Izzy stay there a second longer than she has to. They want me, they'll get me.'

'What! Are you serious?'

'Yes Bas, I'm fucking serious. This isn't up for discussion. It's happening. I'll go to the meeting place, hand myself over, and get Izzy out of there.'

'And we just what? Walk away?' Willow says, the anger in her voice taking him by surprise.

'Yeah actually. That's exactly what you're going to do.'

'No fucking way!' Dav says surprising Shep. He's usually the strong silent type at meetings. 'This isn't happening.'

'I second Dav,' Bas says, his gloved fists clenched tightly on the table. 'We go in as one and get her out. We don't trade.'

Fallon nods in agreement. 'You must be out of your fucking mind if you think we're going to let you do this.'

Nix holds up her hand, silencing the arguments that are flying around the table. 'Enough!' She waits until they all fall silent before she talks. 'Shep. I get what you're saying. I really do, but you can't expect us to let you do this and not fight back. We can't do that.'

'You have to, Nix. I'm not fucking around here. Send someone with me to bring Izzy home. That's fine. But everyone else stays here. I only told you all this so I could make sure Izzy was safe after the exchange. I need you to bring her back here, away from that place. If you want to figure out a way to destroy that fucking contract, go for it. But the exchange has to happen my way.'

He looks around the table, willing his friends to back him on this. Willow is crying. Fallon and Dav are downright furious. Court and Nix are having one of their silent conversations. But it's Bas that worries him the most. His eyes are hard and cold, his fists still clenched in a death grip on the tabletop. He looks up at Shep and he swears he can see tears in his friend's eyes. Bas holds his gaze for a few seconds before growling and looking away.

He'll do what Nix says, Bas always does. But he's far from being on board with any of this.

That awkward silence drags on, but this time Nix doesn't leave him waiting too long. 'Fine.'

'Nix!' Willow says, pushing upright in the chair. 'You can't let him do this!'

'I don't have a choice,' she responds. 'He's right. These people don't sound like ones you mess with. Izzy is human. She's in danger every moment she's there. But I want you to understand something Shep. We *will* come for you. Don't doubt that for one single minute. This is far from over. No member of my team, no friend, will ever have an owner.'

He's struck silent by her words. 'There was me thinking I'm nothing more than a pain in your butt.'

'Oh, you are,' she says with a smile. 'But more than that, you're family. We will fix this.'

'Thanks Boss. I mean that.'

'Good. Right, so you'll be taking two of us with you to the exchange. For Izzy's protection,' she continues quickly before he can argue. 'They'll bring her back to the compound where she can stay. We can protect her here.'

'I appreciate that.'

'Fallon and Bas? You're going with him.'

Willow shakes her head. 'I'm going Nix.'

'No, you're not,' Nix says, shutting her down immediately, which Shep is grateful for. He can say no to Willow until he's blue in the face with no luck, but maybe she'll listen to Nix.

'Nix!'

'I said no! There is no way you can protect yourself, your teammate, and Izzy when you're emotional. You have to stay here.'

Willow isn't in the slightest bit pleased by that order, but she doesn't argue her point. No doubt he'll get it from her once this meeting is done.

'When do you want to go?'

'ASAP,' Shep replies. 'Like I said, I don't want her there for even a second longer than necessary, and they said exchange would be at midnight.'

'Okay. Fallon and Bas, be ready in ten. Bring Izzy back here in one piece.'

Both of them nod, but neither voice a reply. They don't know what to say. Shep decides to stop wasting time and calls an end to the meeting. He gets up then walks over to the door. 'Please take care of Izzy.'

'Of course,' Nix says. 'See you soon, Shep.'

He hurries from the room before anyone gets all emotional with him. It's hard enough as it is, without bringing all their obvious emotion to the party.

'Shep! Hey! Please stop walking. We need to talk.'

Looks like his plan to escape didn't work out. 'No Wills, we don't. The only thing we need to do is to get Izzy back.'

He reaches his bedroom, opens his wardrobe, then locks his guns in the safe. The first thing he'll be told to do is disarm. There's no way those fuckers are getting his guns. Not happening.

'Shep! Stop and talk to me.'

'I don't have time for this Wills.'

'I'm going. You'll need all the help you can get.'

He slams his gun safe closed. 'No! I need you away from this. Away from that bitch. Do you hear me! I can't have her taking another person from my life. I won't let her take you too.'

She's crying, but he doesn't let it get to him. He's too angry, too worried to let it affect him. 'Shep. Please... I'm scared okay. All this is too much. I need—'

'Not now Willow!' He hates shouting at her, but he can't handle any of this right now. The thought of Izzy even spending an hour with his mistress makes him sick. He can't bear it. It's driving him crazy.

'I can't keep you safe out there. Do you not get that! It doesn't matter what I do, how hard I fight, how much I train. I can't protect you. It doesn't matter how good I am at what I do, nothing I do will ever make this better, will ever erase all that shit from my past.

'Izzy is in trouble because of me. If you go out there, I'll just be putting you in danger too. I need you to stay here.'

She tries to hold him back, but he pushes her towards the door. 'Shep! Stop please.'

'Just go, Wills. Please.'

He shuts the door, locking it so she can't burst in again. He's not going to put anyone else in danger. It's not happening.

If this bitch wants him, she can have him.

SHEP

'We're here.'

Bastian's statement brings Shep out of his daze, throwing him back into a reality he wants to run from as fast as he can. He must have been really deep in his head. The drive was going to take about ninety minutes. He doesn't remember any moment of the entire journey.

'Ten men,' Fallon says from the backseat. 'All armed.'

Shep convinces himself to look out the window, seeing his welcoming party lined up in the clearing a few metres in front of the car. Saying they're armed is an understatement. They're set to go to war. Or to meet resistance.

Then the back door of the black BMW is opened by one of the men and a petite woman steps out.

Her.

His owner's blond hair is tied in a tight bun, her makeup perfect, her clothes expensive. If you met her on the street you wouldn't have the first clue how dangerous, how downright cruel she is.

'That her?' Bas asks.

He nods, his voice suddenly gone. This is what she does to him. Scares him. Terrifies him if he's being honest. And he hates that. He fought long and hard to be tough and strong. Now it's all gone. It's like everything he worked for has been for nothing.

'What do you want to do now?' Fallon asks.

What he wants to do is get out of the car, all guns blazing, grab Izzy, kill his bitch of a mistress, and go home. 'Are you not going to try and convince me to rethink my plan?'

'There's no point. I know you well enough to know that much.'

Bas is right. He's made up his mind. This is going to play out the way he planned.

But first he has to get out of the car, walk over there, take Izzy's place, and...

He doesn't want to think about the after part. If he does, he won't get out of the car.

'As soon as they hand over Izzy, you get the fuck out of here. I mean it Bas. Don't take any chances with her. I want your word.'

Bas pauses, then nods. 'You know I don't want to leave without you, but you have my word.'

'Right then. Better get this over with. Catch you later.'

Before they can respond, he gets out of the car and walks around to the bonnet, stopping in front of the headlight, casting a long shadow over the ground.

'Shepherd. Aren't you a sight for sore eyes.'

Her voice isn't threatening in any way, but it makes him want to vomit. 'Where is she?'

Behind him, he can hear Bas and Fallon getting out of the car. They're both heavily armed. Out of all the Blackjacks, they're the two who would go to the local shop loaded with knives and guns.

'Why the friends Shepherd? Don't you trust me?'

'I'm just making sure she gets home in one piece.'

'I'll take that as a no. No matter. I have time to rectify that. Make sure we both know where we stand. Bring her!'

On her shouted command, one of her goons opens the other back door and drags Izzy out. She's pale and visibly shaken but seems to be in one piece. 'Are you okay?'

She nods. 'You?'

His mistress cuts off any further conversation by gesturing to the male standing beside Izzy. He clamps his hand over her mouth as he pins her against him.

'You know the deal Shepherd.'

'I'm not going anywhere until you let her go. Once she's with my friends, I'll go with you.'

She considers that for a moment, before smiling and reaching into her handbag. She takes out a pouch and throws it towards him. It lands at his feet with a clatter.

'Put that on, then I'll do as you ask.'

He picks it up and takes the chain and padlock from inside. It's not the one he wore for twelve years. He managed to cut that one off after he escaped. This chain is new and shiny, but still as thick and heavy as the old one. The padlock is just as heavy, her family seal stamped on both sides.

Behind him Bas growls. He tries to put him at ease by giving him a weak smile, but Bas isn't buying it. Why would he? As soon as he locks that chain in place, his life is over.

'Don't make me wait Shepherd. I'd hate to have to hurry things along by injuring your weak human friend.'

He keeps his eyes on the ground in front of him as he wraps the chain around his neck, fastening it with her padlock. As soon as the lock clicks into place, he feels a bit of himself being locked away with it. More than just his freedom. More than years of his life. The strong, fearless, highly trained Blackjack disappears.

'Please let her go now.'

He's even begging now, and it's been less than a minute with the damn thing on him.

She gestures to her man who releases Izzy, pushing her towards Shep. He meets her halfway but doesn't hug her as much as he wants to. It would just piss off his mistress.

'What are you doing?' she asks, the anger clear in her voice.

'I need you to go with Bas and Fallon. They'll take you to the compound. You'll be safe there.'

'What about you? I'm not leaving you here with that bitch! She told me what she did to you. She bragged to me about it.'

'Fuck! I'm sorry. You should never have been dragged into this.'

'I'm fine. It's you I'm worried about. You can't possibly go back there. You need to fight!'

'Shepherd! Over here now!'

Izzy glares over her shoulder at his mistress, before looking back at him. 'Get in the car with us and come home. You don't have to go with her.'

'I do. She owns me Izzy. Take her,' he says to Bas and Fallon. He can't bear to be near her with this thing around his neck. Izzy shouts out and puts up a struggle when Bas and Fallon pull her away from him. She continues to call his name, begging, pleading with him not to do this.

Without looking back, Shep walks over to his mistress, stopping in front of her. He turns his head away from her touch when she drags her long fingernails down the side of his face. 'Welcome home my pet. Now, remove your clothes. You may leave your underwear on.'

'Please mistress. Not in front of my friends. I beg you.'

'Refuse me again and I will stand you naked in front of your friends.'

He knows she would. She likes to humiliate him. Shep quickly gets undressed, trying to forget that his friends and Izzy are watching this. He can hear Izzy sobbing behind him, as he dumps his clothes in a pile on the ground.

When he's just wearing his boxers, she grabs him by his chain, pulling him closer. 'The next time this comes off is with your head.'

'Yes ma'am.'

'Get in the car.'

He can't bring himself to look back at them. The humiliation is too much already without seeing their reaction to that fucking shit show.

As he climbs into the car, he can still hear Izzy screaming his name, and calling his mistress a colourful collection of names. Even throwing a few at Bas and Fallon when they won't let her go.

He couldn't be prouder of her and her defiance.

'Take us home.'

He shuts off his mind as she settles in beside him and the car moves away. He'll see Izzy again. He knows he will.

He just needs to survive. He did twelve years. He can last as long as it takes for Ethan and Nix to figure out a way to get around his contract.

If they can figure out a way to get around it. He's got to hang on to that hope. It's all he has left.

IZZY

'Here you go. Be careful. It's hot.'

Izzy takes the mug of cocoa from Willow, clasping it in her hands, trying to use it to warm herself. She can't stop shaking. It could be the cold. But it's more than likely anger.

She stares ahead of her, watching the flames in the fireplace dance in front of her. The living room is empty apart from herself and Willow. The rest of the team are working to find a way to get Shep back.

There's nothing she can do to help. Nothing except sit here and wait. Izzy isn't sure why Willow is here instead of with the rest of the team.

But one glance at Shep's sister and she knows why.

Her face is pale and streaked with tears. Izzy knows she looks the exact same.

'How good are the Blackjacks?' she asks, disturbing the silence. 'Will you be able to find a way to get Shep back?'

'Yes.' Willow answers without hesitation. 'We are that good. Ethan and his team are experts at what they do. If there's a loophole, a way to get around the contract, they *will* find it. Shep will be home in no time. I know it.'

'Did you know about his past?'

Willow shakes her head. 'I had no idea. He never said a thing.' She takes a sip of her drink, hugging the cup to her chest. 'He tried to hide the burn scars, but I saw them. I think we all did at one stage, but he never explained how he got them. I asked him about them a while ago.'

She laughs once. 'Big mistake. He was furious. It was like I'd accused him of doing something terrible. He told me to mind my own business and not to mention them again. So I didn't. I kept my nose out of his business. I knew there was something wrong, but I did nothing to help him.'

'There's nothing you could have done Willow. I probably have no right to say this as I barely know him, but he speaks so highly of you. You're his world Willow.' She passes Willow a tissue when she cries again. 'I'm sorry. I didn't mean to upset you.'

'It's not your fault. It's hers. My mother's. I feel like such an idiot. I've been pushing him to be nice to her. I thought he was being stubborn as usual. That they'd had some stupid tiff, and he just should forgive and forget. I had no idea it was anything as horrific as this.'

'Why would you? You weren't to know. He was trying to protect you. That's all he wanted. Just like he wanted to protect me. Now they have him again and...' She doesn't want to think about what he's going through.

'I'm not going to be able to sleep,' Willow says, wiping her face again. 'Would you maybe keep me company for a while? We could watch a movie. I just don't want to be on my own right now.'

Izzy takes the blanket from the back of the couch and drapes it over Willow, then picks up the remote from the coffee table, handing it to Willow so she can pick something to watch.

Being with Willow is helping her. She doesn't want to be alone either. Hearing from that evil, sadistic woman what she did to Shep, how she treated him for years, still leaves her stomach in knots. If she is given time alone to think, she knows her mind will spiral into darkness, to thoughts of Shep being raped over seven hundred times.

To that beautiful man being sold and hurt so badly by someone who should have given her life to protect him.

SHEP

He jerks awake when he's slapped on the side of his face. He looks up at his mistress's bodyguard, a huge fucker with a broken nose. A nose that Shep broke when he escaped the first time.

'I was so hoping you'd find your way back here again. I missed you.'

Shep swallows his smart-arse reply. It won't do anything to help. This dick gets off on hurting him. Always did. Whenever Shep had to be punished, his mistress would call on this guy to take care of it.

He was cruel for the fun of it, and that was before Shep had broken his nose.

Shep tries to stand tall, but he's been hanging by his wrists for hours. Maybe longer. He's exhausted, his arms and shoulders are killing him, and he's freezing cold. The first thing they did was cut off his underwear. It was all part of the humiliation.

'What? Nothing to say?'

'He's coming to terms with the fact he's back here with us again. Aren't you my pet?'

Shep bites the inside of his cheek as his mistress saunters into the room. It's either that, or he's going to scream in frustration.

She grabs his jaw, digging her painted fingernails into his flesh. 'How happy are you right now?' She shakes his head sharply when he doesn't respond. 'Answer me!'

'Very happy,' he grinds out through clenched teeth. 'Can't you tell?'

She laughs as she lets go of his jaw. 'There's the attitude! I was worried you might have calmed down over the years.'

He's all out of responses. His false bravado and over-confidence don't exist in this place. They never have. Here he's scared, alone, and under someone else's control.

As he does his best to lock down the whirlwind of emotions threatening to spill out, she walks around him, her hands exploring, rubbing, squeezing, caressing.

Her nails scrape along his new wing ridges, digging into the skin so hard it's like she's inside his back. 'I have no interest in seeing these abominations. You will not release them while in my house. If you do, I will have no choice but to fix straps around your torso, sealing them in. I've heard that can be excruciatingly painful.'

She slaps him when he doesn't respond. 'Yes ma'am.'

'You should be grateful I'm willing to take you back after being so horrifically disfigured.'

She walks around to face him again, her hand wrapping around his dick and squeezing hard. 'The wings are a compromise I'm willing to make. You are worth it.'

He knows full well she's talking to his dick, not him.

She lets him go, wiping her hand on a cloth her bodyguard passes to her. 'I want him cleaned thoroughly before I use him again. See to it, then hang him back up until he recovers.'

She blows him a kiss as she turns to leave the room. 'See you soon my pet.'

Shep turns his attention back to the bodyguard as he rummages in a cupboard under the small sink in the corner of the room. He fills a bucket with water, then puts on a pair of thick rubber gloves. The

317

bastard smiles at him as he pours nearly a full bottle of bleach into the bucket, then adds a bag of ice, mixing it well. Before he stands he grabs a wire scourer from a packet, dropping it into the bucket of bleach and ice.

The bodyguard reaches into the bucket, taking out the soaking wire scourer. 'Have to make sure every single inch of skin is nice and clean. Don't worry. It'll only hurt like fuck.'

He smiles as he roughly scrubs Shep's side, digging the scourer into his skin before splashing the freezing bleached water over the raw marks.

Shep bites back the hiss of pain. He doesn't want to give this fucker the pleasure of knowing how much it hurts.

The bodyguard glances down at Shep's groin before hitting him with a sadistic smile. 'I think it's time to hear you scream.'

IZZY

She barely got a wink of sleep last night. How could she possibly sleep while Shep was with that woman? Who knows what was being done to him, how he was being treated. It doesn't bear thinking about.

She'd wanted to sleep in his room, to be close to him while she was here, but Nix had put her in a guest room at the other side of the house.

It was too far away from him.

When Willow had called by the room at four in the morning, she was up, staring out the window, her mind going a hundred miles an hour.

Willow hadn't known the reason for the early meeting, but both women were hopeful the rest of the team had come up with a solution, some plan to get Shep back.

Feeling completely out of her depth and out of place, Izzy takes her lead from Willow, sitting in the seat next to her when Willow holds out the chair. Most of the team are already there, looking as tired and stressed as she is.

But Bastian is on a different level. It's not worry she sees in his face. It's pure anger. The intensity is actually quite terrifying.

Nix and Ethan finally arrive and take their seats. Without pausing for a breath, Ethan launches straight in.

'My people have been tearing into this disgusting contract and think we may have found a loophole.'

'That's amazing!' Willow says excitedly.

'It's probably best you don't get too excited. The only thing my team and I can find to stop this right now, is for someone higher up the food chain, to now claim him from the bitch, and become his new legal *owner*.'

'Excuse me?' Izzy says. 'How is that a solution?'

'I know it sounds like more of the same, Izzy, but it's not as bad as it sounds.'

'Sounds pretty fucking bad if you ask me,' Bas mutters darkly.

'If you'll let me finish you'll see what I mean. We have a new owner in mind.'

Izzy follows Ethan's gaze down the table. One by one the Blackjacks follow suit, until Davyn raises his head and looks at them all. 'What? Why the fuck are you all looking at me like that?'

'Because you're a Prime Lord,' Ethan explains. 'You're of higher standing than his current owner.'

Bas shakes his head. 'Are you really suggesting that Shep lets Dav claim him as his fucking property? Is that really the best you can come up with?'

The curt comment drains the colour from Ethan's face. They're not on the best of terms. There's a tension between the two of them. She's sure of it, but right now Shep is her only concern.

'I second what he just said,' Davyn says.

'I apologise if that isn't what you all want to hear, but I'm out of options. The contract is legal. I can't bypass that, and I want to - believe me! If any of you want to see Shep here again, this is the only way.'

'We appreciate everything you and your team do,' Nix says, trying to calm the situation.

Davyn crosses his thick arms over his chest and frowns at Ethan. 'There's a flaw in your plan. I'm disgraced. I don't have a title anymore.'

'Well, technically you do. When you killed your father the house of Oldranson fell to you. Just because you didn't take your seat, doesn't mean it's not yours by right. You *are* a lord, Dav. Shep's owners, for want of a better word, are Primes. The only thing in our world with more clout than a Prime, is a Prime Lord.'

'I don't want to take my fucking seat.'

'What if it means you can save Shep? Would you do it then?' Dav curses under his breath, glaring at the desk instead of Ethan. 'I know you don't want to do this Dav. I didn't say it would be an easy plan, but it's all I can come up with right now. You are perfectly within your rights to walk through that bitch's front door and demand Shep as your property.'

'Will he have to have a chain padlocked around his neck with my fucking crest on it?'

Ethan nods solemnly. 'That is part of the ownership contract I'm afraid.'

'Fuck,' Dav mutters angrily. 'What else?'

'We'll have to pay her what she originally spent on him, but that's in the contract. I'm not sure if it was intentional or not, but the funding received by your mother, Willow, is one-point-five million. That is exactly the total she received for Shep in the first place.'

Willow laughs harshly. 'Nothing you tell me about her would surprise me any longer.' She wipes her face before looking over at Davyn. 'Please do this. I know you don't want to, and I know using your title is a big ask. But I'm asking. Please save my brother.'

'It's not that easy. You're asking me to own a member of this team. To own a friend. If I do this, I could end up owning him for the rest of his life. That's a big fucking decision.'

'I know,' Willow says. 'But this is the only way to get him back. Once he's here we have time to figure something else out.'

'She was bragging about what she used to do to him,' Izzy says. She hadn't meant to say anything out loud.

Davyn targets her with his lone eye, the green beginning to glow. 'What?'

'She told me how she *trained* him. That she would... that she would chain him to the bed and rent him out.' Izzy pauses to wipe some tears from her cheeks. 'That she wasn't sure if she preferred it when he fought back and she had to restrain him, or when he lay there broken and let her do what she wanted. She kept referring to him as her pet, her property.

'I understand I have nothing to do with this decision. But Shep willingly handed himself over to get me out. I'm not going to let him stay there with that cold hearted bitch. I won't let her treat him like that. I won't let her add even one more scar to his skin. No fucking way.

'I know nothing about you Davyn and I have no right to butt in like this. But I am certain, if given the choice, he'd pick you over that vile bitch any day of the week.'

Davyn looks at her for a long time before he leans forward. He's at the far end of the table, but it feels like he's right in her face. 'I like you Izzy.'

'Thanks,' she replies, slightly confused.

'Ethan?' Dav says after a brief pause. 'Get the paperwork ready. Shep is coming home.'

IZZY

'Can I join you?'

She jumps at the sound of a voice behind her. She had been miles away, thinking about Shep as usual, slowly torturing herself over and over again. 'I'm sorry. I was thinking.'

Thea sits beside her in front of the fire. The library in the compound had been a find. The stunning room with floor to ceiling bookshelves, comfortable couches, a huge fireplace, and a coffee machine, had become her favourite place. She could easily see herself spending hours here, buried in a book with a good cup of coffee.

After they save Shep.

If they can save Shep.

'How are you holding up?'

Izzy nods and tries to smile. 'Okay considering. Worried sick, confused, angry, confused again.'

Thea laughs as she tucks her legs under her. 'Oh, that confusion will carry on. I wouldn't expect that to go away in a hurry.'

'How long have you lived here?'

'Just over a year, but I knew about vampires a lot longer, and I'm still getting used to it. It's going to take time.'

'How do you do it? How do you live here with all this craziness? How do you not worry yourself sick every time they go out and fight?'

'I worry a lot. Every time my father and my boyfriend leave here, I have no idea if I'll see either of them again. But over the months, I've had to learn to trust them. Nix trains them hard. They are incredible fighters. Yes, they get hurt and, sometimes, they don't come back for a while. But they *do* come back. Shep *will* come back.'

'I'm sorry about Davyn getting involved. Is he okay?'

Thea shrugs as she looks into the fire. 'I don't know. Did Shep tell you about Dav?'

'No.'

'Dav's father was a truly horrible vampire. He locked Dav in a cage when he was seven and let him out when he was in his fifties. He was beaten, tortured, treated in the most horrific way. He was captured again last year, and his father tried to finish the job by throwing him in a fighting pit. It was a *kill or be killed* situation. Davyn lost the sight in one eye, and nearly lost his life. The team went in to get him and freed him so he could kill his father.'

Izzy blinks for a few seconds as she waits for Thea to say she was just joking. That all that didn't actually happen. But she doesn't. 'You're being serious?'

'That's just the beginning. He was tortured again and had his lips sewn shut so he couldn't feed. Needless to say, Dav isn't keen on having anything to do with his father's legacy or his title.'

'I'm sorry.'

'It's nothing to be sorry about. Dav is strong. He still struggles now and again, but I'm keeping an eye on him. It will take time, but he'll be okay. This is just going to bring back a few memories for him. It's not something he'll complain about though. He'll do it for Shep. He'll do anything for the team.'

Izzy isn't sure she'll ever understand what goes on in this world. It becomes more unbelievable by the day. Everything she's been bottling up over the last few days comes out and poor Thea gets it full force.

She allows the other woman to hold her, as she cries and blubbers all over her. It's embarrassing and she wishes she could stop, but she can't.

After too long she finally gets herself together and smiles apologetically. 'I didn't plan that. I'm so sorry Thea. I just started and couldn't stop.'

'It's fine, Izzy. You've been through a lot. I promise I've cried my fair share of tears over the last few years. If I've learned anything, it's that they will get Shep out. I know they will.'

'I hope so. He's so infuriating, but I think I like him.'

Thea laughs as she passes Izzy a tissue from the box on the coffee table beside her. 'Oh, you like him all right! You like him a lot.'

She laughs as she nods. 'Yeah. You're right. I really do.'

'You know,' Thea says, shuffling a little closer. 'Shep was the one who made me feel at home here.'

'He was?'

'Absolutely! He was incredible. Showed me around, explained how things work, helped me see that I can have a life here. He made a massive difference those first few days.'

Her face drops as she looks into the fire.

'What happened?'

'We kind of fell out. I got into trouble and was captured. The team came to rescue me, but Davyn was taken. He blamed me for that. Rightly so. There are rules. Nix put them in place to protect the team and the humans who live here. I didn't pay attention and Davyn was hurt.'

'I'm sorry to hear that. Are you and Shep okay now?'

Thea shrugs. 'We did sort things out in a way, but we're not back to where we were. I'm hoping that one day we will be. He's a great guy Izzy. Genuinely decent.'

'Can I ask you something Thea?'

'Of course you can! Us humans need to stick together.'

'Are you happy living here? Do you not miss... I don't know, out there?' she says, pointing to the window.

'To be honest, no, I don't miss it. I've got my dad here. And I'm totally in love with Davyn. I wouldn't be without him.'

Izzy falls silent as she looks at the seemingly normal Thea. She doesn't dislike Davyn, but he's as intimidating as they come. From the little she's managed to pick up from Willow, she knows he's a Prime which is why he's so much bigger than the other guys.

When Willow mentioned he's also addicted to blood, she had lost whatever small grasp she thought she had on this new world. She's still trying to get her head around the whole Prime/Hybrid thing without bring blood addiction, or whatever it was called, into the mix.

Learning that Davyn is a Prime who is addicted to blood was hardly encouraging in any way. It just made him all the more intimidating.

'I know what you're thinking,' Thea adds with a grin. 'He does come across as less than friendly, but he is a genuinely incredible person. Massively protective too. It's built into them all. When you're living here you always have a team of bodyguards ready to go to war for you at the drop of a hat. They can be a little controlling from time to time, but they're an amazing group of people to live with.'

Thea pauses before speaking again. 'Could I ask you a personal question?'

'I think after soaking you like I just did it's the least you deserve.'

'You and Shep? Do you see a future there?'

She blushes before she can stop herself. 'There is a possibility I do.

But I can't...'

'Can't what?'

'Realistically, it wouldn't work. It doesn't make sense. Besides, I barely know him. I just don't know if there's anything more than physical attraction.'

'Initially, that's usually what there is. The rest develops over time. I've known of vampires for a few years, and I'm still relatively new to this Blackjack world. But when I saw Dav for the first time... it didn't matter that he was a vampire. I just fancied him.

'When it comes to something like that, sense doesn't come into it. At the end of the day who cares if they're slightly different to us. It's who they are as individuals that's important.'

'I can't read him though. I've tried, but he doesn't open up easily.'

'One thing I've learned from living with them for a while, is that they all have pain in their lives. I don't know much about Shep, but I know he adores his sister, and would do anything for her. I know he's protective of his friends and will fight until he's got nothing left. And I know he's worth taking a chance on.'

'He keeps pushing me away, Thea. I think now I know why. After what happened to him, perhaps he's embarrassed or ashamed? I won't know for sure until I see him. But if he doesn't let me in, nothing is going to happen.'

Thea pulls her into a hug when she cries again. 'Don't let him push you away. I think it's time you push back. Prove that you want him.'

She nods against Thea, hearing the sense in what she just said. She does want Shep. Whatever happened in his past doesn't turn her off in any way. It's up to her to prove that to him.

She just hopes she gets the chance, but that all depends on Davyn and Ethan.

DAVYN

'Are you sure you're ready to do this?'

Davyn grits his teeth as he nods at Ethan. Anger is coursing through him. Uncontrolled fucking rage. Slavery makes him sick. Spending most of his life in a cage was hell. Worse than hell.

The second he was forced to take his father's place as the head of his house, he swore he'd never own any of the vampires in his father's court. If they wanted to stay - fine. If not, he let them go.

Yet here he is, about to lock one of his team into servitude for the rest of his life.

His friend.

As irritating as Shep is, he is a friend.

He slides his hand into his pocket, the lock and chain cold against his fingers. The thick chain will go around Shep's neck, locked in place with Dav's family seal. Shep won't have the keys to that lock. It's something he'll have to wear for the rest of his life, marking him as Dav's property.

'This will save his life Davyn,' Ethan says, clearly sensing he's not on board with this.

Dav looks up at the huge townhouse. He would have preferred to storm the property, take Shep by force. But that wouldn't help. Thanks to that fucking contract, she'd be able to come back and get him again.

The only way to end this is to put himself in that bitch's place as Shep's new owner.

'Are you ready, sire?' He glares at Ethan. 'Sorry. I'm just trying to get into character.'

'Whatever. I'm ready. Just do all the talking. I don't want to say something that'll fuck things up for Shep.'

'Don't worry,' Ethan assures him. 'I've got you, I promise.'

Davyn nods and Ethan rings the bell. A stout woman opens the door, glaring first at Ethan and then at him. Less than impressed by both of them, she turns up her snooty nose. 'Yes?'

'We're here to see your mistress.'

'And you are?'

'This is my master, Lord Oldranson, the Raven King's son.'

It takes her a moment to process all that, but when she does, Dav can't help but be a little grateful his father was such a well-known sadistic bastard. She bows deeply, her eyes widening as she backs away. 'Of course. Please come in.'

She shows them into a small reception room, gesturing towards the couches in front of the fire. 'Please have a seat. I'll fetch my mistress.'

Dav doesn't sit. He's too wound up for that.

'Calm down,' Ethan mutters under his breath.

'I want to kill them, so no, I won't fucking calm down.'

'Whatever you want to do afterwards is your business. First, we need to legally take ownership of Shep. That's the priority.'

'Take ownership? This whole fucking situation makes me sick. All this has to end.'

'I agree, but not now. Not today.'

They both fall silent as the snooty woman comes back to take them into the main drawing room, where the bitch herself is waiting for them, along with someone who can only be her bodyguard. The fucker is big, but Davyn is bigger. One wrong move and Dav will rip that asshole's head from his shoulders.

The bitch quickly gets to her feet, bowing deeply when she sees Davyn. 'Sire. I'm honoured you decided to visit me. I heard many things about your father. What can I do for you?'

Ethan places the piece of paper on the table beside Shep's owner. 'We're here to take ownership of your slave Shepherd.'

Her face changes, the pleasure at his visit changing to confusion.

'Shepherd? No, he's mine. I paid a fair price for him. I can, and will give you anything else you wish, but not him.'

Ethan continues without missing a beat. They were fully expecting this reaction. 'This document states that, as a lord, Davyn holds a higher title than you. As such, he is entitled to take ownership of your slave.'

She picks up the paper and scans it, her eyes widening as she reads the text. 'No. I won't agree to this. He's mine. I paid for him.'

Ethan passes her an envelope. 'That will more than compensate you for your expenses. Now, my lord has paid you and we've told you of our intentions. You know that legally you have to hand him over.'

'He means that much to you? He's a Hybrid, and a damaged one at that with his wings. What possible use could you have for him?'

Davyn clenches his fists, digging his fingernails into his palms. 'It's none of your business,' he replies before Ethan can respond.

She looks up at him and pauses when his glowing green eye and fangs catch her attention. 'Forgive me for upsetting you. I must ask you to reconsider your request. I don't want to give him up.'

329

Davyn takes a step closer, his anger barely restrained. 'And I don't want to ask for him again. If I do, it's going to put me in a really fucking bad mood. I've killed when I've been mildly irritated. You don't want to see me when I'm in a bad mood, trust me.'

His comment serves to persuade her. She licks her lips and nods. 'Very well. Bring him here,' she says to her guard dog.

Her bodyguard bows and disappears from the room, coming back a few minutes later dragging Shep behind him, literally. The guard dumps Shep in front of them on the floor, naked and bleeding.

Davyn growls as he examines his teammate. His skin is raw and bleeding, angry red scratches and cuts covering every inch of flesh, even his groin.

The guard kicks him onto his back, but Shep doesn't react to the contact. No groan, no wince. He is breathing, so hopefully he's just unconscious.

'What did you do to him?' Dav asks, the anger building.

'Cleaned him. You don't expect my mistress to touch him without making sure he was not contaminated first.'

'Cleaned him how?' Ethan asks, leaning over Shep's still body.

'Wire scourer and bleach. Nothing that will scar him long term.'

Davyn growls and moves towards the bodyguard, stopping when Ethan shakes his head. He steps back, barely controlling his temper. 'Remove your lock from his neck. Now!'

The bodyguard takes the key from his mistress and removes the padlock. Ethan replaces it with Davyn's family crest. He hates the look of it around Shep's neck, but if it protects him from bitches like her, it might not be a terrible thing.

Davyn slowly approaches her, making sure his eye and fangs show how pissed he really is. 'He's mine now.'

She pauses, then nods once.

'If I ever get a whiff of you or your men near my property, his family, or anyone in his life, I *will* kill you all. And I promise I am nothing like my father. I make him look like a fucking saint. Do you understand?'

'I understand.' She adds a quick *sire* when he glares at her. Davyn isn't usually one for pulling rank, but he'll take his title and beat her with it if he has to.

'Get a blanket for him.'

She nods and gestures to her bodyguard who comes back into the room with a blanket. Ethan drapes it over Shep's naked body. The contact stirs Shep. He groans, squeezing his eyes shut.

'I'm sorry,' Ethan says quietly. 'Just hang on and we'll get you home.'

Davyn lifts Shep off the ground and Shep groans again. No doubt any contact with his skin is painful. Without looking at the female, Davyn leaves, followed by Ethan.

He walks to the car and gently places Shep on the back seat, then climbs in the front next to Ethan. Without saying anything to each other, Ethan accelerates away from the house, covering the mile to the Bus as fast as possible, without attracting unwanted attention.

Dav looks in the side mirror, watching the house disappearing into the distance. That's the first time he's ever used his title to do something worthwhile, something good. He's grown so used to hating it or ignoring it, out of shame and disgust.

'Are you all right Davyn?'

He nods. 'I am. I didn't realise my title could do something like that.'

Ethan glances at him before looking back out the windscreen. 'Your father was the exception. There is a lot of good you can do in your position.'

'Like you and the Blackjacks?'

Ethan nods and smiles. 'Exactly. I don't have a title - much to my grandmother's annoyance - but vampires in your position can make a difference. It's something you should perhaps think about. Shep wouldn't be in the back seat right now if not for your title.'

'Is he safe now? Will my seal really protect him?'

Ethan shrugs. 'As much as it protects any one of you. You put your lives on the line every day. As much as I wish otherwise, nothing can protect any of you from that.'

IZZY

She checks her watch again. Less than a minute has gone by. Beside her, Willow is tapping her hands on her legs as Thea paces the kitchen area. They're anxious too. Everyone on the Bus is. In front of her, the painfully quiet Bastian is leaning against the wall, his arms to his side and his fists clenched firmly.

'They're coming!' Nix shouts from outside.

Izzy jumps up and hurries onto the street as the large black car pulls up alongside the bus. Davyn and Ethan get out of the car, and she knows something is wrong with Shep. The look on both their faces tells her as much.

'What's wrong?' Willow asks, clearly sensing the same thing she does.

Davyn and Ethan lift Shep out and he screams in pain. They carry him into the bus and lie him on the gurney at the back. Shep is panting and moaning as the blanket is peeled back from his chest.

'Oh God.' Willow voices her sentiment before she can find the words.

Shep's body is torn to pieces, the skin covered in deep angry gouges. Both wrists are badly cut, dried and fresh blood smeared down his arms.

'Bitch must have had him hanging by his wrists. She used a wire scourer and bleach to make sure his skin was clean before she touched him,' Davyn thumps the wall, then walks over to Thea, who instantly wraps her arms around him.

Fletch and Fallon usher everyone away from the table, but Shep's arm shoots out, grabbing onto Izzy's wrist. He opens his eyes and smiles at her. He swallows a few times before he speaks. 'Hey love.'

Izzy laughs and wipes the tears from her eyes. 'Hey yourself.'

He squeezes his eyes shut, as Fletch lays some bandages on his legs to protect them from the straps on the gurney. 'I know I don't look it now, but I really am a big scary vampire.'

Izzy rubs his hand, taking care not to touch any of the numerous cuts. 'You don't have to tell me that. I know you are. The biggest bad-ass vampire that I know.'

He laughs, stopping and hissing in pain. 'Good. I just wanted to make sure you knew that 'cause this really fucking hurts and there's a chance I'm not going to act all macho.'

Izzy leans closer, looking into his navy eyes. 'You don't have to be macho for me, Shep.'

He nods and closes his eyes, sucking in a breath as they continue to work on him. 'Please stay. I don't want you to leave. Please...'

She holds his hand tighter. 'Always.'

He falls silent, instantly freaking her out. 'It's okay,' Fletch says as he moves her out of the way. 'I just sedated him. Bas? Get our boy home as fast as you can.'

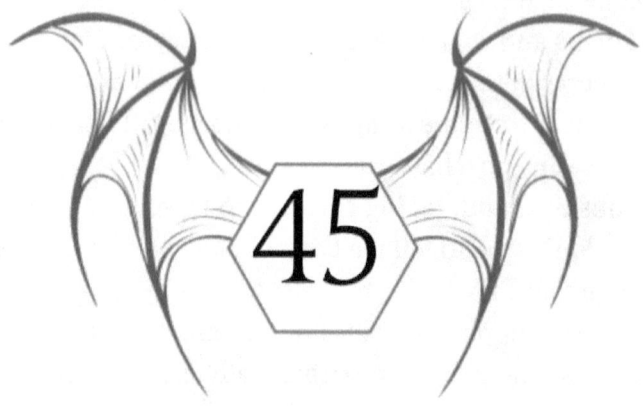

SHEP

His skin is on fire. That's the only way he can describe it. Pure liquid flames course over every inch of his skin from his scalp to the soles of his feet.

Shep concentrates on just breathing, trying to distract himself from the pain. But it doesn't work. He clenches his jaw, trying to keep the scream from tearing out. He can do this. It will take another few hours for his skin to heal. Maybe a day at the most.

'I should let you get some rest,' Dav says, getting to his feet.

He shakes his head no. 'I need to talk to you.'

Dav sits back in the chair, his green eye glowing as he stares at him. Guy seems to be pissed off about something. Whatever. He's just glad for something else to do other than be miserable and feel sorry for himself.

He's desperate to see Izzy, but this conversation needs to happen first. If he knows Davyn at all - which he does - he needs to do this.

'Hurts?'

'Fuck yes.' He laughs, but it dies away when his skin argues back. 'Damn it! It's better than it was, but I'm not having any fun. I wanted to thank you.'

'What the fuck for? I need to apologise to you.'

'What? Now I'm confused. You saved my life Dav. Why would you apologise for that?'

Davyn points to the chain around Shep's neck. 'For that. You've got my crest padlocked around your neck. Technically I own you, Shep.'

He nods. 'I know. Why are you looking all gloomy? It doesn't change anything. Well, unless I don't know you the way I think I do. You want to start bossing me around?'

'Of course I'm not going to treat you like my slave! How the fuck could you suggest that?'

'Hey! I wasn't being serious! Sorry. Badly timed attempt at humour. My timing is a little off lately.'

Davyn sits back in the chair and his shoulders drop.

'You're really bothered by this, aren't you?'

'Of course. Aren't you?'

Shep pushes up, taking a few deep breaths to stop himself from vomiting as the pillow rubs against his back. 'Dav, I've been owned for half my life. When my mother told me she'd sold me, I thought that was it for me. That I'd be owned or sold to some moody fucker who scares the shit out of me. Actually,' he says, pausing. 'I was.'

'You're really not funny.'

'Sorry. What I'm trying to say is, for the first time I'm okay about that. I mean seriously Dav. If I have to be someone's property, I'd prefer it was you.'

'Shep—'

'No. I'm being serious. I can't change what happened, or what I am. My mother is to blame for that. She's the one who sold me in the first place.'

He slowly lifts the chain around his neck, holding the padlock in his hand, trying to calm the shakes he can't get rid of. Even though he's in a warm bed in a heated room, he's still fucking freezing.

The bastard of a bodyguard had washed him down three times with bleach and ice water. The cold mixed with the sting of the bleach was nearly worse than the scourer digging into the fresh wounds – especially on his groin. He'd passed out during that part, thank fuck. He doesn't know who took out the piercing in his dick but he's grateful it's been removed. The way he feels right now, there isn't a chance in hell he'll put it back in.

'Dav, after all the crap I've had to go through wearing one of these chains, I reckon I've just hit the jackpot with you.'

'You're fucked in the head, you know that?' he says, a small grin making an appearance.

'All the best vampires are.'

'You know I have to leave that on? They'll be keeping an eye on you. If any of her contacts see you out without it, she could take you back.'

Shep shrugs. 'I'm not a fan of bling, but what the hell. I can make it work.'

Dav shakes his head as he laughs, which is a rare sight. The guy wasn't a fan of anything cheery. But his past is as fucked up as Shep's, so you can't really blame him. 'Ethan has looked into it. You just need to have any chain with my lock on it. He's getting a thinner chain and smaller lock. It'll look like a regular necklace.'

'Thanks. This isn't exactly comfortable.'

'I can sort that out.' Dav stands up and unlocks the chain, carefully taking it from around his neck. 'Just make sure you put it back on when you leave here.'

'Will do, sire.'

'Fucker,' Dav says, dumping the chain, lock, and key on the table near his bed. 'Izzy is outside. You want to see her?'

'Can I ask you something first?'

Davyn turns around and crosses his arms. 'What?'

'How do you do it? You and Thea, with what we do? With what your father did to you?'

Davyn takes a deep breath and sits back down. 'You want her?'

'Yes, but I don't know if that's a good idea for her. With all this shit that's happened the last... well, few decades, I don't reckon I'm up there with the millions of other better prospects out there for her.'

'And you think I'm a good prospect for Thea? We're all fucked up, Shep. Each and every one of us, but when I was rescued from my father, and I saw Thea...' He pauses and smiles. 'It made everything better. And I know that's corny as fuck, but it's how it was for me.

'I don't feel I deserve Thea. Far from it. And we probably shouldn't work. But we do. I love her and for some fucking unknown reason, she loves me. Past and all, she wants me.'

'Yeah. That's the bit I'm freaking out about. I'm worried Izzy won't want me now she knows what happened to me, what I've done.'

'If she loves you, she will. Love doesn't care about shit like that.'

'But what if I can't be physical with her like that? Not yet anyway. Maybe not for a long while.'

'Tell her that. She'll understand. Thea did with me.'

'What are you talking about?'

'Fuck it! Thea was my first.'

'Whoa. Really? But you're nearly two hundred years old.'

'Yeah, and I was kept in a cage and beaten for a lot of that time. Dating wasn't a priority. And if you tell anyone what I just told you, I will rip your fucking heart out.'

'Hey! I won't say I word, I swear. But thanks for telling me. I mean that Dav. So, Thea took things slowly with you?'

Davyn nods. 'We're still figuring it all out together. It's fucking hard at times. I'm messed up. Learning as I go most of the time. But she's with me every step.' He shrugs. 'Maybe it makes us a stronger couple? Who knows?'

'Are you not worrying all the time about something happening to her by being with you?'

'Of course I am. That's part of the deal. She's human and I'm a vampire. That's always going to be something we'll have to deal with at some stage. But for now, I'm enjoying being with her.'

He gets up and rubs the ruined skin on his face. 'If you want to be with Izzy, then be with her. All the other shit we deal with comes second to that. And you know what? I think after everything we've suffered through, everything we've survived, we deserve to be happy.'

'Don't let her walk away because *you* think it's best for her. If I've learned anything from being with Thea it's that she makes up her own mind about things. Lay it all on the table for Izzy and let her decide.'

'Thanks, Dav. You might be right.'

'You want to talk to her now?'

'Yeah. I do.'

IZZY

She desperately wanted to see him. To talk to him properly now he's awake and more lucid. But she felt it was only right Davyn spoke to him first. Willow also insisted Izzy speak to him next which surprised her. Shep's sister seems to be intent on doing everything she can to push the couple together.

Izzy jumps to her feet when Davyn come out of Shep's room. The huge vampire stops in front of her and fixes his lone green eye on her. It's the first time she's seen him without the eye patch.

The scarring stretches from his forehead and down his eyelid to his cheek. She's surprised he didn't completely lose his eye as a result of the injury. The milky iris of his damaged eye stares blankly at her as he walks over to her.

'Shep wants to talk to you.'

'How is he?'

'In pain but hiding it as usual. He wants you Izzy. He's scared though. You'll need to fight for him.' Then without another word, Davyn walks away, disappearing around the corner.

Izzy faces the door and straightens her shoulders. She's nervous. God knows why, but she is. She knocks, waiting until she hears the 'Yeah' from inside before she opens the door.

Shep may be awake, but he's paler than usual, and the smile isn't nearly as broad as she's used to.

'Hey love.'

'You look brighter.'

'Stop lying. I look shite.' He points to the chair beside his bed, so she sits down. Now she's in the room alone with him she isn't sure what to say. The horrific marks left by the wire scourer have faded a little, but each and every one is still visible. He holds out his hand, so she takes it in hers, rubbing the back of his fingers.

'Are you okay?'

She meets his eyes, unable to stop the tears. 'Am I okay? No, I'm not okay. I'm worried about you, you irritating man. Sorry. Irritating vampire. I didn't think I'd ever see you again. When she put that chain on you and made you strip... I honestly thought you were leaving me for good.'

He tries to push himself further up the bed but gives up and lies back down. 'I'm so sorry, Izzy.'

'Why are you apologising?' Her attention is caught by the chain and padlock on the table. She knows he has to wear that for the rest of his life. Knows he belongs to Davyn, and she hates that thought. 'I shouldn't be loading all this on you. I'm sorry.'

He reaches out, grabbing her hand in his. 'I want you to talk to me.'

'I don't want you to have to remember any of it. I want you to be able to forget. I know that's probably not possible.'

He laughs. 'Yeah. I'm not seeing that in my immediate future. But once my skin heals it'll be a step in the right direction.'

'And what about that?' she asks, nodding towards the chain.

'Ethan is arranging a smaller, less *in your face*, version.'

'That's not what I mean, but that is good I suppose.'

'Oh. You mean having to wear it, full stop?' He rests his head on the pillow and smiles at her. 'I'm fine about it, Izzy. Really. It's Dav. With him the whole ownership thing doesn't mean anything. I get that I'll have to wear it, but what does that matter? It's a necklace. That's it. Besides, you're forgetting one detail.'

'What's that?'

'I'm under the protection of Lord Oldranson. He's got a hefty number of vampires in Ireland under his command. I'm under his protection now. And you will be too. If you want to be I mean?'

'What are you saying?'

Shep licks his lips and adjusts himself in the bed, wincing. 'Fuck! Can you move my pillow down a smidge. Damn thing is digging into me.'

Izzy leans over and carefully moves it lower. 'Thanks love. Can't seem to get comfy at the moment.'

'You didn't answer my question.'

'I need to talk to you properly, but I'm all drugged up and my head is a mess. Will you stay here for now? Here in the compound, I mean. Fletch reckons I should be good to break out in the morning. Maybe then we can talk properly? If you want? I mean you don't have to. I can ask someone to get you the fuck away from—'

She shuts him up by kissing him, delighted when he doesn't pull back from her.

'What was that for?' he asks.

'I was trying to stop you from babbling. And yes, I'd love to stay. Now why don't you get some sleep. Fletch said your skin will heal faster with rest.'

'Yes boss. Will do. Can you maybe—'

She runs her fingers through his hair as she smiles at him. 'I'll stay. Get some sleep.'

He nods then closes his eyes, taking a deep, shaky breath before he settles. Fletch is giving him painkillers but they just seem to be taking the edge off. Even breathing is causing him discomfort.

The wounds are fading though. His tattoos are more visible as his skin heals. He's fed a few times since he woke so that should speed up his recovery. She can't bear seeing him like this.

Izzy kisses the back of his hand then sits back in the chair, rubbing her thumb over his skin.

He wants to talk properly.

When he had said that to her, she was so relieved. It was something she wanted for them. It's something they both need. But she knows Davyn is right. If she wants Shep she's going to have to fight for him. She's going to have to prove to him that she wants to be with him.

It's not going to be an easy fight either. After hearing some of what he went through under the ownership of that bitch, she knows that sex of any kind isn't on the cards for them in the immediate future. It can't be.

Going to The Lair had been about performing as he had been trained to do. She's positive about that. As much as she wants to sleep with him, she will not be with him like that. Not once.

If they're to have any chance of making this work between them, he has to heal first – inside and out. He has to be given back that control he lost years ago.

But that's fine. She can wait however long it takes. He's worth it.

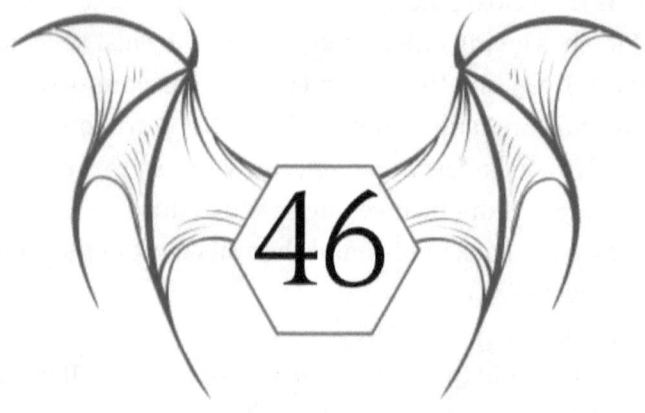

BASTiAN

He slashes his blade across his attacker's torso, slicing his top and skin open like tissue paper. The male screams, pausing long enough for Bas to slice his other blade across his neck. Blood sprays on Bastian's face, but he barely feels it. Nothing exists but pain and anger.

Before that male falls to the ground, he's on the next one, cutting and slicing his body open. Then on to the next. And the next.

By the time he's done, he's the only one still breathing. Bas watches the blood drip off his clenched fists, collecting in pools to either side of his feet.

It's not his blood. None of it is. Nor is the blood coating his face, his clothes, and his knives. He came away unscathed. When you put an expert killer against untrained idiots, that was always going to be the case.

It's been a long time since he went hunting. A long time since he let his rage out like he just did. A long time since he murdered for no reason.

They thought they were tracking him. Following him down the quiet street, blocking him in the corner of the deserted car park. But it was the other way around. He led them there. Took them exactly where he wanted them, then killed them.

He looks down at the team of Order fighters in pieces around him. It only took a few minutes to take down the six fighters. They thought he would be an easy target. Alone and vulnerable.

They weren't innocents. True Order personnel are anything but. Their deaths mean six less issues to deal with.

But it's still six deaths he caused for no reason other than he's angry. Angry at himself. Goddamn furious in fact. Not for killing the males. There's no point regretting that. They would have died at a Blackjack hand at some stage in the future. What he regrets is his time with Ethan.

Every single minute.

Regrets letting him close. Regrets not keeping his own wall up, blocking his emotions. Regrets giving in to that initial urge he had to kiss him.

And now look at him. Covered in blood with bodies by his feet.

What the fuck did he just do?

He's past this. Past killing for the sake of killing. Past killing to make himself feel anything.

He bends down, grabbing a leg in each hand, dragging two of the bodies to the barrier at the edge of the car park. Below him, the sea crashes against the rocks, the spray being driven high into the air each time.

One by one, he hauls the bodies over the railing until they're in a pile at the edge of the cliff. Bas wipes his hands on the coat of the top male in the pile, getting most of the blood off his skin. It'll have to do until he goes home and showers.

One by one, he kicks the bodies over the edge, watching as they disappear into the sea.

Bas drops back onto the barrier surrounding the car park, looking down at the waves below him.

He's only cried a few times in his life that he remembers. Once when his parents were murdered in front of him as a child. Again when his best friend told them what that bitch did to him for twelve years.

And when he walked away from Ethan.

In truth he doesn't regret his time with Ethan. He can try to convince himself of that for the rest of his life. It won't make it any more true. He's been telling himself that since he made the decision to end things with Ethan.

He angrily wipes his face, smearing the tears and blood on his skin. He's experienced true pain in his life. Been tortured, beaten, left for dead. But none of that compares to what he's going through since leaving Ethan's office. This pain isn't easing. The scar left behind won't fade.

Without Ethan, he's back to feeling like a shell. Empty. A ghost.

He swore he'd take a bullet for Ethan. Protect him at all costs. Give his own life to save him. It seems he did in fact do just that.

Walking away to keep Ethan safe has killed a part of himself.

WiLLOW

She was always the nice one. The quiet one. Polite and well mannered as she was raised to be.

But as Willow climbs the ornate staircase to her mother's living room, her thoughts are far from those a well-bred female should have.

Working with the Blackjacks, she's seen more than her fair share of hurt, of pain, of uncontrolled anger. The level of alpha male fuelled emotions is off the charts at times. But she's never felt like that herself before and it scares her.

Her mother smiles sweetly at her, but it's short-lived. As soon as she sees her daughter's face, she reins in her smile. 'Why don't you take a seat.'

Willow lowers on to the couch opposite her mother's armchair. She wasn't doing what she was told. More so sitting to make sure she didn't launch herself at her mother.

'I thought you'd like to know that Shep is safe.'

'I'm glad to hear that,' Lillith replies, looking genuinely relieved. Perhaps she is. Maybe on some well-hidden level she actually does care about her son? Or maybe she's just relieved that it's all over. 'Is he well?'

'No. She scrubbed him with a wire brush and washed him in bleach. He was in agony for days, screaming in pain whenever he moved.'

Lillith swallows deeply, the hand on her lap trembling slightly.

'You sold Shep! Sold him! How could you do that? What did he ever do to make you hate him so much?'

Lilith sips her drink before taking a deep breath. 'I have never, and will never, hate Shepherd. I love him dearly.'

'Love him?' Willow spits. 'How can you say that? How can you sit there and expect me to believe you cared for him at all?

'When your father died, I was left penniless. For years I struggled to keep this house afloat. For years I struggled to provide for you and Shepherd. It was a constant battle. Always pretending to have more than we did so our peers wouldn't shun us.

'And yes,' she continues quickly when Willow opens her mouth to respond to that. 'I know none of that mattered to you, or to your brother. But it mattered to me. It mattered a great deal.'

She bites her tongue, trying desperately to hold back the scream.

How can she speak so flippantly about the life of one of her children? Selling him to keep up with her circle of pompous friends.

'I approached an acquaintance who was kind enough to put me in touch with someone who was extended me a healthy line of credit. Thanks to that, I was able to keep this roof over our heads. Give you everything you needed.'

Willow looks around the vast drawing room, suddenly feeling ill. 'And the payment terms? Did you know in advance, or did you just not care?'

'The initial amount I borrowed was too much to pay back, let alone all the interest on top of that. I suspect they knew that. I was given an alternative method of repayment. They could take you, or your brother as payment.'

In that moment, her mother disappears. It's like she never knew her. A stranger takes her place. Someone Willow knows nothing about. 'So you gave them Shep as payment.'

'I had no choice Willow. It was either him or you. I couldn't let them take you away from me. I know what these people are like. What they would have used you for. I couldn't do it.'

'But you were fine just to hand him over? You knew how he'd be used. You knew, and you still let them take him! I can't believe this... I feel sick.'

'Willow. Please. You must try to understand what it was like for me.'

'For you? For you!' she screams, anger taking charge in spite of her best efforts. 'What about for him? What about Shep!'

'Willow...'

'Tell me what they did to him. Tell me!'

'I'm sure you know. You do not need to hear it from me.'

Willow gets up and kneels in front of her mother. If she stands she's going to have difficulty restraining herself. 'I want you to tell me. Say it!'

Her mother nods, then takes another drink before she continues.

'As you wish. They ran an entertainment business. The burns on his sides were their way of keeping a tally of the total repaid. One burn for every time he was... used for entertainment.'

'Say the words Mother!'

'They sold him for sex Willow. I knew what they were going to do, and I still let them take him.' She closes her eyes as she shakes her head. 'You were never meant to find out.'

'Is that supposed to make a difference? Is this where I say thank you for sparing me the truth all these years?'

'I gave you a life Willow. Everything around you was provided by me to give you a comfortable life. Shepherd has never regretted giving himself up in your place. Not once. Don't diminish his sacrifice by holding this grudge. It's done. We can all move on as a family.'

Willow slowly pushes to her feet, taking a few steps back as her mother's words take a moment to sink in. 'You sold Shep and you think we can just move on. Just like that!'

'I didn't mean it quite as bluntly as—'

'I don't know you. I never have. I didn't want any of this pomp and circumstance, and I never once asked for, or demanded anything in my life. Don't you dare put this on me. Don't you dare! *You* did this for yourself. *You* were living beyond your means. *You* wanted more money. *You* sold your son. *You!*'

'Don't go Willow. We can fix this. I know we can.'

She backs towards the door as she shakes her head. 'No. We can't. You're dead to me. I no longer have a mother. If you ever come near Shep or I again, I won't be so nice next time. Goodbye *Mother.*'

She storms out, angry tears pouring down her face. She's just said goodbye to her mother for ever, but she's not feeling any regret or sadness. Not one bit. The person she thought she knew and loved didn't exist. There's nothing to be sad about.

Shep is her family. The only one she has left. And she will protect him with her last breath.

DAVYN

He takes a drink from his coffee as he waits for Fergus to answer the video call. He'd set up the ancient vampire with a laptop and showed him how to use it for video calls, but the technology is still so alien to Fergus he struggles every single time.

It's been ten minutes and Fergus still hasn't figured out how to turn the fucking camera on.

He finishes his coffee as Thea patiently talks Fergus through it for the umpteenth time. The woman has an endless supply of patience.

She nods to him, turning the laptop around to show Fergus on the screen.

'Sire. I apologise. I am still learning how to use this equipment.'

'No problem. Thea found some entries about various prisons my father supplied to or was involved with. Do you know anything about these prisons?'

'I do not know of these places. Where are these prisons?'

'We haven't found any locations, just that they exist. It seems he was using locals to keep both his fighting pits, and these prisons fully stocked or manned. She's still trying to figure out all the details.'

Fergus's face loses all colour before he slumps back into the seat behind him.

'Are you okay?'

'Forgive me Davyn. I was just... Do you have any idea how many lives have been lost at your father's hands?'

'I'm not sure I want to know the numbers, but I have a fair idea.'

'I cannot blame you. Your father cleared a lot of villages surrounding the castle. I have no idea what these prisons were for, but the fighting pits were quite lucrative.

'I still have a difficult time accepting people were willing to pay handsomely to watch a slaughter. With one vampire being killed in each fight, there was an increasing need to replenish his numbers. As I'm sure you'll remember, the death toll was horrifically high.'

'It's not something I'm going to forget in a hurry.'

Fergus nods slowly. 'I can well imagine. Does... is there mention of names at all?'

Something about his tone and expression sends off alarm bells. 'Who did he take?'

'Pardon me?'

'I don't know you well, but I know that look on your face. I've seen it so many times. He took someone from you.'

'He took family members from a lot of people in the castle. Most of us in fact. We tended to keep any relationships we had with villagers to ourselves. We feared that he would target them if he knew we had connections, and he could have used them against us. But it did not work that way. He took them anyway.'

'Intentionally?'

'Not to use against us. We don't believe he knew who they were.

He just needed the numbers. We believed they all perished. Not many escape the pits. And with all of them shut down since you took over, we feared we would never find out what happened. But if there are prisons, perhaps they are still in operation.'

'And maybe some of the missing vampires are in those sites?'

'A foolish hope I know, but one I'd like to hang on to if possible.'

Davyn looks over to Thea. 'How many more books do you have to go through?'

'At least half a dozen from that year.'

'Fuck. Right, I'll bring this to Nix. See if she can pull more support to give you a hand. Fergus? Thea will keep you posted on this. If you can ask around over there. See if anyone has heard of these prisons. There's a chance the Whelan sister could be there too. My father killed her boyfriend and mounted his head, but she vanished. This could be where she vanished to.'

'Of course. I'll let you know if I hear anything.'

'Fergus?' Thea asks, interrupting the conversation. 'Who did you lose?'

Davyn didn't want to push the man on the topic. He was right. Everyone in the castle has lost someone. Davyn lost his mother. He has no doubts his father killed, kidnapped, sold, or just gave away whoever he wanted. It's how he operated. The selfish dick was all about himself, his power, his funds, keeping his ridiculous Raven King title.

'I lost my son, Thea.'

All plans to keep out of it come crashing down when Davyn hears that. 'I didn't know you had a son?'

'He would be the same age as you, sire. He was twenty-six when he disappeared. He had just transitioned a few weeks before. He was a strong boy Davyn. My bloodline is Prime, but until my son was born, our line had been relatively weak. For some reason, he made up for all my shortfalls. Perhaps it was his strength, his size, which was his downfall. He would have made an excellent fighter.'

350

'Or someone who could have stood up to my father.'

Fergus nods, a small smile turning the corners of his mouth. 'I do not doubt that for a moment. He was not a fan of your father.'

'Sounds like someone I'd get along with. What's his name? We'll keep an eye out for him.'

'Quillan, sire. His name is Quillan. I have to believe he is still alive. I have all this time. Until I see his body, I refuse to believe otherwise.'

'If I find any mention of Quillan, I'll contact you immediately,' Thea says.

'I appreciate that.'

Dav needs to talk to Nix, so wraps this up. He's not ready to get into any deep and meaningful chats with Fergus about his son. 'We'll be in touch.'

He ends the video call, then slumps back in his chair. 'Fuck! This is like a damn Pandora's Box.'

Thea hands him the drive with a copy of the information she's collated so far. 'But it's a box that needs to be opened. This is your legacy Dav. I know it's not what you want, and it's not what I want for you. I want you to be able to put all this behind you. But we need to fix this. We need to find out what happened to these people.'

'We?'

'It's always *we*, Dav. I'm with you through all of this. You saw Fergus's face. Even that tiny glimmer of hope that Quillan is still alive gave him something to fight for. Your father kept meticulous records. We have names buried in those pages. We will find out what happened to them. Think of all the families you can bring closure to.'

'It could be where Murt's sister ended up?'

Thea nods enthusiastically. 'I really think she's in one of these prisons. Your father killed her boyfriend and put him on display. Why not her? He didn't put women in the pits, did he?'

'No. Only males.'

'So, he didn't kill her. She didn't go to the pits. That leaves the prisons. You never know, she could be alive and well, locked away waiting for someone to find her.'

He leans over to give Thea a kiss. 'I love you.'

'I love you too. Now give that to Nix. This is bigger than either of us can handle on our own.'

He takes the drive and heads up to Nix's office. Her door is open, so he goes straight in without knocking and sits in the chair opposite her.

She peers over her laptop at him. 'Come in, please.'

He ignores her comment and places the drive on her desk. 'Thea found that my father supplied vampires to secret prisons, as well as his fighting pits. According to Fergus, he emptied villages around the castle to get his numbers up. There are too many books though. Can you send that information to Ethan and see if he can spare anyone to help Thea?'

Nix picks up the drive, turning it over in her hands. 'She did well to get any of those records collated so fast. We might have to bring her in as a team member. I'll get this to Ethan. Is there any mention of where these prisons are?'

'Nothing so far. Could be where the Whelans or their missing sister are?'

'Good point. I never thought of that. Leave it with me. I'll sort it out. Can Thea keep doing what she's doing?'

'Yeah. She wants to help out. Fergus's son is also missing.'

Nix takes a long breath. 'Okay. It sounds like we're going to be working double time over the next few weeks or months.'

'We can handle it.'

She smiles at him. 'I have no doubts. I have to say, I'm proud of you.'

'For what?'

'You've turned something truly horrific into something positive. That takes a lot of guts and bravery. No one would have questioned you if you'd decided to walk away from that castle and never look back.'

'Thea and this ownership thing with Shep changed my mind. She's backing me. Plus, I don't want to own that fucker for the rest of his life. He's irritating.'

Nix laughs at that. 'But we all love him.'

'Whatever. I just don't want my crest locked around anyone's neck. Even if it is helping them. There's no need for shit like that.'

'I couldn't agree more. We'll get there Dav. And just for the record, you have the full support of the team and access to all Blackjack resources. We'll back you too.'

'Thanks Nix.'

He leaves her to contact Ethan and heads back to Thea to help out as much as he can.

He may not have wanted anything to do with Ireland or that castle, but maybe Lord Davyn Oldranson can tear up the rule book and leave a legacy he can be proud of.

SHEP

As he watches Willow train, Shep realises for the first time how fucking awesome his sister is. Until that moment he'd been looking at her as an overprotective big brother looks on a little sister. But she's so much more than that. She's a valued member of the Blackjacks and has been for ages.

He was just too stubborn to see it.

Even when faced with a fighter the size of Court, she's holding her own. No wonder she could drop him on his ass so easily.

Willow hasn't been near him since he was released. He's worried sick that she's ashamed to have him as her brother. He wouldn't blame her. He's meant to be the strong dependable one. Knowing he was used like he was doesn't say a lot about his ability to protect anyone.

He waits outside the training room, watching through the window until she's finished. This conversation is going to be awkward enough, without having it while she's still hyped up from the session.

About ten minutes later, the siren goes off signalling the end of the training exercise. She speaks to Court for a moment before grabbing her towel off the bench and wiping her face. Court nods at him as he walks past, leaving Shep alone with his sister.

As soon as Willow sees him, her entire demeanour changes. He was expecting that, but enough is enough. Nothing that happened is on her. And he's going to make sure she knows that.

'Hey. I was watching you for a bit. You kicked ass.'

She smiles at him, but it's for show. 'Thanks. I'd better go and have a shower.'

'Sit for a minute.'

'I really—'

'Please Wills. Sit down.'

Her internal struggle takes longer than he thought it would. Not a great start, but she does eventually sit. He joins her on the bench, sitting back slowly so he doesn't aggravate the wounds on his back that are taking their sweet time to heal. 'What's going on between us Wills?'

She glances at him before looking back at the ground. 'Nothing. We're fine.'

'We're far from fine! You can't even look at me without frowning. I miss you. I miss my sister and I want her back.'

'I'm here Shep. I haven't gone anywhere.'

'Are you ashamed of me now? I wouldn't blame you if you were.'

That does the trick. She turns around to face him, shaking her head. 'No! I could never be ashamed of you. What happened... it wasn't your fault Shep. None of this was.'

'It's not yours either.'

'That's not true. It is my fault.'

He suspected she felt that way, but hearing the words come out of her mouth knocks him sideways. 'Oh Wills. What the fuck are you talking about? How the hell is any of this your fault?'

'She sold you and saved me. Our mother decided I was more important than you were.'

'She sold me because she knew I'd survive. She knew I was too stubborn to give in.'

The look she gives him screams *yeah right*.

'Okay so maybe that's not why. I don't know her reasoning, and I don't really care. The only thing that matters, that's ever mattered to me, is your safety. And look at you now! You're every bit as formidable as I am in the field. And that's the only time I'll ever say that!'

She smiles at that. 'I learned from the best.'

'Court is damn good.'

'I meant you,' she says, looking up at him. 'How can you bear to look at me after what happened? You were hurt for so long, while I lived in that fucking mansion with everything I could ever want. I was free, and you were a possession. You must hate me so much.'

'Firstly, don't curse. That's one habit you can do without picking up from me. And I could never, ever hate you. Neither of us had any control over what happened. It was all down to *her*.'

He takes her hand, hanging on to it when she tries to pull back. 'Not one day went by when I had a bad thought about you. I swear that's the truth. I don't want this to come between us. Please Wills.'

'So, what now? Do you just wear that thing around your neck for the rest of your life? Does Davyn own you until you die?'

'Yeah. That's the way it works. But it's not a big deal. I've had a chat with Dav about it. He's as thrilled about the prospect as you are, but I'm genuinely okay about it. I trust Dav. Nothing will change except that I won't be looking over my shoulder anymore. I'm safe Wills. Having his seal around my neck means no one can touch me. It's a good thing.'

'Does Izzy see it the same way?'

He shrugs. 'She understands. It's just a necklace Wills. That's it. Without it, I'm in trouble. With it, I'm safe. Please don't see it as anything sinister, or life threatening. It's not. Far from it.'

'I'm sorry Shep.'

'What for?'

'For being such a terrible sister.'

The tears are flowing down her face now. Shep wipes them away with his thumb, trying to compose himself before he speaks. He's not great with all this emotional stuff. 'Why would you say something like that?'

'Because I am. I've spent so long going on and on about you making things right with our mother. You asked me, told me, begged me to let it drop. But I couldn't. I thought I was doing the right thing. I thought that if I could get you to see sense, I would get my family back together again.'

She laughs harshly. 'Make you see sense! I thought you were just being a stubborn fool Shep. I'm so so sorry. I should have just trusted you and let it go.'

'Hey. Stop crying. It's not your fault. You were just doing what you thought was right for our family. You had no way of knowing that she had destroyed whatever family we had, decades ago. I love you Wills.'

'Can you ever forgive me?'

'Nothing to forgive. Can I ask you a favour?' She nods, wiping the tears from her cheeks. 'Can I give my sister a hug?'

She collapses into his arms, crying against his chest for a few minutes. But he couldn't care less. He wouldn't have blamed her if she couldn't handle being around him.

'We good?'

She nods against his chest. 'Yeah. We're good. I love you Shep.'

'Love you too.'

'So,' she asks as she gets herself together. 'Is it too soon to ask you about Izzy?'

He gets up, trying to shake off all the emotion, and get back to being her smart-ass brother. 'Ask what?'

'Is she staying here with you?'

'What? Here? No! Why would she?'

'Because you're in love with her and she's in love with you, that's why. Nix will let her stay if that's what you want. You know she will.'

That may be the case, but he's not so sure it's a good idea. Izzy has an apartment, a life, college, a job, and her world doesn't include him.

'Ah, I'm a bit of a free bird kind of guy. And she's got her own things going on. '

Willow pushes to her feet as she laughs. 'Wow! Still fighting it.'

'Fighting what?'

'Your feelings, that's what! You are allowed to have a personal life Shep. Court and Nix do it. Dav and Thea do it. You can too.'

His hand travels up to the lock around his neck before he knows what he's doing.

'Ah. So, you tell me it's fine and doesn't mean anything, but yet you don't think you're good enough for her because of it?'

'No! I didn't think I was good enough for her before I had that. Maybe I'm just meant to be the inappropriate bachelor of the group? Maybe this is as good as it's going to get for me?'

Willow grabs his arm, stopping him from pacing, which he wasn't even aware he was doing. 'Do I need to drop you on your ass again Shepherd? Cause I will if you keep spouting rubbish like that! If you want Izzy, tell her! Let her make up her own mind about what she wants. She deserves that at least. Stop hiding.'

'Hey! I'm not hiding from anything.'

She pokes him in the chest, the grin not taking away from the seriousness of her jab. 'Are too.'

'Am not!' he says, swatting her hand away.

'Are too,' she says, ducking his next swipe, sauntering away as he glares after her.

FALLON

His scent is everywhere. It's filling her nostrils, hitting parts of her body she'd been ignoring for too long. But Austin is awakening her like no one has for decades and that's terrifying her. She's not ready to feel again. Not ready to have anyone swaying her emotions.

She lowers him into his wheelchair, those emotions of hers being stirred again when she sees the elation on his face. He enjoys being taken out into the fresh air by her, and she will gladly take him out every single night if it means she can see that smile.

He seems happier since he's been allowed out of his room. Healthier and stronger too. He's far from having the physical build of one of the males, but he's catching up faster than she expected.

Perhaps the non-human blood flowing through his veins is helping.

His rougarou blood.

The more time she spends with him, the more confused she is about the entire situation. She's spent limited time with the wolf species - whether from Ireland or beyond - but she can't see any sign of that in him.

'Are you all right cher?'

She really wishes he'd stop talking to her like that. She likes it too much. 'I'm good. Are you hungry?'

'Always.'

Fallon pushes his chair back in through the double doors and into the main house. She stops at the kitchen, requesting dinner from Gwen, before bringing him back to his room.

It's far from the vast bedrooms herself and the rest of the team have, but compared to his cell, it's roomy and comfortable.

'I still don't understand how y'all can live out here without anyone finding you.'

She positions his chair next to his bed, locking the brakes in place. 'It's fairly unpopulated out here. We have privacy. Room to be ourselves.'

Austin heaves his body from the chair to the bed, pulling himself back so he's sitting against the wall. 'You're lucky cher. And I guess I am too. I couldn't have asked to be rescued by a better team. Y'all are being so kind to me. I hope I can repay you one day.'

Gwen interrupts by arriving with his dinner. 'I've brought you fish and chips. I thought you could do with a bit of a treat. I even included my famous mushy peas.'

'Thank you Gwen,' he says his eyes widening when she lays the tray on his lap.

Fallon is surprised when Gwen comes back in a minute later with a second tray. 'For you dear. Enjoy.'

She looks down at the fish and chips on the tray then over to Austin. 'You can sit on the bed if you want.'

She does, resting her tray on her lap. 'Sorry about this. I wasn't expecting her to bring me dinner too.'

'Why are you apologising? I'm glad she did. Between you and me cher, it gets a little lonely in here. It's nice to have someone other than the TV to talk to.'

In spite of wanting company, she can't find anything to talk about. He's not offering up anything either. With no memory it's probably difficult to find a topic he knows much about.

'Can I ask you something Fallon?'

'Sure.'

'What am I?'

She freezes with the fork halfway to her mouth. 'What do you mean?'

'I have no memory, but that doesn't mean I can't see things. Your brother has not been alone with me lately. But you have. I think you've figured out something about me, and you're afraid to leave a weaker human alone with me.'

What the fuck does she say now? Nix and Fletch would probably want her to produce some line, something tame so he's not freaked out. But he has nothing, and no one in his life. The Blackjacks are all he has, and he should be able to trust them. Trust her.

'We received intel that a rougarou was kept in the lab you were rescued from.'

'What's a rougarou?'

'It's a type of werewolf. There isn't much known about them. We didn't even know they existed until we received that intel.'

He brushes his hand over his short brown hair as he digests that. 'Okay. So why do you believe I'm this...what did you call it?'

'A rougarou. Your blood isn't fully human. There's something odd about it. We've never seen it before.'

'But that could mean a lot of things.'

'True, I guess the strongest hint is that the rougarou is from Cajun legends.'

He frowns as he looks down at the foot of the bed. He's confused and scared at the same time. But then his face changes, the smile putting her on edge.

'Thank you.'

'What?' His reaction isn't what she was expecting on any level.

He shuffles down the bed, bringing him closer to her. 'Do you have any idea what it's like not to know who you are? What you are?' He hits his fist against the side of his head. 'There's nothing in here Fallon. Nothing about me. About my past. About a family, friends, a life. It's empty.'

'I just told you there's a chance you're a werewolf.'

'Yes cher. But I'm *something*. I'd happily be this rougarou or whatever, instead of being nothing. I'm trapped in a body that isn't working properly. My head is empty of all memories. I've been kept in a glass cage and experimented on like I didn't matter. I'll take whatever information, even if it's not proven, or just a guess. I don't care. I'll take it.'

'You keep surprising me Austin.' She didn't mean to tell him that, even if it is the truth. She just told him he could be a werewolf and he's happy. But after he explained why, she understands. It all makes sense.

'I'm glad I can keep someone like you on their toes,' he says with an incredibly sexy smile.

'Oh, you do that Austin, believe me.'

'Is there any way of proving or disproving your theory? I'd like to know for sure if there's a chance I'm going to change on the first full moon.'

She laughs, still surprised by his reaction to the whole situation. 'We're doing research. Finding out everything we can. It might mean more—'

He holds up a hand. 'Let me guess - tests?'

'Yes. More of them. We'll figure this out Austin.'

'Until you do, I'll abide by whatever new rules you have. I'll keep away from people. Stay in here if you think that's safer.'

She rests her hand on his leg before she knows what she's doing. He may not be able to feel it, but the contact hits both of them. He looks up at her, his brows furrowed. She continues, trying not to make it seem like a big deal. 'There's no need for that. We'll keep an eye on you, but things stay the same. We're not going to lock you up again.'

She removes her hand, stuffing it in her pocket as she gets to her feet. Enough of this. She needs to leave him alone for a few hours and train. Work off some of this emotional shit she's unleashing. 'I'll leave you to it. I have work to do.'

'Of course cher. Thank you so much for telling me the truth. I'll do whatever I can to help.'

'See you later.'

She closes and locks the door behind her, leaning back against it and closing her eyes. This is bad. So so bad. She needs to keep her distance, not have unplanned romantic dinners with him. If he is a rougarou they have no fucking idea what he'll be like. He could very well decide to tear their heads off and eat them.

Or he could be an asset like they've never had before.

One thing is for sure, she's walking a dangerous line. One she had planned to keep away from for the rest of her long life.

There's a real chance Austin will be the one to claim what's left of her heart.

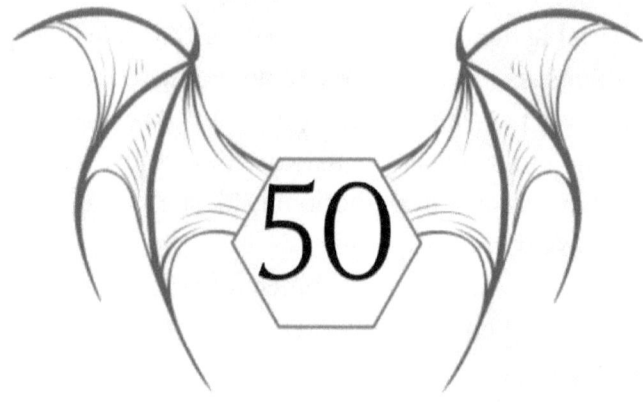

SHEP

He stays in the shower until the water runs cold. He still feels dirty. The bitch had only touched him that once before he was cleaned, but he can still feel her on him. It's been like that for decades, why should it change now?

At least his skin is better again. It's still a bit red where her bodyguard went a little heavy with the scouring pad, but he'll live. And it didn't leave any scars. He's got enough of them as it is.

Shep gets dressed in a pair of jeans, a t-shirt, and his Converse, before sitting on the end of his bed and trying to calm himself.

Izzy will be coming to his room in a few minutes. He wanted to talk to her in private so thought it would be the best place.

Thankfully, Gwen and her team had worked wonders on his space while he was in the medical centre, making sure it was spotless. It doesn't feel like his room at the moment. He's always been a little chaotic in his personal space. It's probably where his mind has been too. Always fighting against the memories and the shame.

But he doesn't really feel like himself either, so it's probably fitting. He's fine about his newfound situation with Dav. He's got no worries there at all. It's his relationship with Izzy he's struggling with.

He looks over at the door when someone knocks. 'Yeah?'

'It's Izzy.'

Show time.

He stands, smoothes his t-shirt, then opens the door. He can't help but smile when he sees her. Her long black hair is out, falling to either side of her face and down her shoulders. The white fitted shirt is tucked into skinny jeans, teamed with a pair of brown heeled boots. Fuck, this woman is hot! Then she smiles at him and the hot jumps up a level.

'Hey love.'

She shyly tucks her hair behind her ear, then stuffs her hands into the back pockets of her jeans. 'I'm a bit early. Sorry.'

'It's fine. Come in.' She steps inside his room and goes over to the couch, sitting down to the far left. He closes the door, discreetly rubs his sweating palms on the legs of his jeans, then sits beside her.

'You look much better. You're healing so fast.'

'Yeah. Cool vampire genes.'

The awkward silence continues for a few minutes. It's up to him to start this off. 'So, I wanted to talk to you about...well, everything I guess. I didn't want you to find out all that stuff the way you did. I didn't want you to find out all that stuff, full stop. Things are just...'

'Complicated,' she says with a small smile. 'You know you can't keep saying that. I want to help you, but you need to give me more than complicated.'

'I know. I like you a lot Izzy. I really do. I just really don't want to have sex with you.'

Of all the ways he could have phrased that, he went for the worst way possible.

'Wow! Okay,' she says, wrapping her arms around herself. 'I appreciate your blunt honesty.'

'No! That came out all wrong. I don't want to have sex with anyone. I hate it.'

She reaches out and takes his hand, but his damn reflexes kick in, pulling it out of her grip. 'Okay, you're going to have to talk to me Shep. I won't touch you. I'll just sit here and listen, but I need to know what's going on. The full truth. Lay it all out for me. Please.'

Right on cue, the burns on his skin itch. He looks at Izzy, hating the sadness on her face. He's done that. He's hurt her and that's the last thing he ever wanted to do.

He stands and kicks the end of the bed. 'Fuck! I'll ask Bas if he can drive you home.'

He jumps when she grabs him by the shoulder, spinning him around. 'No Shep!'

'No? No what?'

'You are not getting rid of me so easily. I know you want me. I'm not being big headed at all, but you are attracted to me.'

'I can't be with you like *that* Izzy! I'm not going to be with you after what I've done. I can't do that to you.'

She points to the couch. 'Sit down!' She repeats it a little more forcefully when he hesitates. 'Thank you.' She sits beside him again and turns to face him.

'Okay, so this is what's going to happen. You're going to talk to me. You're going to tell me everything that happened. Get it all out. Then maybe, while I'm still sitting here, we can have another discussion about where we go next. If we're to have any chance of getting past this, I need to know what's going on in your head. I'm not going to judge you, Shep. Please tell me.'

He takes her hand and slides it under his t-shirt, placing it over some of the burn scars running up his side. He presses her hand against the scars, as he focuses on the wooden floor in front of him.

'My mother likes to live an extravagant life. Always had to have the best of everything. Which was fine while my Dad was alive. But when he died... well, she was left to figure things out for herself. And it backfired. She borrowed money from people she had no right borrowing money from. Anyway, long story short, they eventually gave her a deadline to pay them back... or they would help themselves to her belongings. Well, she couldn't pay, so she was offered an alternative.'

He pauses and rubs the back of his neck. He's never spoken about this to anyone. He knows his old mistress told her some of it, but he wants her to hear it from him. Hear the truth instead of whatever disgusting version that bitch told Izzy.

She's listening to him without interrupting which he's grateful for. He needs to get this out in one go. 'The alternative payment was Willow or me.'

Izzy's hand trembles against his side, but she doesn't say anything.

'She picked me. It's a good thing really. If given the choice I would have picked me too. Anything to keep Willow safe. That's the most important part. It didn't matter what they did to me, as long as they kept away from her.'

Shep squeezes his eyes shut and curses to himself. 'So, my mother just handed me over and went on her way with Willow. It turns out that as well as lending money, the guys she owed money to also had a *hospitality* business. I was rented out by the hour to pay for her debts. Sick fucks had a unique way of recording how much my mother still owed. One burn for each visitor to my room.

'I was kept chained to the bed most of the time. If the guest was smiling when they left my room, I was marked, and the debt decreased. I tried resisting at first, but my body wasn't always on the same page as my head. Vampire males have a damn impressive libido. Didn't really matter either way. If I wasn't willing and able they'd give me something to change that.

'I couldn't do anything to stop what was happening, so after a while I gave up resisting. I hated every minute of it, but it became my life. I guess I got used to it.' He stops talking but can't look over at her. This is so much worse than he thought it would be.

'So, about a year later I figured out the debt should be paid, or at least close to being settled. But my *mother* never came back to claim me. All they needed was for my mother to come to them and ask for me back. But she never came. So they kept me.'

'How...' she pauses briefly. 'How long did they keep you?'

'Twelve years, give or take.'

'Oh God...'

'They could have just let me go, but I guess I was worth too much in revenue. They weren't going to kiss that goodbye. Don't know why, but apparently I became a favourite with some of the upper-class females.'

She lifts up his t-shirt so she can see the burns clearly. 'How many scars do you have?'

'Seven hundred and fifty three. They started with my legs.' He pulls up his jeans to show her the burn marks running up the sides of his leg. 'Just glad they stopped before they ruined my arms. I wouldn't have been impressed with that.' He laughs once. 'Sorry. Bad joke. Not used to talking about it.

'I knew I was there because of my mother's debt and thought that I'd be let go once it was paid off. I figured if I did what I was told - and did it well - the debt might be paid off faster. I was their prisoner. There wasn't anything else I could do. So, I just went along with it.' He closes his eyes for a moment, then focuses on the floor again.

'I can't tell you how much I hated it. The stench of too many expensive flowery perfumes. The feel of *them*. The things they'd say to me. The way they'd look at me. I hated every single second, but I still did what was expected. I honestly thought I'd get out sooner that way.'

He scrubs his hand through his hair as he laughs harshly. 'How wrong was I! By that time, I had regulars. Bored mates of distinguished members of vampire society. I was raking it in for them. Why the hell would they kiss all that goodbye by letting me go? The owner of the club was married. His wife had a thing for me. She used me a lot.'

'Your mistress?' Izzy says.

'Yeah. Her. She called me her *pet*. Fuck, I hated her more than I've hated anyone in my life! Even more than I hate my mother. She never hurt me, as in hit me, or anything like that.

'It was more about how she treated me. Like I should be grateful she was giving me her attention. I had to ... I had to thank her after. Like it was some fucking privilege that she let me near her. She made me feel like I was nothing. That a whore like me should be grateful for any attention.

'She used to wear this really sickening perfume. It was something with rosewater in it. Fucking rotten stuff that would coat everything - my skin, my hair, my nostrils. It didn't matter how much I showered afterwards, I couldn't get rid of the stench.

'I think I shut down when I realised I wasn't getting out. I went through the motions. When I thought there was a way out, an end in sight, I had a small bit of control. It was pathetic, but better than nothing.

'But, after I realised I was there for the long haul, I had nothing left to fight for. I accepted I had no control over what was happening. I was told repeatedly I was a toy. Something with a limited use. Something that could be disposed of when they were done with me.

'I can't tell you how much I hated when someone opened that door, but I also needed someone to open the door. That doesn't make any sense.' He gets up and rubs the back of his neck as he paces. He's close to throwing up. His stomach churning violently as the memories are brought to life again.

'You see, once the door closed, I was alone again Izzy. There was nothing to do but think. To replay everything that happened. To hate myself even more for wanting that door to open. After a while, I hoped someone would come in - offer some distraction from what was going around in my head.'

'How did you escape?'

'They got sloppy. I reckon they thought I was broken. No fight left. Didn't keep a hold on me when they took off my chains.

'I had some fight left all right. I took a few of them down on my way out. Helped myself to some clothes. But I bumped into the bodyguard when I got down to bottom floor. He was so surprised to see me I got the upper hand. I shattered the bastard's nose before I made a run for it.

'I broke into a workshop. Found a bolt cutter to cut her chain off my neck, then lived rough for a few months. When I was sure no one was looking for me, I hooked up with Willow again.'

'Why didn't you tell her about any of this?'

He snorts. 'Yeah right! Like that's a conversation I'm going to have with my sister. I'm her big brother Izzy. I'm the one she can depend on no matter what. I didn't want to destroy our relationship.'

'I don't know what to say.'

'You don't have to say anything. It is what it is. And for the most part I was treated well. I wasn't worth anything if they hurt me. I was fed, allowed to work out, had my own room. Just wasn't allowed to leave.'

'Or to say no. Twelve years of being...' she sniffs and wipes her face as she turns away from him.

'Hey? What's up?'

'I'm heartbroken for you. It's horrific.'

He wipes her tears away, slightly confused by her reaction. He wasn't expecting her to cry for him. The only reaction he'd been building up to, was her making a swift exit from his life. It doesn't take a genius to realise she's disgusted by what he just told her. It's written all over her face and nothing he says is going to take that away.

It's ruined. They're ruined.

No one is going to want anything deep and meaningful with someone like him.

He frowns as Izzy takes his hand in hers. 'I know that can't have been easy to talk about it but thank you for trusting me with the truth.'

He shrugs. 'It's no big deal.'

'Stop it! Don't keep trying to brush this off. It's important, Shep.'

'Sorry. I can't stop doing that.'

He looks down at her hand over his. It feels nice. Maybe she gets it? Is there a chance she could accept him? He wants her to. More than anything he wants her to still see him as a strong male. It's petty and egotistical, he knows that. It shouldn't matter if she pities him. It makes sense that she would. It's not how anyone would want to spend twelve years of their life.

But he survived. He came out the other side. It's vital to him that he's still thought of as the strong warrior, the strong Blackjack, the male who would kill to defend his sister, his team.

Izzy.

He's never been more sure of anything before. Izzy is right up there with everyone else he cares about. He would kill to keep her safe without a second thought... if she'd let him. There's still a strong chance she's just being nice to him after what he told her. There's a big difference between that and wanting him.

'Can I ask you something Shep?'

'Shoot.'

'The Lair. Being with people there. Why do you do that? Why can you go there, but not be with me? I'm trying to understand, but I'm struggling with that part.'

'Join the club,' he mutters. His stomach does that whole nauseating somersault of shame it does whenever she mentions that place. 'I need it, Izzy. It's all I'm good at. When I'm doing that I somehow feel validated. Worthwhile even. I can't believe how messed up that sounds out loud.

'It's all I know how to do. Nix and the others, they think I sleep with everything that moves, because I like it. It's like this in-house joke.' He laughs briskly. 'Can't really blame them. I've never told them I have to do it. That if I don't let this ball of whatever the hell it is in my chest out, it'll destroy me.

'Going to The Lair. Doing what I do. It helps. It's the only thing that does. But I hate it! I hate having sex. I get nothing from it. I just lie there and let them do what they want to me. I've never once been in control. Never once been the one on top. I can't even remember the last time I actually came when I've been with anyone.'

'Fuck!' He abruptly pushes to his feet and walks to the far side of the room. 'I can't do this. Why are you still here? Why haven't you run for the fucking door?'

She stands, walking over to him again. 'Stop running away from me.'

'I'm not!' He looks around the room and smiles sheepishly. 'Okay, maybe I am. I do like you. I just...' Just what? What can he offer her by asking her to stay? A friendship? A kiss and a cuddle? Some fucked up nonsexual relationship? She deserves more than that. More than him.

IZZY

Hearing the truth about what he went through tore her heart to pieces. It was so much worse hearing it from him, than it was to hear it from that woman, but she needed him to do that. She needed to hear it in his words. She also believes he needed to tell her in his own words. To get it out so they could move on.

If they can move on.

'So, when you say you hate sex. What do you hate about it? Is it the act itself? Is it someone touching you?'

'All of the above. It was just something I had to do to survive.'

'And you've never finished when you've been with someone?'

He shakes his head. 'I wasn't allowed to *come* until after the client did. I was beaten if I did. So, I just got used to not *coming* while I was having sex. I'd take care of myself after, if I needed to, but never while I was with someone.'

'Were you with men or just women?'

'Mostly women.' He shrugs as he looks down at the ground. 'I didn't get a say on who came into the room.'

'When I touch you, what happens in your head?'

'I freak out. I'm okay touching you. I really like kissing you and holding your hand and stuff like that. But when you try to make a move on me, my head just goes off track. I don't mean to, and I know it sucks for you. I'm sorry.'

'You have nothing to apologise for. Everything you're saying makes sense, do you hear me? Everything.'

'Okay, but that doesn't really help us move things along. I've had sex with so many people over the years, and I hate telling you I can't be like that with you. You deserve more than I can offer. But I need you to know that when I say I can't, it's a compliment.'

He curses and scrubs his hand over his face. 'I can't believe how fucked up all this sounds.' He taps the side of his head. 'It all makes sense up here but when I say it out loud, it's messed up.'

'It's coming out perfectly Shep. And believe it or not, I do take it as a compliment.'

'You do?'

'Yes. But that doesn't mean I don't want us to find a way to work through this - for you as much as for me.'

'Why? There's nothing stopping you from walking out the door and going back to your life. You'll be safe now. You can forget about all this and go back to normal.'

'I don't want normal. I want you.'

'Should I take that as a compliment?' he asks.

''Yes you should. You've been honest with me Shep, and I can't tell you how much that means to me. So, I think it's only fair I return the favour.'

His face drops. He's expecting the worst.

'I'm deeply in love with you Shep.'

If the situation wasn't so serious, Izzy would laugh at the look on

Shep's face. He genuinely wasn't expecting her to say that. She had to though. If there was ever a time to say it, it was in that moment.

He still hasn't moved a muscle. She doesn't even think he's blinked yet. 'Shep?' She waves her hand in his face. 'Hello? Are you okay?'

'What? Yeah. I'm... sorry did you just say that you love me?'

'Actually, I said that I'm deeply in love with you. There's an enormous difference.'

'Are you sure?'

She laughs loudly. 'Sure there's a difference, or sure that I love you?'

'The loving me part.'

'Of course I'm sure. Why wouldn't I be sure?'

'Because of everything I just told you. I wouldn't blame you for not wanting anything to do with me.'

She holds out her hand, waiting until he takes it in his before she continues. 'I just told you that I'm in love with you Shep. I'm not going anywhere.'

When he smiles, she nearly cries. It's filled with such relief. He honestly thought she was going to leave him.

'But what about you know, being with you like that? I don't know how long it will be.'

'That's fine. Things have been so hectic it would be nice to get to know you better first anyway. I have an idea if you're game?'

'I'll give anything a shot for you.'

God she loves this man. 'Give me an hour, then come downstairs to the living room.'

'An hour? To do what?'

'That's none of your business. Just do what I say.'

He salutes. 'Yes ma'am. Whatever you say.'

She hurries away from his room and goes down to the kitchen, finding Gwen at the stove stirring pasta sauce in a huge pot. 'I need your help with something.'

'What is it dear? Is Shep hungry again? I can't keep up with that vampire's stomach.'

'No... well actually yes in a roundabout way. I'd like to have a proper first date with him. Everything's been so crazy with his wings and... well, that other woman. I'd just like to show him exactly what he means to me without...' She really wishes her mouth had stopped a few words ago.

Talking about her lack of anything sexual with Shep isn't where she wanted to go with Gwen. She barely knows the woman, plus she's old enough to be Izzy's mother. 'Sorry. I didn't mean to say all that.'

'I was young once myself I'll have you know. And I heard what happened to him. I understand what you want to do.'

She links arms with her and leads her across the hall to the living room. 'How about you get this place sorted and I'll look after the food? I know the way to that vampire's stomach. Basically, it's anything edible, but he does have a few favourites I can rustle up.'

'Thanks Gwen. I really appreciate it.'

'Nonsense! If anyone deserves a bit of happiness it's this lot of vampires, believe me. Now chop chop. There are candles in the drawer by the far wall. I'll make sure everyone keeps away from here tonight.'

'Thanks Gwen.' Izzy looks around the huge living room, focusing on the massive fireplace. That'll have to be lit for starters. She finds everything she needs at the side of the mantle and gets to work lighting it.

When Shep arrives an hour later everything is ready. He pauses at the doorway and looks at the room, his mouth open. 'What's all this?'

She takes his hand, leading him inside, before closing the double doors behind him. 'I thought we could have a proper date. Our first one didn't quite go to plan, what with the whole *drinking someone's blood* thing.'

'Yeah. Not my best move.'

'No, but I want you to see that there can be more to us than sex. I have no idea what you're going through, and I'm not going to tell you that it will all be okay in time, or anything like that.' She takes his hands in hers and looks into his blue eyes. 'But what I can say is that I love you Shep. I want to be with you - sex or not. I just want you.'

She's never known him to be lost for words, but she's got him. Instead, he checks out the room she's spent the last hour preparing. The fire is lit, candles along the mantle and on pretty much every surface there is.

On the coffee table in front of the fire is a mouth-watering meal. As well as his favourite antipasti platter of marinated mozzarella balls, olives, cheeses, and breads, there's a huge bowl of pasta with garlic bread.

'Gwen said you have Netflix, so I thought we could stick on something, eat dinner, and relax. Is that okay?'

'Okay? Fuck, Izzy. I don't know what to say. This is amazing. It's perfect. Thank you.'

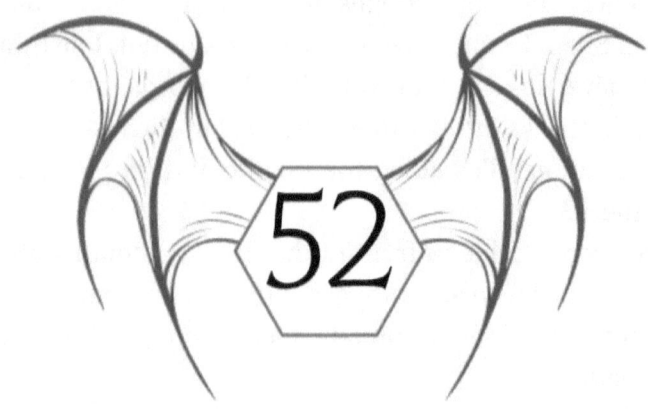

ETHAN

It's late. Apart from a handful of staff, everyone else has gone to their homes. Back to their friends and family. Back to their loved ones.

But he's got nothing to go home to. No one waiting for him. No one to talk to about his day, share a meal with, climb into bed with.

Ethan wipes his face as he turns to look out the window behind his desk. He can't stop the tears. What reason does he have to be upset?

He hasn't lost anything. Not really.

He didn't *have* Bastian. They shared their bodies - nothing more.

The lie is like a blow to his gut again. Who is he kidding? Bas had his heart. He had willingly handed it over without even knowing it was happening.

And now he's alone to grieve a relationship that never really existed except in his head.

He doesn't have any photos of them together. Doesn't have any trinkets or mementos. There's nothing in the world to even hint that they had a friendship, let alone anything more.

But did they even have a friendship?

He wipes his face again, willing the tears to stop. He needs to get over this before it gets in the way of his job.

Ethan spins around when someone steps into the room. 'What are you doing here?'

Nix closes the door, before walking across the room and taking a seat in one of the chairs at the other side of his desk. She crosses her legs, brushing her dark hair back from her shoulder. 'I thought you might need a friend to talk to.'

He attempts a smile as he turns on his laptop, pretending to have some work to do. 'Why do you say that?'

Nix reaches across and slowly closes the laptop. 'Because you're sad and doing a terrible job of hiding it. We've known each other for a long time Ethan. I know you better than anyone else in my life. I know when you're upset, so don't try to tell me otherwise. I'm not going to buy it.'

His first instinct is to keep saying he's fine. But the tears decide to come out again, bringing the truth with them. Nix gives him time to get himself together, which he's grateful for. He already feels pathetic enough as it is, without being comforted in that moment.

Nix goes over to his bar at the side of the room and fixes them both a drink, placing the glasses on his desk, before sitting down again.

'I apologise,' he says after taking a sip of the whiskey. 'I didn't mean to do that in front of you.'

'You've seen me cry dozens of times. It's what friends do from time to time. What happened between you and Bastian?'

He looks over at her. 'Bastian? Why do you assume something happened between us?'

'He's been your bodyguard for months. As far as I was aware, he was doing an exceptional job. Then unexpectedly you request he be taken off your detail and Fallon put in his place.

'Now, I might be reading between the lines here, but I can't help but think that there's more to this than a mere personality clash. Besides, it's Bas we're talking about. I can't think of anyone who has ever had a personality clash with him.'

He should keep up his farce, but he can't. He needs someone to know. Needs there to be some record somewhere that this happened.

'I made such a foolish mistake Nix. I broke my own rules and now I'm paying for it.' He takes another sip, hoping the drink will help to dull his pain. Being mostly human means he can get drunk, unlike his vampire friends. Every now and again his diluted blood has its perks.

'You fell in love with him, didn't you?'

'I've been an idiot Nix. I never meant for it to happen. I really didn't. But I just couldn't resist him. And he did nothing wrong! This was on me - not him.'

She holds up her hands. 'We're talking as friends Ethan. I'm not here to judge anyone.'

'Yes well you can judge me. I deserve it.'

'Can I ask you something?'

He nods, as he takes another drink.

'You hesitated when making your decision to send us to Ireland to take down Davyn's father. Was that because of Bas?'

'As I said, feel free to judge me. I saw your request and I just froze. I pictured him lying on a bed with his lips sewn shut. Every time I closed my eyes I saw Bas with Davyn's injuries. I couldn't do it.'

'But you did.'

He laughs. 'Not by choice. Bastian came to see me. He could see exactly what I was doing and reminded me of our agreement. The team must always come first. I didn't realise until that moment how far I'd let him in, how deeply I cared for him. How in love I was.'

'Past tense?'

'Yes. Like I said, I broke our agreement. I demanded more of his time.'

'Demanded?' she asks. 'I can't see you demanding anything Ethan.'

'I'm guessing that's how he saw it. I believed we were okay. It was hard not being able to have anything meaningful with him, but I was doing what I could to keep my feelings to myself. Perhaps I failed?

'A few nights ago, I asked him to stay with me. We were together and as usual, it was incredible. But when I woke he was gone. I knew then I'd pushed him too far.

'Then he came to me and said that we had run our course. He walked away. I am trying so hard to be professional about this, but it hurts so much Nix.'

He doesn't mind when she hurries around his desk to hold him. He needs it more than he thought.

'I'm so sorry Ethan. I don't know how to make it better for you.'

'It's my burden.'

'Oh would you knock it off. I'm here for you. Use me.'

She sits on the edge of his desk, leaning over to brush the tears from his cheeks. 'Have you tried to speak to him?'

'It's done Nix. And he's probably right. I need to concentrate on our work. I can't let my heart make my decisions for me. It will cost lives, and I'm not prepared to do that.'

'I remember someone telling me a while ago that I am allowed to have a personal life, as well as being a Blackjack. I don't suppose you remember who that was, do you?'

He leans back in his chair and smiles as her. 'I believe that was me.'

'It was. And I followed your advice. Because of that I'm now with Court and happier than I've ever been. Do you not deserve the same?'

'If only.' Ethan swallows the rest of his drink, placing the glass back on his desk. 'But I fear that's not going to happen. I can't be gay, Nix. My grandmother would never allow it. Our work is too important to cut off our main income stream. In time that may change, but for now, I must keep up appearances. I must continue to live a lie.'

'That's not fair on you Ethan. You shouldn't have to hide who you truly are.'

He shrugs. 'It won't be forever. Until then I want to focus on the fact that we are fighting for those unable to fight for themselves. That is far more important. And I won't distract Bastian. With our numbers so low, you need him focused.'

'You can be focused and still be with Bas.'

'No. He's made it clear it's over. I'll be fine. I just need to give myself a stern talking to. What I will ask for though is some time. Would you mind if I kept away from the compound for a while? I don't think I'm ready to see him yet.'

He can't imagine a time when he will be ready, but he does need to get over this. His life's work is the Blackjacks. Bas is one of them. Their paths will cross again, but not yet.

'Of course.' She stands and holds out her hand.

'What?'

'Do you honestly think I'm going to let you sit here alone all night? Not happening. I'm driving you home, we're going to order takeout, and we'll watch some ridiculous comedy on TV.'

That sounds perfect. He takes her hand, grabbing his laptop before he locks his office, and allows her to lead him to the elevator.

Enough crying. Enough of feeling sorry for himself. He won't let his weakness in any way affect the Blackjacks or their work. He's just going to have to push his feelings for Bastian away, bury them deep where they can't interfere.

In time the pain will ease... he hopes.

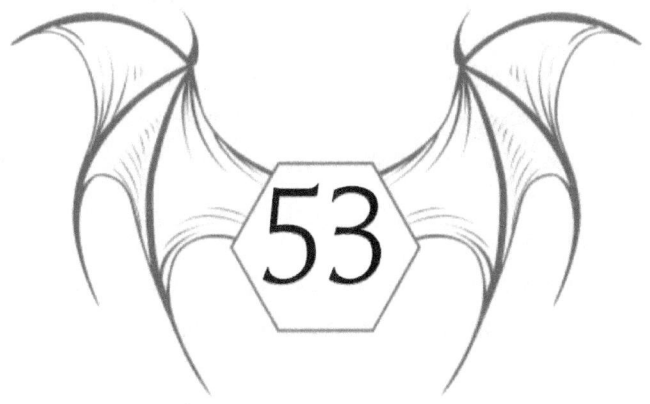

SHEP

'I am so stuffed.' It takes a lot to actually fill him, but Gwen managed it with the banquet she supplied. Shep slouches back on the couch, his arms spread along the back as he groans. 'So, so stuffed.'

Izzy shuffles closer to him, tucking in against his side. Instinctively he tenses and he hates it. 'Sorry.'

'Do you want me to move?'

'No. I like it.' He drapes an arm around her, holding her close.

He really likes holding her. With her, it's never felt wrong or forced. He flinched and pulled away, but that was instinct. It's what he's always done. And it's probably something he'll do for another while. But at least now she knows why. She knows it's not her.

This is his chance to have someone in his life who cares about him for who he is, not for what he can give them. And that means the world to him. She means the world to him.

He's never done anything like this before. Never just watched a film and eaten tasty food with someone who wasn't his sister, or a team member. It's strangely comfortable but also intimate, in a way he never thought it would be.

While they watch the film they hold each other, talk about their likes and dislikes., get to know each other better. The only touching that takes place is holding hands, and her beautiful body lying against his.

But it's perfect.

Everything about Izzy and how she is with him is perfect. It's what he needs. He needs normal. He needs gentle. He needs understanding.

He needs her.

'Izzy?'

She sits up and smiles at him. 'Yeah?'

'I love you.'

Her incredible smile makes his fucking year. 'You do? Really? I didn't tell you how I feel so you'd say the same to me. Not if you're not ready.'

He takes her face in his hands, holding her close. 'I love you Isabella. I know you deserve better than I can give you, but I'm going to be selfish here. I want you. I want you more than I've wanted anyone in my life. I feel different with you. I'm a better person with you, if that makes sense.

'I'm going to just go for it here, so sorry if I'm running instead of walking, but do you think you'd consider staying here? With me I mean? You can have your own room of course, but I thought it might maybe be an option? You could finish your coursework without having to worry about The Lair. I'll look after you financially for as long as you'll let me.'

She sits up straight and hits him with a strange look.

'That's a weird look. You okay?'

'Did you mean all that?'

'Yeah. Every word. About the loving you part and about the moving in here part. All of it.'

'Do you not have to check with Nix first?'

'Fuck no! She's cool about stuff like that.'

'And you really want me to move here? Like give up my lease on my apartment?'

'Okay, so how about I cover that for the rest of your lease, just in case you decide you can't stand me, or I'm an obnoxious git to live with? At least then you'll have somewhere to escape to. But as for The Lair, you won't need to work there to cover your costs. I'll do that. You can just focus on getting your course wrapped up.'

'I just want to give you advance warning here. I may be about to hug you.'

'Go for it!'

She squeals and pulls him into a bone crushing hug.

'Is that a yes? Also, I can't breathe!'

She releases him, smiling apologetically. 'Sorry. And yes, It's one hundred percent a yes. I'd love that.'

'Brilliant! I can bring you to your place tomorrow if you want to grab some stuff.'

'It's a date.'

He squirms on the couch, trying to get comfortable, but his wings aren't on board with that. They're unhappy about something, and he's not got a clue what.

'Are you okay?'

'Yeah. Fucking wings are pissing me off.'

'Why don't you let them out for a while? It can't be comfortable having them squashed inside you for so long.'

'Would you mind?'

She stands up and moves the coffee table out of the way. 'Get them out. There's nothing they can destroy.'

'That was a once off. I'm not planning on doing that again.'

He pulls off his t-shirt then stops trying to keep his wings inside. Less than a minute later the two huge limbs are out. 'Fuck, that's actually better,' he says, stretching them to each side.

Izzy stares in amazement at the wings as he moves them, the sensation still completely weird.

'Can I touch them?'

'Go for it!'

She runs her fingers along the thick flesh. 'They're beautiful. Everything about you is.'

He notices that she's moved her attention from the wings to his burns.

'You shouldn't be embarrassed by them.'

'My wings or my scars?'

'Both.'

'The wings I can get used to. The scars are fucking horrible.'

'Actually, I was thinking that each and every scar is testament to your strength, to your bravery, to your love and commitment to Willow. That's nothing to be ashamed of. Far from it.'

He looks down at his chest then back up at her. 'Really? You think that?'

'I wouldn't say it unless I meant it.'

Maybe she's right. Each of the scars lining his legs and side signify survival. His survival.

'Thank you for saying that. And thank you for tonight. I've never had someone do anything like this for me. I've never just spent time with someone. I'm just worried that you'll get bored with me. And I wouldn't blame you. I can't expect you to hang around waiting for me to get myself sorted.'

'I told you Shep. I love you. Of course I want to be with you like that at some stage, but I understand why you can't right now. And to be honest, I'm fine with that.'

'You are?'

'I have no idea what it was like for you in that house with *bitch woman.*'

'I like that name. It suits her.'

'Oh that's one of the tame ones, believe me. I'm here for the long haul. We can spend the next few months, or even years getting to know each other. We'll take it slow. Take it at your pace. If it's just kissing, holding hands, and snuggling like tonight, I'll be happy. If after a while you want to take it further, we'll do it on your terms. Small steps.'

'You're fucking awesome, you know that?'

'Don't be ridiculous. Of course I do!'

SHEP

As he takes his seat in the meeting room, he can't help but smile to himself. A week ago, he didn't think he'd ever see the room again. Now here he is, still a member of the team, in love with a beautiful woman who is willing to take things at a snail's pace with him. And he's free.

Okay so Dav is officially his owner, but he's not worried about that fact in the slightest. This morning, he was given his new, very swanky chain, and he couldn't be happier with it. The platinum necklace is a hell of a lot thinner than the industrial chain *she* had locked around his neck. Instead of a heavy padlock, Ethan had a special lock made.

Shep had actually been a little speechless when he saw it. The lock has been made in the shape of Dav's pauldron, the horned devil stamp with his crest on the back. It still locked the chain around his neck, and to those who knew what they were looking at, it marks him as

Dav's property, but to the rest of the world, it's a necklace with a pendant on it.

Considering how his life could have played out, he's not doing too badly.

Bas sits opposite him, but his smile isn't enthusiastic in any way. His mate is downright miserable. Has been since he ended things with Ethan. Shep wishes he could help, do something to drag his friend out of his head, but he's at a loss what to do. He doubts anything he says is going to make the slightest bit of difference.

And it appears that he's not the only one struggling.

Ethan hasn't been to the compound since they ended things. He's usually here at least once a week - sometimes more often. He's avoiding Bas. Maybe they agreed to keep away from each other for a while? Whatever is going on, it's between the two of them. Not that he's being selfish or anything, but he's got enough to deal with in his own life, without trying to figure out another couple.

And he's still got a lot to figure out. He will though. He's not ashamed anymore. Not embarrassed or disgusted by his past. He knows it's something he's going to get through with Izzy's help.

'What the fuck are you smiling about?' Bas asks from across the table.

'What?'

'You've got a stupid grin on your face,' Willow says, nudging him in the side. 'You're in love. It's so cute.'

'What's cute?' Nix asks, as she and Court take their seats.

'My brother and Izzy.'

Nix smiles as she settles into her seat. 'You know, I have to agree. It's nice to see you smiling for a change.'

'Hey! I smile a lot.'

Nix gestures to his eyes. 'Not there. You smile, but it's never reached your eyes. Not until her.'

The fact Nix noticed that has taken him aback. She really does know them better than they know themselves sometimes. 'You might have a point Boss.'

'I usually do,' she responds with a smile. 'So, how are you getting on with your new piece of jewellery?'

'I actually like it. I'm relieved Dav's crest doesn't have a rabbit or anything like that on it. I can handle this devil thing. What is it anyway?' he asks Dav.

'Fuck knows! It was my grandfather's pauldron. I think it's a horned demon. Definitely not a rabbit.'

'A horned demon! I can pull that look off, no problem.'

She hits him with a look that tells him to be serious. 'Honestly, it's all good Nix. I see it as a necklace. The only change it's going to make to my life is that I won't be looking over my shoulder anymore. There's nothing to be down about.'

'Glad to hear it. Ethan has logged the relevant paperwork making it all official. Until we find some way to eradicate this disgusting practice, you are legally Dav's. That woman will never be able to claim you again.'

'Glad to hear it,' he says, repeating Nix's statement.

'Okay, so back to the reason for this meeting. I'm just going to jump right in. Rhain.'

The groans and rumbles of cursing take over the meeting, until Nix holds up her hand, silencing them.

'I trust you've all got that out of your system. Now, Shep, when you were at his house, you reported that he was taken by force.'

'Yeah Boss. In his undies too. He wasn't happy about it.'

'No less than he deserves,' Bas mutters, his look a little scary. The male is in a seriously dark place right now.

'Perhaps,' Nix continues. 'However—'

'You can't be serious?' Court says, jumping in before anyone else can. 'You want to save him? Rhain?'

'I know he's at the bottom of our friend list, but he has been extremely useful over the last few months. If he hadn't given us that drug to give to Shep, he could be dead right now.'

'Yeah, you got a point there Boss,' Shep says, 'But, I wouldn't have needed it at all if he hadn't created the other drug that gave me wings. It's kind of like patching someone up after shooting them. It was all down to him.'

'I know, but according to Ethan's reports, Rhain wasn't aware of everything The Order was doing in the labs. That drug wasn't his project - it was The Order's.'

'And my memory?' Court says. 'Austin's memory? Do we just forgive him for that?'

'I know what you're saying, I really do. And I'm not saying for one second that we forgive and forget anything. Far from it. But he's also the key to maybe unlocking those memories again. That vampire is a fountain of knowledge - both about The Order, and whatever was going on in those labs. He's an asset we can't leave in their hands.'

'What's Ethan's position on this?'

The whole table turn their attention to Bas. Shep isn't sure if the growl was intentional or not. Knowing Bas, probably not. He's usually got a good hold on his emotions.

Nix frowns but doesn't comment on the growl. 'We're in agreement. We need Rhain. We need the information he has.' She leans forward, taking a long breath before she continues.

'We're fighting a war. A war we're struggling to keep on top of. The Order was somehow able to give Shep wings. They altered a Hybrid and made him Prime in all but blood. They were keeping a rougarou in the lab. Why? If Austin is what we think he is, what did they do to him? Have they altered him? Tried to mix a rougarou with a vampire? We need to know.

'Besides, the role of the Blackjacks is to fight for vampires who can't fight for themselves. Right now, that's Rhain.'

'Fuck!' Court sums up what everyone else is thinking. 'You really want us to rescue him?'

'I think we need to.'

'But he's dying Nix,' Bas says. 'His Fever can't be cured. Are you going to risk us, to save a dying bastard like him?'

'Well, Ethan has a solution for that too.'

Shep glances at Court as their second in command catches on. 'No fucking way! You want me to give him my blood? Not a snowball's chance in hell! He kept me prisoner for years so he could take it. I'm not jumping at the chance to hand it over to him now, out of the goodness of my heart.'

'I know,' Nix says, trying to calm the situation. Good luck to her! Court is pissed. 'We're a long way from that point. Right now, this is a job just like every other one. I understand you are all against this, but I see Ethan's point. This is bigger than our personal dislike of Rhain. He could tip the balance in our favour.'

'He could get us all killed.'

'Yes Bas. I realise that.' She slides a file into the middle of the table. 'This is everything we know about Rhain. His businesses, his homes, any information Ethan and his team were able to find on him. We work this like any other job. He's a vampire who has been taken by force by The Order. His life is in immediate danger. That's all that matters. We are going to find him. I don't want to make this an official order, but I will if I have to.'

'Fuck!' Bas's curse surprises everyone, but that's the only comment that is made.

'Good. Ethan and his people are trying to find potential locations where they might be holding him. We'll move out as soon as he has some intel.'

'What about the Whelans?' Dav asks. 'We still looking for them?'

'Of course,' Nix says. 'Nothing has changed there. Ethan has split his support team in two. One half will look for Rhain and the other the Whelans and the prisons. He was able to determine that there has been talk of at least three prisons in Ireland. He's still working on the exact locations, but it's a good start.'

'Ireland is a big fucking country when you don't know where you're looking,' Dav says.

'I know you're frustrated. We all are. But we're the best of the best. We will find out what happened to them, and to Fergus's son Quillan. Until then it's business as usual. Fallon and Dav, you're on patrol tonight. Stay safe. Dismissed.'

Bas charges from the room before Shep can ask him what the fuck is wrong. Not that he doesn't know. It's Ethan. They've got this cheery version of Bas to deal with for the foreseeable, which should be fun.

'Hey! Wait up!'

Bas stops at the end of the corridor and turns to face him. 'What!'

'Hey! What did I do?'

Bas scrubs his hand over his face as he curses in Spanish. 'I'm sorry. I'm not in a great mood.'

'Oh you think? I might have picked up on that when you growled at the meeting. That's a first for you. You really don't like Rhain, do you?'

'And you do?'

'Okay, so I'm not best mates with him or anything, but I kind of get where Ethan and Nix are coming from. He has helped us a bit over the last few weeks.'

'That hardly wipes the slate clean.'

'I know. Nix and Ethan have their heads screwed on. They know what they're doing.'

Bas shakes his head but doesn't reply. 'You know what you need?'

'What?'

'You need to beat me up.'

'Excuse me?'

'It's been ages since we had a go at each other in the training room. I've got loads of energy to blow off, and you're about to explode. Come on mate. Pretty please!'

Bas holds his glare for another minute, before breaking into laughter. 'I really hate you at times.'

'Ah you don't. You love me really.' They walk down to the training room in a comfortable silence, which Shep breaks as they get to the locker room. 'You know, I'm still here for you whenever. Just because Izzy is with me doesn't change anything.'

Bas pulls off his t-shirt, hanging it in the locker. 'I know, but I appreciate you saying that. And I'm sorry about my mood. I'm finding things difficult.'

'Have you seen him at all since you went your separate ways?'

'Not alone. And now he's staying away from the compound, so the odds of seeing him are slim. He's avoiding me.'

'Or maybe just avoiding a painful situation?'

'Perhaps. '

They continue getting changed in silence, but this time Shep leaves him to it. He's never seen Bas like this before. He's also never known Ethan to avoid the compound for this long. Anyone with half a brain can see how crazy they are about each other.

After nearly losing Izzy to his own stubbornness, he feels for the two of them. Maybe in time they'll realise how they feel and stop playing games or ignoring what's in front of everyone's faces.

SHEP

Once he's able to pick himself off the floor of the training room, after Bas kicked his ass, again, Shep has a hot shower, then stops by the kitchen, grabbing a tub of ice cream and two spoons from Gwen, before making his way to the library. Izzy is spending most of her days in there, studying in peace and quiet, while the rest of them train.

Both herself and Thea had taken over the room, Thea sorting through papers from Dav's father on one of the large tables, and Izzy at the other, college books all over the surface.

He loves that the two women have clicked so well. It can be lonely here when the team go out for hours on end. It's good they have each other to talk to.

He knocks on the door, before slowly opening it and peering

inside. It's just Izzy at the moment, her smile when she sees him making his fucking week. 'Hey gorgeous. Time for ice cream?'

She shuts her laptop. 'Are you kidding me? There's always time for ice cream.'

He drops onto the couch, cursing when she sits beside him, her elbow digging into his ribs. 'You know it's a three-seater couch? You don't have to actually sit on me.'

'But I also know what you're like with ice cream. I don't want to be too far from that tub.'

She reaches up to kiss him, her hand sliding around the back of his head to comb through his hair. For someone who is still getting used to kissing, he's getting the hang of it. He could kiss her for hours and still want more.

'So, any news?' she asks as she settles back in the chair and digs her spoon into the tub.

'Yeah. We're going after that bad guy I told you about. Rhain.'

'Going after how?' she asks around a mouthful of ice cream.

'Saving his ass I guess. We have to find him first.'

'Are you okay about that?'

He shrugs as he digs his spoon into the tub again. 'I guess I'm okay with it. I'd prefer not to have wings, but he did give me that shot that saved me. Maybe he's not all bad. Maybe. Whatever. He's probably going to be dead by the time we find him.'

'Oh wow! That's cheery! I thought you were a highly trained group of warriors?'

'Of course we are! How dare you suggest otherwise! Anyway, I don't want to talk about that asshole. How was your day?'

'Good,' she says, snuggling closer to him. He loves the feel of her body against his. She's being an angel with him, keeping things slow between them, while still moving him along in the right direction. A direction he wants to go in.

And for the first time it's somewhere he believes he'll be able to reach, with her help. It's somewhere he's looking forward to reaching.

They'd slept in the same bed last night. They were both dressed, but it was a massive step in the right direction for him, and for them as a couple.

He'd also stopped all trips to The Lair. With Izzy in his life, he no longer needs it. He doesn't need to have meaningless sex with random strangers. He just needed someone to love him. Someone to see beyond all that stuff and like him for being the messed-up vampire he is.

'I should get my assignment wrapped up tomorrow so I can take the rest of the night off. Are you free, or does Nix need you for something?'

He shakes his head. 'Nope. I'm all yours. You got something in mind?'

'Well, I've been wanting to ask you something for a while and life just got in the way.'

'A hell of a lot of fucked up life got in the way.'

'Yeah. That's probably a better way of describing it,' she says. 'Okay, so do you think you could take me out on your bike? I've never been on a motorbike before and just thought—'

He doesn't let her finish the sentence, grabbing her by the hand and pulling her from the room.

'Shep! What are you doing?'

'You want to go on the bike, you're going on it.'

'But what about the ice cream?'

'Some things are more important.'

She laughs as she races to keep up with his long strides. Deciding to get things going faster, he picks her up, throwing her over his shoulder. 'Oh my God! I'm going to throw up ice cream all over your back!'

'I don't want you to change your mind.' He places her back on her feet in the garage and passes her a helmet. 'There you go.'

She leans back against the wall, laughing to herself. 'You know I could have just walked. You didn't have to carry me.'

'You liked it.'

'You think?' she responds, as he takes his keys from the safe.

'I know it.' He passes her a jacket from the hanger and shrugs on his own one, before picking her up and placing her on the saddle of the bike. Shep helps her fasten her helmet, before climbing on in front of her and putting on his own helmet. He starts the engine and the bike roars to life. Izzy's hands wrap around his waist holding him tightly, as he rides up the tunnel leading to the garage entrance.

As soon as they reach the road, Shep accelerates. Izzy presses against him, her small body nestled tight against his back. 'You good?' he asks over the mike in the helmet.

'Woohoo!' she screams in his ear, instantly making him grin like an idiot.

'That's a good woohoo right?'

'Fuck yes! Does it go any faster?'

'Hang on.'

He pushes the bike harder, the roar of the engine going perfectly with Izzy's cries of delight in his ear.

He's a long way from getting his shit together. A long way from getting over what happened to him. But even being like this with Izzy is such a big deal to him.

He has no idea what the next week holds for them, or the next month. But he does know one thing. He's happy, and madly in love with this stunning woman. Being with Izzy makes him happy, and he thinks he makes her happy too.

She loves him. Messed up and all, she loves him. And right now, maybe that's enough for both of them.

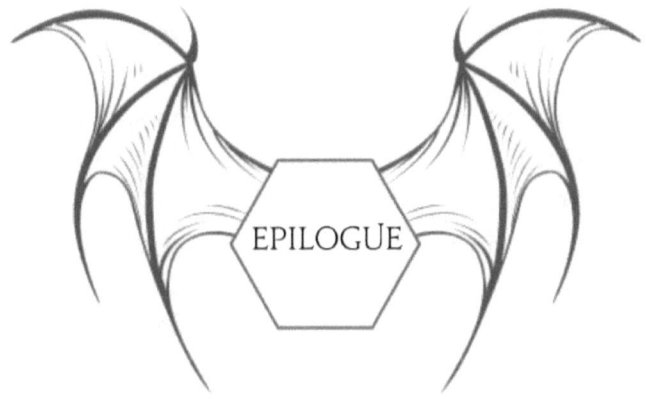

RHAiN

Growing up he had been lavished with all the finest things his parents could give him. The best clothes, the most extravagant houses, private education, dozens of servants to make sure his every wish was granted.

He never wanted for food, for money, for shelter.

Affection, love, and things like that were in short supply, but he grew up strong because of that. He never cried, rarely showed pain, kept his emotions firmly under control. It made him a formidable male. Someone who excelled at business, who fought hard for everything he wanted, and never gave up.

He's a winner. He succeeds. He never shows weakness.

When Barton falls back against the bars of his cell, sweat soaking through his shirt, he can't help but smile to himself.

Even chained up and being beaten, he's still winning.

It's not much of a win, but in his current situation, a win is still a win.

Barton wipes his face on his arm and sneers over at him. 'What are you smiling at Rhain? Has Fever finally taken your sanity?'

Rhain doesn't acknowledge that with an answer. He's chained to the wall in a stone cell, his wrists and ankles firmly shackled, his wings stretched out, each one pinned to the wall by a thick metal stake. A beating is the most excitement he's had for a few days. He'll take the distraction.

The fact the wall he's chained to is behind another half-built wall isn't putting him at ease in the slightest. The double-door sized hole in the bricks is large enough to accommodate his body and allow Barton to hit him, but he has the worrying suspicion that it won't be open for long.

Barton roars as he rams his fist into Rhain's stomach. 'Stop smiling! Do you not see how much trouble you're in? You're not getting out of here Rhain. You will die here, chained to the wall in your underwear.'

Barton is probably right. This is the end for him, but that doesn't mean he's going to give Barton the satisfaction.

Barton wipes his face again, then reaches up to grab a handful of Rhain's hair, pulling his head back. 'I used to fear you Rhain. Every time I was sent to see you I feared for my life. Did you know that?'

Rhain keeps his eyes on Barton's. Past tense? No. Rhain can still see the fear in the male's eyes. Barton swallows and drops his gaze.

That's it, you pathetic cretin. Look away. You still know your place.

'All you had to do was keep your mouth shut. That's all. Now you're here and I'm in charge of you. I get to make decisions that will directly affect your life. How does that feel?'

'You are delusional.' He hates that his voice isn't as strong as usual, but he's tired, weak from lack of food, and in pain. He just hopes he's still hiding it as best he can.

'Is that right?' Barton replies with a less than confident smile. 'How do you come to that conclusion?' Barton points to the feeding tube and IV Rhain was fitted with yesterday. 'I decide when you feed. I decide when you get your precious serum. Me!'

'You are no more in charge of my future than I am. If you kill me right now, you will perish a few hours later. I am still far more important to The Order than you are. How does that feel? A prisoner is still higher up the food chain than you.'

Rhain groans when Barton hits his stomach again. The blows are far from powerful, but this isn't the first time he's been beaten. He won't show it, but it is beginning to take its toll on his body.

'It is you who are delusional Rhain. While you are here I own—'

His final words never make it out of his mouth. The only thing that does make it out, is a small gasp of shock, followed by a trickle of blood.

He slowly looks down, confusion growing on his face when he sees Rhain's wing disappearing into his body.

'I just killed you Barton. How does that feel?' Rhain pushes his wing forward, shoving Barton off the talon at the end, dumping his body on the ground. Rhain waits until Barton draws his last breath, before he slumps in his chains, exhaustion and pain washing over him.

His right wing hangs limply by his side. No doubt he's done irreparable damage to it by tearing his wing off the spike impaling it. He hadn't planned on killing Barton, but he has no regrets about that part. The agony is worth it.

But then he hears clapping. Slow and steady from outside his cell.

'You really don't like playing with others, do you?'

The female strides into his cell, the two large males with her immediately securing his wing back to the wall, creating a new hole in the flesh.

Clearly afraid he is going to tear them free again, they insert a second stake in each wing, this one clamping over the finger bones. There's no way he'll be able to get free without breaking the bones in his wings.

She brushes the back of her hand down the side of his face. 'So handsome, so dangerous, even when chained as you are. I must thank you for taking care of Barton. It was amusing to watch.'

'You knew I'd kill him.'

She shrugs, as she wipes his blood from her hand, smearing it on his chest. 'I can't say it bothered me either way. I did hope you would. I understand he's been a particular irritant to you over the last few years. I must admit I felt the same about the fool. So,' she says, turning to face him. 'One irritant taken care of. Now what are we going to do with you?'

He keeps his mouth shut. The head of The Order isn't someone you answer back. Court's ex girlfriend won't kill him personally, but she doesn't have to. There are enough vampires who answer to her who would happily do that job for her. Barton may have thought he was the one to hold Rhain's life in his hands, but it is her. It's always been her.

'Why did you tell them about me? Why did you tell Court?'

'I'm dying Ma'am. I'm tired of the lies. They asked and I told them. The only thing they know is that you are the head of The Order. Nothing more.'

She nods. 'I believe you. And yes Rhain. You are dying. But revealing my identity to him might just bring about your death in a less pleasing way than you had anticipated. I ordered you to take Court's memory for a reason. You know that.'

She grips his neck, pushing his head back. 'You have opened a Pandora's box that should have remained closed. Court was never to remember. Thea was never to know. You have displeased me greatly by opening that mouth of yours.' She digs her fingers in, squeezing hard. 'No apology?'

'Is... there...any... point?' He has no idea why she didn't want Court to know who she is, but that hardly matters at this stage. He has disobeyed her.

She laughs at his response. 'No. Probably not.' She releases him, tapping his cheek before she takes a few steps back. 'I have had to come up with a particularly suitable punishment for you. I know you enough to be sure you would take anything and everything I throw at you.

'It's that tenacity that drew me to you in the first place, Rhain. I had planned for you to stand by my side as we lead vampires back to greatness. I found you attractive, Rhain. Strong and obedient. You are still attractive but your obedience is lacking. Now you're an annoyance. One I have to deal with.

'But not yet. Maybe not this month. Perhaps not this year. And I know you don't mind waiting. You believe you have only a certain length of time left.' She gestures to one of her goons, who pulls a syringe out of his jacket pocket and injects the contents into the IV in his arm.

'What was that?'

'Your serum, Rhain. Oh yes, I was able to acquire some from your servant Geraint. He was most helpful before he lost his head. I have quite a bit, so don't get any ideas about escaping your punishment by dying. I have control of you and your Blood Fever. I am going to seal you in here until I'm ready to deal with you...whenever that may be.

'Until then you will stay here alone and in the dark. I suggest you use the time to consider everything you've done to irritate me.' She turns away, leaving the cell. She waves over her shoulder before she disappears around the corner. 'See you soon. Brick him in.'

Rhain holds the panic at bay as the men who entered the room with her start closing up the opening in the outer wall.

As the wall grows in height, gradually sealing him in, he forces himself to remain strong, composed, unaffected.

Which is far from how he's feeling.

Internally, the panic takes hold.

He's afraid of the dark. Has been ever since his father locked him in the basement of their house as a child. It was his punishment for answering back. A harsh one at that. Those two days in the windowless damp basement had both terrified him, and forged him into the vampire he is today. He swore in that moment that he would never let anyone push him around again.

If only his father could see him now.

Another line of bricks is cemented in place. The wall is now at eye level, the bricks mere inches from his face. Only a few more rows to go until he's sealed in. The two tubes connected to him are placed on top of the wall, one brick left out to make room for them. At least he'll have some light from that one gap.

As punishments go, she's excelled herself. He doubts he would have come up with something so severe.

She could easily leave him bricked into the claustrophobic space between the walls for years. Feeding him by tube. Giving him his serum to keep him on the brink of sanity. Perhaps insanity. He's already struggling to keep his iron façade in place.

He can't be here for days, let alone years. If she had left his wing free he'd slit his own throat right now without any hesitation. But it's too late for that. There isn't enough room to move his wings even if he could free them.

Rhain closes his eyes, concentrating on breathing in and out to push his fear and panic down. If he lets them take control, he's going to give her exactly what she wants - obedience.

Rhain opens his eyes again, the silver glowing in the dim light as the last brick is slotted into place. He focuses on the space with the two tubes snaking through it, watching until the light goes out as the men leave.

Then there's silence.

Fuck her!

He didn't survive over three centuries by being obedient. He didn't survive by breaking – not to his father, not to Geraint, not to Barton and certainly not to her.

He smiles, baring his teeth. If she thinks he's going to fall at her feet just because he's her prisoner, she's got another thing coming.

He closes his eyes, blocking out the bricks right in front of his face. Blocking out the feel of tube down the back of his throat. The pull of the IV as it hangs on the other side of the wall. The suffocating fear threatening to tear the scream from him.

He's Rhain.

He's survived worse.

He'll survive this.

Then he'll kill that bitch.

Thank you for reading *Defying Shep*.

I hope you enjoyed spending more time with Shep and the rest of the Blackjacks. There's plenty more to come!

The sequel, *Defending Rhain* is coming next.

Do you fancy staying updated with news about my books?

• Join my mailing list at: www.kafinn.com/

• Like me on Facebook: www.facebook.com/kafinnauthor

• Follow me on Instagram: www.instagram.com/kafinnauthor/

• Keep up to date with new releases:
https://books2read.com/ap/nE2Kdj/KA-Finn

Also, if you have a moment, I'd appreciate if you could review *Defying Shep* at the store where you purchased it. The Blackjacks and I would love to know what you thought of the book.

Thanks for your support!

K.A. Finn

Coming next.

BLACKJACKS BOOK 4

DEFENDING
RHAIN

www.ingramcontent.com/pod-product-compliance
Lightning Source LLC
Chambersburg PA
CBHW020506020726
47493CB00001B/210